THE SEA WITCH

FOR THE LOVE OF THE VILLAIN

BOOK ONE

REBECCA F. KENNEY

First Edition: November 2022

Kenney, Rebecca F.

The Sea Witch / by Rebecca F. Kenney—First edition.

Cover art by Doelle Designs

TRIGGER WARNING

age gap between fantasy characters,
violence, abuse, torture, gore, murder,
sexual threat, self-harm,
explicit intimacy/spicy scenes, inexperienced/virgin female main
character

PLAYLIST

"Whisper" Burn the Ballroom
"Poor Unfortunate Souls" Jonathan Young
"Under the Sea" The Lost Bros version
"Kiss the Girl" Chase Holfelder
"Surface Pressure" No Resolve
"Poor Unfortunate Souls" VoicePlay, Rachel Potter
"Stay" No Resolve
"Your Song Saved My Life" U2
"So Close" Jon McLaughlin
"Graveyard" Halsey
"Arsonist's Lullabye" Hozier
"Chasing Echoes" Poets of the Fall
"Old Angels" Pastelle, XENEN
"In It" Ruelle
"Sweet Dreams" Aviators
"Get You Alone" Sleeping Wolf
"Nothing to You" Payson Lewis
"Dark Dance" Burn the Ballroom
"Deep End" Daughtry
"A Good Song Never Dies" Saint Motel
"I Won't Say (I'm in Love)" The Lost Bros
"Animal" The Cab

1

THE SEA WITCH

I have never belonged to the sea.

It's been mine, but I've never truly let it possess me. I am a creature of two worlds—land and sea, the wayside and the water.

I bear no allegiance to either element or its denizens. I have no coddling compassion, no tears for the weak and the wandering.

As I stand here, at the brink of a black cliff, with the white froth churning far below and the tang of scales and salt in my throat, I feel no pity for the ship I can see in the distance, borne aloft by waves as high as the cliff itself.

The sailors aboard that ship are doomed. Their bodies will settle onto the sandy floor of the ocean, where they will swell fat, then float, and then sink again one last time. They will be bones in my domain.

Well... not my domain, exactly. *His* domain. Tarion, King of the Sea. The very thought of him curdles my stomach.

But he and I share at least one principle. We do not try to save the humans when the ocean chooses to claim them.

Lightning snakes from the sky, a searing white flash—splits the mast in two, I think, though I can't see well through the tossing sheets of rain. My eyes are better than a human's, but they have their limits, especially in a storm such as this.

The ship crackles with fire, and I breathe out, an eager sigh. I love fire.

After several minutes of glorious burning, the ship crumples. Collapses, and disappears in a hiss of steam beneath a spiral of black smoke, under the ponderous canopy of the storm. More lightning, with purple edges this time. Beautiful.

I savor the bitter crackle of savage light in the air. I spread my arms to embrace it—the sweet aura of untamed destruction.

Nothing can quell the ocean's fury, or steal her prey.

But…

A flash of white in the sea, not frothy and formless, but neatly shaped. A tail—iridescent scales. The glitter of gems.

Frowning, I shield my eyes and peer through the rain.

I can make out bare shoulders and a face, little more than a pale blur. And another face, bobbing close to the first.

Lightning snaps again, capturing the tableau below me in its harsh light.

Among the tossing waves, a mermaid struggles, clutching a dark-haired human male. She's dragging him toward the narrow bit of beach beside the cliff where I stand.

He must have leaped from the ship when it began to burn, and was quickly overwhelmed by the sea. She's trying to save him.

I sink to a crouch so I can lean farther over the cliff's edge. My claws delve long grooves into the rock.

This does not happen. Cannot happen. The denizens of the sea do not pity or spare the scum of the land. We leave them to drown, just like they leave us to burn and blister if we happen to lie wounded on their beaches.

It is the law. Not my law, or Tarion's, or the law of Perindal, ruler of the human kingdom. This law transcends us all.

If the human had made it to land of his own effort, or if he'd been helped by another of his kind, I might leave it be. But he has been claimed by the ocean, and I crave his death. I am not a gentle being. Any heart I possessed shriveled into a brown husk long ago.

The mermaid has nearly made it to shore now, despite the sucking force of the waves, despite the bulk of the man she is towing. Her skin gleams pale, her body undulating, tail thrashing. She's tiny, but powerful. Determined.

I should crawl down there and make sure the man dies, despite her efforts.

My body shifts its shape, legs disappearing, tentacles uncurling. I retreat from the brink and begin my descent, not down the sheer face of the cliff, but along the right side, where jutting rocks offer some shadow and concealment while I make my way to the beach.

For a handful of moments I can't see the mermaid or the man she's trying to rescue. Quickly, smoothly, I crawl down from the height, the suckers on my tentacles clinging to the rocks.

I pause in a darkened crevice, where the rain racing off the edge of a wet black rock conceals my form. Between two more rocks I can see them—the mermaid and the man. She's struggling to push him through the shallow surf, farther onto the sand.

He's tall, well-muscled. Young. As she gives him another shove, his head lolls back, his handsome face exposed to another flicker of lightning.

I bite back the snarl that rises in my throat.

I know him.

The young man lying on the beach is Kerrin, son of Perindal. He's the crown prince of the human kingdom bordering this part of the sea—the only kingdom I concern myself with at all.

I've seen the boy before. He's probably two years older than the last time I saw him, when he was sailing out of Delmuth Port, bound for faraway lands where he would study the art of diplomacy and perhaps find a bride.

He has returned. And judging by his physique, he's been studying the art of war as well as the finer points of diplomacy.

A soft, sweet, musical voice makes my ears twitch. But the mermaid's words are anything but lyrical.

"Shit," she says to the unconscious prince. "Why are you so rutting heavy?"

I almost laugh. Because immediately after she says it, she glances furtively around, as if she's afraid someone will pop out and reprimand her for using such language.

The half-shy, half-rebellious expression on her face tells me everything I need to know. That, and the sparkling diadem clasped in her dark red hair.

This is no ordinary mermaid. This is one of Tarion's daughters. A princess of the sea, and a virgin, if I'm not mistaken. The innocent offspring of my nemesis.

Her skin is white as the lightning. An elaborate corset of pearls, shells, and crystals covers her ribcage and most of her chest, but the effort of dragging the prince ashore has stressed her above-water breathing abilities, and with every gasp her plump, soft breasts surge in the most enticing way. The gills along her neck are fluttering, trying to process more air, despite her best efforts to keep them sealed. She isn't used to exerting herself while above the surface.

11

Long curls of blood-red hair are plastered along her wet skin, as if someone lovingly painted swirling shapes over her flesh.

A vision creeps into my mind—my monstrous, hulking form crawling out of the dark recess and startling her. One tentacle across her mouth to muffle her screams—my other tentacles coiling and clamping around her tail. Claiming her mouth, and then her body, as mine.

It's a wicked thought, one I immediately dismiss with a pang of revulsion at myself. Much as I hate her father, I would never take my vengeance in that way.

But I may have another use for her.

The storm is dying, dissolving as quickly as it arose. A few stray beams of fading sun pierce the mass of clouds.

In the strange sunset light, the mermaid's hair is haloed with fire, and the planes of her face glow like starshine.

She has crept partway onto the wet sand now. She places her cheek near the prince's mouth—feeling for his breath, perhaps? After a moment she frowns and pushes his head aside experimentally. A little water dribbles out between his lips.

Her delicate dark brows pull together, and her mouth tightens. After a moment's thought, she thumps her fist twice against the man's chest.

When nothing happens, she does it again. "Fucking breathe," she says, in that sweet, dainty voice of hers. I have to cup my palm over my mouth to keep from chuckling.

The prince jerks and chokes out some water. He's breathing now, but he doesn't open his eyes.

The mermaid princess makes a tiny mew of delight. That little sound—gods. She probably sounds like that when she's aroused.

She scoots closer to the human prince, laying aside wet locks from his handsome face. He's crisply, perfectly beautiful, and every touch of her fingers worships that beauty. Her face softens with wonder and desire—no, not desire, exactly—something purer, more innocent.

Longing.

"I wish I could stay," she whispers to him. "But no one can know I saved you. Do you know *why* I saved you? Because I saw you laughing with your men, and you looked so free and happy. Someone so pretty, so young, and so gloriously free can't just—*die*. You have so many land-things to do, like—like walking, and going up steps, and reading paper books, and cooking with fire."

She says the last word reverently, and I realize I'm smiling. Not smirking—I'm grinning widely, like a damn fool. I haul in the expression, glowering at her from my crevice even though she can't see me.

"Sweet sailor," she says softly. "I'm so glad I was able to rescue you. Gods, I wish I could be—I wish—" She glances down at her close-set scales, their dark iridescent sheen tinted with orange-gold from the rays streaking through the broken stormclouds.

She flips her tail, flinging sparkling drops. Her caudal fin glows translucent in the sun.

"I wish I had legs," she murmurs.

And there it is.

The desire I can grant for her. The one that will seal her father's fate, if I play my cards right.

I'm an excellent hand at cards. I've played in taverns all along the coast. And I'm absolutely certain I can win at this game.

With a sigh, the mermaid leans over the prince again, her fingertips floating above his damp chest, not quite touching. He's breathing faintly but steadily.

They're a lovely pair—I have to admit it, much as it curdles my gut to think so. Both are gorgeous specimens of their kind—a daring contrast, him with his lightly tanned skin and black hair, the girl with her pallor and her scarlet locks. He's twenty-five, I believe, and she must be about the same age.

By contrast, I'm an old man. Two hundred fucking years and counting.

I'm so tired of existing.

But miserable and weary as I am, I refuse to end myself, out of sheer spite to the entire world and its gods. I have to believe one day I will find my joy through revenge.

And this little mermaid might be the one to bring it to me.

2

AVERIL

I have never belonged to the sea.

Ever since I was a fingerling, freshly spawned, I've had an itch to be elsewhere.

It's the urge that has driven me far into splintered shipwreck graveyards, past the jaws of sleeping monsters, into the deepest trenches of my father's domain, until even my resilient body begins to creak with the weight of the ocean above.

I'm not afraid of things that are different, or unknown. I want them, I welcome them.

I break rules on purpose, as far as I dare. I don't tell anyone when I break them, though, so perhaps I'm not as brave or rebellious as I'd like to imagine.

My father's realm is rife with danger. I acknowledge that, and I'm smart about my choices—usually. Maybe the choice I made today wasn't so smart. I saved the handsome, laughing human I saw on the ship. He leaped overboard when the mast split, but the smoke and terror overcame him—or maybe he wasn't a strong swimmer. So I wriggled through the waves, claimed him, and dragged him ashore.

As I lie on the beach beside him, I can imagine what my older sisters would say if they knew what I've done.

Serra would stare me down accusingly. Then she'd fling herself toward the man, and with nails like knives she would slash his throat, leaving his blood to soak the sand. "The ocean wants a sacrifice, and shall have it," she'd say.

She's the most religious of my siblings. Takes after my father in that way. Worships the ocean as Life-Giver, spends hours simply floating in clear water, meditating. So boring. Her mate is the same way, though sometimes I wonder if his devotion originated from his goal of being Crown Consort one day. He certainly became more devout when he began courting my sister.

Yes, Serra would have the most savage reaction. Some of my sisters would sneer at me for sparing a human life, while others would look aghast.

The nearest sister to my age is Ylaine, mated to Ardoc. I miss her more than the others. She used to accompany me on some of my journeys into the forsaken or forbidden parts of the ocean. I always felt braver with her along. She was so skittish and fearful that my own sliver of courage looked like a plank by comparison.

Ylaine is the only one of my sisters who knows about my collection of human artifacts, and my secret desire to walk on two legs and explore the earthen parts of the world. She might understand why I feel drawn to this stranger.

It's not just his lovely features, or the toned, elegant lines of his body. Something about his manner sucked me in, lured me closer than I ever go to the humans' ships. He was joking with the other men, and his laugh rang boldly across the water, even as stormclouds gathered overhead. As if he was daring the world

17

to doom him. As if he held in his soul the same gleeful recklessness that I feel, the same compulsion to fly higher and dive deeper than anyone else will.

I sensed an echo of myself in him. The Soul Echo that each of my sisters mentioned when they found their true mate.

A terrified, wild delight bubbles in my chest at the thought that maybe this *human* is my mate. There's a rightness to the idea, a sort of strange justice that someone from an entirely different race could be *The One* for me—the man for whom I've been saving my body and my heart. Everyone in my father's realm thinks me strange already. They cannot wait for me to find some decent, law-abiding merman and settle down with him. It would serve them all right if I found my Soul Echo in a human male.

I'm sure I hear a Soul Echo between me and the pretty human. I'm almost absolutely certain of it.

And I'm hearing something far louder than an inner voice. Shouts carry across the sea, voices from a battered skiff bobbing along the waves. Several dark shapes are in it—a handful of surviving sailors. In a moment, they will notice me and the man I saved.

I can't stay here. Can't let the sailors find me. My father says if the humans catch us, they'll strip our scales and use them for currency, before roasting our flesh as a delicacy for their noble families.

I'm not sure if any of that is true—I rather doubt it, because my father is prone to exaggerate when he wants his children to obey. But I'd rather not risk being peeled and flayed.

The skiff is drawing closer, so I ease back into the water and slither quietly away under the surface.

I tuck myself behind a rock, peering around it long enough to make sure the men notice my beautiful, rescued sailor.

He's beginning to stir and lift his head. They will care for him, and he will live.

That should be enough for me.

But it's not. I want more.

I want *him*.

The violence of the wanting startles me. It's a gnawing, craven, acidic hunger, devouring itself and me along with it. I curl my body slightly, pressing a hand to my chest. Yes, this must be the Soul Echo. And this human has to be my mate.

Cautiously I peer around the rock one last time.

The skiff has nearly reached the narrow strip of beach. One of the humans is standing up in it, his body rigid, his face alight with eager disbelief.

"Your Highness!" he calls to the man lying on the sand.

Your Highness?

What the fuck?

Ugh, I really must stop saying that to myself or it's going to slip out in my father's presence one day. Or I'll say it in front of my sisters and one of them will tell on me.

"Profanity is beneath us," my father intones whenever one of us uses a word he deems vulgar. "We are royalty, and our speech should signify as much."

Apparently the man I rescued is royalty, too. A prince. Which makes him all the more imperfectly perfect for me.

The kingdoms of sea and land have never been friendly, but there used to be a sort of tentative truce. Until—well, I'm not sure what happened. I could never get a straight answer out of our court historian. She says my father has forbidden the recounting of "that terrible tale of treachery and torment." The historian is dreadfully alliterative. And dreadfully annoying.

So is my father—exasperating in the extreme. He seems to think I'm still in my gawky adolescence, when I'm fully grown at twenty-four years.

19

Maybe he holds onto me so tightly because all my sisters are already mated. I'm the last one—his youngest, and physically the smallest. Though I'd like to think I'm as strong as any of them. I've had the same combat training. *More* training, in fact, if I count the various dangerous expeditions I've conducted on my own.

I risk another peek around the rock. The last one for sure this time. And then I'll go.

The skiff has been pulled up on the beach, and the prince— oh gods—he's moving. Standing up, with the help of another sailor.

The prince strips off his wet shirt, his paneled torso gleaming in the fading sunlight. Carved ledges of muscle seem to point down, beneath the pants sagging around his hips.

I've caught glimpses of human male parts, thanks to the habit sailors have of pissing over the railing of their ships. But I'd like a closer look. I'm so curious about human genitals— male and female. I'm told the private bits dangle openly between their legs, while ours lie concealed beneath scaly flaps. We eliminate waste from apertures under those flaps, too—openings separate from the sexual parts.

Sexuality fascinates me, like everything else does, but it's one area I've yet to explore. Merfolk mate for life, so experimentation with the opposite gender—or any gender—is forbidden. We're supposed to save ourselves for our One True Mate. As mermaids, our inner pleasure points lie deep inside, impossible to reach with our fingers, only accessible by a merman's long, flexible penis. I've heard whispers of one mermaid who was caught using an eel to pleasure herself—she was banished from the kingdom by the priestesses. Despite my curiosity about carnal delights, I've never tried anything of the kind.

But sometimes I yearn for a new kind of pleasure. And I want love—wilder and more beautiful than the bonds between my sisters and their mates. I want something fiercer, deeper, all-consuming.

My mate might be the man walking away from me along the beach right now, in the company of the surviving sailors. They're following a narrow path, sand and shale, winding between the bluffs and disappearing beyond. They're going somewhere I can't see, or follow. Damn this tail.

As the men's shapes recede, growing smaller, wending along that path, I crawl onto the top of the rock I've been hiding behind. It's a risky move. One of them might see me.

Maybe I want them to.

The prince waves another man on, ahead of him. He's the last of the procession.

Maybe I want him to turn around. To notice me. To know that I saved him. To speak to me, and—

He halts on the path. And he starts to turn.

My heart takes a flying leap out of my chest, and I slide off the rock with a splash. I streak away as fast as I can, slicing through the waves, gills flaring wide with excited panic.

He turned around. He looked. Did he see me? He couldn't have—I moved too fast.

I plunge deeper into the welcoming depths of the ocean. My eyes switch focus, pupils expanding and shifting so I can see clearly in the darkness.

I don't usually venture into this area of the sea. This stretch of the ocean is home to a dark entity, a prominent figure in some of my father's most dreadful tales.

The foulest enemy of all civilized merfolk.

The Sea Witch.

Scary stories don't usually deter me, but anytime I've ventured near here, I've encountered a thicker-than-usual

21

population of toxic pufferfish, poisonous eels, hazardous urchins, and deadly anemones—as if every denizen of this region has been corrupted, and they're now in league with the Witch, daring anyone to enter his domain.

When I was saving the prince, I swam through these waters without considering the danger. I was too intent on getting him to safety.

But suddenly the danger I'm in becomes startlingly real.

Because three figures have just swept out of the gloom, and they're closing in around me—a triangle of solemn faces.

I have never seen any merfolk like them.

3

AVERIL

The three mysterious merfolk swim on my level, one directly in front of me and the other two on either side. I could plunge down to the murky bottom, or charge upward, to the surface. But they're so close now—they might catch me.

Spines march along the arms of the male to my right. His tail is enormous, striped and fanned out, just like a lionfish. He wears two wide belts crisscrossed over his broad chest, and the hilts of weapons protrude above his shoulders, jutting from their sheaths on his back. The lionfish male's face is deeply scarred, and one of his finned ears is missing its pointed tip. Red-brown hair clouds the water around his head.

The male on my left has a broad, rippling tail like an eel, with a belt of woven metal and bone at his waist. From head to tail, his skin is a seamless gray with a hint of dark green in places when he moves. His fingers, arms, and body crackle faintly, sparking with energy now and again. Long nails, serrated teeth, gray eyeballs with slitted yellow pupils—he's rather terrifying.

The third stranger looks oddly translucent, his organs hazily visible through his flesh. A long, thin appendage arches from his forehead, bearing a teardrop bulb that glows with an oddly enticing light. I find myself staring at that glimmering bulb, drifting closer to him.

His features are gelatinous, almost fluid in appearance, and his eyes are milky-white—but I barely notice, because the light bobbing in front of his face blurs my thoughts, weighs my eyelids, and slows the movement of my gills.

I think, if I touched that glowing bulb, it would feel good. I want to try it.

"We're supposed to talk to her, Ekkon," says the lionfish male. "Not lure her in to be eaten."

His words spark in my brain, and I blink, frowning at the distraction from the light.

"Hush, Liris," hisses the transparent creature. "You'll break the spell."

"Forgive my partner's questionable methods," says the lionfish, Liris, apparently addressing me. "We invite you to come with us and meet the Sea Witch. The two of you have a common interest."

His words are an annoyance. They're getting in the way of my focus on the alluring orb. I try to block him out, but as he keeps talking, the charm of the glowing light dissolves, and my thoughts clarify.

A muted voice in the back of my mind is suddenly freed, blaring *danger, danger* through my consciousness.

I don't wait for Ekkon to reinstate his hold on me, or for Liris to finish his speech.

I dive. Straight down, quick as I can—and I'm fast. No mermaid visits the places I go without learning how to put on a burst of extra speed to avoid predators.

Arrow-straight, I shoot for the bottom, then with a pulse of my tail I push myself level again, skimming along the ocean floor. I can lose them—I can get away—

But a thicket of brightly-colored tentacles rises in front of me, its vivid orange and lurid purple screaming another warning.

Poison.

Too late. I can't halt my body—my momentum carries me straight into the tangle of poisonous anemones.

A second later, I realize these creatures are more sentient and mobile than regular anemones. Their tentacles thicken and tighten around my limbs, securing me in a deadly net. My skin is already stinging, my torso and tail beginning to droop, heavy and numb. I try to thrash, but it's no use. I can't move.

Prickles of pain dance along my arms, my chest, my neck. I twist and buck, managing to lurch onto my back, but I can't drive myself upward out of the thicket. The slim, rubbery tentacles are moving in, covering my face, closing me off from the open water.

Like all mermaids, my throat, lungs, and voicebox are uniquely designed to help sound carry underwater. I force out a scream, hoping it will shear through the gurgling deep, but my vocal cords are poisoned, my cry weaker than it should be. Useless.

Maybe the ocean is punishing me for stealing her prey. Maybe this is my penance for saving a human life. Father always says it's the law of the world—the denizens of one element must not save those claimed by another.

If this is my punishment, I'm happy to pay it. I'm happy the prince will live, free and beautiful, with his smooth, gill-free neck and his long legs. But I wish this didn't hurt so much— gods—the pain flooding my body is so intense I scream again. A tentacle noses into my open mouth, entering my throat, choking me.

Eyes blown wide, I watch the anemones knit together in front of my face, blocking my sight. Just a small opening left, through which I glimpse the quiver of blue water, and something black—a darting shadow.

And then agony pierces my spine, and I arch mutely, my throat clogged with the anemone, my gills spasming helplessly. My vision darkens.

A blaze of white, forked light.

Sizzling energy scars through the tentacles around me, and the scent of the water turns acrid, bitterly tinged with scorched anemone and leaking poison.

Someone grips my upper arm, hauls me out of the shattered tentacles. A clawed hand yanks the piece of anemone out of my throat, and I gag. My gills are working again, processing the water, feeding my lungs.

But they're still slow, still affected by the poison. Agony races along my nerves, and it would be a relief to twist and flail, but I can't move.

"Toxic paralysis," says a voice—I think it's the lionfish, Liris, but I can't be sure. My eyes are swelling shut.

"She doesn't have long," Liris continues. "We have to get her back to the cave. Graeme, you're the fastest, and I can't risk my spines grazing her and making it worse. Take her and go."

Graeme must be the male who's part eel, the one who crackled with energy and blasted apart the anemones. I hardly care where he's taking me. I'm a swollen mass of pain, my thoughts blurred and sinking.

Dimly I'm aware of the current of our speed as Graeme tows me through the sea. My eyes are sealed shut now. But I can hear, beyond the rush of our passage, a chorus of moaning voices—hundreds of them. They sound smaller than merkind, fainter, wispier. Like the remnants of a thousand shredded souls.

My father told us the Sea Witch tears apart the spirits of those who dare to bargain for favors from him. Listening to the haunted choir filling the void around me, I can believe it.

If I could feel anything but pain, I'd be afraid. But all I can think about is relief. I want relief from this pain, whatever the cost. I'd give anything to be on the other side of it, looking back at its memory. Feeling like myself again.

I want to live.

The fearful chorus fades into a deadly silence. The water around us has changed—there's a faint warmth in it, and the crisp tingle of magic. I've only felt magic once before, when a mermaid sorceress from another settlement came to perform for one of my sisters' mating ceremonies. Her magic was limited, but she could make beautiful dancing figures of colored light that twirled through the sea.

This magic is much stronger. It vibrates along the edges of my pain-cracked skin. The water slipping over my tongue tastes rich and wild, potent and—and male. Merfolk give off pheromones regularly, sometimes subtle, other times stronger depending on their fertility cycles. While some emit a blended agender scent, most produce pheromones that are either male or female.

I'm not scenting much from Graeme, but the other entity in this space tastes and smells overwhelmingly masculine.

Graeme slows his frantic speed. "The girl, as requested."

Another voice speaks—a voice like black stones grinding along the icy bottom of the ocean, in the deepest trench known to merkind. I've never heard a voice so deep.

28

"Shit, Graeme," it growls. "What have you done to her?"

"She fled from us. Right into a nest of noxcoils."

"Fuck," rumbles the voice, and my whole body shivers. My pain is less now. More of a creeping, cold numbness. I have a feeling that's a bad sign for my survival.

"I'll have to heal her." The growly voice is nearer to me now, and I try to scream, because I can't stand being this close to so much wicked power when I can't see its source.

"Quiet, little one," murmurs the deep voice. "Graeme, the yellow vial in the top cabinet. Don't open it, just hand it over. And the little pouch from the drawer below that. Good."

Something curls around my body—an arm? Seems too thick to be an arm. Not the right texture. But then, my sense of touch is being distorted by the swelling and numbness.

The voice grinds out strange words I don't recognize. Thick fingers insert themselves into my mouth, pressing something onto my tongue.

"Swallow, sweet child," coaxes the voice, and something strokes my throat—not fingers, exactly—oh gods, I can't bear this, being touched by someone I can't see—by the dreaded Sea Witch, no less. It must be him.

If there's one thing I hate, it's helplessness. And ignorance—I hate not knowing about things. I want full knowledge, complete understanding. I need to see, to know—the urgency swells inside me and I manage a faint quiver, limbs to tail.

"Still fighting, I see." The appendage around my waist tightens a little. "Good. It will take a few moments for the antidote to take effect. Keep struggling, keep breathing. Stay awake."

The "few moments" feel more like entire hours. Days, perhaps. I squirm again, and a rasp of protest escapes from my swollen throat. There's a deep hum of approval from the Sea Witch—I assume the voice belongs to him.

He's saving me, but not out of kindness. He wants something from me.

Liris, the one with the lionfish aspect, mentioned something about a common interest. I want to speak, to protest that I can't possibly have anything in common with a horrible witch who abuses his power and destroys lives.

But all I can do is breathe, and struggle faintly, and make raspy, unhappy sounds.

Finally my eyelids feel less puffy and heavy, as if they're shrinking back to their normal size. Finally I can open them, just a crack, and look around.

I'm in an underwater cave. To my right, as far as I can skew my gaze, there are cabinets and drawers covering the cave wall. Above, golden worms creep along the arched ceiling, their glowing, bulging bodies lending light to the space.

And to my left—

A scream sticks in my throat, and I try to jerk away—

The Sea Witch.

He is enormous. Brutally muscled. His arms—my gods— bulging biceps, tattooed forearms, and veined hands. Every muscle in his abdomen is deeply defined, right down to the place where his brown skin merges into the body of an octopus— massively thick tentacles, pale gray with hints of mottled blue.

I've never seen such a thing. Merfolk usually have neat, sleek fishtails—not lionfish tails, eel tails, or octopus tentacles that move with a mesmerizing, sinuous power.

Swallowing, I pull my gaze away from those undulating appendages, back to the more normal-looking parts of him.

He has long hair that's either black or deep purple—I can't quite tell which. Like his tentacles, his hair seems to have a mind

30

of its own, shifting and curling in ways that have nothing to do with any current.

As if his powerful body and tentacles weren't overwhelming enough, his face is heart-stopping. Granite features, harsh and bold. Full lips forming a wide mouth, cocked at the corner, as if my shock amuses him. Heavy black brows, and a pair of piercing eyes with deep bluish-purple irises.

No gills anywhere, that I can see. His underwater breathing systems must be internal, somehow. Perhaps he has altered himself magically.

He is monstrous, virile, terrifying. I don't want to be near him. I want to leave.

"You seem frightened, little mermaid," he says, in that deep, deep voice.

I can't quite speak yet. My vocal cords are loosening, but my throat is terribly sore, maybe because of the tentacle the anemone shoved down it.

"I can only imagine what your father has told you about me," he continues.

My eyes widen.

"Oh, yes, I know you're one of Tarion's spawn. The diadem in your hair, and your fancy corset." His eyes travel to my chest, and the corner of his mouth quirks higher. "Marks of royalty, those. And I keep a closer eye on Tarion than he likes to believe, or I like to admit."

His tentacles writhe restlessly, and one of them skates up the rocky wall of the cave, its tip curling and uncurling.

"Your father and his merfolk think me the worst of beings, but in truth I'm merely a devotee of balance," he says. "Magic is cruel and visceral—and I'm talking about real magic, not whatever paltry, pretty flimflam you may have seen at court. True power, real transformation—they demand sacrifice. A yielding of something, to balance what is received. I have sacrificed much during my life, and so I have power. Which means others are jealous of me, and concoct stories that will make them feel better about their own failures and weaknesses."

My father isn't weak. I try to speak the words, but I only manage a croak.

He frowns. "Where's that sweet voice of yours? It should have been restored by now—unless—" He pries my lips open again. The sensation of his strong fingers probing the inside of my mouth sends a tingle through me.

"Ah, so there was a direct internal application of the venom," he says. "Your throat is more inflamed than I thought, and your voice is almost gone. We can't have that, can we?"

He whirls, his tentacles swirling fluidly through the water. A quick dart over to a cabinet, and he returns with something that looks like a pearl. He places it on my tongue. "Swallow."

With difficulty, I obey. The pearl seems to dissolve on the way down, soothing the scratchy soreness in my throat.

"You lying monster," I say immediately. "My father isn't weak."

"Ah, the princess's dulcet tones are restored," he drawls. "What a delight. Now, if you'll hold your tongue for a bit, I'll explain why I had my friends bring you here."

"Friends?" I gasp. "Those things are your friends? I thought they might be your servants, or..."

His smirk vanishes and his face hardens. The rich bluish-purple leaks from his irises, spreading until his eyes are entirely that color, corner to corner, not a hint of white left, except for his pupils, which are weirdly pale now.

My gills flutter, the air supply to my lungs stuttering.

The Sea Witch stretches taller, the mass of his tentacles pushing him up until he towers over me, a looming storm of magic and menace. "Those *things*, as you call them, are worth more to me than your wretched father's entire court, and all his precious daughters. They were cast out—abhorred for their differences, like I was. Like I *am*. If you're going to remain undamaged in my presence, Princess, I would choose your words more carefully. Attempt to open your mind a little wider than your upbringing has allowed thus far."

Maybe it's not a good idea to antagonize the extremely powerful Sea Witch who just healed me and could easily snap my spine with one tentacle.

"My apologies," I say in my sweetest voice. "I've had a strange day, and a near-death experience. Fear makes me foolish."

He sinks a little lower. "As it does to us all."

"Your friends mentioned a 'common interest' we share," I continue, though it grates against my soul to think of sharing anything with this brutal menace of a man.

"Yes. I apologize if they gave you a fright, my dear. You see, this was too perfect an opportunity to pass up—you, here, in my domain—and the prince, within our reach."

My pulse quickens.

"The prince?" I say, with attempted nonchalance. "What prince?"

"Why, the one you saved from a shipwreck less than two hours ago." The Sea Witch glides around me, his tentacles caging my body without ever touching my skin. "Have you forgotten him already? Strange, I thought you seemed rather besotted with the handsome lad."

I pinch my lips together, refusing to answer.

4

THE SEA WITCH

The little mermaid is nearly back to normal now. When Graeme brought her in, she was a swollen blob, her skin taut and mottled by poison, her body completely numb. Since I administered the antivenom, her distended torso has regained its slim suppleness, and she can move again. She's trying to be still, trying not to show agitation in my presence, but her slender tail keeps rippling and flicking restlessly.

Her plump pink lips are pressed together, as if to hold in more words I might find offensive. Her large eyes shine, curious and wary. She has unusually thick lashes for a mermaid, and her features are delicate and charming. In a word, she's beautiful, which is lucky for me. It will make her seduction of the prince so much easier.

"Normally I prefer to plan these things carefully," I tell her. "But in this case, time is of the essence. You and I have both been given an opportunity to obtain something we crave."

"And what is it you think I crave?"

"Human shape, so you can enter the prince's life in a way you can't in your current form."

Her gills flutter faster at her throat. "Even if I did want that, no one can give it to me."

"Oh, but I can." To prove it, I alter my own body, vanishing my tentacles and giving myself a pair of long, strong human legs, with a bit of dark smoke to shield my genitals from the little mermaid's gaze. Not that I'd mind her seeing me naked, but she's suspicious enough already. Best to keep the focus on what I can offer magically, not carnally.

I switch to my tentacled form again, a smooth transition that makes the girl's mouth gape.

"What the f—I mean, how did you do that?" she asks.

"Magic, my dear. And I'll do it for you, too, provided you agree to certain terms. But as I said, time is short. Your rescued prince and his remaining sailors took the path up to a small coastal town, where they will no doubt spend the night being coddled and celebrated by the villagers. They may perhaps spend a few more days there, recuperating from the ordeal and searching the beach for survivors. After that, they will have half a day's journey south to reach the summer palace at Crystal Point, which was no doubt the Prince's original destination before the storm struck. You have very little time to arrange a meeting with your prince before he is swept back into court life. This is your one chance, and my only offer."

I watch her pupils dilate, desire mingling with caution.

"You just said that real transformation requires sacrifice. What would I have to sacrifice for this metamorphosis?" She meets my gaze boldly.

"I possess a certain amount of natural power, so I can transform your body into a human's right now, and it will remain so as long as you stay within a limited distance of me," I explain. "But when you're with your prince, you cannot be always in

5

It sounds too good to be true. And it's too sudden, too strange.

I'm no fool—I know the thing the Sea Witch will ask of me is probably wrong, or dangerous. Or perhaps it's simply a task he cannot do for himself, though I can't imagine how someone with his power could lack anything. He can obviously make himself legs and go on land whenever he likes. If he wants me to steal something or spy on someone, why can't he do it himself?

"And you won't tell me what the task is?" I hedge, eyeing him.

"Not yet. You see, magic is stronger when there's a bond of trust between the parties involved."

I cock my head. "You made that up."

"Perhaps. Who's to say?" He grins, sudden and savage, but there's a spark of real humor in his eyes, and I feel the barest answering twitch at the corner of my mouth.

He's right about one thing—I've longed for legs since I was tiny. My inner restlessness has propelled me from one risky part of the ocean to another, but the coastline always hovers in my mind, an unexplored region, an untouched paradise. I want desperately to go there.

And the prince—the lovely male I saved today—his image fills my mind, too. The curve of his dark lashes, brushing his cheekbones as he lay unconscious. The fall of his wet black hair, bouncing into curls after just a few moments in the air. The planes of his handsome face, the angle of his jaw, the strong slant of his throat.

Every line of his body enchanted my eyes, drew me in, teased my mind with naughty possibilities. Even now, thinking of his gleaming chest when he took off his shirt sends a delicate prickle of delight through my tail.

And then there's the echo I felt—the kinship with him. The tugging *want* that tells me he's a person I need—maybe even my mate.

I want his body, and his beauty. I want his easy laughter and the camaraderie I witnessed between him and the other sailors. I want to know more about him. I want to step into his world.

The Sea Witch has been waiting while I pondered. The only sign of his impatience is an occasional twitch of his tentacles.

"It's possible to communicate without speech." My words are more a confirmation to myself than a question for the Witch. I've never shied away from a challenge before. I can conquer this one.

"Yes, it's possible," says the Sea Witch. "Allow me to show you."

He surges toward me, a tempest of sinuous tentacles and hard muscle. He catches my chin with his fingers, his dark hair feathering in the water around us both. I'm frozen, captured by the intensity of his hooded gaze.

close proximity to me, within my magical range. Which means I need something to tether your transformation. I need an intrinsic part of you. Your voice, for example. As long as I carry your voice, your human shape will hold, no matter the distance between us."

"That's ridiculous." She flips her tail, pushing away from me. She bumps into one of my tentacles, and horror crosses her face briefly.

I'm used to being despised and deemed monstrous. Still, her instinctive revulsion angers me more than I like to admit.

"You can't *take* my voice," she continues. "How would I speak to the prince? How would I enter his life and make his acquaintance?"

"I could take your eye instead, or a hand, or your hair," I growl. "Or I could take your virginity. The act of sexual awakening would provide enough magical energy for a tether."

She recoils again, her eyes impossibly wide, like two innocent blue oceans. "The voice will have to do, I suppose. Though I'm not sure how I'll communicate with him—I've heard that humans write the Common Tongue differently than we do under the sea."

"I can teach you how to attract him without your voice or any written words," I tell her. "Human men are simple. A lovely face and a beautiful body are more than enough to lure them. Many would prefer you without a voice."

She frowns at that, her chin tilting up defiantly. "And what do you get out of this? You said it's an opportunity for us both to get something we crave, but you don't *crave* my voice—it's simply a tether, an exchange, right? So there must be something else you want."

Oh there is. Something I ache for, with every savage, bitter bone in my body. Vengeance, and a reclamation of what is mine.

But I answer lightly. "For now, let us say that at some point during your acquaintance with the Prince, I will ask you for a favor. And when I ask, you will agree, and you'll perform the task as soon as possible. If you complete it successfully, I will have the power to restore your voice and make your human shape permanent. If you fail, I will swallow your voice, and it will be mine forever."

"Is it murder?" She blinks at me with horrified fascination. "Are you going to ask me to murder someone?"

"Murder? No, nothing so dreadful. Not murder, or dismemberment, or anything bloody."

"Oh." She bites her lip, the juicy flesh dented by straight white teeth. She's thinking it through. Pondering everything I've said, looking for loopholes and tricks. Clever little thing. But I've been honest with her, for the most part. It's a straightforward offer.

"We should do it now, or not at all," I tell her. "As I mentioned, your opportunity to meet him is limited. Once he's back in the Summer Palace—"

"I know," she snaps. "Give me a minute. I wasn't expecting any of this today—seeing *him,* then the storm and the peril, and then your friends, and you—*this*—"

"But today isn't the first time you've longed to visit the human world, is it?" I murmur. "I'll wager you're someone who pushes boundaries, or perhaps swims right past them. You enjoy skirting around the rules, don't you, little one? Think of it—this could be your only chance to own a pair of feet, to wriggle your toes in the sand, to walk upright under the sun. You could taste their food, read their books, listen to their fireside stories and songs. You could sleep in a bed, climb stairs, ride a horse."

"A horse?"

"You see? There's so much you don't know. So much the handsome prince could show you." I drift nearer. "So much I can

37

give you. Things you've wanted. All you have to do is yield me your voice, and do me one small favor when I ask it."

Her expression fluctuates—less caution, more desire. It's all I can do to refrain from a triumphant grin.

She can't say no to this offer.

I've got her now.

She's mine.

As he appraises me, his eyes gleam with lascivious heat. His tongue passes lightly over his full lower lip, and his mouth tilts up at the corner.

I can't breathe. My gills and lungs are paralyzed.

His expression shutters suddenly, turning cool and disinterested as he backs away. "I communicated with you just now. What was I saying?"

"You were—um—" I swallow, gathering my hair in both hands and twisting it. "You looked as if you wanted to—to—"

A smirk flickers across his mouth. "You can say 'fuck,' you know. There's no one here to object. It's a crude human word that merfolk have picked up, but I rather like it. So feel free to say it—unless you're a prude as well as a virgin. The latter is simply a matter of choice or opportunity—the former is a stunted state of mind I'd rather not waste my time with."

"I'm not a prude," I say haughtily. "And yes, you looked as if you wanted to fuck me."

"Exactly. A fake desire, which I communicated to you without saying a word. You can do the same with your prince—communicate all sorts of emotions, from curiosity to vulnerability to lust. What are words but vehicles for emotion, anyway? You'll do fine without them. And I'll be here if you need help. Believe me, I want you to win his heart."

That makes me very suspicious indeed. But I only say, "How will I contact you?"

"All in good time, love," says the Sea Witch. "First, I must know—do we have a deal?"

"We have a deal." I hear myself saying the words, but I don't really believe them. I can't grasp the fact that in a short time I might actually have legs. It still seems impossible.

"Good," rumbles the Sea Witch. He backs away slowly, his tentacles snaking out to seize a few different objects—two tiny jars, a spiral shark-eye shell, a limpet shell, and a ball of twine.

Keeping his eyes on me, he cuts pieces of the twine with his sharp fingernails. His tentacles deftly loop the twine through a small hole in each shell. Then he douses both shells with the contents of the jars.

The curly snail shell he fastens around his neck with his own hands, while two of his tentacles approach me, their tapered tips holding the ends of the other makeshift necklace.

"The shark-eye will remain with me, and will contain your voice," he explains. "The limpet shell is yours. It will allow me to see you whenever you want to be seen, and to speak to you."

"Will I be able to see you as well?"

"If I allow it." His tentacles are lifting my hair, deftly knotting the cord at the back of my neck. I grit my teeth, trying not to recoil from their touch. The appendages are softer than I expected—not rubbery or slimy, but almost velvety, even in the water. It's an odd sensation, and goosebumps rise along my arms.

The limpet shell floats near my chest, tethered to my neck. I flip it over, noting the glossy turquoise of the inner lining. Beautiful.

Energy thrums through the shell and the cord, prickling against my fingertips. Startled, I drop the necklace. Both the twine and the outer surface of the limpet have transformed into what looks like pure gold.

"Nothing to worry about," croons the Sea Witch. His necklace matches mine now, a gleaming gold. "It's simply the spell taking effect. In a moment I will begin your physical transformation. But first, we should discuss the ruse through which you will enter your prince's life."

"Ruse?" I blink at him.

"You can't tell him you're a mermaid. You need some other story, some foundation on which to base your pretense, even if you cannot speak the tale." He taps his full lips thoughtfully.

43

"You're a noble lady from some distant land. Your ship was caught in the same storm that destroyed his, and you were the only survivor. You've temporarily lost your voice because of the terror and trauma of the shipwreck. I'll give you some jewels to corroborate the ruse. And you should have a gown. I think I've got one stowed away."

For a moment I'm overwhelmed at the thought, at the wonder of a *gown*—a real human gown to cover my real human legs. I can't wait to wear it.

Now that I've committed to this, I feel less anxious and more excited. "A story, jewels, and a gown. I'm ready. Let's do this."

"Patience, little one," chuckles the Sea Witch. "It will be night in the surface world now. I'll take you ashore, and we'll practice a while until you can manage comfortably on your legs. Then you'll wait on some scrap of beach until a human finds you—or until you grow too impatient and you toddle up to the village on your own, which seems far more likely. Is there anything you need to do here before you go?"

I hesitate, chewing my lip—a bad habit of mine when I'm thinking. Serra snaps at me whenever she sees me doing it. "Now and then I run off for a couple of days. My father is usually too busy to notice right away, so I have some time before he realizes I'm gone. When I return he always punishes me, but I don't mind."

"How does he punish you?"

"Silly things, like taking away some of my jewelry, confining me to my room, not allowing me my favorite treats, sending me to bed early."

The Sea Witch cocks his head. "It's as if he thinks you're still a child."

"Exactly."

Those unearthly eyes of his travel from my face down to my chest. "But you're not a child," he says, low. "Far from it."

I can feel blood rushing to my cheeks. "That's—that's beside the point. The point is, he won't miss me right away, and when I go back, the punishment won't be terrible, as long as I'm not absent too long."

"If," says the Sea Witch quietly. "*If* you go back."

6

THE SEA WITCH

The mermaid princess stares at me. Realizing, perhaps for the first time, what it will mean for her if she succeeds in winning the prince's heart. It will mean a choice between land and sea. A choice I've never been able to make—one I've had the power to avoid.

I let her ponder the future while I move into a nearby chamber and collect the items we need—some jewelry, a gown and a few undergarments for her, and a pair of pants for me. I place them into a bag, secure the flap, and sling the strap of the bag across my body.

When I return, the mermaid's chin is set. She's still determined to do this. Plucky little thing.

"If you're ready, we'll go," I tell her.

"Go?" She frowns slightly.

"I prefer to do the transformation in a shallower area. You'll be losing your gills along with your tail, and the shift can be disconcerting. I prefer you don't drown while you're trying to adjust."

"Oh." Her cheeks flush slightly. "That makes sense."

I eye the diadem in her hair, and she touches it self-consciously. "Should I take this off?"

"I think so. On one hand it fairly shrieks 'princess,' which might be alluring to your chosen prey, but on the other hand it also screams 'mermaid' with equal volume, which could raise some alarms. Best to leave it here. I'll take care of it for you."

It takes her a moment to disentangle the piece from her hair. When she hands it over reluctantly, I tuck it into one of my cupboards and snap the latch into place.

"Come." With a powerful pulse of my tentacles, I spur myself out of the cavern and through the tunnels leading to the entrance of my lair. I don't have to look back to know she's following.

It's a relief to be moving, with fresh water flowing around me, bathing my senses. Back in the cavern I could smell and taste her far too strongly—a delicate, succulent fragrance, a tempting feminine warmth. The desire I "faked" during my demonstration of non-verbal communication was all too real.

But I've felt desire for females before. It means nothing, and is easily resisted.

Her musical voice pursues me as we swim. "You're right, my father still sees me as a child. But you called me a child too. 'Sweet child,' you said."

"I apologize. It's the dramatic difference in the years between us. To someone like me, you seem newly spawned."

"How old are you?"

I halt, whirling sharply to face her, my tentacles crawling up the sides of the exit tunnel. The mermaid's eyes widen with alarm.

"How rude to ask my age, little princess," I growl.

47

"I meant no disrespect. I was only curious."

"You're a very curious sort, aren't you?"

Her lips twist wryly. "It's a flaw."

"Is it?" I hold her gaze. "I am over two centuries old. Old enough to be your ancestor."

"You don't look it. You look my age. Is that magic?"

"Yes."

"Can I learn the magic? Or—buy it?"

I chuckle. "You haven't even gotten your legs yet, and you're already bargaining for longevity and youth as well? One boon at a time, love."

I continue my swim, leaving the cave system. Beyond the stony walls of my lair, my garden sprawls over the ocean floor— a throng of dangerous plants and creatures, all of them of the sharp, toxic, or carnivorous variety. They rise in a thick riot of color, reaching nearly to the surface, undulating into the distance. They protect me and delight me.

"They're lovely," murmurs the girl. She's floating to my right, keeping a careful distance from my tentacles and from the fronds of the plants. "Lovely and terrible." Her eyes flick toward me for a second. "Those friends of yours—Graeme, Liris, and Ekkon—they live here with you?"

"Yes, though they have their own quarters. They are a mated triad."

Her eyebrows lift. "Oh."

"Triads aren't allowed by your father's priestesses, are they?" My lip curls in a sneer.

"No," she says slowly. "The priestesses teach that every mer has only One True Mate."

"Ah yes, the law of the 'One True Mate.'" I can't keep the venom out of my voice. "And what if your 'mate' betrays you? Or dies? Or changes? What if you find someone else you prefer?

What if the two of you grow apart? What if your heart and body need more than one person to be fulfilled? What then?"

"I—I don't know."

I smile at her, savage and dark. "Enough talk. We need to pass through this area, and I can't risk you getting poisoned again, so I'll take you through myself, as Graeme did before, when he brought you to me."

Realization dawns on her face, but I don't give her a chance to protest. My tentacles shoot out, snaring her, dragging her through the water and bringing her body flush with mine. Two of the tentacles pin her to me, while I use the rest to propel us both ahead.

I know this garden like I know my own skin. With the mermaid's slim body tucked against me, I dart and duck, dip and sway, slither through gaps and slide under fronds.

She twitches in my grasp. "Let me go."

"No."

Her tail quivers, flexing just enough so I can feel her strength. She's no match for me, not really, but if she wanted to, she could give me a challenge. But she must recognize the danger of trying to swim this area by herself; she doesn't try to break away.

Her hair flows back over my right shoulder, mingling with my own. I struggle against the urge to look down, to admire the delicate features so close to mine.

Her corset presses against my chest, a hardened casement of pearls, shells, and jewels encrusting her body, preventing me from feeling her soft breasts. The armor of her innocence.

These corsets that Tarion makes his unmated daughters wear—they're designed to be worn for a long time, and not removed for months. Removing the corset means its destruction. It's another way for Tarion to guard against the corruption of his precious girls. I will take great delight in cracking open the little princess's corset when we reach the shallows.

7

He's so huge. Strength radiates from him—strength and danger. My teeth grate against each other, and it's all I can do not to scream as I'm pinned against the monstrous Sea Witch, towed through his deadly underwater forest.

Again I hear the chorus of mournful, wispy voices, threading through the waving fronds of the garden. "What are those sounds?"

His answer thunders through his massive chest, vibrating in my body. "The ones who broke deals with me."

"You killed them?"

"They doomed themselves."

Mother Ocean, what have I done? I've made a deal with this creature of legend, with this horrible witch, and now—now I think it's too late to back out. The necklaces bind us. I haven't given him my voice yet, and he hasn't given me legs, but I suspect that breaking the arrangement at this point would make the Sea Witch very, very angry. I don't want to know what he would do to me.

Closing my eyes, I focus on the face of the human prince. I think of him awake and laughing, brimming with life, adventure, and humor. I think of him lying peacefully on the beach after I saved him, so young and vulnerable and beautiful. Mine. He can be *mine*.

I can do this.

When I open my eyes, we're soaring through clear water, with the sea bed rising gradually to meet us as we near the shore.

The Sea Witch hasn't released me, so I squirm. "I can swim on my own now."

His tentacles relax, allowing me to push away. "Fine. Keep up."

"I'm fast," I retort. "Maybe even faster than you."

"I doubt that." He angles upward, and I follow his trajectory until we break the surface. It takes me a moment to seal my gills and switch to lung breathing.

The night sky arches above us, deep blue-black frosted with stars. A shimmering moon, blurred at the edges, floats between ragged strips of cloud, the leftovers of the storm.

When I glance at the Sea Witch, my stomach jolts. His rugged face is upturned, its planes softened with silvery light. His massive collarbones gleam wetly, and the curled golden shell lies just below the hollow of his throat. He lifts one tattooed arm, sweeping dark, damp locks back from his face. His hair definitely has a purple tint. I've never seen such a color.

"This depth should work," says the Sea Witch. "Are you ready?"

"Am I ready for legs, right now?" I gasp a laugh. "Gods, no. And fuck yes."

He laughs, sharply and loudly, with a surprised look, as if I startled the sound out of him. He clears his throat, reining in his smile, then mutters a long string of words.

"What is that language?" I ask, but then I forget to listen for an answer because something is happening. Magic is buzzing over my body, coursing along my skin and scales, delving into my bones. My tail thrashes, whips, and splits apart in a blaze of hot pain. There's a crackling snap at the base of my spine—a grinding sensation of new bones thrusting out of my pelvis, pushing downward, lengthening.

I can't scream, because my throat is changing too. The spongy area beneath my gills, the passages that guide air to my lungs—they're evanescing. I touch my neck, and my gills shrink beneath my fingertips, leaving smooth skin behind.

Pain spears through my lower half—what used to be my tail—my spine arches backward, and my mouth opens in voiceless agony.

"A moment's anguish, princess," says the Sea Witch. My body bucks, flailing in the throes of the change, but I catch a glimpse of him. His eyes are flooded with dark purplish-blue again, and his pupils are two milky moons. "You've got to pay to play. The gamble for the gain."

Bastard. Wicked brute. Conniving monster—oh gods, oh Mother Ocean, I'm going to split wide open and bleed out into the sea. A thousand swordfish are lancing through my lower body—a million lionfish spines are grazing my raw nerves. It's a fierce rival for the pain from the anemone's poison.

Worst day of my life.

My vision blurs until I don't know if I'm seeing the indigo sky or the Sea Witch's hair, the pallid moon or his unearthly white pupils—everything is blue and purple, and swirls of inky black and points of silvery light—

And then it stops—all the pain, gone. A sense of wholeness, of newness—but I'm sinking. I'm sinking straight down, until I touch the sandy, grainy floor of the ocean—until my *feet* touch the—my *feet*—

The water has closed over my head.

I didn't get a good breath before I went under and my lungs are already tightening.

I try to swim, but I don't have a tail anymore and these strange flimsy appendages, these legs, they're just flapping uselessly—

A tentacle writhes around my waist, hauling me back up to the surface. I pop up, streaming water, gasping for air.

The deep tones of the Sea Witch break through my confusion.

"Your skin, your hair, your eyelashes, your eyes themselves—they're all different now. You're fully human. You don't shed water as easily or dry as quickly in this form. You can't see in the dark, and your vocal cords are altered, optimized for air." He grips my chin. "Look at me. Do you understand? It's not only the legs. All of you has been changed."

I nod, choking on a half-sob. With shaking fingers I scrape the hair out of my eyes. Though it's the same dark red color as always, it feels different. The texture is finer, and it's more thoroughly soaked with water than usual.

"We'll go ashore now," says the Witch. "I'll get that corset off you and you can put on the gown and jewels. But before we drape your new legs in skirts, I must teach you to walk."

8

The little mermaid doesn't realize that this is new for me as well.

I've never made a deal of this kind. Though a couple of merfolk have asked me for legs, I've always denied that such a thing was in my power. I've kept that magic for myself.

She's the first one I've changed. For a few moments, I was sure I'd killed her. Not that I'd much care. Tarion has enough spawn to keep him occupied.

But something inside me flinched when I saw her struggling mutely, lashed with bone-breaking pain.

I'm confident in my magic. But even someone with as much experience as I have occasionally makes mistakes. One wrong word in the spell, a wavering of intent, a foggy picture of the results instead of a clear vision, and the entire thing can go very wrong.

As I help the girl toward shore, one tentacle wrapped around her waist below her corset, I eye my handiwork. She looks right. Looks human. I think the transformation has worked as I planned. Her body has rebuilt itself as it would appear if she'd been born human.

The water is to my waist now, and dropping lower. I let go of the girl, and she stumbles, flailing in the water, trying to stand on her new legs. I press another tentacle to the small of her back, bracing her.

She shoots me a savage glare, so I shrug and withdraw, leaving her to struggle alone.

When she manages to stand upright for a moment, the water skims the line of her hipbones. Beneath the bottom edge of her corset, her stomach sucks concave with every excited breath. She looks at me, triumphant—then teeters and crashes into the water again, her red hair unfurling like blood in the surf.

Grumbling and swearing quietly, she crawls ahead into shallower water. The two moon-white globes of her new bottom surface through the foam.

My cock hardens, beginning to protrude from the slit that conceals it. In this form, it's hidden at the center of my tentacles. But once I switch to human male shape, my arousal will be harder to conceal.

I thought I could handle this. I've gambled in human taverns where bar wenches sat on my lap and popped out their tits for my pleasure, and I wasn't this hard. I hate that a daughter of Tarion's is affecting me so strongly.

It's not just her ass that allures me. It's the tension of her body, the determination in the way she moves. Her gritty silence. She has been through excruciating pain twice in one day, and she has barely complained. Not what I expected of someone so slender, so small compared to me.

She has a spirit far bigger than her body, that's for certain.

She's standing up again. Fates save me.

That beautiful bottom, twin cheeks perfectly rounded, tucked against creamy thighs. Long pale legs. Hips with an unconsciously tempting tilt as she props herself upright.

I move forward, my tentacles lifting me, carrying me along through the shallow surf until I can see her from the front.

Human women usually have hair on their bodies, while mermaids don't. She seems to have retained that mermaid quality despite her human limbs—odd, and it probably represents a weakness in my spell, but the view of her bare sex is something I can appreciate. It's small and perfect, like her—a triangle of neatly parted flesh, with a hint of pink between the lips.

She's rooted to the spot, staring down at her legs. They quiver beneath her. Her hands cup her hips, then slide downward, over her thighs. Her fingers find the space between her legs, and her gaze flashes up to mine. "What?" she whispers. "What is this?"

"I'll explain everything, once we get you on land." I tear my gaze away and nod to the strip of pale beach ahead. "We have a few hours before dawn. I need to have you ready by then."

Since she seems to dislike my tentacles, I extend my arm, a courtly gesture I've not used in long time.

"I don't need your help," she says.

"My dear, all of this is you needing my help. Who gave you these fine legs and that sweet little pussy?"

"Pussy?" She frowns.

"Human slang, referring to the female genitals. It may also refer to a cat, a furry animal with an affinity for eating mice."

"Mice?"

"Even smaller furry animals, palm-sized, with long tails, large ears, and a hankering for cheese."

"Cheese?" she asks, almost desperately. Her eyes shine, pools of moonlight and eagerness. She wants to know it all, everything, immediately.

I used to feel that way about magic. About the sea. About the world.

"One thing at a time. For now, take my arm, and let's get you to shore."

9

The legs feel a little clumsy and gangly, but I like them.

I'm not sure I like the nubby bits between the legs, though. They're strange. I don't care about being exposed to the Sea Witch, because the genitals don't really feel like *mine*. He seems fascinated with them, though. Maybe he's staring because the spell went wrong and they're malformed. That would be terrible. It would make my eventual mating with the Prince more difficult—or even impossible.

The skin of the Witch's forearm is warm under my hand, a distinct contrast to the chilly night breeze blowing over me. My skin stipples into goosebumps.

"Bend the knee, move the leg forward—good," he says, as I take a step. "Now your other leg. It's difficult in thick wet sand. Even humans struggle with that. It will be easier once we get to the flat part of the beach. Keep going."

This is the same beach where I dragged the prince after I saved him. And there's the path, the one that disappears between the bluffs—the one he took with his men. I picture him standing there, shirtless and beautiful, smiling at me, urging me on. Extending his hand, asking me to come to him, to be with him.

My next steps are more steady, more certain. I loosen my grip on the Sea Witch's arm, confident that I can do this, buoyed by the vision of my true mate.

And then I sway and pitch forward, landing face-first in the sand.

It's in my eyes, coating my lips. Grains grit between my teeth.

I've had sand in my mouth before, in the ocean, but not this much. And it has never stung my eyes like this. I gasp and try to spit it out.

The Sea Witch pulls me up into a sitting position. His deep voice thrums at my ear— "Hold still."

A stream of water sprays against my face, rinsing my eyes, cheeks, and lips. I stick out my tongue, and with a chuckle he rinses that too.

My eyes blink open in time to see him fling the arc of water back into the sea. "You can control water?"

"In small amounts. I used to wield much greater power over it."

"I thought only the King of the Sea could do that. My father Tarion has power over water. He does a water show for the court every solstice."

The Witch's features tense, a muscle jumping along his jaw. "How diverting for everyone. An excellent use of such power."

"Y-yes," I say cautiously, sensing the darkening of his mood. He's sitting too close to me, if it can be called sitting— with his tentacles bunched under his torso. A few of them wriggle along the beach like thick bluish-gray worms.

We're on the wet, packed sand left behind by the tide. I stretch my legs out, pressing the lower edge of my corset against my belly so I can get a better view of the parts between my legs. "This is called a pussy? Is that how it's supposed to look?"

"It's called many things," says the Sea Witch curtly. "And yes, it looks perfect. I mean it looks fine. Good enough."

I probe the area, frowning. In mermaid form, the two openings for elimination and breeding are very obvious once you lift the scale-flap. In this form they seem to be smaller, and in different places. "Where do humans eliminate waste?"

"You have a very small hole at the front for pissing, one at the back for shitting, and a slit in the middle for sex. Stop touching yourself."

"I'm curious."

"Then touch it later, when I'm not around. Gods." He looks away.

It's a little frightening, having these new parts, but it's exciting too. I risk a few more touches, and I'm surprised when a little zing of delight runs up through my belly. It happened when I poked a small nub of flesh right at the top of the pussy.

"What is this for?" I touch it again. "It feels nice."

The Sea Witch glances my way again, and I notice a deep flush across his face. "For someone who knows the word 'fuck,' you know precious little about human anatomy."

"So teach me."

He rises on his tentacles with a strangled groan. "Gods, what have I gotten myself into?"

"This little bit here is for sex, isn't it? For pleasure? Which means I shouldn't touch it. Pleasuring yourself is stealing the future joy of your one true mate."

"The priestesses taught you that nonsense?" He laughs sharply. "I assume they teach that only to the females, and let the males do as they please."

But I don't respond. I'm too busy squeezing the flesh of my legs. Then I hitch one foot onto my knee so I can inspect my feet. "I love these." I wriggle them. "Like tiny stubby fingers. What are they called?"

"Toes."

I glance between my legs again. Since I shifted my position to inspect my foot, that area is spread wider. "Oh, I think I see the opening for sex now."

"Princess," says the Sea Witch, in a desperate growl, "you should put on some clothes."

10

THE SEA WITCH

I haven't wanted to fuck someone so badly in well over a hundred years. Every tentacle I have is creeping toward her, yearning to touch her—my cock is so hard it's almost painful, completely extruded from its slit. I can't bear this. I need relief, or I really might push her down into the sand and have my way with her.

I wouldn't. I won't. But she's sitting there, wide open, inspecting herself, exposing the most delicious-looking pussy I've seen in a long time. I might die if I can't taste her.

Tarion's daughter, Tarion's daughter. Enemy. Rival. She's the catalyst for my revenge and nothing more. I'm not fucking my mortal enemy's spawn. Though it would probably enrage him to know that I had, if I did.

Which I won't.

I unsling the satchel from my body and pull out the gown, undergarments, and pants. I say a quick spell to dry the clothes, then I throw the gown and underthings at her. "Put these on. I'm going to change behind that rock."

She holds the clothing, confused. "How do I put them on?"

I groan again. "Haven't you observed humans before?"

"There's only so much you can observe from the water, or from a distance."

"Fine. I suppose I'll have to dress you as well."

"I think I can figure out how they work," she says, bristling. "You go and change."

I walk around the boulder and switch to human form. Shifting used to hurt, but it's painless by now, a seamless change. I brace my bare back against the rock and circle my burning cock with my fingers.

"I think it's incredible that you can alter your form at will." The girl's sweet voice wafts through the cool air, and I bite back another groan as my cock twitches in response. "What else can you change into?"

"None of your business," I grit out, stroking frantically along my shaft.

"Should I put the gown on over my corset?"

Damn it. "No, don't do that. I need to take the corset off you. It's a sure sign of your true origins."

"Come here and help me take it off, then. I can't do it myself."

Fuck.

"I'm—busy," I choke out.

"Can you remove it with magic?"

"No."

"You must have shifted by now. What are you doing back there?"

Growling, I pull on the pants, tucking my aching cock into them. It pokes outward against the fabric, an obvious betrayal.

"You are the most annoying mermaid I've met in a hundred years," I throw at her.

A moment's silence. Then, "Well, you don't have to like me, do you? Just hold up your end of the deal and we'll be rid of each other soon enough. I don't much care for you either. And I say that with the deepest respect for your power."

I scoff, half-smiling. She's still afraid of me. Good.

If only my control over my form extended to physiological responses like arousal. I take a moment to breathe, to enumerate the wrongs of my past, to wallow in the darkness and the loss. Then I push myself away from the boulder and stalk toward her. I'm still half-erect, but she's unused to human males, and she's focused on the clothes. Perhaps she won't notice.

Her lips part as I approach. "You're very tall as a human."

"I am." I place my hands over the top of her corset. My fingers slip between the firm cups of the corset and the surging flesh of her breasts. The edge of the golden limpet shell around her neck bumps against my knuckles. "Are you ready?"

"You keep asking me that. I'm always ready—just do it."

I tighten my grip and begin to pull. The muscles in my forearms strain as the corset gives way, slowly, shells and pearls and bits of shiny rock popping loose.

"I've heard that these things are built or crafted onto you, so they cannot be easily removed."

She nods. "The first layer is wrapped around us and adhesive is applied, and then the corset-crafter adds more layers, one after another, along with embellishments. Sometimes it takes days to finish the process. But the result is a long-lasting piece we can wear securely for months. I've had this one for nearly a year."

"Humans have a different view of clothing. They change it every day."

"Every day?" Her eyes widen, silver-blue in the moonlight. "How fascinating. So they have many clothes. Will I have many clothes?"

"If you can make the prince like you, yes." With a grunt, I pull outward, ripping the corset halfway down the center. "Gods, this is well-made."

"It's going to feel so strange with it off." Her voice jerks as I yank repeatedly at the remaining stubborn part of the garment. Finally it breaks free, and she steps back, wriggling out of it. The corset falls to the sand, a discarded shell. I pick it up and hurl it far out to sea, where it splashes and sinks.

The princess is nude—a lithe, lovely shape with full, pert breasts, a trim waist, and the most alluring curvy hips. She sighs, cupping the underside of her breasts briefly. It's strange to think that she hasn't touched them in months. Must be a relief to be out of that confining case.

For one of Tarion's pious spawn, she certainly has little compunction about being naked in front of me. Most likely because she views me as a beast, a monster, a wicked creature not worth thinking about beyond what my magic can do for her. In that respect, she's much like all the other merfolk.

She shakes out the undergarments I gave her—a chemise and a pair of lacy drawers. "How…" her voice trails off. Meditatively she puts one dainty foot through the armhole of the chemise, nearly toppling over in the process.

"By the Deep, you're helpless," I snap, kneeling on the beach. "Hold onto my shoulder and lift your foot."

Her small fingers clasp my shoulder, and I hold out the lace-trimmed undershorts for her to step into. Her fragrance dizzies me—a warm, enticing deliciousness I want to nuzzle into. But I drag the garment up her legs without leaning any closer than I must.

67

She manages the chemise herself after that, while I turn my back and think very hard about very terrible things until my arousal diminishes.

Once I set her loose here, I will head up the coast to the next town and I will fuck the first willing woman I find. That's all I need—a good lay. It's not that I'm attracted to this girl specifically—any warm body will do.

"You said I should practice walking before I put the dress on," the girl reminds me.

"So practice." I seat myself on a low rock nearby. "And while you do, I'll tell you about human manners and behavior."

For a couple of hours she staggers around the bit of beach in the moonlight, while I tell her everything I can think of, everything that she might need to know. There's so much to explain, and not enough time to thoroughly test what she's retaining. I can only hope that her lack of a voice will help keep her true origins a secret. She can't betray what she can't speak.

It's unfortunate that I must take her voice. It's lilting, melodic—rather charming. But I need a strong tether to maintain her current form even when she's far from me. I must have a part of her, and her voice is the safest, least harmful option.

"How am I doing?" she asks, mincing toward me across the sand with careful steps. Her long red hair billows around her slender body, and her eyes are alight.

"You look like a bowlegged snipe," I say.

She narrows her eyes, opening her mouth to say something cutting in return, but she bites it back, probably concerned about magical retaliation from the legendary Sea Witch. "I'll practice more."

"Watch me." I rise from the rock and saunter along the strip of beach. "Keep it loose, see?"

With her brow furrowed in concentration, she mimics me a little too well. I can't help snickering. "That's a very manly swagger indeed."

"You said to imitate you." She flushes.

"Try it more like this." Crushing down my pride, I do my best imitation of a barmaid's hip-swaying walk.

When I turn around, the princess has both hands clasped over her mouth, and she's giggling into them.

"You dare laugh at the Sea Witch?" I step into her space, towering over her.

She doesn't flinch. More giggles leak between her fingers. "You want me to walk like *that*?"

"Human men find it appealing."

"Why?"

"Because it makes them think of sex."

"Why?"

"Because of the ass moving, and the—never mind. Do it."

Still smirking, she sashays down the beach in her underthings. Then she turns to face me and comes back, her hips tilting dramatically with every step. "Like this?"

Yes. Yes, exactly like that. "You still look like a snipe. But closer to the mark."

"I'll try it again," she says earnestly. "If you think it will make the prince want me for his mate."

I have no answer. Entranced, I watch her saunter away.

Perhaps I am not much better than a human male, after all.

She is infuriating yet intoxicating, naïve yet sensual. Of course the puny prince will want her. How could he not?

11

When the first rays of dawn lighten the sky, the Sea Witch rises on his long legs. They're clad in loose pants that seem to bulge oddly in the front at times. Some human fashion, I suppose.

I'm tired of practicing my walk, and though I'm grateful for the brief education the Sea Witch has given me, I'm eager to start learning and exploring on my own.

I pull on the gown, delighting in the swish of fabric against my legs. Then I add a necklace in addition to my golden shell, and I clasp bracelets around my wrists.

The Sea Witch watches me dress, with a guarded expression I can't read.

"Will they come down to the beach and look for survivors, do you think?" I ask. "Or should I go up to the village?"

"They will come." He steps back, eyeing me. "You should be more rumpled and torn, as if you've really been in a shipwreck. Come here."

I approach him cautiously. His fingernails are broad and blunt, but as I watch, he alters them, turning them into claws.

"Hold still." He slashes at me, ripping through the bodice of my gown.

I whimper at the sight of the shredded fabric. I can't help it; I love this gown, my very first, and I hate seeing it torn, even if it's necessary for our ruse.

My whimper catches the Witch's attention. He freezes a moment, eyes snapping to mine. Then, with bared, gritted teeth, he keeps tearing at the dress—across the stomach, along the shoulder—he even drops to one knee and ravages the hemline until it is mostly shredded. A few times he nicks or grazes me with his claws, but I don't make a sound.

"You wouldn't have come away from a wreck without a scratch," he says. An explanation, not an apology.

Still on one knee, he glances up at me. "At least you look properly exhausted."

"Neither of us has had any sleep. But you can go back to your cave-hole and rest, while I have to wait to be rescued, and then I'll have to sleep in a human bed, which will feel very awkward, I suspect."

"And what do you sleep in at the palace back home?" He rises, his mouth hitching in a sneer. "A lovely gilded hollow lined with mother-of-pearl and stuffed with the softest undersea ferns?"

"Actually, yes."

He stares at me for a moment with those indigo eyes. Then his lips twitch up at the corner.

I'm smiling too—can't help it, even though I don't *want* to smile at him, or with him.

He reaches out, thumbing my chin. Then the backs of his knuckles trail along the side of my neck, down to my chest.

Heat surges over my skin, blooming along the path of his touch.

His fingertips linger against my breastbone before collecting the limpet shell. "Remember, this will allow me to observe you and your surroundings. I'll speak to you through its power, though no one else will hear my words. So if you're in trouble, I can advise you. But don't abuse the connection. I have more important things to do than watch a little mermaid toddle through her first day on land."

His words sting, and I flush hotter. "I won't call on you unless it's important."

"Never forget that you and I have a deal. You must win the Prince's heart, and when you do, you will perform a single task for me. Only then will I return your voice. Which I plan on taking right now." His broad hand slides up to my neck again.

I swallow anxiously against the press of his strong fingers. "Wait, wait… I'm not sure how to win his heart. There's the walk, but what else? What can I do?"

The Sea Witch's face is stony, merciless. Part of me wants to cringe and beg for his help, while another part of me wants to rise up tall and challenge this hard, cruel man, to show him my own strength. To prove I'm his equal.

"Subdue that wild spirit of yours," he says quietly. "Show the prince your vulnerable self, soft and helpless. He'll want to save you and protect you. Relax your face a little—I can still see your rebellion peeking through. Widen your eyes, and let your lips part. Just so. Look at him the way you're looking at me now, and he will be—" He hesitates, clears his throat— "he'll be enchanted."

I nod, trying to memorize the way this expression feels so I can replicate it.

"One more thing before I take your voice," says the Sea Witch huskily. "What is your name?"

"Averil. Yours?"

His dark brows pin together. "No one cares to know my name. I am 'the Sea Witch,' the ghoul of your father's folktales, the monstrosity that haunts the deep."

"I don't want to call you 'Sea Witch,' or ghoul, or monstrosity."

"You won't be calling me anything," he says blandly. "You won't have a voice. Now sing for me."

I blink at him. "Sing?"

"A continuous flow of sound makes it easier for me to isolate and seize your voice. Sing."

Why does his request make me feel so awkwardly shy? Merfolk love to sing. We sing beneath the water and above it, and in times long past, some of our kind used their voices to lure unwary humans into the deep. While much of our knowledge is carved in symbols onto stone beneath the waves, more of the mer history is woven into songs and chants. I know many of them. So why can't I remember a single one?

"Sing," urges the Witch. He bows over me, tall and dominant, his purple-black hair whispering around his shoulders, tossed by the sea breeze. He smells of darkness and fierce wind, of salty waves and white stars. His fingers tighten around my throat.

A whisper of melody spirals up inside me, and I begin to sing. It's no song I've heard before. It's a golden chain of notes, entirely new—lovely, desperate, melancholy, and wordless. The music weaves with the wind and the susurration of the waves, until the song is no longer mine, but his. It slips out of me, threads of gold visible in the air, slithering into the necklace he wears, winding around it. The Sea Witch's fingers twitch spastically against my neck, and his head tips back, his eyes closing as if in pleasure.

"Mine," he breathes.

I want to ask him how it's possible to take a voice. Voices are generated when air moves through vocal cords, so how can he transform such a thing into magical energy and steal it from me? Did it even work?

When I try to ask the questions, and no sound comes from my empty throat, I know that it did work.

He has my voice. I have my human body.

We have a deal.

No more delays. If I want my voice back—if I want to explore the human world and win the heart of the beautiful prince—I must follow this through to its end.

The Sea Witch releases my neck, grinning, wickedly satisfied. His canines are longer and sharper than those of most merfolk.

He's backing away, retreating into the sea, the surf foaming around his bare feet, then his knees, thighs, waist—he shucks off his pants under the water and his tentacles snake out, thick and powerful, rising above the surface like trees, but with sinuous, tapered ends that curl and writhe.

"Tides be in your favor, little princess," he says in that depthless voice of his. "When you are alone tonight, think of me, and I will speak to you."

My breath catches in my throat. Of course he will want to check in, to be sure I'm accomplishing the task of charming the prince. There is no other meaning behind his words.

His eyes still locked with mine, he ducks beneath the water. And he's gone.

The beach feels strangely empty without his huge, magnetic presence.

I inhale. Try to speak, just to test the spell. My voice remains absent, and my human shape stays intact.

Sighing, I flop down on the sand. Might as well try to relax until I'm found by the search parties.

I don't intend to fall asleep. But somehow I find myself waking up, blinking into the bright morning sun as a dark shape leans over me.

"See there, Brixeus," says a young male voice. "I told you I saw a red-haired woman in the sea! You thought I was imagining things—ha! She must have been stranded from some other shipwreck, prey to that terrible storm! Bring the apothik over here!"

I squint, then gasp as I make out the handsome face of the man I saved yesterday. He's smiling at me, beautiful as the sun itself, delight in his eyes.

"My lady, can you hear me?" he asks eagerly. "Can you tell me your name?"

I want nothing more than to tell the prince my name. But I can't. I can't tell him anything about myself, nothing precious or important or silly or sad.

As I lie in the sand, blinking up at him, dread sinks into my soul, and I realize what a foolish bargain I've made.

What have I done?

What if the prince doesn't feel the Soul Echo, the call between mates? What I've done all this for nothing? What if I never get my voice back?

Liquid wells in my eyes, trailing from the corners and dripping along my temples. These must be *tears*. Human tears, a sign of deep emotion, as the Sea Witch told me during our lesson last night. He said as a human, I'd be able to cry. I'm not sure I like the feeling, but there's a bit of relief in it.

I lift my tear-filled eyes to the Prince's eager ones. Tenderness grows in his gaze.

"Forgive me," he says. "I shouldn't ask you anything, not yet. You've been through something terrible. Worst storm I've ever witnessed. Once the apothik checks you, we'll take you somewhere safe and comfortable."

I nod, while more tears slip from my eyes.

There's a man standing behind the prince—tall and slim, dressed in impeccably neat clothes. His skin is deep brown, nearly black, and his gray hair is shaved close to his skull. White gloves cover his folded hands, and his mouth is a grim line.

"Be cautious, Your Highness," he says. "We have no idea where this woman comes from. She could be an enemy spy."

"Nonsense, Brixeus," says the prince. "You're paranoid."

"I have reason to be, my lord. The recent attempt on your father's life—"

"Which came to nothing, since he remains alive. This girl is clearly harmless, and she needs our help. Ah, Cassilenne, there you are! Come and see to the survivor's comfort, if you will. Tell me if it's safe to move her."

The woman he's addressing crouches beside me. Her long black hair swings in a loose braid, tendrils curling around her face. Her skin is tanned, her dark eyes rimmed with thick lashes.

"Hello there," she says, laying gentle fingers along my cheek. "Do you have pain anywhere?"

I shake my head.

"Watch my finger, please." She holds it up, moves it right and left. "Good. Can you tell me your name?"

Again with that question. I open my lips, but only air comes out. I tap my throat, giving her a worried frown.

"You can't speak?" She frowns as well, exchanging glances with the Prince. "Please do not worry. Such conditions can be brought on by terrible experiences. It may pass in time. Until then, we will take good care of you. Can you move?"

I nod, pushing myself into a sitting position.

The apothik Cassilenne gives the prince an encouraging nod. "She can be carried up to town. I recommend a bath, hot liquids, and plenty of rest."

"Of course, of course." The prince leaps up, only to bend down again, tucking his hands under my body. "I'll take her there myself."

He scoops me up, and my belly quivers with delight at being pressed to his crisp white shirt. He smells delightful—like flowers, spices, and luxury. His shirt is partly unbuttoned, and as I curl against him my fingers brush solid, heated skin, soft over hard muscle.

My heart tugs, drawn toward him with all that I am. As he carries me along the beach and up the path, I let myself admire his strong throat, his crisp jawline, the mobile softness of his mouth, the flick of his long eyelashes.

He is perfect. He is everything I want.

"I'm Kerrin," he says, smiling down at me. Such kindness and warmth in that smile. It saturates my heart like the heat of the sun.

I try to mouth my name to him. *Averil.*

"Ariel?"

A-ver-il, I mouth again.

"Avawel. Avril? Ah, don't worry about it. I'll just call you 'Beautiful.'"

My cheeks heat, and I glance away, smiling. The prince laughs, picking up his pace. His left hand shifts as he carries me, cupping the side of my breast as if by accident. "You know, Beautiful, it's odd that I should encounter someone like you. Someone without a voice, after—" He shakes his head with a light laugh. "It doesn't matter. But perhaps the Fates intended something special with that storm. Something wonderful! What a lucky day, after all!"

Another merry laugh rings from him, and I smile wider. But there's a shade in my heart, because I saw him laughing with those sailors on his ship, and some of them drowned, yet he doesn't seem to think of them at all. Perhaps he did not really know them. Or perhaps he's the kind of person who chooses to focus on the pleasant, hopeful side of life, not the sadness.

What a truly wonderful man.

12

THE SEA WITCH

What an insipid fool, chortling and laughing after so many of his own men perished yesterday. They're likely the same crew that shipped out with him when he left for his foreign travels. He knew them well, yet he can forget their loyalty and service, snickering over some perceived luck of his own. Idiot.

I did not go up the coast and find a woman. I started to, and then I began to think of the princess lying on the beach, helpless and innocent, dressed in a tattered gown, and I imagined some drunken fisherman coming upon her and tearing off her clothes, thrusting himself inside her. The vision was so sharp I turned back and slunk through the darker waters at the foot of the cliff, watching the princess sleep until she was found by the right people. Then I went ashore myself and prowled along the path leading to the village, keeping to the shadow of the trees, watching the prince carry the girl.

He adjusts his grip more than once, unnecessarily. Takes a feel where he can. He's enamored with her body already.

I must warn her not to yield him too much ground physically until she is sure of his heart. My purpose won't be served if he uses her as a quick lay—he needs to want all of her to be his, forever. He needs to ask for her hand. Only then will the right chain of events be set in motion, the events that will lead to my revenge.

I will not go into this town, not with Brixeus present. He would recognize me. I could alter my features, of course, but he might wear rings or carry charms to dispel such magical disguises. I cannot risk my presence being marked. So when Prince Kerrin and his rescued maiden pass the first house on the outskirts of the village, I return to the sea.

When I reach my lair, the others are waiting for me. Liris, running his fingers anxiously along his spines. Graeme, dark gray and narrow-eyed, his eel's tail flickering with barely contained lightning. Ekkon, floating in the glow of his own lure, his translucent body undulating slightly to stay in place.

"Well?" Liris asks. "Did you make a deal with her?"

"I did."

He hums anxiously. "Risky, dealing with Tarion's own daughter."

"Let him come for me," I snarl. "I will be ready. I'll have the prince proposing to her within three days, and when he does—"

"Three days?" Graeme chortles, his eyes and teeth flashing electric white. "You're no matchmaker, Zoltan. You can lure women for a night, but arranging a commitment, an engagement, between two strangers, within just three days? It's lunacy. Impossibility."

"The girl must secure the prince's heart before he heads for the Summer Palace at Crystal Point," I retort. "Or else he may leave her behind. He has to take her along, and their connection must be strong enough to withstand the complexities of court life and politics. At this time of year, the king is usually on holiday at the Summer Palace, and he will have brought along a passel of peevish nobility. A new royal romance will be something for them to either deconstruct or obsess over, and I must make sure it's the latter."

Graeme exchanges a look with Liris. "You've concocted some wild schemes in the past, but this is by far your wildest, I believe."

"Indeed." Liris swirls nearer to me, careful not to brush his spines against my tentacles. "Will you not give this up, Zoltan? What you seek is out of reach, and you have only the barest chance of success with this plan. I don't want to see you disappointed again, my friend."

My fingers curl into fists. "This is the most promising plan yet. The best chance I've ever had to reclaim what's mine. What harm is there in trying it?"

"The harm," says Ekkon, in his distant, singsong voice, "lies in the darkness that will descend upon you if you fail. We've seen you in that dark place. We've dragged you out of it, with difficulty. We would rather not have to do it again."

"I won't trouble you, then," I snarl. "If I fail, I'll go far away. None of you will have to see me or speak to me anymore. But that's not what you want either, is it? Because if I leave, there's no one to alter your forms so you can fuck without hurting each other."

Liris looks away, and Graeme hisses through his teeth. Ekkon merely blinks, a ghostly smile on his translucent face. "That would be unfortunate," he says faintly.

"I enable you to have some measure of physical fulfillment to grace your otherwise esoteric mating bond," I tell them. "And I do it without bargain, without price, except that of friendship. The least you can do in exchange is to allow me this chance at my own happiness."

"Happiness?" Liris looks back at me sharply. "Is that what you seek? I thought you wanted revenge."

"They're the same thing."

"No," he says gently. "Ah, no, they are not."

13

AVERIL

I haven't seen Prince Kerrin much today, but I don't really mind, because the hours have been so full of other incredible things.

I've made some observations of humans on ships and ashore, but nothing I learned by observation compares with experiencing things myself, witnessing them up close. I've been out of the water, on rocks or beaches, but never for long, since my scales and skin would begin to feel dry and itchy after too many minutes out of my natural element. Yet with my new body, none of that matters. I can exist in the air, on the land, as if I was born to do so.

It's odd to be planted and pinioned to the earth instead of floating freely, but the adjustment isn't as dramatic as I feared it might be.

It's a good thing my voice is gone, or I might let out too many exclamations of wonder and too many eager questions, spoiling the secret of my origins. As it is, I have to hold myself in check, trying not to startle or gasp or flinch or leap at every new thing. I have to keep my reactions under control.

When I do overreact to something, the two maids tending me simply cluck their tongues and say, "Poor thing, had such a fright, didn't you? No wonder you're a bit jumpy. Anyone would be. Have a sweet, dearie. Another sip of tea. Would you like a blanket, dove?"

The two maids expect me to relax in the comfortable common area of the inn where the prince is being housed, when I would much rather be flying around the room, touching every single thing, or running outside to survey the gardens and the town. Whenever the maids leave the room, I hop up and explore my surroundings, only to be shooed back to the couch when they return.

At last, one of them comes in and says brightly, "Well, dearie, since you seem to be feeling well enough, how would you like to dine with His Highness this evening, at the mayor's house? Finest place in town. Not up to royal standards, but we do what we can. The prince has sent over a dress for you, to replace your torn-up gown. If you feel up to going, I'll help you dress."

I leap up, nodding enthusiastically. At least the nod and the head-shake are shared signs of assent and dissent between the peoples of land and sea. Otherwise I would be in a much more frustrating position.

As the maid helps me dress, I try to fake an understanding of how each garment should go. Apparently I fail, because she looks at me sharply several times. "Hit your head, did you?" she asks. "Lost a bit of your memories? I had a cousin what got clocked real good once. Literally clocked. I mean a big old heavy clock fell right off the mantelpiece and struck his skull while he was adding logs to the fire. Couldn't remember his wife for a week, or so he said. Went off gallivanting in the next town for a few nights, slept with nigh on half a dozen women before he regained his senses and came back."

I blink at her, stunned. Under the sea, cheating on your mate is a sin punishable by excommunication and exile.

"Don't look so shocked, dearie." She chuckles. "You got a man?"

Do I have a man, or a mate? Maybe. I'm not sure yet.

I shake my head.

The maid gives me a conspiratorial smile. "Well then. Let's see if we can't deck you out well enough to turn the royal head. I'm Ems, by the way. Maid at the inn by day, mother of two babes by night. One of those babes is my big strapping husband." She chuckles. "Needy as the little one, he is."

I smile at her, wishing I could tell her about my sister Ylaine. She has a tiny daughter now, and her mate Ardoc is the sweetest hunk of useless male I ever met. Utterly adores her and their daughter, but so helpless sometimes, especially when he got cuttlepox a few months ago. Ylaine told me he moaned and groaned until she was sure the entire undersea kingdom could hear him.

I can't share any of that with the maid. Which annoys me. But my frustration fades a bit when she arranges my newly human hair into an elaborate scarlet coiffure my maids under the sea could never have achieved.

The dress the Prince sent me is blue like the calm ocean beneath a sunny sky—the perfect complement to my fair skin and dark red hair. It scoops even lower in the front than my corset did, and it plunges deep on the other side too, revealing most of my back, but I don't mind. I'm still wearing the jewelry the Sea Witch gave me, and my own pearl earrings.

"Are you all right in this?" the maid asks with a faint frown, tugging at my neckline. "If you'd be more comfortable in something else—"

I shake my head, smiling, and she nods. "Well… you look lovely. The Prince's equerry, Lord Brixeus, will be here soon to escort you to the mayor's house."

As she turns away, I catch her hand. Then I touch my chest, looking at her earnestly, gratefully. Hoping she'll understand my thanks.

A warm smile spreads over her face, and she pats my hand. "There now, dear. It was a pleasure. Take care of yourself tonight. Here's hoping you will recover and we can get you back with your family."

She leaves then, too swiftly to see my face fall.

My family. My father, my sisters, the court—my people.

I left them with barely a thought. Impulsive, reactionary, like I always am. Selfish. Because when they realize I'm gone, and not just on one of my usual forays, they will feel angry, betrayed, and hurt.

Guilt coils in my heart, and I remember the words of my father's favorite priestess: *Loyalty to one's progenitor is paramount above all else. If we fail to be grateful to those who made us, we are worth less than the sand that swirls in the waves.*

I've defied my father many times, in small ways. This is by far my biggest act of rebellion.

But is it really rebellion, or is it simply my choice? My decision, as a full-grown mermaid, to live the life I desire?

Maybe it's not rebellion, but liberation.

I'm still pondering that when a rapping sound startles me. A man stands in the doorway—the tall, elegant, dark-skinned one who cautioned the prince that I might be a spy. Lord Brixeus, equerry to the prince—whatever that means.

I'm not sure why he bumped the door with his hand in that way. Some human method of announcing one's presence, perhaps? Rather abrupt, in my opinion.

"Milady," Lord Brixeus says coolly. "I'm here to take you to your dinner with His Highness. And on the way, I have a few questions for you."

I walk beside Lord Brixeus as smoothly as I can. The cobblestones of the street are perilous indeed, and the skirts of this gown are stiffer and more voluminous than the first one I wore, so I avoid introducing any of the hip-swaying that the Sea Witch taught me, lest I topple over.

People stare as we pass. Odd that they'd be staring at me—I'm fully human, according to the Sea Witch. Unless he left some telltale mark or sign, something undone that hints at my otherness and attracts attention. I wouldn't put it past him. By all accounts he's a trickster and a villain who persuades people to take on bargains they can't fulfill.

I know this, and yet I bargained with him myself. Idiotic. Risky in the extreme. Why did I think I could do this, mincing along like a human girl, masquerading as one of them? I'm bound to be found out the minute I sit down at a human dinner table. I ate some food earlier, back at the inn, but this will be a formal meal. The Sea Witch gave me instructions for an occasion such as this, but I'm afraid I didn't grasp everything. What if I—

"Where do you come from?" asks Lord Brixeus. "What kingdom?"

I glance up, surprised. He's glowering at me, dark brows pinned together.

I tap my lips and throat.

"Yes, I'm well aware that you claim to be unable to speak," he says. "Convenient, that. But you and I both know there are other ways of communicating."

Of course. I summon the pleading, vulnerable expression the Sea Witch told me to use, the one that should make men want to rescue me and help me. It feels wrong on my face.

Lord Brixeus's frown deepens. "I am not the prince. No fakery will win my heart, I assure you. I can see that you are not what you seem. But who you are, exactly, I do not know. No matter—rest assured that I will be watching your every move, woman. One false step, one attempt at harming the prince, and you will be ended on the spot. Do you understand?"

My eyes widen, this time in real consternation. I stop, laying a hand on his wrist, shaking my head, frowning up at him, willing him to see that I mean Kerrin no harm.

Lord Brixeus pulls away. "Strange woman. Walk on, and do not touch me again."

Threatening though he is, I feel a grudging respect for him. After all, he's only doing his duty as a loyal subject to the Crown.

Most of the houses in the village are modest—some kind of white stone-like material, crisscrossed with wooden beams for support, with red-tiled roofs and flowers overflowing from boxes hung in front of the windows. I marvel at the abundance of scarlet, purple, blue, and yellow blooms. I love the color and glory of the life under the sea, but this is beautiful, too. I want to touch every flower. But I must walk primly beside Lord Brixeus until we reach our destination.

The mayor's house looks similar to the others, only wider, taller, and deeper, with even more flowery windowboxes. A man opens the door, and Lord Brixeus ushers me through into a room with a polished tile floor. We are directed down a hall into a larger room, one glittering with tiny bits of fire on long sticks— they're called candles. The Sea Witch told me about them. There are two tables shining with dinnerware—I know about those because of items I've gleaned from shipwrecks.

People stand throughout the room—several men in fine coats and a handful of women in gowns, waving fans. Faces of every color, bodies of every shape and size. Beautiful humans, all of them. I'm overwhelmed by their loveliness, and I let a smile of utter delight spread over my face. It's returned, first with looks of surprise, then by tentative answering smiles.

A rotund, cheerful-faced man steps forward, drawing a curvy woman with him. "I'm Throanfeld, Mayor of the town," he says. "This is my wife Julen. We're so happy you were found safe, and that you are well enough to join us."

They both look genuinely happy, and my smile widens. I wish the Sea Witch could see how well I'm doing, how pleasant everyone is being. Well, except Lord Brixeus, but I'll win him over.

The golden limpet shell grows a touch warmer against my skin. But before I can think anymore of that, the mayor's wife, Julen, takes my arm. "We heard about the loss of your voice, dear. Don't worry about a thing. You'll sit near me. Unless the prince wishes otherwise." She lowers her voice. "He seems quite taken with you."

"Sshh, love," chides the mayor mildly. "Don't embarrass the poor girl. We're about to sit down to dinner. When his Highness arrives, we'll—"

"I have arrived," says a clear, merry voice, and my heart flutters, warmth flooding my cheeks.

When I turn to face him, Prince Kerrin halts, a hand splayed over his heart. "My gods. You were beautiful on the beach, but by the dragons of the sea, you are *stunning* now. I chose the dress well, did I not?" He glances around the room, a charming grin cocking his mouth.

Murmurs of assent and admiration ripple through the room. I squirm a little. I'm not sure why. They were all looking at me before, but now it feels as if their stares have changed—turned keener and hungrier in the wake of the prince's comment.

"Come, Beautiful," says the prince. "Sit with me." He holds out his arm.

The mayor's wife lets go of me. I'm sorry about it, for some reason.

But this is what I want. The prince's attention. Time with him, so I can feel the Soul Echo again and ascertain whether or not he's my mate. Sometimes the bond is immediate, and sometimes it takes a while to be sure.

Lowering my head briefly, I accept the prince's arm. A memory flashes through my mind—the first man who offered me such accompaniment. The Sea Witch's tattooed, sinewy forearm. My new feet slogging through thick, wet sand.

The prince leads me to the head of the table, while the other guests shift and rearrange themselves, finding chairs. They don't sit until he does, and at his gesture I sink awkwardly into the chair beside him.

"I hope Brixeus was good to you," says Prince Kerrin, low. "He may be a suspicious old bastard, but he means well."

I give him an understanding smile.

"You should smile all the time, Beautiful," he says. "You're absolutely ravishing when you do."

He likes it when I smile. I make a mental note to do it as much as possible. One more way to win his affection without words.

I glance down at the table. And my heart nearly stops, the sensation of phantom gills fluttering at my throat.

So many, many forks and spoons. Large plates with smaller plates on top in seemingly neverending circles. An array of glass and pewter drinkware. One of the goblets is half full of ruby liquid. And in the miniature bowl at the center of my stack of dishes, there's a tiny twist of paste topped with a fleck of green and a sprinkle of reddish-brown dust. Is it food?

I don't know what to touch first, what to do. When I look up cautiously, trying to get a hint from the other guests, everyone seems to be looking at me.

Desperate, I turn my thoughts inward. The Sea Witch said I could call on him through the shell. He can talk to me without anyone else hearing. He can help me get through this, if he's there, if he will listen.

I press all my thoughts into one concerted pulse. *Sea Witch, I need your help.* I grit my teeth against my pride. *Please.*

14

The princess's anxious plea ricochets through the snail-shell on my chest, vibrating in my mind.

I've been watching her from my lair for a few minutes—it seems she subconsciously wished for my observation. Which pleases me more deeply than I'd like to admit. And now she's actually begging for my help.

The shell translates her thoughts, sending them to my brain in her sweet, musical voice. *I can't do this. Help me. What is all this? Why are they staring?*

I tap the shell again, broadening my view of the girl and her surroundings. The scene appears all around me in grainy color, a moving picture in floating particles, sand coalesced and magically arranged to replicate her form and everything she sees.

"The prince's lady begins the meal," I tell her aloud. "That's why they're looking at you. Pick up the wine glass and drink a sip or two. Then take the tiny garnish fork near the silver goblet and touch it to the paste. Put a dab of it on your tongue, then nod."

Oh gods, I was afraid you wouldn't answer.

She obeys me immediately, sipping the wine and tasting the garnish. When she nods, the servants immediately remove the tiny tasting dish, and the meal begins with a clink of dishes and a ringing of silverware.

My eyes lock onto the little three-pronged garnish fork still pinched between the princess's tapered fingers. It looks similar to the one that I—

Thank you. Her voice interrupts my reverie.

"Can't have you panicking and spoiling the plan," I retort.

She's sipping the soup now, her inner voice making all the delighted sounds she can't voice in person. Her soft moans send a tingling arousal through my entire body, from fingertips to tentacles. How does she do this to me? I hate it.

"Stop focusing on the soup," I snap. "Pay attention to the prince. Men like women who focus solely on them."

But I want to eat, she whines. *It's so delicious. Have you tasted soup before?*

"Of course. Many kinds."

There are many kinds? Oh my gods. I want to try them all.

The corner of my mouth twitches up. Furious, I slap my own face, hard. Difficult to do underwater, but it's a necessary personal chastisement.

After one more bite of soup, Averil turns her attention to the insipid prince, who's regaling the table with tales of his exploits abroad—beating this duke in a duel and that princeling in a game of Chips-and-Daggers. So he's a gambler. That is the first thing about him that has piqued my interest. When he mentions my favorite game, Headsman's Yoke, I'm even more intrigued.

"I'll teach you a few games," I tell Averil. "So you can play cards with him. Express some interest, right now."

Play cards? she says vaguely, but she acts on my nudge, leaning closer to the Prince and looking up at him with keener attention.

"Do you like games, Beautiful?" he asks, smiling down at her.

"Say yes," I hiss. "But look uncertain or modest about it."

She smirks, shrugs, and nods.

"Excellent," says the prince. "I'd play you tonight, but you should go to bed right after dinner, and get some rest. Perhaps tomorrow we can have a game."

There's a power in the way he speaks to her—an ownership. He expects to be obeyed. Of course he does—he's a rutting prince, heir to Perindal's throne.

He's very forceful. Averil's inner voice is admiring, yet a little unsure. *He wants what's best for me. That's so kind of him. Very thoughtful. Just how a true mate should act.*

If she mentions the "true mate" nonsense one more time…

"Ah, yes, but pray don't plan on any games tomorrow night, Your Highness," says the mayor. "We're organizing a little gathering here in town, to express thanks to the gods for sparing your life from the shipwreck, and to light candles for the sailors who were not so fortunate."

"How kind of you," says the prince. "But that sounds so doleful. I'm sure the deceased men would much rather we celebrate them in joyful fashion. A banquet and a dance, I think, would be better suited to the occasion. Better yet—a festival of masks! I do love a good masquerade."

Asshole. A self-absorbed, disloyal asshole, just like his father.

The mayor exchanges startled glances with his wife, but quickly recovers his composure. "Just as Your Highness wishes, of course. I'll see it done."

"We must have your very best provisions and decorations for the party, mind you," says the prince, raising his cup to the mayor. "And where is the next course? Some meat, I hope. I feel as if I've been waiting forever for the main event." He laughs, and the other guests chuckle politely with him.

He lacks patience, Averil says inwardly. Finally she is slightly displeased with him. *But everyone has faults. I'm not particularly patient myself—*

I interrupt her. "Now I have to teach you two things— gambling and dancing. Once they put you to bed and things become quiet, slip out the back door of the inn. I'll meet you there, and we'll go somewhere I can teach you without being interrupted or suspected."

Will there be more soup?

"No. Stop thinking about your stomach. And pace yourself—you don't want to become ill from all the rich food. Another thing—don't yield your body to the prince yet. It's his heart you want to secure first, not his cock."

He's my future mate, she exclaims inwardly. *Giving myself to him will be perfect and beautiful when it happens. You don't have to be crude about it.*

"To use one of your secret favorite words—right now he wants to fuck you, and that's all, trust me. Heed my warning, do you understand? He's likely to try something tonight. Don't give in. Not even a kiss yet. Save that for tomorrow."

A kiss... oh... She freezes right in the middle of poking her serving of gravy-laden roast with a spoon.

I narrow my eyes, sensing her anxiety. "What is it? And eat your meat with a fork, not a spoon. Gods."

I haven't kissed anyone, she replies. *I'm not sure I know how to do it well.*

My stomach flips over. "Well, I suppose that's another thing I'll have to teach you."

15

AVERIL

After dinner, the prince makes excuses for leaving early and
walks me back to the inn himself. Two servants trail us, one of
them carrying a package of some kind.

Prince Kerrin breezes past the innkeeper and the staff with
cursory thanks for their hospitality. While he's speaking with
them, I slide my hand down his arm, curling my fingers against
his palm.

He glances at me, arching a brow and giving me one of his
gorgeous, heart-warming smiles. And I feel it again—the thrill,
the Soul Echo, the pull between us. The certainty that I could be
happy with him, forever. We could explore the world together—
not just this kingdom, but others. He'll be a king one day—he
can take me anywhere. Of course, he'll have duties—but my
father takes holidays, and I'm sure Kerrin would too.

Kerrin weaves his fingers with mine so that we're palm to
palm, the heated centers of our hands pressed together. Thrills of
connection course up my arm, and I'm practically breathless as

he leads me upstairs. I've never felt like this before. He has to be my one true mate. Nothing else could feel this good, this right.

"Your room is near mine," the prince says, pointing to a door. "Just there. But before you retire, I have a gift for you." He takes the package from his servant and places it in my free hand. "I want you to wear this to bed, and think of me." His voice sinks to a throaty whisper. "Maybe I'll come see it on you later."

If it's an article of clothing like the gown he gave me, it makes sense that he would want to see how it looks and fits; so I nod.

The prince smiles, lifting my knuckles to his lips. A brief press of his mouth, a long look into my eyes. "Until then, Beautiful."

He turns with a courtly spin, snaps his fingers at his servants, and enters his room.

I slip into mine, holding the package in one hand, pressing the other to my belly, which keeps swooping uncontrollably. I'm smiling wide as a basking whale.

I explore the room first. I've been given a nice one, by the look of things—there's even a tiny privy closet with something the Sea Witch grudgingly explained to me on the beach—a toilet and a pipe system. In the sea we simply swim away from others to relieve ourselves. Sometimes there are zones where elimination is prohibited, but we don't attempt to contain, purge, or channel the waste like humans apparently do. The sea takes care of all that.

I have a little difficulty with the process in my human form, but I refuse to even think about the Sea Witch while I relieve myself, lest I summon his gaze accidentally and he witness every shameful detail.

When everything is satisfactorily disposed of, I clean my hands in a bowl of water. There's a hard, strong-smelling chunk of something in a dish beside the washbowl. I can't remember what the Witch called it, or how to use it. I run my fingers over the object, but it only gets slimy, so I dip my slippery fingers in the bowl again until the sliminess is gone.

Next I inspect the package, relishing the smoothness of the strange wrapping. Paper, I think, although I haven't had much chance to see paper up close. When paper comes down below, it becomes soggy and falls apart quickly.

Inside the wrapping lies a filmy scrap of white cloth. I lift it out, shaking it gently until its folds fall.

It's a garment. But it's much scantier than the gown I wore tonight.

I disrobe down to my drawers and carefully work the flimsy thing over my body. It's nearly as translucent as the body of the Sea Witch's strange friend Ekkon. The hem barely covers my genitals and my breasts are perfectly visible through the thin material of the front. Gauzy lace sleeves drape my arms.

This must be what human women wear to bed. It's certainly more revealing than anything I ever wore under the sea. Shrugging, I remove my jewelry except for the shell necklace, and I lay the pieces on a tall dresser.

A sharp tapping at my door, and I jump. A moment later, a head pokes in—not Ems, but the other maid who cared for me today.

"I'm heading home," she says. "But Ems told me to be sure and check on you first. I brought you a nightdress…" But her eyes widen as she takes in my garment. "I see you already have a finer one. Well, I'll just leave this here anyway. If you get cold." She drapes a thick ivory garment over a chair. It has buttons, and would probably cover my body much better. "Just put the lamp out when you're ready to sleep."

I stare blankly.

"Ah, yes, the lamps are the newfangled kind. Perhaps they don't have these wherever you're from. The innkeeper and his wife are very progressive. He has a brother in the capital, you see, an inventor. And noble guests often take their rest here during the warm months. So close to the shore and the Summer Palace." She walks over to the dresser and points to the glowing lamp atop it. "See this key? Turn it this way, and the light will go down. Keep turning, and it will go out altogether. Reverse it, and the light returns."

At my grateful nod, she gives me a little curtsy and leaves the room.

I wander to the human bed, marveling at how stationary, how grounded it is, like everything else here on land. When I crawl onto it, it's so soft and pillowy that I want to moan aloud. But I can't. So instead I sprawl on it, limbs relaxed, and I smile against the smooth fabric.

A few moments later, there's another rap at the door, and someone immediately steps into my room.

I sit up, trying to straighten the thin nightdress.

Prince Kerrin closes my bedroom door behind him. He's shirtless, wearing loose pants. His black hair is tousled, his cheeks flushed. There's a goblet in his hand, and his lips shine wet.

"Drink?" he asks, extending the goblet.

I shake my head.

The prince is staring at me hungrily, rather like the Sea Witch did when he was showing me how to communicate an emotion without words.

It's just as the Sea Witch warned, then. Prince Kerrin is eyeing me like he wants to fuck me. That's the coarse human phrase. At court under the sea, we would say mate, copulate, merge, synchronize, or any number of elegant words.

But the Sea Witch said I must not do that with the prince yet. I need to win his heart first.

The prince sways a little, stepping toward me. "Stand up, Beautiful. I want to look at you."

I rise from the bed, marking the dilation of his pupils as he comes nearer. But when he reaches for me, I recoil.

I don't know why I withdraw. If he's my mate, I shouldn't.

I want him, I do. Just—not now. Not yet.

He blinks at me, his brow furrowing as if he's confused, hurt, maybe a little angry.

I can't stand for him to be angry. He might decide he doesn't like me at all.

Impulsively I seize his hand and set my mouth to his knuckles, like he did to mine.

"You're an odd one," he says, with a half-smile. "I suppose you're tired?"

I nod fervently.

"Very well." His tongue slides across his lips as he scans my body again.

One step nearer he comes. His free hand cups my waist suddenly, a hot press of hard fingers dragging upward, hitching the hem of the nightdress even higher. His teeth are set, slightly bared. His nostrils quiver.

I hold my breath, waiting, tense.

In the deep, no one forces another to copulate. The priestesses teach that mates shouldn't deny each other, but beyond that, a forced coupling is punished to the worst degree.

The prince wouldn't force me. He's too good for that. If he presses, I will yield, because I want to please him.

Or perhaps I will use my training as a warrior, and stop him.

I let that bold impulse flash from my eyes to his.

And then I remember that the Sea Witch told me to subdue my rebellious side in Prince Kerrin's presence. I let the fire fade, and I force my fingers to uncurl.

The prince's eyes blink, as if he's momentarily confused by my reaction. Then he backs away, with a clumsy wave of his cup. "Another time, then."

I give him a small smile.

When he leaves, I resume breathing normally.

I wasn't afraid, only nervous because this body is new, and my connection to the prince is new, and I want everything to be right the first time I join with my mate.

But I didn't like the look in his eyes, or his hard grasp of my waist. In that moment I felt none of the pleasurable delight I experienced when he led me upstairs. And that troubles me.

Tonight at dinner, the prince's behavior bordered on unkind a few times, especially to our hosts. Maybe that's acceptable among humans. But it reminds me unpleasantly of my sister Serra, of the callous, cruel way she treats our servants and the lesser nobles at court.

I sit crosslegged on the bed, chewing my lip, waiting for the creaking footsteps and distant voices of the inn to settle a bit before I go to meet the Sea Witch.

Mates don't have to be perfect. But I do want mine to be kind.

With a blanket wrapped around me, I manage to sneak downstairs once most of the noises of the inn have quieted.

When I step cautiously out of the back door, there's a cloaked man leaning against the wall outside, smoking a long pipe—some traveler or other, also housed at the inn. We ignore each other, and I hurry past a strange-smelling outbuilding to a low wall with a gate. We have doors and gates at home as well, though they look somewhat different and they always fill up an entire frame or opening. A waist-high gate like this would do nothing under the sea. One could simply swim over it.

I manage to figure out the latch quickly and I step through. But there's no one waiting for me, only a dark, empty dirt path bordered by more walls and hedges. The hedges are singing, or chirping—shrill sounds that seem to come from somewhere among their leaves.

Curious, I step closer, fingering one of the leaves, delighting in its velvety underside and glossy surface. It has sharp edges with points, and I prick myself on one. I can't let out a cry—just a breath. Blood beads on my finger. Under the sea it always spiraled away instantly.

Lifting my finger, I inspect the crimson dot.

"Put it in your mouth." A deep, growly voice, deep as sin.

I whirl, and there's the strange pipe-smoking man. Taller than I realized, and very broad in the shoulders and chest. He throws aside his hat, baring his face to the moonlight and the distant glow of the courtyard lamps.

I squint. There's something familiar about him, but—

Sighing, he hooks his pipe between his lips and pulls open his shirt. There's the shark's-eye shell, shining golden.

My mouth gapes.

"It's a glamour." He touches his face. "Not a true transformation, like yours. This is a temporary illusion to protect my identity. I can let you see through it."

And suddenly, I do. I see him, as he looked on the beach last night. His rugged features, his violet-blue eyes, his full mouth, which quivers as if on the verge of a smile before clamping into a grim line.

The Sea Witch gestures for me to follow him along the path, so I do.

But then I catch his arm. I point to the hedge that's singing and then touch my ear, begging with my eyes for him to explain.

"Insects among the leaves," he says. "They make sounds with their legs and wings."

I move toward the bushes, but he grabs my wrist. "No time for that, O curious one. Come along. I've borrowed a horse."

My gaze whips back to his, while my heartbeat quickens. If he has a *horse*, the singing insects can wait.

"I thought you'd like that." The Witch smirks. "Of course I can't let you ride alone—you'll fall off and break an ankle. So you'll be riding with me."

I nod, not really understanding or caring, and I hurry past him while he chuckles softly.

A shadow shifts ahead, a bulky form moving in the dark. Something makes a rough, quick, purring sort of sound—maybe a snort. I've never heard anything quite like it. Moonlight gleams on a shiny kind of fur, like a sea otter's pelt, but shorter.

The horse is huge. Grand and gorgeous. I feel like sinking down and worshiping it. I stand with both hands over my mouth, frozen in awe.

"Reach out your hand," says the Sea Witch.

Tentatively I stretch out my arm. The horse extends his long neck and face, his immense velvety nostrils flexing.

"You can stroke his nose."

Gently, gingerly, I do. He's so sleek, so warm. So alive and beautiful and powerful.

I glance back at the Sea Witch. His arms are crossed, and his biceps bulge against the tight sleeves of the ivory shirt he's wearing. "Enough fondling. Time to mount."

He comes up to me and touches the blanket I'm holding around my shoulders. "What are you wearing under here? Is this a nightdress?"

I nod, opening the blanket to let him see.

His eyebrows lift, and his mouth opens. For a moment he looks away and doesn't speak. Then he says, "The prince gave you this?"

Again, I nod.

"Did he try to touch you? Bed you?"

Another nod. My whole body is burning. I pull the blanket tightly around myself again.

"All right. I can't take you into the *Fiddling Albatross* looking like this—they'll think I'm paying for your company. When we get there, I'll glamour this into a dress with more— um—with *more*."

His hand dips lower suddenly, catching my leg under the knee and hoisting it high while he braces my back with one hand. Before I can struggle, or think past the startling sensation of his fingers in that tender spot, he plants my foot in a loop of metal and leather.

"This is a stirrup. You can use it to mount. That's the saddle, where we sit to ride. Reach up as high as you can and pull. You're a shrimp compared to this horse, so I'll have to give you a boost. Try to get your other leg over the saddle. Just like riding a dolphin. Ready?"

I throw him a reproachful look.

"I forgot. You're always ready."

He pushes and I leap. I can't get a grip on the saddle—I'm trying to hold the blanket as I mount, but my foot slips out of the stirrup, and I crash back against the Sea Witch. At the same moment the horse snorts and shifts impatiently, bumping the Witch hard. He's off balance, so when I slam into him, we both go down, while the blanket slides into the dirt.

He's lying under me, a wall of muscle between me and the ground.

"Get off me," he snarls.

I try. I push against him, attempting to get up. My bare thigh slides between his. There's an odd hardness below his belt. Something solid, perhaps a weapon he's carrying under his clothes.

"Damn you, shrimp, get *off.*" He shoves me up, scrambling out from under me. "Let's try this again."

This time I manage to get astride the horse, with my skirts scrunched up high on my legs. *Just like riding a dolphin,* I repeat in my mind, but he doesn't seem to hear me. I suppose since he's here seeing me in person, the remote mental connection of our shells doesn't work.

The Sea Witch grips the front of the saddle, right between my legs. There's a flash of awareness, a tingling heat as my body registers the nearness of his fingers to that little sensitive nub of flesh I found earlier, and for a moment—just a moment—I wonder how it would feel if he touched it.

Then his huge body lands in the saddle behind me, his front crammed up against my backside. That strange hardness again, pushing at my rear…

"Fuck," says the Sea Witch in a strangled voice. "This is not going to work. You need to sit behind me." He dismounts immediately. "Scoot back. Way back."

Glaring, I move, trying to hold my scanty nightdress in place. He awkwardly manages to get up in front of me, elbowing me in the face in the process.

"Hold onto my waist," he orders. "No! Not that low. Higher."

With a sharp sigh, I move my hands higher.

The horse starts moving with a jolt, a rocking motion I didn't expect. It's not particularly comfortable, but once we're out of the narrow path, the Sea Witch speaks a string of unrecognizable words again and the horse launches into a smooth run, so fast that the night wind whips my hair back and the landscape flies past us in a blue-black haze.

"A spell for extra speed," he says. "Convenient for travel."

We're already out of the village, speeding along a road at the top of the bluffs. To my right, sparkling black and silver, lies the sea.

Without my blanket, the chilly air rushing off the ocean cuts right through my frail garment. I press myself to the warm, broad back of the Sea Witch. It doesn't feel as strange as it should, being this close to such a malevolent, powerful being. Maybe because I know we have a deal, and the deal protects me from him, for now. And he is my only source of heat. In my mermaid form, I'm far more resistant to temperature changes. Not so with this human flesh.

I want to ask the Sea Witch about the other physical differences between humans and mermaids, the less obvious ones. And I want to ask him how it feels to have so much power at his disposal. Whether anyone else could learn or obtain such power. How much of it he was born with, what it cost for him to gain the rest. Where he came from, if he ever had a mate…

The string of questions continues, growing longer and longer in my head until I'm sure I won't be able to remember them all. I could write them down for him—he knows how my people write the Common Tongue. But I'm not sure he'll allow me the time for questions. There's so much I have to learn tonight.

One of the larger clouds looming overhead releases a fine, misty rain that slicks my nightdress to my cold skin. I shiver, cuddling closer to the Sea Witch's back, tightening my grip around his body. His shoulders twitch, but he doesn't protest.

"We're almost there," he rumbles. "Before we reach our destination, I should return your voice. Temporarily. While you're in my presence, I don't need to hold onto your voice to keep you secure in this form. But know that if you drift too far without yielding your voice to me again, your voice will snap right back into this shell, by force. And it will hurt."

Golden tendrils slither over his shoulder, snaking toward my mouth. I part my lips, and as the tendrils rush in, my throat warms and hums—my voicebox vibrating to life.

"You could have given my voice back the moment I saw you tonight," I accuse him. "But you waited until now."

"Yes. Because I didn't fancy hearing your questions all the way to the tavern."

"Oh." I almost laugh. It's irritating that he didn't return my voice sooner, but it's also pleasing, somehow, that he knew I'd have a long list of questions for him.

The horse pulls up suddenly outside something that, at first glance, looks like a couple of blackened shipwrecks jammed together, with lights winking through a few smudged portholes. A ramshackle building, to be sure.

Over a clumsy slab of a door swings a metal sign—an albatross holding an instrument. I've got one of those instruments in my collection. A fiddle, our court historian said when I asked her. I didn't tell her I'd found one or kept it, of course. Having human artifacts isn't forbidden, but cultivating an assortment as large as the one I've got would certainly give the priestesses cause to raise their eyes and question my obsession with humanity and land-things.

"Welcome to the *Fiddling Albatross*," says the Sea Witch, dismounting. "I'll help you down."

Looking up, he lifts his arms. But his eyes flare wide as he takes me in—my soaked nightdress, completely transparent now. I don't much care; it's nothing he hasn't seen before. He made this body, after all.

I jump down, and his huge hands catch me just above the waist. His thumbs graze the underside of my breasts.

Our bodies are pressed together, my rain-melted scrap of fabric against his wet shirt and pants. Pants that are once again stiffly, annoyingly prominent.

"Whatever weapon you're hiding under your pants, you should take it out," I tell him. "It's poking me."

His face freezes in an expression akin to horror. "I really don't think you want me to take it out."

16

Averil tilts her head curiously. "Why don't I want you to take it out? It must be uncomfortable, concealing whatever that is—a weapon or a tool—"

I move back with a frustrated groan, stepping around her to seize the horse's reins. I lead the horse toward a long open shed with an overhanging roof, where other horses stand tethered over a trough.

It's too much to hope that the curious princess will leave the subject alone. Of course she can't. She follows me, dripping and practically naked and shivering.

"I—I just don't understand—why you won't explain," she says through chattering teeth.

I knot the reins around a post and then whirl back to her, pushing her clear of the horses in case one of them kicks, steering her around a lump of shit on the ground.

Gripping her shoulders, I shake rain out of my eyes. "It's my cock," I hiss. "That's what you felt."

She frowns. "That can't be. Penises are soft and long and flexible, at least among mermen. Not that I've seen one up close, but… oh, and human penises are much shorter, but they also seem soft-ish. Not long and hard like *that*." She nods to my pants.

"Human penises are soft when they're not aroused," I say. "And as for the length, few men are as well-endowed as I am in this form."

"Aroused," she whispers. "Oh. You mean—because of me?"

"You're practically naked."

"But you've seen me naked."

"To check your form. To be sure my magic worked correctly. Doesn't mean I'm immune to the sight. Heartless monsters have dicks too, and desires to go with them." Rage burns in my chest, and I squeeze her shoulders harder. "The physical response doesn't mean I actually want you. Far from it."

"Well, that's—good."

"Yes. Now that your sordid curiosity is sated, let's go inside and get some dry clothes. I can't glamour away the wetness and the chill, so I'll have to bargain with the innkeeper, see if he has any spare garments for us."

She's quiet, subdued, probably processing the new information, but the moment I haul open the heavy door to the tavern, her entire face lights up again. She lunges toward the warm glow, the merry voices, the clank of mugs and plates, the rattle of dice. I have to dart forward and hustle her into a dark corner of the entry, between two long cloaks on pegs.

"Like I said, you're practically naked," I snap. "Stay here, out of sight, until I get the clothes."

The tavern keeper, Bolc, thinks himself my friend, though to me he's merely an occasional acquaintance. In exchange for a little magic to fix some soured ale, he goes into his storeroom and fetches two sets of homespun clothing and a threadbare cloak. Bolc doesn't know the true extent of my magic, or my real origins, but he seems to enjoy the idea that a mysterious conjurer deigns to visit his humble establishment from time to time.

I return to the girl and wrap her in the cloak before hurrying her through the common room and upstairs. Bolc told me of an unoccupied room in which we could change, and we make quick work of it. I manage not to look at the girl, though the knowledge that she's changing in the room with me, her fair flesh soft and damp and bare—it's almost enough to make me come all over the floor.

But I am master of myself, slave to no wide-eyed little mermaid with long red hair. I resist. I overcome.

It helps that she keeps asking me questions about the tavern. By the time I've answered twenty of them as curtly as possible, my dick is calmer.

We descend the stairs, and the serving girl gives me my usual table in a back corner, after shooing away a couple drunken idiots. There's a box of beaten copper on the table, worn shiny by greasy fingers, greenish at the corners. I open it and take out a couple decks of ale-stained cards and some chipped dice.

"Your first lesson," I say, but Averil isn't listening. She's staring around the room, with that look she gets where her entire face becomes a shining sun of pure wonder, tinged with avarice—the hunger for knowledge.

Watching her, I remember the first time I came here. I hadn't been on land in a long time—at least not around humans. I arrived on a night like this, only it was storming much harder—thunder that rocked the rafters. But everyone inside felt safe, warm, and happy, and they roared right back at the thunder whenever it boomed, lifting their cups, drink sloshing and spattering on the weathered wooden tables. I slunk into a corner, and when the pretty tavern wench winked at me, I managed to wink back. That night I gambled, I drank, and I fucked. I felt alive again.

This place, lopsided and greasy as it is, has been a haven for me. I've always come here alone. And now I have brought my enemy's daughter to my place of refuge. A mistake, most likely. When all this is done, she will despise me more than she does now. Her memory will sour my haven forever.

But I can't really believe that in this moment, when the sweet glory of her face is lighting up the whole room.

The tavern girl I slept with that first night moved on and married years ago, but the two others who work here now have both taken my dick before. One of them approaches our table, side-eyeing Averil. She doesn't seem jealous, only mildly interested.

"Drinks, sir?" she asks.

"One pitcher of ale and two mugs." I hesitate, watching the princess flick through the playing cards with rabid interest, "— and a hot chocolate."

When the drinks are delivered, Averil inspects her foamy mug, sniffing cautiously. "What is this?"

"Taste it."

She sips, while I watch her carefully. When her eyes dilate, I grin. And then I bury the grin in a mug of ale.

"This is magic," she breathes. "Utter magic. I could drink this forever. What is it called?"

"Hot chocolate."

"And what's your name?"

I almost answer automatically. But I bite my tongue. "Clever girl. No."

She smirks, licks foam from her pink lips. "Worth a try."

I can't sit here watching her savor the chocolate, or I'll lose my mind. So I say brusquely, "I hope you can drink and learn at the same time."

Headsman's Yoke is too advanced, so the game is Chips-and-Daggers, which involves laying cards in certain sequences along the open space in the middle of the table. The two players can claim certain cards and leave others, but it takes skill and knowledge to know when to collect and when to let them ride. Depending on which cards show up, the action may be leisurely, or it may proceed at a frenzied pace. When a player gains a full trace of cards, they win.

After I explain the rules, the princess and I try a slow round, and then we play a game in earnest. I hold back, leaving spaces open for her sometimes, moving more slowly than I usually do. When Averil wins the first trace, she frowns at me, but she only says, "Another game."

Once more I restrain myself from showing my full skill, and when she gains the trace, she slams both palms on the table and stands up, glaring.

"Stop letting me win," she hisses.

"I'm teaching you."

"You don't teach someone by handing them success. They have to earn it. They have to work hard and lose and lose until they gain it."

A roaring flush runs through my body, because she's beautiful like this, stormy and indignant, and despite her human form she has never looked more like a princess of the sea.

"I agree," I say. "I agree completely. I wasn't sure someone of your father's line would have that philosophy. He always believed in the easy way. Taking what he wanted with as little work as possible."

Her brows slant more sharply inward. "You never said you know my father."

116

"Knew. Long ago. Before he became the Sea King, and I became the toxic ghoul of the deep, the bedtime story he used to frighten his spawn."

I can't keep the bitterness out of my tone. I should not give her this much of the truth; she might guess the true target of my scheme. Rebellious though she is, she wouldn't agree to being part of a direct plot against her father.

"I knew the human king, too," I offer, to reroute her suspicions. "Perindal, father to the prince. And he's still the same treacherous bastard now that he was then."

"So your deal with me has something to do with King Perindal. You plan to harm him somehow."

"You won't be hurting anyone," I say.

"You avoided the question."

"You didn't ask one," I growl. "You made two statements."

She's still standing, leaning far across the table, clearly enjoying the height advantage it gives her over me. Our profiles are much closer now, barely a breath between us. Her small white teeth are clenched, bared beneath her plump, parted lips. Her eyes fairly spark with blue fire, and her long red hair tumbles onto the table, dragging a few of the playing cards out of place.

I stare boldly into her face and give her a grin that's more like a snarl.

Her eyes dip to my mouth.

My nerveless fingers release the cards I'm holding. My heart pulses, hotter and larger than ever. *Kiss me.*

"Another game." Her breath skims my lips. "This time, don't hold back. I can take it."

I feel as if I'm dropping, tossed into the deep with a boulder for a heart and it's plunging me down, down into a chasm I can't swim out of. No magic will help me, because this is its own magic—a kind I wasn't prepared for. I did not guard myself well enough. I am a fool—a drunken, doomed fool, drowning in the ocean of the princess's eyes.

"One more game," I say hoarsely. "And then I teach you to dance."

17

The music starts before the Sea Witch and I finish our third game, and it's so enticing I don't play as well as I'd hoped. Not that I could beat him anyway—his fingers fly over the cards so quickly I can barely see them at times. Somehow I'm confident he's not using magic. He has his own kind of pride. He wouldn't cheat to win, not at this game. Maybe with someone else, but not with me.

Why am I so sure of that? And yet I am.

The music though—pipes, a couple of drums, a pair of fiddles like the one on the tavern sign, all of them playing a merry, jaunty tune. We have music under the sea—drums and pipes, but they are much different. Music below the surface is wild, deep, and mournful. It reverberates and ripples through the water. This music is quick and giddy, short sharp notes that skitter freely through the thin air.

The notes quiver in my blood and bones, and I can't help moving my shoulders and feet a bit. When the Sea Witch gets a full trace of cards, I leap up and hold out my hand. "Teach me."

He rises heavily, sighing. "Remember, this is all in pursuit of you not embarrassing yourself too terribly at the masquerade tomorrow night. You'll need to charm His Highness with your movements. As we're dancing, watch the other women, too. Notice how they move. Especially that one. And her." He points to a couple of the women already dancing with men in the clear space between the tables.

I nod, determined to encompass it all somehow, to learn everything I can. When we arrived, I was tired and cold and sleepy, but now I'm warm. The chocolate drink and the card-playing have given me energy.

The Sea Witch pulls a string of leather from the lacing of his shirt, cuts it in two with a sharp claw, and ties up his hair in a knot with one piece. "Turn around."

I turn my back to him, and he gathers my damp locks, binding them at the nape of my neck. My skin tingles wherever his fingertips touch, and I think of his hands on my shoulders when we spoke outside.

The physical response doesn't mean I actually want you. Far from it.

But he gripped me with such ferocity…

Gods, the intensity of his eyes…

My heart beat so fast in that moment. I'm not sure it was fear.

The first dance he teaches me is the same merry jig everyone else is doing. It seems impossibly complex at first, especially for someone like me, with new legs, but no one mocks me. Any chuckles at my expense are good-natured, accompanied by nods and cheery, boozy grins.

Another jig after that, and another. I barely have to touch the Sea Witch—hand to hand a few times, his palm burning against mine—a touch at my waist, or at the small of my back.

I observe the women while I listen to his deep voice issuing instructions. But I watch him, too. He's so tall, so immensely broad of body, with such long legs—he should be clumsy, but he isn't. He's all lithe energy, controlled power and surging muscle. His shirt is too tight around his arms and it gapes open in front, showing a generous triangle of his well-cut chest. The shell necklace swings as he moves, its magical glow subdued to a golden twinkle. I like the tapered shape of his torso, his trim waist, the way his hips jerk and swerve through the movements of the dance, the smooth way he spins, the quick clatter of his boots as he jigs sideways and then back again.

He looks human. Not like the deadly monster and terrible conjurer he is. Not like a bargainer of souls and denizen of the deep.

He seems to belong here. Yet he belonged down there too, in his lair surrounded by his lovely, toxic garden.

After a few jaunty jigs, the music shifts, the fiddles slowing into a more graceful tune. The Sea Witch hesitates, his chest heaving. We're both lightly damp. The dress I'm wearing has a high enough neckline to cover my shell necklace, but I touch the hollow of my throat just above its edge, frowning at the wetness beading there.

"Sweat," explains the Sea Witch. "Human bodies purge heat through moisture during exercise."

"Fascinating." I stroke the back of my neck, feeling the *sweat* there as well. I lower my voice, craning up to whisper to him. "Your magic is incredibly detailed and comprehensive."

He blinks. "I—thank you."

"Should we dance again?" I ask.

"Yes, but a different kind of dancing. The kind the prince will want to do with you." His throat jerks as he swallows. "I hold your waist and you hold my arm, here. And then our other hands—like this. Now we step, to the back, to the side. Back in

122

your direction, and then to this side. A simple square to begin with, and then we'll go from there."

I frown, focusing very hard on the steps. After a few moments he says, "Averil," in that dark, deep voice, and my head jerks up, my stomach thrilling.

"Stop thinking so hard," he murmurs. "Feel the music."

One of the musicians is beating his drums faintly now, like a distant heartbeat, and he's crooning low, smooth words I can't entirely grasp. It's an unfamiliar human dialect, I think. But when I stop focusing on the steps, and I listen, I can *feel* the emotion of the song, and the wandering, tempting sway of the music.

"Let your body take over," purrs the Sea Witch. "Let me guide you."

His palm presses at the back of my waist. My breasts brush lightly against his chest—or rather his ribcage—he's truly so fucking tall. His hips are level with my belly, and as we move together, I feel the nudge of hard flesh through his pants.

Arousal. He's aroused by me, fully clothed as I am, in this plain dress that covers me from neck to ankles.

The entire surface of my skin blooms to life, warming and waking. Flutters dance between my legs, along the lips of my genitals. Delicate, insistent sensations, slithering upward through my abdomen, heating my core.

I tip my head back and look up at him.

He's looking down at me, darkness and want and latent anger swirling in his eyes.

"I'm sorry," I whisper. "You don't have to touch me, I can find someone else to dance with."

"My reaction is not your fault or your responsibility," he growls. "And no one else is going to touch you tonight, do you understand?"

I inhale sharply and nod.

The Sea Witch and I don't speak again for a while, or let our eyes meet. We only breathe against each other while the rhythm surges through us, moving our bodies in tandem.

Under the sea merfolk dance, in our own way—interlacing movements, synchronized swimming conducted to a rhythm. And there are mating dances, performed only on a pair's joining day. Humans are much freer with such intimate activities, it seems.

"Do they dance like this every night?" I murmur.

"Almost every night." His voice rumbles through my body.

"And you dance with others?"

"I do. I've danced with many women here. Fucked many of them, too." He says it in a hard, bright tone, like he wants to shock me.

"So you've never had a mate?"

"No. I don't believe in the concept." He catches my hand and twirls me around, and I follow the movement with a gasp. "Dancing and sex are a relief. They bring me pleasure. Why deny myself, waiting for some 'one true mate' who may never appear?"

In secret moments, I've had similar rebellious thoughts. "Why indeed?" I murmur. "Especially for someone like you, who—um, well…"

"Someone like me?" he intones. "Go on."

"Someone isolated. Someone who doesn't like others."

He pulls me tight against his body. "Someone who lives in a deep, dark cave surrounded by poisonous creatures."

I risk a tiny smile up at him. "You have to admit, those things might be a bit of a turnoff to any potential mates. But you know that already. That's why you do it, to keep others away. Except those who come to bargain. If they dare your death traps, you know they're serious enough to make a deal."

I've been speaking low, but he still glances around, as if he's afraid someone will overhear. He pulls me out of the dancers, tows me along past our corner table and into a back passage. There are two figures there, grunting urgently in the shadows, one of them pinned against the wall while the other ruts between their legs. I avert my eyes, following the Sea Witch, my fingers still hooked in his.

He opens a door. Pushes me into a pitch-black room. A snap of his fingers, and a light flares to life, floating above our heads. It looks like a tiny octopus made of golden dust, moving steadily in place, tiny glittering tentacles dangling. By its light I can see that this small room is lined with shelves and supplies.

"That's beautiful," I breathe, staring up at the glimmering golden light-creature. "How do you—"

He presses a thick finger to my mouth. "An illusion of sorts. Don't talk about my magic and my deals in the common room."

I shove his hand aside. "No one heard."

"But they could have. You and I are both unglamoured here. The tavern keeper and I arranged a long time ago to set a sigil on this building, one that removes glamours, so no one can magically disguise themselves. The precaution serves both his purposes and mine, usually. But in this case, though we are far from the town where you're staying with your prince, it's still possible someone could recognize you if you draw too much attention to us."

"To *you*, you mean. Because you don't want to be connected to me in any way. And you glamoured yourself in the village, which means you're afraid someone will recognize you. Someone you were acquainted with back when you knew Perindal. Lord Brixeus, maybe?"

The Sea Witch's jaw clenches, and his irises began to leak inky purple-blue across the whites of his eyes again. I watch the effect, fascinated.

"You," he grits out, "are entirely too clever for your own good."

"Thank you."

"Not a compliment."

"Isn't it, though?" I allow myself a pleased smirk.

The Sea Witch licks his lips, watching my mouth. "It's time for your last lesson of the night," he says huskily. "You'll be kissing the prince tomorrow. You should practice."

"Oh. Yes. I want to learn to do it right. The human way. You don't mind, do you? I'm sure you've kissed plenty of humans."

"I have. But don't your father's priestesses frown on such interactions with the opposite gender? Aren't you afraid you'll sully yourself?"

Heat crawls into my cheeks. "It's for my true mate's benefit. And you don't really count, because you—you're— we're not friends. We have a deal, and that's all. This is part of the deal's fulfillment. Nothing meaningful."

Why does my voice sound so breathless?

"Of course," says the Sea Witch, with a grin more dreadful and terrifying than any I've yet seen from him. "I don't count. Pucker up, little mermaid. Let's practice."

"So how do—how do we begin?" I tuck my hands behind me because I don't know what to do with them. In the sea, my arms could float gracefully at my sides, or swirl through the water. As a human, they simply—hang there. Awkwardly.

"Pretend I'm your prince," says the Sea Witch. In the golden glimmer of the magical light overhead, his face is shadowed, its angles more dramatic than ever.

He's handsome. I've known it, distantly, from the moment I met him, though my fear of his brutal size and his magic clouded my admission of it. He's not pretty like Prince Kerrin is—but his face is like the rest of him—magnetic.

126

I can do this. "All right. You're Prince Kerrin."

"And we've been dancing at the masquerade tomorrow night," he rumbles, "and you've been rubbing that lovely little body against me until I can't hold back any longer. I need you."

He moves in, crowding me against the shelves. My breath quickens, half frantic and half enchanted. My mouth feels dry. Should I lick my lips? I do, and the Sea Witch nods, his eyes piercing mine. "Good. The tongue across the lips—do that for him tomorrow night."

"I will," I breathe, and I do it again, more enthusiastically.

Humor sparks in his gaze. "Not too sloppily, and not too often."

"Oh."

"It's all right." His large hands come to rest on my cheeks. An unexpectedly gentle touch from such a powerful man.

He tips my face up, and his eyes close as his mouth descends. The smooth skin of his lips grazes mine, pressing in slowly. My own lips are instantly sensitized, heated and tingling. A swift lance of delight squiggles straight down the center of my body, plucking at the tiny nub between my legs.

The Sea Witch pulls back. "It's customary to move your own lips a little. To respond to the person kissing you."

"How?"

"Whatever feels good. Return the pressure, lean into the kiss. Again."

Grasping my waist this time, he kisses me, and I rise on my tiptoes, pushing my mouth to his. The zing of pleasure through my core happens again, intensifying right between my legs. I sway, but he holds me steady, pulling me slightly closer, with our bodies aligned, like they were in the dance.

Now I understand why the priestesses say we shouldn't experiment with anyone but our intended mate. Because kissing the Sea Witch feels wonderful. It's almost enough to confuse me about my feelings for the prince.

If the prince is my mate, why does my body respond like this to the Sea Witch?

The physical response doesn't mean I actually want you. Far from it.

The Soul Echo. That's the difference. I've felt it for the prince, and not for the man kissing me. At least—well—I suppose I don't truly know what a Soul Echo sounds like, but—

"Averil," rumbles the Witch, his mouth moving against mine. "Stop asking questions."

"Sorry."

"Don't apologize for being yourself." He withdraws slightly. "Was that enough practice?"

"A little more, I think," I breathe. "Is that—is that all there is to it?"

"One more thing. Something the prince may try. Don't be afraid."

I let my body yield, compressing to his, and this time the roll of hard flesh under his clothing isn't strange—I like it, and I think it would feel good in that little sensitive spot between my legs. I almost rub myself against the hardness as I stand on my toes and meet his mouth one more time.

The Sea Witch parts his lips under mine, and I mimic him. His breath flows warm into my mouth. He tastes like bitter ale, and salty sea, and crisp magic.

And then his tongue glides between my lips, probing into my mouth. It traces a slick path across my tongue, a languid caress, and my whole body erupts into glorious heat and craving. My thoughts blur, and suddenly my hands have a purpose—winding around his broad body, urging him nearer.

When his tongue withdraws, I delicately slip mine into his mouth. He gives a shuddering groan, his chest heaving against my breasts. His hands start to move up my body, but they halt just below my chest, then leave my waist. His palms slam against the shelves on either side of me.

We break apart for a bare instant to breathe, and then we're kissing again, delirious and dizzy. Somehow my arms got around his neck. Somehow one of his hands is grasping my nape, under my hair. Somehow my hips are rocking urgently against his body. Somehow—somehow this went too far.

I break the contact, turning my face aside. My lips feel swollen, hot and wet. There's wetness between my legs too. Mermaid arousal involves the generation of additional fluid, so I suppose human arousal is similar, though the liquid is likely of a different consistency.

"Enough," says the Sea Witch, breathing heavily.

"Enough." I swallow, my fingers fluttering across my mouth. "Did I do all right?"

He lets out a hoarse laugh. "You're a natural talent."

"Thank you. And you're—very good too."

He sets the back of his wrist to his mouth, muffling a strangled sort of scoffing noise. Then he goes to the door and holds it open. When I pass him, the narrow space between our bodies feels as if it's been electrified by his friend Graeme— charged with a buzzing, brittle heat.

We head up the passage to the common room, and then the Sea Witch goes upstairs to fetch the wet things we left in the empty chamber. We say a brief goodbye to the tavern keeper and make our way through the dwindling crowd to the door. The Sea Witch snags the cloak he wrapped around me when we first came in—it has mostly dried, and he bundles me in it again before hustling me outside.

The misting rain has stopped, but the clouds are thicker, the night darker. It's the cold, aching dark between the setting of the moon and the rising of the sun.

Weariness floods my mind and body, and my eyelids feel unsupportably heavy.

"If I have to sit behind you on the horse, I might fall asleep and topple off," I say ruefully. "Can't I ride in front?"

Another choked laugh from him, and he blurts out, as if he can't hold the words in, "If we do that, I'm going to come in my pants against your pretty ass. Is that what you want?"

18

Averil blinks up at me, rosy lips parted, eyes blown wide with mingled shock and interest. "Come?"

"Release. Ejaculate. Fucking explode."

"Like the emission of the male during mating? That's a pleasurable act, I've heard. So—you would feel good?"

"Yes," I growl. "And no. I would hate it."

"Because you hate me." She says it with perfect certainty and understanding. "You hate everyone, except your three friends, and a couple of acquaintances."

"Yes." The word grates out between my teeth.

She's still flushed from my kisses—I'd bet all my cards she's sopping wet between her legs. But another emotion enters her gaze—pity.

"You don't have to live like this, you know," she says softly.

"You've been acquainted with me for a day and a half. You know nothing about me."

Her mouth curves, a knowing smirk.

Which drives me insane. She *doesn't* know me. Can't know me.

I don't let people know me, except maybe Graeme, Liris, and Ekkon. And even they don't understand everything about me.

"Say hello to the horse," I order. "I'll return in a moment."

I stride into the dark, circling the inn, around to the back. I tear my pants open, releasing my heated, painfully stiff cock. It's been erect for hours, and I can't stand it any longer. Frantically I pump my hand along it, grinding my teeth to keep from groaning as forcefully as I want to.

All night. All night it's been like this. I want her so badly I can't think. Fuck. Shit shit shit—

My whole body tightens, chills racing over my skin as I erupt, shooting cum into the dark. Nothing but bushes and an outhouse back here. No one to see.

My shoulders heave as I tease out the last of the pleasure. Then I refasten my pants again and messily tuck in the shirt. My hands are shaking.

It felt good, but it wasn't true relief. I suspect I won't feel truly, blissfully satisfied unless I get to bury myself in the luscious body I made for the princess. Unless I get to hear her moan and mew and plead, and call my name while she begs me to make her come.

Once won't be enough. I'll make her scream again and again, until she's limp and boneless.

But that will never happen, because I have a plan. A purpose. A goal I must reach, and reaching that goal means delivering her into the heart and the bed of the prince. To avenge myself on her father, I have to give her to the whelp of my *other* great enemy, Perindal.

She's a pawn. A tool, nothing more.

I stalk back to the front of the inn, where she's standing awkwardly near the horses.

"You can sit up front." I prepare the horse and boost her up into the saddle. She doesn't ask questions—a little odd, but perhaps she guesses what I did, and understands why there's no erection prodding her backside when I mount behind her.

I enhance our speed again on the way back, slowing the horse as we approach the village. The princess's warm body is slumped against mine, her head lolling on my shoulder. I'm afraid when she enters the inn, she'll stumble sleepily around and crash into something, or tumble down the stairs, but I can't risk taking her indoors myself. Even a glamour won't protect her from censure if she's seen returning this late with a strange man.

There's other magic I could do if I'd brought supplies, but my natural abilities are limited. I have access to a little illumination magic, a little water and wind magic, limited glamours for personal appearance—and my strongest ability, physical transformation. For anything else, I need other ingredients. One of the rings I wear enables the enhancement of a mount's speed, not my own. And every time I use it, it needs a couple of hours to renew its strength and effect.

Once we're in the lane behind the inn, I lift Averil down and pat her flushed cheek quickly. "Wake up. You have to go inside."

"Hmm." Her lashes blink open. "Gods, I'm tired."

"You've had a long couple of days. Go in and sleep. If anyone sees you enter, act like you were confused and wandering. They'll excuse it as part of your trauma from the shipwreck. Don't forget to change back into that bit of lace the prince bought you, and hide this dress somewhere, maybe under your bed. Oh, I nearly forgot—I need your voice back."

"No," she moans softly. "Oh, I did enjoy having it again."

"Can't be helped," I murmur. "Sing for me. Softly now."

She rouses enough to sing me a breathy little song, a variant of one of the dance tunes we heard at the *Fiddling Albatross*. Her voice spirals out of her throat, rejoining me, curling into the shell against my chest. I wrap my hand around the pendant.

"Go," I tell her. "And remember what you learned tonight."

She bites her lips, shooting me a knowing glance. And then she's through the gate, crossing the innyard. Vanishing into the building.

A frigid wind rushes across the yard, striking me full in the chest, chilling me to the bone. The world is suddenly cavernous and cold, a rushing emptiness in which my power seems pitifully small. I look up to the sky, swirled with icy stars, and I want to cry out, to scream, to roar, to plead for something I can't put into words, not yet, not now.

My jaw tightens, and I close my eyes, breathing through the panic.

Then I renew my grip on the horse's reins. "I've borrowed you long enough, my friend," I tell him. "Let's get you home."

19

I'm exhausted. So tired I fell asleep on the horse, lulled by the rocking motion and by the warmth of the Sea Witch's chest.

But when I creep up to my room, change back into the nightdress, and crawl onto the bed, I find myself unable to sleep. My entire life, I've slept in my pod at home, lulled by the faint movement of the water. I don't need a strong current, just a little motion. Something. Not this stark stillness. There's a stagnation of the air that I can't stand.

The inn creaks occasionally—a good thing, since it disguised the squeaking of the staircase as I returned to my room. And there's a faint gurgle of pipes, a sporadic snore, an occasional rattle or clang from somewhere. The sounds are all too sharp, too caustic.

Sighing, I flop over among the tangle of fabric on the bed. Sheets and blankets. They seemed comfortable earlier, but I don't like them at all right now.

I get up and fumble with the window. I think there's a way to move the pane of leaded glass—I've experimented with opening and closing the portholes of shipwrecks, so I should be able to figure it out. But I'm afraid to exert too much pressure on the frame, and the latch doesn't want to budge. So I flounce back to the bed, leaving the curtains parted to admit the faint starlight.

My skimpy nightdress opens, revealing the lace-trimmed undergarments I'm wearing. They still feel damp on the inside from when I was kissing the Sea Witch.

Chewing my lip, I stare at the area between my legs. It looks soft and small and pillowy under the thin fabric.

Decision made, I go to the lamp on the dresser and turn it up, just a little. A tiny glow so I can see what I'm about to do.

If kissing the Sea Witch was good practice for being with my true mate, shouldn't I take it a step farther? Shouldn't I acclimate myself to every aspect of my new human body? Just so I know what to expect when I finally do join with the prince.

When the Sea Witch left me alone with the horses, I didn't stay in that spot. I followed him. It was dark behind the tavern, so I couldn't see as well as I would have liked—but he was touching his cock, that much I guessed. Letting himself "explode," as he said, so he wouldn't disturb me with his arousal when we rode together on the horse. The sounds he made—stifled groans, fraught with pain—or pleasure? Those sounds roll through my mind, quivering in my soul.

I shimmy off the underwear and prop myself against the pillows on the bed.

Spying on the Sea Witch was wrong—as wrong as it would be to have him here, watching me. Looking at me with those stormy eyes while I slide two fingers into the crease between my legs and spread myself, as I begin delicately probing the tiny bud, the one that reacted so delightedly when he was kissing me.

He'd frown and growl. *Stop touching yourself. Don't do that in front of me.*

137

The thought makes me smile, even as I gasp, because this feels so good. Simply delicious.

I swirl a fingertip over the little nub, wiggling it gently, then faster. Every shift in motion corresponds to a new kind of thrill. More wetness is seeping from me, and my breath comes shallow and sharp. I'm not sure how to take this play to its completion, to the pinnacle. And I want more than this. I crave hands gliding over my skin. I fix the image of Prince Kerrin's beautiful face in my mind, imagine his hands cupping my body... but then my mind skips to the moment when the Sea Witch's broad palms moved up my sides, then vanished before touching my breasts.

What if he hadn't stopped?

What if he had crushed himself against me with all his brutal force? Squeezed my breasts with his fingers while he kept kissing me, while his warm tongue filled my mouth with salt and fire...

My hand is moving by instinct now, quick and frantic, the same motion over and over. I can't stop. I don't care what the priestesses would say—none of them can see me now and it's practice, just practice—my back arches, my head tipping back. I'm desperate—I would screech aloud if I could. I want something I can't quite reach—almost—

No. No, I can't do this.

I pull my wet fingers out of my human parts and fling myself over onto my belly, burying my face in the pillows.

Am I stealing from my mate's future pleasure?

Is this wrong, what I'm doing? More wrong than making a deal with the Sea Witch? Why do I even care, when I've gone so far past what anyone in my world would excuse?

I have already exiled myself.

Fuck.

I can't say it aloud, but I think it over and over.

Sometime amid the swearing I move onto my side, and I notice that the limpet shell is faintly warm, tucked between my breasts. It's almost—humming.

Horror blazes through my chest.

I thought of the Sea Witch. I pictured him watching me.

Did I activate the shell? Summon his gaze? But I didn't actually call him, and I didn't hear him answer. Surely he was already back in his woeful cave-lair, sleeping, and he didn't see any of what I just did.

I don't try to probe for his thoughts or call to him. I grip the shell in my fist, shut my eyes tight, and imagine myself drifting through shafts of sunlight in some blue lagoon far away.

No one wakes me until noon, and then I'm offered a milky bath sprinkled with fine herbs and florals, while I'm fed a luncheon on a silver tray. The Prince, I'm told, went out riding, but he'll be back soon. He'll want to see me when he returns.

Once I'm dressed in a frilly blue gown, Ems the maid asks if I want a book to pass the time. I can't read the letters humans use to write the Common Tongue, but I accept the offer anyway, just to have the pleasure of the pages in my hands.

Ems takes me down to the inn's common room, to a table by a wide-open window through which pours the limpid light of early afternoon. She gives me a book of folktales. "These will be easy on your mind, my lady," she says. "In case the wreck did some damage, you don't want to be straining yourself."

With the help of the images on each page, I begin trying to decipher the correlation between the way we mermaids write spoken language, and the way humans do it. But before I've

139

made much progress, Prince Kerrin barrels through the door of the inn, breezy and beautiful, cheeks flushed from his ride. He grins upon seeing me and strides over immediately, stripping off his gloves and tossing them to Lord Brixeus, who catches them but looks grim about having to do so.

"Beautiful!" cries the prince. "So good to see you. You're looking—well, still tired, but lovely in spite of that. Ah, that smile." He caresses my cheek. "I'd give my kingdom for your smile. Look at it, Brixeus. Isn't she the most perfect rose you ever saw?"

"Very lovely, Sire," says Lord Brixeus dryly.

The Prince shrugs, scooting onto the bench across from me. "What does he know? He's an old married man. I'll be the judge of beauty around here." He flashes me a dimpled smile. "So, Beautiful, care for a walk? A drink?"

"A drink, Your Highness?" Lord Brixeus raises an eyebrow. "You've been dipping into your flask all morning, and you'll be drinking at the banquet tonight."

"Be off, *father*." Kerrin waves him away with a laugh. "I can hold my drink."

"As Your Highness likes, of course. Shall I have wine sent in, then?"

"Yes, yes. And let no one disturb us for a while." Prince Kerrin leans across the table, gathering my hand in his. With his other hand he pushes aside the book I was reading. "Let me tell you about the jumps I did with my horse this morning. There was one stile we took—I thought my horse wouldn't clear it, but I pulled him right over. Confidence is the key, see? With confidence you can do anything. No chances taken, no victories gained. I believe in risking it all. That's the only way a man can really feel alive."

I squeeze his hand, letting my eyes flame into his. *Yes, I understand. That's how I feel, too.*

He talks more, including many horse-related terms I'm unfamiliar with, but I simply nod and smile, giving him my full attention. He barely notices the wine when it's set on the table, which I count as a victory of my own.

"Lord Brixeus is my equerry, you know," he goes on. "Handles travel arrangements for me, the purchase and care of my horses, that sort of thing. But he serves me in other ways too. Handy fellow. Considers himself an advisor of sorts, I do believe, though he's best when he sticks to his area of expertise." His handsome face falls, sadness creeping into his eyes. "When I was abroad we picked up a few excellent horses. They were in the hold of the ship when it went down. Expensive stock. Glorious bloodlines. A pity to lose them."

I pat his hand. The loss of the animals is tragic, but I wish he would show the same grief over his lost men.

After more conversation about horses, I withdraw my hand and begin miming the stacking and dealing of cards.

"Oh, you want to play a game?" Kerrin's eyes brighten.

I nod eagerly.

He calls for cards, and after more exaggerated motions from me and many confused looks from him, he decides we'll play Chips-and-Daggers, which is what I've been trying to suggest the whole time.

The prince takes off his riding coat, lays it aside, and rolls up the sleeves of his ivory shirt to his elbows, baring strong forearms. As he deals the cards with consummate grace, I inhale his scent—spicy, luxurious, with a hint of sweat and horse from the ride he took. I love the blended fragrance. I love the lines of his fingers—less thick and strong than the Witch's. Just as masculine, but more elegant and well-groomed, strung with exquisite rings.

My lesson in Chips-and-Daggers is still fresh in my mind, so I'm eager to play. Maybe I'll even win my first game.

Before we begin, Kerrin takes a long drink of wine. He offers me some, but I shake my head. I want every mental faculty as sharp as possible for this game.

We begin, and instantly I notice a difference in the way Kerrin plays. He tosses down cards sloppily, without the Witch's deft attention to keeping the piles clearly defined. He calls "pause" a couple of times so he can swig more wine, while I chafe at the delay and use it to spot more openings for my own cards.

The prince wins the first game, barely. I don't believe he realizes how close I came to beating him. I *must* beat him. I want to show him that I'm clever and quick—a worthy opponent. A woman with a mind to match his. Someone he could count on. A clever partner. A valuable mate.

While he deals again, I breathe deeply, trying to soak in the moment so I can savor it forever. The dancing movement of a tree just outside the window, dappling the cards with sunlight and leaf-shadow. The smooth-worn wood of the table under my fingers. The sharp, fruity sting of the prince's wine-scented breath as he leans playfully toward me, tracing the line of my nose with the stiff edge of a card. His merry laugh. The flex of muscle in his tanned forearms. The crisp curls of his black hair, bobbing over his forehead.

He's beautiful. A delight. Living with him like this would be wonderful. And I know it would be challenging, too—he will be king one day, with many responsibilities. I need to prove that I can excel, that I can learn, and that I can conquer what comes my way.

So when he's finished dealing and the game begins, I am utterly savage. No mercy, not a half-second's hesitation. My thoughts feel like lightning flashes, flicking through possibilities, sorting my choices and carrying out the motions instantly.

When I collect the trace, just a few minutes into the game, the prince drops his cards and stares at me.

"Such good luck you had there," he says, sipping more wine. "Very well. Again."

Not luck, I want to say. But I merely give him a little smile.

I win the next game as well, taking the trace right before he does. This time he flings down his cards so hard I jump.

"Rotten luck I'm having," he snaps. "See, that last card slipped through my fingers, or I would have gotten the trace. And you put that five too close to the eight—I didn't see it."

We play again. When I win the third time, the prince lets his entire hand fall to the floor and he sits there glowering, his mouth tight.

This is not going as I planned. I don't understand what I'm doing wrong. He should be impressed, not angry.

Cautiously I turn my thoughts to the necklace I wear, calling in my mind. *Sea Witch… are you busy?*

Of course I'm busy, he answers immediately. *You think I'm floating aimlessly in my cave, waiting for a summons from a spoiled little mermaid princess? Not fucking likely.*

I hold back a smirk. *I'm playing cards with the prince, and I've won three games of Chips-and-Daggers. But he's not pleased at my intelligence or quickness. He seems upset.*

Of course he's upset, growls the Witch. *He's a primped-up little poppet who believes himself superior to everyone else. He can't stand being bested. Let him win.*

But I thought I should show him what I can do, I protest.

The Sea Witch cuts me off. *Let him win. Again and again. Watch his mood improve.*

After collecting the other cards, I pick up the prince's discarded ones. Then I stay on the floor by Kerrin's chair, offering the stack to him with my most pleading and vulnerable expression.

143

The prince looks at me, pursing his lips. "One more game. This time make sure you're putting the cards in the proper spots. Think through your moves. Don't rush."

I nod meekly, but a vague resentment heats my chest.

I don't like having to submit before him and beg him. I don't like his attitude about losing. And I don't like him trying to teach me what I already know, what I'm clearly doing better than him.

If I had nothing else at stake, I might give up on him now. But I'm not ready to yield my legs yet. I've only just begun exploring the human world. And if I want to spend more time on land, in this form, I have to keep up my end of the bargain with the Sea Witch. I have to try to win the prince's heart. And so I must believe that Kerrin's heart is worth winning, even if I'm already seeing parts of it I don't like.

Surely there's more to Prince Kerrin than this. There must be nobility, tenderness, endurance, persistence, and kindness. I'll have to dig deeper and get him to reveal those traits to me.

It's comical how much Kerrin perks up once I let him win a couple of games. But I grumble to the Sea Witch in my head the whole time, pointing out moves I could be making, while his mocking laughter rumbles through my brain.

You really hate holding yourself back, don't you, love? the Witch snickers.

Who wouldn't? I snap mentally. *And stop calling me 'love.'*

Whatever you say, shrimp.

Brute.

Minnow, he retorts.

Ghoul. I slap down a card. *Wicked trickster.*

Trickster? Mm, I like that, he purrs. *Little sinner.*

My fingers freeze, pinching a card too tight, and Kerrin collects the trace with a howl of victory.

Little sinner? I ask the Sea Witch. *What do you mean by that?*

Why, nothing at all. But I do wonder… are you ever able to finish what you begin?

My cheeks flame. Is he talking about last night? Did he see me toying with myself after all?

So quiet all of a sudden, Princess.

Begone. I don't need your help anymore.

As you wish. Until tonight then.

Tonight? I ask, my heartbeat skittering.

Didn't I tell you? I can practically hear the Sea Witch grinning. *I'm coming to the masquerade.*

20

What does the Sea Witch mean, he's coming to the masquerade?

He can't. Can he?

Before I can try to sort through my confusion and ask any more questions, Prince Kerrin rises from the table, reeling slightly. "I think I'll have a nap before tonight's festivities. Care to join me?"

Flushing, I stare at his extended hand.

Maybe lying side by side with him on a bed would be a good thing. Maybe the intimacy will prompt him to unburden his heart about deeper, more important things. Perhaps it will strengthen the connection between us. Maybe he'll kiss me. I do like kissing very much, and I'd like to try it with him.

When I place my fingers in his hand, he pulls me closer swiftly, cupping my waist. His eyes are hooded, his lips full and perfect and damp, ruby-red from wine and his natural color.

"Come with me then," he whispers.

Nerves thrilling, I follow him upstairs to the second floor. We're trailed by three dutiful guards, whom he slurringly orders to wait outside as he guides me into the airy, well-appointed room he's been given. Then he shoos away a valet who's been folding clothes into a drawer.

As the chamber door shuts, the prince pulls me over to the bed, tumbling himself and me onto it with a cheerful laugh.

Three big windows stand open in this room, gauzy curtains fluttering in the light breeze. The prince falls back onto the richly colored pillows, black curls tossing around his face. I'm half on top of him, gasping a voiceless giggle, the lightweight gown I wear sliding off my shoulder, showing the strap of the chemise beneath. The padded chemise is barely enough to contain my breasts—I'm used to far more support and coverage from my corset. I feel as if my chest is hanging out of the gown's low neckline.

The prince seems to like the view. His eyes fix there, where my breasts surge eagerly with the breath of everything I cannot say.

He lifts a hand, running his fingers across the swells of my flesh. The sensitive skin tingles at his touch, and I feel a warming sensation between my legs.

Relief floods my body. I was half-afraid I wouldn't feel a strong enough attraction to him, after—well. After last night, with the Witch.

Twisting my long red hair aside, I lean down, draping my body on top of the prince's, my breasts squished against his chest. My mouth hovers over his, his soft breath mingling with mine. Such lovely, long, dark lashes he has. And such a perfect nose… almost too perfect.

I brush that last little thought away and lean in.

The moment my mouth brushes his, Kerrin grips the back of my head and crushes me hard into the kiss. His tongue pries my lips open, forging inside, pushing and poking into my mouth.

Then he's moving, rushed and desperate, bowling me over, pressing me down into bed under his lithe, muscular body. He's strong, urgent, pushing my legs apart with his knee, settling in and rolling his hips against my center, groaning against my mouth as he enjoys the friction.

He shifts, raking his fingers up my thighs, bunching my dress at my waist, stroking along my leg with one heated palm.

I'm startled, uncertain, swept underwater by the current of his compelling passion.

But I can't let the prince have my body too soon, because the plan is—forget the plan—because *I don't want this*. Not now.

All I wanted was some kissing, some closeness, and now—how do I get him to stop?

He scrapes down the top of my underwear, grasping my bare hip.

I push against him, but he only mumbles blearily. Too much wine. The night he changed me, the Sea Witch told me about brewed alcohol and its effect on the human brain. We don't have such drink under the sea, but we have other substances that produce a similar effect.

The prince isn't himself in this moment. And I can't speak to him, or explain what I want.

In my mermaid form, I'm a fighter as well as a princess, and though my body may be different, it still holds that strength, that training. I can't hurt the prince, or I might ruin my chances at winning him over—but I can make my meaning clear.

He's reaching between us, fumbling with his pants. I tense, preparing to communicate a firm, unmistakable sign that I do not want him to mate with me—but then he exhales and his body slumps and slackens. He shifts partly off me before going completely limp, his breathing heavy and regular.

His beautiful, rosy, drunken face is on my breast. He's fast asleep.

For a few moments I wait. Should I stay here and rest under him, or at his side? Wait until he sleeps off the wine and regains his usual demeanor? Not that I've seen much of his usual demeanor. It's usually filtered by wine.

At last I push him carefully off me, rearrange my clothing and slip out of the room. The three guards barely look at me. As if they're used to flushed, disheveled women leaving their master's bedroom.

The thought annoys me.

The prince hasn't been saving his body for any "true mate." Why should I have to? Simply because it is the way of my people, of my father's religion? Because it is part of my culture, my family's way of behaving? Because that is what all my sisters have done?

I twist my hair anxiously, angrily. I wanted to be different from them all, didn't I? That's why I came here—because a simple merman mate wasn't good enough for the wild, adventurous Averil, the littlest mermaid. I thought I was special. That I deserved something more, or something different. And now, here I am—trapped in this bargain with a prince I'm not sure of anymore.

I shut myself in my room, plopping onto the bed to think.

Kerrin just lost a ship, a crew, and his prize horses. His father was recently the victim of an assassination attempt. Of course he's distressed. Of course he's upset, drinking heavily, sensitive to his own failures. Of course he's aching for a little pleasure and comfort. It makes sense. I just need to be less demanding, more understanding of his needs, how he's feeling.

Tonight at the banquet, at the dance, I'll have another opportunity to interact with him. It will be better. It has to be. Because if I don't win the prince's heart, I won't be able to do the Sea Witch the favor he wants. And he will either swallow my voice forever, or take away my human form forever, or both. Maybe he'll even shred my soul, and I'll be a wailing spirit in his toxic garden for centuries.

I press my fingers over my face, feeling the pricking at the backs of my eyes, the trickle of hot tears. Silently, voiceless, I cry.

Because in my hubris, my desire, and my recklessness, I have truly made the worst possible mess of everything.

Ems the maid brings me a deep blue gown flecked with silver for the masquerade. It has hints of purple when I turn in the glow of the common room fireplace—an unsettling reminder of a certain person with darkly purple hair and deep violet eyes.

Ems fights with my hair a long time, getting out all the tangles I've put into it. I'm not used to the way this human hair behaves—my mermaid hair is more slippery, and tangles far less. But at last Ems manages to get it braided and bundled into a fine arrangement that pairs beautifully with the midnight-blue, silver-trimmed mask she places over my eyes.

She tries to convince me to switch my limpet necklace for a different one, but when I cover it protectively with my hand, she nods. "I understand. A family heirloom, maybe. Special to you, when you've lost so much." And she pats my cheek.

While I'm admiring the play of the light on my gown, the prince comes down to the common room, accompanied by a valet, a couple of guards, and Lord Brixeus. He walks to me immediately, draws me aside, and lifts my hand for a penitent kiss.

"Beautiful, I must apologize," he whispers. "I haven't been myself lately. I—we could have had a fine time, you and I, but I was clumsy and I was— Believe me, I will make it up to you."

His eyes plead for understanding.

I reach up, pressing my palm along his cheek. He sighs, relieved. "Thank you. I suppose the great thing is, no one needs to know about it, right? I won't tell them, and you—well, you *can't.*" He cups my chin, caresses my lip with his thumb. "You don't know what a relief that is. After all the women I've been with during my travels, all the ones who have gossiped about me, told lies, ruined my marriage prospects—to finally have someone who cannot betray me—it's a wonderful thing."

All the women. I try not to let that phrase bother me, but it does. The injustice of it, that he should be allowed so much experience when I am not. Perhaps I should *take* some experience for myself. Perhaps I should experiment a little more with someone else before giving my body entirely to this man.

The prince's gaze turns distant for a moment. "Did I sometimes forget myself, in the heat of wine and passion, and share a few royal secrets, make a few injudicious errors, show the strength of my desire a little too forcefully? Perhaps. Unfortunate, but such things happen. There should be a vow of binding silence over what passes in the bedroom, don't you agree? Especially if one wants to try something new and salacious occasionally—why should it be gossiped about the next day for all to hear?"

He takes both my hands, looking intently into my eyes. "Why should I not have someone lovely and graceful, someone sweet and pure and *silent?* And who cares if I know not where you come from? You're of wealthy origins and noble birth, that

151

much is plain, and it is enough. You, Beautiful, are perfect. You are everything I—"

"Your Highness." Lord Brixeus's tall, dark-suited form appears at the prince's elbow. "We should make our way to the festivities. They'll be waiting on your arrival for the opening banquet."

"Of course." The prince nods, accepting the gold-feathered mask Lord Brixeus hands over. The valet ties the mask string, and then I take the prince's arm.

Two more guards join us, and we proceed out of the inn, along the village street toward the square. The sky is still colored with the orange-gold of sunset, painted with streaks of dark purple cloud... like the Sea Witch's hair...

I begin eyeing the crowd, looking for anyone who matches his height and build. Most of the people milling about in the street and the square are less fabulously attired than the prince and I—they're villagers who have brought out their best garments to be a part of this occasion. They wear masks cobbled together from all sorts of things—bones, buttons, beads, lace, netting, feathers, wood, paint, canvas, seashells. Some masks are gaudy, some gorgeous, and others downright gruesome.

Though some of the men in the crowd and around the banquet tables are burly, tall, broad, or all three, none of them seem to be *him*.

So I put him out of my mind, and I enjoy the delectable spread of food. In fact, I enjoy it so openly that the prince lays a restraining hand on my arm. "Please do not eat quite so much," he murmurs. "It's unbecoming to a woman of your station, especially one at my side. I would hate to imagine you becoming as gigantic as my dearly departed mother."

Startled, I gape at him.

"Died of a weak heart, she did. Four years ago." He nods sagely.

I'm less horrified by her death than by the way he just spoke about her. I may be slender myself, but richness of flesh isn't despised under the sea. There are women of all shapes and sizes enjoying themselves here tonight, and why shouldn't I be one of them?

I contemplate reaching for another piece of soft, honey-soaked bread, just to spite him. But a burst of wild music begins, signaling the start of the dancing.

The night is darker now. The village square is hazy with torchlight and smoke, rich with savory scents and spiraling laughter. Bonfire glow bathes the faces of the rowhouses; shadows dance across the pale plastered walls. There is something mystic and magical in the sound of the instruments, in the way the notes swirl through the night, coiling around my soul and body, urging me into the dance.

Prince Kerrin smashes down his goblet, heedless of splashed wine, and leaps up. "Dance with me, Beautiful."

I'm not very good at dancing yet. This could be a disaster. But I go with him anyway, and I try to keep up with the steps as best I can. It's a dance of pairs, a merry, fast-moving one, and I clasp the prince's hands, laughing silently with him as our feet move in tandem. Our eyes lock, and his are bright with pleasure, bright with hope—bright with the beauty I saw in him at a distance on that first day. His is a soul that could be beautiful. Maybe it has been marked and mottled by dissolution and selfishness. Maybe I can help him, restore him to what he should be.

I *want* to help him. And I let that fervent desire shine through my eyes, until his gaze softens with a wondering tenderness I've never seen from him before.

When the music ends, he clasps my head between his hands and kisses me.

Our masks graze lightly against each other as Kerrin's mouth takes mine, warm and soft. It's a delightful kiss. A mostly sober kiss. A kiss to erase the uncomfortable memories we made earlier today.

The crowd around us erupts into cheers. Breaking the kiss, the prince lifts his head, laughing, and raises a triumphant fist to them all. As if he has just won some great prize.

I suppose I'm flattered to be the prize.

More music, and this time it's a dance of changing partners. I'm very confused by the circular movement of the lines, the way they flow together. Half the time I have no idea who I'm supposed to be dancing with—I simply smile at everyone until my face hurts.

I'm at the edge of a revolving circle, in a line of women, when suddenly all of them do a quick turn and break off into pairs, seemingly with the first man who happens to be in front of them. I hesitate, my smile dropping, lost for a moment.

Broad gloved hands seize mine, and a large male figure looms over me. The man wears a mask covering his face from his upper lip to his hairline—just two deep holes through which I catch the faintest glitter of eyes. His hair is inky black. His long legs are encased in leather pants, and his massive chest is buttoned into a fine coat of swirling brocade, deep purple and gold, over a ruffled shirt.

That full, wide mouth and ruggedly carved jaw—I'd know them anywhere.

He smells like spiced wine and wicked poison. Like salt and leather. Like the sea.

155

21

THE SEA WITCH

Averil knows me at once. I see it in the telltale flush that creeps up her chest and neck, flooding her cheeks with bright color.

She can't speak to me, but she huffs out a little breath of displeasure, unhappy that I've disturbed her evening with the prince.

"I'm helping our cause," I murmur, drawing her into the dance. "You've done well thus far. But nothing will make the prince desire you more than a little competition. A man like him will want to secure you for himself once he sees you're attractive to others."

I flip her around, her back to my front, and I catch her wrists, spreading her arms wide. She's splayed against me, and I duck my masked face to the curve of her neck, skimming along that tender flesh. Her pheromones are not as strong in this form, not like they were under the sea, but the delicate fragrance of her skin sends a bolt of arousal racing straight to my cock.

The music has dropped into a more dramatic melody, a dance of passion and darkness. I whirl the princess around again, and she crashes into my chest with a soft gasp, facing me, pinned in place by my arms. I move with the rhythm, grinding my body against hers.

Out of the corner of my eye I see the prince, dancing with a buxom lady, but watching me and Averil with growing displeasure.

"He has noticed," I murmur. "He's beginning to grow jealous."

Averil bites her lip, throwing me a sharp, reproachful look.

"Trust me," I say. "Remember, the magic is stronger when we trust each other."

She rolls her eyes, but I sweep her into a spin that makes her gasp again. Yes, I will whirl all the sharp little thoughts out of that busy brain of hers. I will make her a slave to sensation.

She fights me at first, pulling back as I move her through the steps. And then, suddenly, wondrously, she yields. I can sense the change—the bend of her spine, the new fluidity of her limbs, the relinquishment of her soul to the music.

Her creamy neck arches, confidence in the angle of her chin, and her blue eyes flash boldly into mine.

Wildly, wondrously, we dance. Hips pressed together, then shifting apart, heated space opening between us. Hands meeting, moving, limbs sliding against each other. Whirling, bending, swaying through the melody as it sinks and swells.

Every nerve in my body is burning. I want nothing more than to tear off every vestige of human attire, explode into the tentacled monstrosity that I am, and drag this beautiful girl down into the depths with me, where I will make her writhe in desperate ecstasy on the tips of my tentacles.

As the song ends, she crashes against me one more time, her breasts heaving, face tipped up to mine, and the wildest expression in her eyes—a princess of the sea, a daughter of the ocean, bright and savage and scintillating with repressed desire.

And then she is yanked away from me. Claimed by the hand of the prince. Towed away through the crowd, while he glares back at me with all the ferocious rage of a toddler whose favorite plaything was taken.

New figures block the retreating forms of the prince and the girl—three muscular guards and Lord Brixeus himself, confronting me. Thank the gods for my mask.

"Now then, good sir," says Brixeus blandly. "You must understand you've made quite the scene. You're a passerby and a traveler, no doubt, and yet you've managed to offend the Crown Prince. He requires that we make an example of you. Unfortunate, but there it is. These gentlemen will escort you outside of town where you can be on your way."

"I only danced with a pretty girl," I say, keeping my voice low and rough.

"Yes, but you see, that pretty girl is the prince's favorite, and the way you danced with her is unacceptable to His Highness. He considers it a personal affront. An attack on his property, for which there must be punishment." Brixeus nods to the guards. "Take him, and do as we discussed."

I grin beneath the mask, but Brixeus is already turning away. Not the faintest flicker of recognition.

I allow the guards to hustle me away, between the buildings and out of town. When we reach a muddy back lane, the abuse begins. A smashing blow to my face, one that partly crunches the mask. A kick to the back of my legs, and then more kicks and punches, bringing me to my knees. They tear off my coat, rip my shirt to shreds, drag off my boots and throw them aside. Quickly, quietly, I cast a single light-based illusion, rendering the shell necklace invisible to them, lest they try to tear that away, too.

I could fight them off easily, with muscle or magic. But I let them beat me, because I cannot give myself away. Let the prince think he has conquered a rival. Let the events of this night cement his desire to lay a permanent claim on the girl he rescued.

Pain explodes through my jaw, my cheekbone, my ribs, my stomach. It's a brutal, clarifying pain, and when it's over, I lie prone in the muck long after the boots of the guards have tromped away. Yielding to a masochistic impulse, I suppose.

Before I can decide to gather myself up and leave for the sea again, there's a noise from the alley that empties into the muddy lane. Soles scrape on stone, a coarse sound against the jovial murmur of the distant music.

A figure appears, stepping from the cobblestones to the soft earth. Approaching me.

Averil scrunches up her skirts and runs over to me before sinking to her knees in the mud. Her fingers flutter over my ruined clothes, my cuts and scrapes. Gingerly she removes the dented mask, wincing at my bruised face. She taps her throat rapidly, then points to my chest, her eyes frantic.

"Ah." I let the invisibility glamour drop, revealing the necklace again. "It's still safe, love. Don't worry."

She closes her eyes briefly in relief, then taps the shark's-eye shell, a clear demand.

"I can't restore your voice right now," I say. "Not this close to everyone else."

She screws up her face angrily, her small fists tightening. Then she pokes my bruised cheekbone, hard.

"Ow."

Her eyes widen with insistent demand, and she taps her throat.

"Fine," I growl, allowing her voice to unspool from the shell and return to her body.

159

"Gods-damn you," she hisses. "Why did you let them hurt you?"

"Part of the ruse, love. Your prince has to feel that he has defended his own honor and secured his claim against a challenger." I let my head tip back into the mud. "It wasn't so bad. I've had worse. Now you should return to the handsome Kerrin—he'll be hunting for you soon, if he hasn't already drowned his senses in more of that delicious spiced wine."

"You're a fool," says the princess. Her face is shadowed, but I can see the angry glitter of tears in her eyes.

"You're offended by the way I danced with you." I push myself up on one arm, stifling a groan. "Just an act, shrimp. Nothing more."

"That's not it. I'm—you're badly hurt. You need help."

"That's why you're upset?" I laugh softly. "I can heal this easily once I get home."

"Oh." She inhales sharply, then blows out a long breath. "That's good."

"Anxious for the monster's well-being, princess?" I croon. "That seems like a waste of your emotion."

"I'm not anxious," she snaps.

"Clearly."

"I just— Some things happened, last night, and today—"

"Ah, last night." I let my mouth quirk in a mocking smile, and her eyes latch with mine, instantly alarmed.

"You *did* see me," she breathes, spreading her fingers over her cheeks. "You disgusting beast."

"Your mind summoned my gaze. I merely enjoyed the show. Wasn't much to it, unfortunately. You didn't seem to understand what to do. Would you like a lesson?"

I expect her to refuse at once. When she hesitates, my stomach rolls over, a slow thrill pulsing through my abdomen while my dick hardens.

"Would you like a lesson?" I say, lower.

"What is it called?" she whispers. "That bit, the part that feels good?"

"Your clit?"

"Yes, that. And was I doing—I was doing *something* right, or almost right. I—" Her fingers crumple the rich fabric of her gown. "It's not fair that Kerrin has had so many pleasurable experiences with other women. Like you have. And I've had nothing. I don't even know how to—what I—" She rams the heel of her hand against her forehead.

"You want experience. Pleasure. Before you are mated to someone."

"That's wrong, isn't it?" She stares at me desperately. "I've been taught that it's wrong."

"All in your point of view, love." A muscle jumps in my jaw as I clench it, trying to control my breathing. Trying not to betray how very interesting I find this turn of the conversation. "Your father worships the ocean and the old gods in the old way. He didn't used to be so strict, though, believe me. Time has changed him, made him fearful. The fearful seek control, and one of the best-loved tools of a fearful, controlling ruler is religion."

"So you're saying he and the priestesses have simply made up all those rules."

"I'm saying I don't believe the old gods would care, one way or another, if you had a little fun before you bind yourself to the prince. As I've told you, I don't believe in true mates. I've found many women worth respecting, and many who gave me a good time—favors I made sure to return in full. But I've never found anyone I wanted for a mate. I support your pursuit of the prince because there is something I want, as you know— something you owe me. But your father and the priestesses aren't here, little sinner. And Kerrin has not claimed you yet.

161

You belong to yourself, for now. A bit of practice couldn't hurt. And no one would ever need to know."

She's staring at me, watching my chest rise and fall under my ruined shirt. She reaches out with one finger, tracing a cut, then examining the sticky scarlet residue left on her fingertip.

"You're the only one I could experiment with, and you know it," she breathes. "But as you've said, you dislike me. You don't really want me."

With every bit of my bone and body, yes, I do.

But this is not about me, or our goals, hers and mine. Against all my will, I find myself urgently wanting her to experience the kind of nerve-shattering bliss I know I could offer, the kind her insipid prince will probably never give her. She should feel that glory once, before she ties herself to Perindal's foolish son.

"I could—remove myself from the situation," I say slowly. "Leave you untouched by my hands. My tentacles alone could service you, give you an experience you would never forget. An hour or two, like a sinful dream, and then it would be over. No one the wiser, and you would still be unmated by a human."

She avoids my eyes. "Would you—would they, your tentacles—go inside me?"

"Yes."

A shaky inhale, and she purses her lips. "Maybe. But now I should go back. And you should heal yourself. I wish you would let me help you."

"I don't need your help."

"Of course not." She starts to rise, but I catch her wrist, pulling her close with a sharp jerk, so her mouth nearly brushes mine.

"Sing for me first," I order.

Averil's lashes dip, her gaze finding my mouth. She wants to kiss me, I know it.

"You kissed your prince today," I murmur. "Was it everything you dreamed?"

"And more." There's an edge to her voice, but before I can inquire further, she's singing to me, slow and sweet, yielding her voice again. The familiar hum of its warmth curls into the shell against my breastbone.

"Go back to the prince," I tell her. "But tonight, if you cannot sleep, I will be on the beach where I gave you legs. You can meet me there, and it will be like a dream. A gift to yourself before you take a mate. No stain on your conscience, unless you allow it."

The shadow of heightened color deepens in her cheeks, and her pupils dilate, but she only rises and hurries away.

After she's gone, I haul myself up stiffly, grimacing at the twinge of torn flesh and the spike of pain through cracked ribs. I make my way out of the village, down the path to the strip of beach by the black cliffs. The cliffs where I watched the sea take the prince's ship.

Blasted damn prince. I hate him.

Yet without him, I would not have this one chance to get the thing I need, the thing they took from me, the object I made sure they could never wield, the one *they* made sure I could never reach.

I will have it, no matter what I must pay.

I stow my clothing in a chest I've hidden, buried in the sand by the cliff. My tentacles unfurl, a welcome return to my natural shape. In moments I'm back in the sea, forging through its welcoming depths, saltwater stinging my wounds.

I'm mending myself with a tincture or two when Liris ripples into my lair, a flurry of striped fins and variegated spines. His scarred face looks unusually serious.

"The Sea King is looking for his daughter," he says.

"Let him look."

"You don't understand. He's out of his mind. He's hunting for her everywhere. He says if she isn't found in two days, the priestesses must do a reckoning to discern what has happened to her."

That makes me pause. "A reckoning? That's an arcane rite. A brutal one, involving the bloody sacrifice of three merfolk. Surely the people would never allow it."

"Tarion's power is absolute, Zoltan. Not like when you ruled and everyone had a voice. He and the priestesses can do anything they want, to anyone. They will go through with the sacrifice, believe me. And you know where the girl is. Do you want that blood on your hands? Does *she*?"

I grit my teeth, hissing as I smear jellied poultice into a larger cut. The wound bubbles and seals instantly.

"At least tell the girl what her father is doing," Liris urges me. "She should know about it. Let her make the choice, to stay or to return."

"She and I still have a deal. A bargain has been struck. She either fulfills her role in this, or she loses her voice, and more besides. You know how it works."

"Surely there's a way to—"

"There isn't. I need more time, Liris, just a little more *time*. What Tarion does in his rages is no fault of mine. You cannot blame me for the results."

Liris gnaws his scarred lip. "If he suspects you at all, Zoltan—if he believes you've had anything to do with her disappearance, this venomous garden can't protect you, and neither can we. He'll devour us all."

"We have other haunts he doesn't know about. In fact, you should take Ekkon and Graeme to the Sounding Waste, to the maze there. You'll be safe. Stay hidden until this is over."

Liris hesitates, then bows his head. "Very well. We'll go tomorrow, as long as you promise you'll be careful. Stay on land as much as possible until it's done, so Tarion can't get to you."

"I will."

"And Zoltan, maybe tonight, you could..." His voice trails off as he looks hopefully at me.

"Alter your forms so the three of you can fuck each other? My pleasure." I grin at him. "It has been a while. I'll perform the spell now—I have somewhere to be later. Go find the boys and get busy."

Liris races off, and I shake my head, still grinning. I don't even need to see the three of them to alter their forms, I'm so used to doing it. Remove the toxic lionfish spines from Liris. Eliminate Graeme's lightning, dull his teeth a bit. Dim Ekkon's lure so it won't overcome his mates' minds, and give him a more solid appearance, as he always requests. Just the way the three of them like it. They'll be busy for the next few hours, and as long as they stay in their quarters, near my lair, the effect of my magic will hold.

I try to keep myself busy. I try not to listen to the groans and breathless screams echoing through the halls of the cave complex as my friends take their pleasure.

I float in my sleeping area, my tentacles creeping up the walls around me, holding me in place, and I picture the scene of the masquerade as I left it. By now the dancing should be slowing, simmering down as villagers grow weary, or perhaps more drunken. The prince will likely keel over soon. The mayor may perhaps make some attempt at a speech, commemorating the lives of the sailors who died in the storm.

Lord Brixeus will likely follow up with a speech of his own—one of thanks to the villagers for their hospitality—a speech no doubt dripping with heavy implication that the prince should soon leave the village and head for the Summer Palace at Crystal Point, where his father awaits him.

Prince Kerrin won't be able to excuse the delay much longer. But will he take Averil with him, or will he leave her behind in the care of the village, like a stray kitten? I hope my challenge tonight was enough to stir him up, to make him feel more possessive of her.

If they go to the Summer Palace together, I'll follow them. But I must keep my distance from the king and his retinue. Perindal may or may not have a conjurer or two in his employ, but he will at the very least have magical protections in place around himself—charms to dispel glamours and disguises, to alert him if the dreaded Sea Witch of his past comes to call.

Not to mention the fact that the Summer Palace, also known as the Queen's Palace, is wreathed with protective magic, bonded to its very walls, so that I, specifically, may not enter. Perindal paid dearly for that protection, and I know he still keeps his chief treasures there—including the thing I want back. It's hidden deep in the bowels of that castle, and I will have it. Averil will fetch it for me.

But first... there is the matter of Averil herself, and the specific kind of tending she requires. Will she meet me on the beach, I wonder?

When my friends have had a few hours to themselves, and their passionate cries have ebbed, I lurch upright and leave the cave, wending my way through my gardens until I approach the shore and the shallows.

My heart is pounding. I can feel each beat, throbbing through every tentacle I possess. My cock is huge and heated, prodding boldly from its slit, hard and demanding.

Doing this for the girl, without touching her with my hands or fucking her myself, will be the most difficult thing I've done in a long time.

Yet I am determined to set all else aside for a little while, and use every bit of sensory talent I possess to thrill her thoroughly. She may pretend it was a dream afterward, but she will remember this night for the rest of her life. Every time she goes to bed with the insipid Prince, she'll remember me, and the pleasure I gave her.

And the delight will not be entirely one-sided. My tentacles are sensitive. I will be able to feel her soft flesh, the tremors of her body, her smooth skin. I will be able to watch her come undone for me.

I crawl out of the sea, dripping, my muscles hard with tension, with anticipation, my arms rigid from shoulders to claws.

And there she is, sitting on a rock, waiting in the moonlight. Wearing the flimsy scrap of a nightdress the prince gave her, a cloak puddled on the ground at her feet.

When I come out of the water in a shower of glittering drops, she leaps up, her spine straight and her head lifted. Her decision made.

Slowly I approach her, tentacles creeping across the shining wet beach. Her feet are bare, each toe dimpling the sand.

I speak to her quietly, afraid she will startle and flee. I am so desperate to do this. "I won't give your voice back, because you might not be able to keep from screaming, and we can't risk discovery. But someday I will make you scream until the sea itself trembles."

It's a foolish vow, one that probably betrays too much of what I desire. But Averil is too jittery and expectant to notice. She's blushing, fluttering with arousal already, dizzied yet determined.

"From now until the moon sets," I whisper, "nothing I do to you with my tentacles will count. I won't touch you with my hands, or kiss you, or speak to you. Anything else is fair game, as long as it brings you pleasure. Anything. You yield complete control to me. Agreed?"

She shudders. Shudders *toward* me, a voiceless yearning. And nods.

I let out a long rumble of satisfaction, letting my tentacles surge forward and surround her.

Deftly I use their tips and suckers to peel off the nightdress, until her whole beautiful body is bared to me, shining vulnerable and soft in the moonlight.

The cliffside hollow from which I watched her save the prince that first night. That's where I'll dismantle every inhibition she has and usher her into a universe of exquisite pleasure.

I catch her up in my tentacles, and I carry her away into the dark.

22

The Sea Witch didn't ease me into this dream—he swept me into it, carrying me off like a monster might steal his prey.

Once I gave my consent, he did not ask if I was ready—he knew that I was. I always am, for him.

We're in a dark, damp hollow beneath an angled shelf of rock. He's hiding in the blackness, his torso swathed in shadows, erasing himself from this moment so I don't have to disentangle any difficult emotions—I can simply enjoy the sensations alone.

I'm lying naked on one of his velvety tentacles, its curve following the arch of my spine. Another thick length of tentacle drapes across my breasts, its small suction cups working my flesh, teasing my nipples into aching points. The stimulation sends a fresh flood of liquid between my thighs.

A tiny sucker pumps gently over my clit, coaxing out little pulses of brightening pleasure, while the tip of another tentacle nuzzles into the crevice of my bottom, teasing the puckered hole there, nudging inside just barely. The tempting, wriggling movement in that private place sends lightning skating up my tailbone, along my spine.

A blunt tentacle probes along my slit, rolling in the slippery wetness, dipping between the lips of my sex in slow sweeps, like a tongue licking deeper, deeper, each time a little deeper. A deep ache wakes inside my core, a hollow yearning to be filled, *now, please, please—come inside—*

The slippery tentacle noses maddeningly along my sex again, before plunging into my body in a rush of glittering, glowing, overwhelming sensation.

I am suspended, surrounded, penetrated. Soaked with sweat and slickness and unutterable pleasure.

I am letting him take me apart.

I am coming undone, slowly, yet still holding onto something while he tries to make me let go...

The dainty suction on my clit increases, intensifies. Tentacles quiver against my rear, palpate my breasts—they're stroking my neck, slithering across my mouth—and the one in my pussy keeps plunging, steady and slick, deep inside me, over and over, pumping me toward something, something...

The suction vanishes from my sensitive bud, only to be replaced by a tentacle tip, like a finger, rubbing quick and delicate. I can't bear it, can't bear it—oh—gods—

A sharp, searing line of ecstasy shears through me, straight from that blazing point of contact all the way up my belly, my chest, my every nerve ending. I arch, speared and spasming, blazing—nothing has ever been this beautiful, or this filthy.

Pleasure is cracking me open. Shattering me into bright, keen fragments. An explosion of starry bliss, the first climax I have ever felt.

He doesn't speak. But I hear a low hum of male satisfaction from the darkness where he's shrouded, watching me explode—watching me come.

His tentacles stroke me, soothe me, then lift me, winding around my arms and legs, turning me over and splaying me wide until I'm suspended face-down, my limbs extended. It's so dark I can barely see the rocky floor of the hollow. I might as well be floating in the sky, bound by a cosmic god, wrung out for his pleasure.

A rippling appendage slides down my belly, rubbing between the lips of my sex, grazing the sensitized bud of nerves again and again. I thought maybe it was over, but no, no—more pleasure is coming. I can feel my body's senses leaping forward, flinging me headlong into this new, delicious world of sensation.

Tentacles coil around my breasts, squeezing lightly, their tips plucking at my nipples. I gasp, still voiceless.

But someday I will make you scream until the sea itself trembles.

I cling to the thrilling memory of his deep voice—I imagine it reverberating through my very bones. And then I'm being filled again—a tentacle slicked with my own juices gliding inside me. Another is pressing into my rear, going deeper this time, writhing into my bottom. Two channels filled and pulsing, while my clit quivers under the ministrations of another tentacle.

When the second climax hits, I nearly pass out. My limbs go stiff and straight, shaking, vibrating with glimmering, exquisite sensation. Every nerve is illuminated as if by pure white lightning. I want to scream. I have to. Sweat films my forehead, my breasts, my whole body. I'm a mess—a trembling, spasming, glorious, wretched mess.

I'm still being filled, still surging with the slow, resolute rhythm of the two tentacles inside me. For a long time they squirm and pulse and pump through my channels, while his other tentacles surround my body, upholding me, caressing me.

Then the tentacles in my rear and my slit begin to move in tandem, faster, faster—inhumanly fast, impossible—I can't bear it—oh oh *oh oh*—and I crash again, splintering into bliss, shining flakes of me flung out into the wild night, into the cosmic darkness in which there is only my body and his monstrous, shrouded self.

When the third climax is over, I hang there, helpless and sated and nearly inert.

Awareness trickles back into my consciousness.

The fragrance of the sea—salt air in my lungs. The faintly venomous, crisply magical scent that always seems to linger around the Sea Witch. The rushing surge of the waves on the strip of beach beyond the cave. The sated, pulsing warmth of my insides, empty now, and weak with delight.

I'm too spent to know what I should do, where I should go. Who I should be after this.

My body is lowered down from the height, curled among comforting velvety tentacles. Carried out of the cave into the water, where the salty surf welcomes me, soothes me.

The Sea Witch doesn't touch me with his hands, not yet. We are still in this sequence of pretend, this artificial separation we've created between our goals and my wicked desires. But he washes my body with his tentacles, draws me back to shore, and sends a soft whirr of air over my skin to dry it.

Once I've managed to get dressed, he finally speaks. "It's over. We will not speak of it again. And it does not count."

I nod. Though I'm not even sure what I'm agreeing to. Saying a thing "doesn't count" is merely an excuse. And I know it, but I don't care.

"Can you walk?" he asks.

Again, I nod. I'm deliciously sore, but I feel incredible, too. I know the path back to the village well now. I can return alone.

Part of me doesn't want to look at him, and see the tentacles, and think about what I just let him do to me.

But it seems untrue to myself and unfair to him if I can't face what I've done. So before I ascend the path between the dunes, I turn back, and I look straight at him, as he rises tall atop those coiling tentacles, his hair tossed in the breeze, his great arms folded over his chest.

I give him a small smile and a wave. Because he deserves it. He gave me all the pleasure I craved, and demanded nothing from me at all.

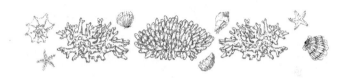

The prince summons me down to breakfast in the common room much earlier than I expected.

I'm a little groggy, a little grumpy, and a bit dizzy in the head because I've been staying up far too late and not getting nearly enough sleep. Though last night's lateness, to be fair, was my own fault.

I'm half afraid Kerrin will see something in my face, that he'll guess the wicked things I allowed the Sea Witch to do to me in that beachside cave. My indulgence of my curiosity and my desires took me to a place I never imagined I would go. I still can't believe I let it happen.

But it's over, and it didn't count. It's not as if I let the Sea Witch touch me with his hands and invade me with his cock. That would be entirely different and inexcusable. And it's not as if I gave the Sea Witch any pleasure in return. I didn't touch him or tease him to climax. I didn't curl my fingers around his thick—

"Good morning, Beautiful," says Prince Kerrin, and I startle, looking up from my cup of tea, my cheeks hot.

He sent a servant to bring me down early, yet made me wait here for quite a long while. I'm starving.

"And what does his Highness desire to break his fast?" asks the innkeeper, approaching us with an obsequious bow.

"Poached eggs, sugared fruit tarts, cold ham, hot bacon—crispy, not limp—and toast with honey," the prince says carelessly.

"Very good, sir. And for the lady?"

"She'll have the same."

I force a smile as the innkeeper meets my eyes, and I try not to care that the prince didn't attempt to ask me what I wanted. If he had, I couldn't have answered. Still, I would have appreciated the chance to try communicating my own wishes.

"I trust you slept well after—after last night's festivities?" Kerrin's forehead wrinkles, as if he's trying to recall precisely what happened. "After I sent off that brute who was pawing you, I do believe I had a little more wine than I intended."

Since I can't speak, I can't remind him that he dragged me out of the dancing, back to the tables, where he began to drink copiously and bellow about "nasty uncultured yokels who think they can paw another man's woman." During his tirade, I slipped away and found the Sea Witch lying wounded—and by the time I returned, Kerrin was unconscious on the banquet table, drooling onto a napkin that Lord Brixeus daintily wedged beneath his cheek.

Lord Brixeus and I exchanged a long look over the prince's snoring form. A wordless understanding.

Freed from the prince's jealousy, I danced a while longer, until the mayor and Lord Brixeus made a couple of speeches and the gathering began to thin. After that, I return to the inn to change, before slipping away into a wicked waking dream of tentacles and shimmering darkness.

"I've been wondering something," the prince says, interrupting my memories. "Can you write, Beautiful? I suppose you would have by now, if you could. But can you?"

I nod, and then I shake my head. With my finger I trace several symbols from the mermaid language on the table. I dare not write anything permanent, lest someone recognize the source of the only written language I know.

"I don't know those letters." The prince frowns. "So you understand the Common Tongue, but you can't write it? You can only write in some other language?"

Wincing, I nod.

"Amazing." He grins, eyes bright with pleasure. "You were sent to me by the gods, I swear."

A frown pulls at my brows. Why is he so pleased by my inability to communicate?

The prince moves on from the topic, standing abruptly and stalking away from the table. "I've come to a decision, Beautiful," he says. "This little town has given me all it can by way of rest, and no other survivors have crawled onto the shore. So after breakfast I'm leaving for my father's summer palace at Crystal Point."

My stomach drops.

He's leaving.

I have to make him take me along. Otherwise my deal with the Sea Witch will be broken, and I will lose everything.

I lower my gaze, letting tears come into my eyes. Easy to do, since I'm faced with the loss of my human form, my freedom on land, my voice, and my father's love. I'll be lucky if I'm not exiled from court for life, after all I've done.

The prince crosses to me with long, quick strides, sinking to one knee at my side and tipping my chin up with his long, ringed fingers. "Oh, no, Beautiful, do not cry," he croons, running his thumb gently under my eye, collecting a tear. "Did I say I would leave you behind? Never. You will come with me, my little beauty. At least, I'll allow it if you can give me a smile. You can do that, can't you, darling? A smile for your prince?"

Blinking, with tears studding my lashes, I give him a tremulous smile. It feels like a betrayal of myself. I have never felt less like smiling.

"Good girl." Kerrin pats my cheek. "And while we're talking of it, Beautiful, I must know—you like me, don't you? We get along well together. We would make a lovely match of it, you and I. I must confess I like you better than so many of the preening princesses I've been forced to suck up to during my travels. Most women are just insufferable, don't you think? The incessant chatter about inane topics—drives me batty, to be honest. But you—you don't annoy me much at all. And I think you'll annoy me even less once we get a little better acquainted." He slides a warm hand along my thigh, squeezing lightly.

I keep the smile on my face. A traitorous tingle races along my leg, from the place where he's touching me straight to my center.

I must be the most wicked, wanton little mermaid to ever live. So much pleasure last night, and now I'm melting again, eager for more—in spite of the way Kerrin has behaved to me and others.

What is wrong with me? Am I doomed to be enslaved to my body's nonsensical reactions? Have I no self-control at all?

When Kerrin moves in, I let him kiss me. It's nice, so I continue kissing him until the breakfast arrives. The damp slickness of my underwear makes me feel secretly naughty as we eat together, but Kerrin barely acknowledges me—he nibbles disdainfully at the food while giving orders for our things to be packed up at once in preparation for a hasty departure to Crystal Point.

177

There aren't many possessions to pack, since he lost so many of his own things in the shipwreck. In fact, I'm not sure how he accumulated all the clothing, weapons, and jewelry he's been wearing since I arrived. Perhaps he simply took what he wanted from this town's merchants and shops.

The prince demands a carriage as well—the finest that can be had on short notice. He and I will ride ahead while the servants and guards follow.

I should let the Sea Witch know what is happening. I call on him silently, feeling the telltale warmth of the shell necklace as he responds.

The prince is taking me with him to Crystal Point, I say. *We're leaving within the hour.*

I told you he would, responds the Sea Witch in my head.

There's relief in his tone. Of course there is. This is what he wants, the unfolding of the events that will lead to my mysterious task, this favor he wants me to do in order to fulfill our bargain.

Why do I feel so helpless and tiny at the thought of going alone with the prince to the Summer Palace? The idea of so much distance opening up between me and the Sea Witch—it's disturbing. Not because I like the Witch or care about him at all—simply because his magic is my anchor to this form. And he's been very helpful. I might need him. I *do* need him.

And you, I say cautiously, *will you still be able to help me? I'll be farther away. I can still speak with you through the shells, but what if I need more assistance, more training, more—*

His voice interrupts my thoughts. *I'm coming with you. I'll have to keep my distance—I have more enemies the nearer I get to the king—but I must stay close so I can manage this situation. Not that I don't trust you, shrimp,* he adds dryly, *but the stakes are much too high to leave anything to chance.*

178

Joy threads through my heart, and it's all I can do to keep my face calm and placid as I munch the tasty bacon the prince deemed "too crisp."

The Sea Witch is coming with me. He'll still be nearby. It's reassuring, that's all. There's safety in his proximity. More safety than I sometimes feel in the presence of Kerrin, son of Perindal, prince of this kingdom.

The prince's father was recently the subject of an assassination attempt, I tell the Sea Witch. *Do you think there's a risk to the prince himself?*

Interesting, muses the Witch. *I suppose it's possible. Court is a savage place, princess. You know that, being a royal yourself—but you've been somewhat sheltered, since you're the youngest and therefore a less valuable pawn in the games of state.*

Thank you for that, I retort. *I've always loved thinking of myself as the least valuable pawn.*

I'm only saying you're unprepared for the level of schemes and vitriol you'll encounter in a human court, says the Sea Witch. *Watch yourself. Continue to be the sweet, lovely, wide-eyed, voiceless thing the prince cherishes, and you'll be able to stay on the path we need to follow. Not too much curiosity. No investigations or clever intuitions.*

None at all?

You can't help yourself, can you? His voice carries a smile. *At least keep them to yourself. Don't risk our goals.*

I want to ask what our goals are, exactly, because I have the strangest feeling mine have changed. And once my task for the Sea Witch is done, I'm not certain what I will want—to retain my legs and remain on land, or to return to the sea. Somehow I don't know if I'll be quite happy with either one.

And I'm not sure I can be happy as wife to this prince, who is now castigating the inn's cook for cooking the bacon precisely

179

as he requested, while seemingly oblivious to the fact that for half the meal we shared, I was carrying on a conversation with another man inside my head.

23

THE SEA WITCH

When I follow Averil, I borrow the same horse I took from the mayor's stables before. I like the stallion—good-tempered and responsive, yet with an unbroken spirit.

I've always despised the breaking of animals, whether of land or sea. Better to work *with* the will of a creature, to partner alongside them, rather than crushing a bright nature in the name of dull obedience.

I'm far less patient with humans and merfolk. Prince Kerrin, for example, is a prime example of a man who could use a good breaking. I wonder what it would take to crack through his hollow selfishness and find the meat of a worthy man beneath. If anyone can unearth his true potential, it's the red-haired princess riding in the open carriage with him.

I can see flashes of them through the trees—his gold circlet glinting amid raven curls, her hair shining like a scarlet flame. He has taken the reins from his driver and he's whipping the flanks of the horses, urging them down the bumpy coastal road at a breakneck pace. Showing off for the princess, no doubt.

She looks to be enjoying it. She's leaning forward, smiling.

Rolling my eyes, I pull the horse farther into the meadows that run alongside the road. I need to keep a safe distance, lest the prince's retinue take note of me. I'll ride the forest paths for the rest of the day, keeping out of sight and hoping that careless idiot prince doesn't snap Averil's neck and his own on the way to the palace.

The image of Averil lying in the road, her neck crooked and her blue eyes empty, jumps into my mind in a searing flash of pain.

I nearly whirl the horse around and ride to them, drag the carriage to a stop, pull her onto my own horse, and run away with her, somewhere he can never touch her or put her at risk again.

But I shove the impulse aside and focus instead on the delight of riding through the warm, hazy, spice-scented woods, in shade flecked with sunlight, taking an occasional pull from the waterskin at my side.

I carry a large leather satchel with me, packed with some clothing and magical supplies. Not quite what I'm used to working with under the sea, but I can make do. The principles and properties of my magical concoctions are similar whether I'm working in air or water, although the ingredients and amounts sometimes differ.

If the prince is the sort of man I suspect he is, he'll slow the journey during the afternoon—find some excuse to laze by a river and drink, and perhaps nap before they travel on. I have plenty of time to reach Crystal Point before they do and find a room for rent on the outskirts of the town where I can be near Averil, yet not so near that anyone of import notices me. I'll wear a glamour, and a hood or a hat as well, as a double precaution.

Hours later, I'm riding along the road among grassy, sea-scoured bluffs, admiring the crystal-blue of the ocean to my left and the outline of the Crystal Palace far ahead, when an alarmed call throbs through the necklace I'm wearing.

Sea Witch, I don't know what to do.

"Fuck," I mumble, pulling the horse into a copse of trees and swinging out of the saddle. When I touch my necklace, the scene unfolds around me, assembled in shimmering motes of dust and dirt, rather than sand and water.

Averil reclines on the sloping green grass by a stream, the remains of a grand picnic scattered around her. The bodice of her dress has been pushed aside, and the prince is draped on top of her, mouthing her breast, laving her nipple with his tongue.

A hot, wild anger bellows in my brain, roaring, rushing outward into hers.

"Is he forcing this?" I grit out.

No, no. I wanted it. Allowed it. But I—you said I shouldn't give in to him until I was certain of his heart. I wasn't sure if I should give him everything yet.

I haul in a ragged, burning breath. "Do you *want* to give him everything?"

I don't know. It feels good, but—

I shudder, hanging on her words, but her thoughts sink into a blissful sigh as the prince runs his fingers beneath her skirts, heading for her center.

This is what we planned. This has been my intent all along. This act is the natural outworking of our scheme to insert her into his heart and his bed.

So why do I feel as if I will die if I must witness it?

"Do what you like with him," I say curtly. "If he goes too far, refuse him, preferably without wounding his pride. No easy task, I admit, but you got yourself into this. I have things to do."

Wait, she says, but I close the connection.

What do I care if she fucks him by the stream? Now or later, it matters not to me, as long as Kerrin proposes to her. As long as he takes her to the place where every future queen of this kingdom goes on the day after her engagement to the Crown Prince. As long as he unknowingly grants her the access I crave.

Why should I care what they do together? Why should it inflame my soul like bubbling acid, gnawing me until I feel my very bones aching?

I hate them both. Especially her.

I will destroy the pair of them without mercy. When Averil realizes what she has done for me, the chaos she has enabled, the destruction I will bring upon her father—then she will be sorry she ever touched the puling, mawkish prince.

I will have my revenge on them all.

24

Kerrin has just began stroking me through my underwear when Lord Brixeus strides up. "Your Highness," he says, careless of my bare-breasted state. "We should continue our journey to your father's palace."

"Am I never to have her then?" says Kerrin petulantly. "Fuck you, Brixeus."

"Yes, milord," drones the equerry. As he turns away, his eye catches mine for a moment. His expression is deeply, bitterly disdainful. It's clear he thinks me some crown-chasing slut at best, and at worst, a conniving spy.

Perhaps I am both of those things. I'm strangely unsettled about letting Kerrin touch me, even though it felt good, even though I'm bound to no one else, even though I've decided to let myself explore my own desires a little more.

So why do I have the crawling, uncomfortable sense that I was doing wrong by permitting his mouth at my breast and his hands on my body? Is it because, deep down, I think he's unworthy of me? Or perhaps it is something else.

As Kerrin and I ride in the carriage that afternoon, he keeps trying to persuade me to put my hand on his crotch and rub his cock, whose hardened shape I can discern through his tight pants. But he doesn't ask outright, and I pretend not to understand, just as he rarely attempts to understand me.

Our journey takes us along a pretty coastal road, within full view of long pale beaches, grassy dunes, and verdant forests. At last, a high point appears ahead, where the Summer Palace stands bright and beautiful against the clear blue of the afternoon sky. The town clustering around the point features red-tiled roofs and bountiful windowboxes like the village we just left, except the houses here are bigger, the shops more numerous, and the cobbled streets wider and better kept. The streets are steeper, too, winding up toward the central attraction—the white stone palace with its gleaming gold-tiled peaks and flashing crystal windows. Balconies lace every level, and pennants flutter from the slim towers. It's altogether beautiful.

We enter the gates to the sound of trumpets—a hastily assembled passel of musicians, by the look of their flushed faces and the slightly off-key timbre of their music. The prince wasn't expected, having traveled in a hurry. Apparently he sent no one ahead to tell the palace staff of his impending arrival. Yet he will expect them to have all things perfectly ready for him.

I am ushered from carriage to courtyard, up some steps, and along hallways. The prince doesn't offer his arm, yet I have no doubt he intends for me to follow him closely. So I keep my eyes open and my mouth shut, and I try to move with the grace I usually possess under the sea. Here it's a clumsier elegance of earth-bound feet and legs swooshing through skirts. But I hold my head high, nonetheless, and attempt to act every bit the princess I am.

Court at home is a place of colonnades and hazy multicolored glow-lights, where priestesses and dignitaries float

187

in ornate alcoves and supplicants spiral outward from the royal bower in long lines, waiting to speak with my father.

In the Summer Palace, the human court is on holiday. Gaudily dressed courtiers hang on each other's arms and shoulders, eyelashes flickering with gold flakes or green glitter, mouths wine-stained, lips issuing spirals of colorful smoke. The throne room is a scattering of couches draped in half-clad bodies.

The throne is empty.

A tall, angular woman rises from a sofa beside the throne, twirling a long-stemmed smoking stick. "Your Highness! Lord Brixeus! What fun. Crown Prince, we were so relieved to hear that your life was spared after that terrible storm. Such an honor to see you back home again, after your years abroad. I'll see to it that a great feast is held in your honor tonight."

"What is all this chaos, Lady Felton?" Lord Brixeus says grimly. "Where is His Majesty?"

The woman sidles closer, hushing him with a long finger. "The king is still recovering from the poisoning attempt."

"Still?" The equerry raises his eyebrows.

"Trust me, the apothiks are doing all they can. Thank you for sending Cassilenne to us—she has been invaluable. Most skilled young physician in the kingdom."

My eyes widen at the mention of the apothik with the braid, the one who tended me when I was first found on the beach. I haven't seen her since that day, nor did I think to ask about her.

"Brixeus didn't send her to Crystal Point—I did," Kerrin says airily. "I wanted my father to have the best care, even if it meant I myself was left without a healer to attend me."

"His Majesty should have recovered by now," Lord Brixeus murmurs. "When we received word of the attempted assassination, the messenger said the king had not ingested much of the poison. Such a small amount should not lay him low this long."

"Perhaps this was a unique kind of toxin." Lady Felton shrugs.

"And they caught the man who did it?" Lord Brixeus is frowning deeper now. "I suppose he was interrogated. What did he say? Who sent him?"

"Oh, he died before they could torture the truth out of him," says Lady Felton.

"And the poison, was there any remaining? Did anyone study it?"

"By the gods, you ask many questions." Lady Felton laughs, but there's ice in the sound.

Lord Brixeus's face tightens. "I was merely wondering if perhaps the poison was of unique origins, something our apothiks do not know how to treat. Maybe a toxin not from the land, but from the sea."

"What?" The prince frowns, looking confused. "What does that mean?"

"It means your father has old enemies," Lord Brixeus replies. "Enemies who do not forget."

My heart clenches. Old enemies from under the sea?

Could it be that the Sea Witch is behind the attempt on the king's life? The Witch said I wouldn't have to harm anyone—he didn't promise that *he* wouldn't. He could have been lying to me earlier, when we discussed the assassination.

Yet the Witch doesn't seem to be able to get close to King Perindal himself. How could he have managed to poison him?

"I want to see my father," Kerrin demands. "I haven't seen him in ages. I have things to tell him, and someone for him to meet." He snags my wrist, hauling me close to his side.

Lady Felton's impossibly long lashes droop as she surveys me. "Forgive me, your Highness—we'd heard that your search for a bride had been—unfruitful. Troubling, of course, since you must secure an engagement before the end of your twenty-fifth year. But can it be you've found someone after all?"

"I have. And I would like to present her to my father for his blessing. We've been traveling, so please take her away and have her freshened and dressed so she can meet him. She's a mute, so don't bother trying to talk to her."

Heat rushes into my face at the callous dismissal, but Kerrin follows it up with a sunny smile and a long kiss to my mouth.

"As you wish, Highness," says Lady Felton. "Come, child, let's make you fit for a king."

She says it with the faintest mocking lilt, which Kerrin doesn't seem to notice. He's heading straight for a doorway in the far corner of the throne room, where the apothik Cassilenne stands silently in a blue gown, with her braid over her shoulder.

Something in the way the prince hurries toward her, with more strength of purpose than he usually shows—it piques me. Did she travel abroad with him? Did she also escape the shipwreck in the skiff full of survivors? It's possible she was there, and I didn't notice her that night. Or she may have come ashore with others at some point. Perhaps she is merely a friend from his youth who happened to be in the seaside village when his ship wrecked nearby. Which would be an odd coincidence.

What is she to Kerrin? A physician only, or something else?

The questions in my mind and the tension in my body only increase throughout the rest of the afternoon and evening. Kerrin drags me into a dark, cavernous bedroom and presents me to his father—a sweaty, pallid man, swathed in sheets, who's barely alert enough to recognize his son.

"I found her, Father," Kerrin says. "My future bride. A noblewoman. Beautiful and graceful, just what you wanted for me. I intend to ask for her hand. Tell me I have your blessing."

The king mumbles something unintelligible.

"A nod of assent is all I need, Father," says Kerrin, striding forward, laying his hand atop his father's sweat-damp head. "Yes? Good? I have your approval?" He presses lightly on the king's head, which tilts forward. "You are witnesses to the king's blessing," Kerrin says to the chamber servants and guards. "Lord Brixeus, you are witness as well."

Lord Brixeus does not answer. He stalks grimly from the sickroom.

I leave the chamber feeling panicked and alarmed, pitying a king I barely know. He seems so helpless, not at all the formidable enemy the Sea Witch made him out to be. I suppose years ago he must have been great. Even a few weeks ago, perhaps, before the poison. I'm not accustomed to human economics and I have little to go on except my visit to the seaside town, but from what I can tell, Perindal's kingdom seems to be pleasant and prosperous. He must have managed it well.

Next comes the banquet—a garish dinner during which I must sit primly beside the prince and smile at everyone. Once they find out I can't speak, few people seem to think me worth the barest attempt at communication.

My coiling discontent tightens and burns, especially when the prince leaves the banquet and doesn't return for a long time. I sit gracefully posed, bright-eyed and smiling, taking tiny sips of wine while watching the dancers and jugglers Lady Felton ordered for the occasion. Their performances are alluring, I must admit. Far different from anything I've seen under the sea.

But at last I grow tired of waiting for the prince, and during a particularly vibrant performance by some acrobats, I slip out of the banquet hall and wander along the corridor down which Kerrin disappeared.

It's quiet, lined with alcoves draped in heavy curtains. From one of those half-concealed spaces comes a faint glugging, slurping sound, and a low male moan.

I creep nearer, leaning around a stiff fold of drapery.

And there is Prince Kerrin, his pants open and Cassilenne's braid wrapped around his hand. She's on her knees sucking his cock, her head bobbing fervently, drool leaking from the corner of her lips.

"Fuck, I've missed this," gasps the prince. "The girl we found—she's sweet, and gorgeous of course, and perfect for the plan, but she's so prudish. Doesn't understand desire at all. Not like you do."

Cassilenne slides her mouth off him with a wet pop. "Maybe you and I can teach her a few things before this is all over. I do like her. It's a pity—"

"It's a pity my cock isn't in your throat right now," says Kerrin, hauling her mouth onto his shaft again. She chuckles around him, then gags a little.

I move away from them as quietly as I can, but I'm barely able to place one foot in front of the other. Nausea roils in my gut, and an icy flush rolls over my skin.

Everything I knew is crashing together in my mind, like columns tilting and toppling, bearing each other down in a cacophony of destruction. My thoughts keep jumping, disjointed and frantic, through the sour truths I've just learned.

The prince doesn't want me as his mate or consort—or if he does, it's not the way I'd like to be wanted.

He mentioned "the plan." And she said, "It's a pity." Neither of those things sound good. Rather ominous, in fact.

Lady Felton said the prince must secure an engagement before his twenty-sixth birthday.

Kerrin presented me to his father and the court. Yet he has his cock in the apothik's mouth right now.

She's so prudish. Doesn't understand desire at all.

His words. About me.

I'm shaking with rage. I want to scream.

I thought this piece of wretched human filth might be my mate, but instead he's using me somehow, for some plan of his. He thinks me a helpless stray, a lucky find, a voiceless pawn he can plug into his schemes.

Well, two can play his game. Because I'm neither as helpless or voiceless as he thinks. So I will stay here, and I'll pretend to be the dutiful wide-eyed girl he rescued. I'll toddle along after him—but once my bargain with the Sea Witch is complete, I will have my choices back. And then Kerrin, son of Perindal, will feel my wrath.

The rage rushes through me, glorious and freeing. It scours away all my doubts and guilt. I don't have to feel conflicted about my dislike for Kerrin anymore—at last I can fully admit that I was wrong about him, that he deserves my censure. And in the face of this betrayal I will become the thing Brixeus feared I was—a spy in the palace. Just because I am silent does not mean I am powerless.

I do not cry. Tears are for humans. But I gather my skirts and return to the banquet hall.

When Kerrin comes back to his seat at the dinner table, I shed a brilliant smile over him.

And when, at the end of the night, he calls for silence, kneels before me, and asks for my hand in marriage amid the cheers of the court, I gasp and nod and flutter and kiss him—a bargain sealed in burning lips.

One I fully intend to break.

25

THE SEA WITCH

Averil calls me shortly before midnight. *I demand to see you.*

"Demand?" I rise from the cot where I'm sitting, in the small room I've rented for the next week. "Since when do you demand things of me, shrimp?"

When and where?

There's a savage strength to the mental timbre of her voice. Something has happened to her, changed her. Perhaps she slept with the prince and discovered a deep love for him, a commitment to the crown and to her new life on land. The thought sickens me. But the vengeful anger I felt earlier has ebbed somewhat, and I regret cutting off our connection when I did.

"Can you even get out of the palace?" I ask her.

Leave that to me. I've been sneaking out of my father's domain and circumventing his guards since I was freshly spawned. When and where, Witch?

"South side of the point, on the outskirts of town. A place called 'Flay's Kitchen.' Tucked between two rocky peaks, one shaped like a raven. Lots of gulls hanging about. Can't miss it."

She cuts the link between us, and I massage my forehead, confused. But excitement churns deep in my belly, because I'll see her soon.

I grab my coat and leave the boarding house. My new residence is an hour's walk from the outskirts of Crystal Point, far enough to be safe, yet near enough to let me get to Averil quickly by magical means if I need to.

It will take her some time to get out of the Summer Palace and make her way to "Flay's Kitchen," so I leave my stolen horse in the boarding-house stable and walk the distance myself. In addition to my coat, I wear a scarf and a broad-brimmed hat, along with a glamour. Should anyone have charms or other means to dispel glamours, the physical disguise should help conceal my identity.

I'm not sure how many people in this area would still recognize me, though. It's been a few decades since I walked openly among them, owning my magic, my title, and my friendly connection to the human king.

Those were the golden days, before I made an unfortunate choice and was so harshly punished for it.

When I reach "Flay's Kitchen," I lean against the wall outside, waiting for Averil.

She arrives on foot, swathed in a dark-blue cloak, limping a little. She's unused to walking so far, and she's wearing a pair of ridiculous silken shoes they must have given her at the palace. It pains me that I didn't consider her comfort, that she had to trudge this far on her soft, new, human feet.

There's a brittle, seething energy around her, a ferocity in the way she rips back her hood and peers into the shadows beneath my hat. I allow her to see through the glamour at the

195

same moment I release her voice. The golden strands slither into her parted mouth, and she nods sharply. "Good. You came. I have things to tell you. What is this place?"

"Ah, you'll see." I leap ahead of her, pulling open the door of the building. A savory scent of hot, delicious, peppery broth rushes out, and she freezes for a moment.

Her wide blue gaze meets mine. "Is that soup I smell?"

"This place is known for its variety of delicious soups," I tell her. "For one low price, you can eat as much soup as you want." A stupid grin spreads across my face, even as I try to hold it back.

Averil stands in the open doorway, staring at me, shock and wonder churning in her eyes. Her gaze softens, her brows bending slightly as if she's truly seeing me for the first time. The sweet tenderness flickering over her face—it's enough to turn a man into a muffin. I cannot bear it much longer.

"Soup," she whispers.

"Soup," I say hoarsely.

Someone shouts at us to come in or go out, so I force down my surging emotions, usher Averil into the eatery, and manage to find us a private corner tucked against a window. I order half a dozen different bowls of soup, and by the time they arrive, rain has begun to spatter against the leaded glass beside our table.

Sitting there, in the glow of the candles and lamps, with the chatter of the eatery around us, the rain darkening the night, and the fragrance of creamy soup in my nostrils, I am strangely at peace. I watch Averil sipping broth. The way her lips purse to blow on the hot liquid is the most exquisitely sensual thing I have ever seen.

I can't help remembering what she looked like in the dark beachside hollow, naked and writhing on my tentacles. Nothing could have improved that sight, except perhaps less distance between us.

But she would never want such proximity with me. Only with her puling prince.

"So was your first mating with the prince everything you imagined?" I growl, and then I fill my mouth with a large spoonful of soup. It's boiling hot, and I splutter and choke. "Fuck, fuck!"

Averil giggles compulsively, choking on her own soup, and for a moment the two of us cough and beat our chests and laugh and wheeze until the tears ooze from our eyes.

"I didn't mate with him," she says at last. "He's not the man I thought he was. Far from it, in fact."

Delight and dread spiral up in my heart. Gladness, because she sees his unworthiness. Caution, because she cannot back out of this deal. Doing so would harm both of us, in different ways.

"You must keep pursuing him," I tell her sternly. "That is part of our agreement."

"I'm well aware." There's a vengeful cunning in her eyes I've not seen there before. I'm disturbed by how much I like the look on her. "I will continue seducing him, trust me. Although I don't anticipate the need to continue the ruse too long."

"You think he will propose soon?"

Her eyes narrow, and she opens her lips as if to say something. Then she clamps her mouth shut again and merely nods.

"Good. Once he asks for your hand, tell me at once."

"There are other things I need to tell you," she says, and she describes King Perindal's sorry state, as well as the suspicions that a poison from the ocean might be involved. "I must know, Sea Witch—did you poison the king?"

"I did not. Interesting that Brixeus should suspect a toxin from under the sea. Do you think your father might have arranged it?"

Averil shrugs. "He doesn't speak much of humans, except to warn that they will flay and eat any mermaids they find on their shores. From all I've seen, that's not true."

"Some humans might do that." I wince. "Mermaid flesh and scales do indeed carry magical properties. And for those born without innate magic, such substances can be tempting indeed."

"So magic can be borrowed, bought, or taken if you're not born with it." Her blue eyes bore into mine.

"Yes."

"Teach me then. After all this is over. I want to learn. I want power like yours—youth and long life."

I quirk an eyebrow at her. "Power like mine corrupts and changes you. As I've told you, it requires great sacrifice and dedication. It is cruel, and I wouldn't wish its effects on you."

"Why not?" Her voice is still musical, but brittle, pitched low so no one but I can hear. "I'm your enemy's daughter. You hate me, or at least dislike me. You couldn't even touch me with your tentacles without cloaking yourself in darkness and pretending you weren't there. You shouldn't mind if I suffer some cruel side effects."

The truth clogs my throat, but I swallow it down. "And why would I teach powerful magic to my enemy's daughter?"

"What if I promised never to use it against you?"

"Others have made me similar promises, and broken them."

"Oh." She takes another pensive mouthful of soup. "I suppose there's no chance of you teaching me anything *else* then."

The way her lashes lift—the subtle, sensual hint in her expression—my stomach drops, and my dick twitches.

"Is there anything else you wish to learn?" I ask, low.

"I happened to witness something between Kerrin and a girl of the court—an apothik." Her features harden, and her face takes on a more brilliant shade of hectic color.

Ah. This, then, is responsible for her change in demeanor. Her prince has shown his true colors, taking pleasure with someone else. A cheat and an asshole, as I thought. And Kerrin's betrayal has wounded her deeply.

"She—had her mouth on him," Averil whispers. "He liked it. What if I learned the same skill?"

My stomach sours, a bitter darkness dredging up from the bottom of my soul. "You want to learn this skill so you can keep your prince's attention?" And inwardly I add, *I thought you had more self-respect than that.*

"Maybe I want to keep his attention," she murmurs. "Or maybe it simply looked rather fun." Her lashes flick up, and her mouth curves, a sinful little smile. "What do you say, Witch? For the sake of our bargain, are you willing to give me a lesson?"

26

The Sea Witch stares at me as if I just offered to bite off his head. Perhaps he fears I might do exactly that.

His muscular throat bobs with a hard swallow, and his eyes darken under his heavy brows. "Let's be very clear about what you mean," he says thickly.

My heart is juddering in my chest, wild and uncontrollable, free and reckless. I'm angry, and I'm viciously delighted. I have never felt this way in my life.

Slowly I draw my foot out of its delicate slipper, and I lift it under the table, nudging it between his legs. I press the toes he gave me over the hard bulge under his trousers. He sucks in a sharp breath, and his gaze snares mine, a sizzling heat rolling off him as he leans closer to me.

"Little princess," he purrs. "I think you are playing with something you don't understand."

"And I think you underestimate me, as people so often do," I retort. "I know what I'm doing, especially after what happened in the cave."

Even as I say it, a pang of uncertainty smarts in my soul. Maybe it was disgusting to him, watching me lose myself in that carnal way, sweating and writhing as I did.

"Maybe you'd rather forget the cave," I murmur, tapping my foot across his crotch. "I suppose it must have been… difficult to watch."

"Best sight of my life." His voice is a harsh snarl, as if someone kicked the words out of him.

My toes pat the lump under his pants. His cock responds with a hard, hot throb against my foot.

"So you do want me a little," I whisper, pressing firmly.

"Gods-fuck," he barks. "You keep doing that, and there will be no lesson in pleasure, because it will be over."

My heart swells—it's a molten, rapid creature, fluttering in my throat. "Where can you teach me?"

"First, you should drink some water. I'm not having your spicy soup mouth all over my dick." He winces.

I sip from a mug of water on the table, trying not to assume why he does the same, or why he sloshes the water around in his cheeks so thoroughly before swallowing.

Does he plan to do something to me as well? My body responds to the idea with a flood of warm, wet arousal. I will be a swollen, slippery mess before this is over.

"Come." The Witch rises abruptly, throws a coin at the serving boy, and orders, "Hold our table." The boy nods, and the Sea Witch hurries me out the door of the eatery.

There's a slanted roof shielding the front entrance from the rain, and the overhang continues around the side of the building, protecting a couple bundles of hay and a generous stack of firewood from the elements.

The Sea Witch tosses his hat and scarf onto the woodpile, then leans back against the outer wall of the building, between the firewood and a glowing orange window. His features are rock-hard, a muscle jumping near the corner of his jaw and another flexing at his temple. His massive hands begin working at the buttons of his pants, releasing them one by one.

Then he stops. "You don't want to do this," he says, glowering. "You're angry at the princeling. Betrayed and pained. I know the feeling." He starts buttoning himself up again. "You're young. You don't know what you want—"

"How dare you," I hiss.

His brows contract in confusion.

"This is where you draw the line?" I snap. "Not when I bargained my voice for a human body? Not when I let you do the filthiest things to me in that hollow by the sea? You think I don't know what I want *now*? Because I'm young? How. Dare. You."

His eyes widen as I march up to him and take his jaw in my hand. I'm terrified and exhilarated by my own daring, emboldened by the blend of awe and avarice in his eyes.

"I may be young, and occasionally foolish, but from what I've seen, even a man of centuries may be a fool." I tighten my hold on his chin, drawing his face down to mine. His breath bursts warm over my lips. "Kiss me, fool."

He captures my mouth with a desperate groan that drives a hot spike of desire straight between my legs. Fingers tangling in my hair, he whips me around and shoves me against the wall, hunching over me with that great tall frame of his.

Nothing about his urgency frightens me or makes me pause, because I want him just as badly, maybe more. It's as if some fervent, wanton, winged thing in my soul longs to crawl right out of my body and leap into his, to possess him, preen over him, to become part of his form and thoughts forever. Or maybe I'm losing my mind to some hideous sorcery. If so, I cannot think of a better way to spend my time than grinding my scorched skin against his, praying to the gods for all my clothing to disappear so I can feel every rippling muscle and hard plane of the Witch's body.

He's devouring my mouth, one huge hand wrapped around my neck and the other in my hair. Salt and sweet fire, magic crackling against the edges of my teeth. The slick glide of his tongue over mine.

I whine, desperate, and twist my body until he leans back, giving me space. My shaking fingers make quick work of the remaining buttons on his pants.

"Wait," he gasps. "Wait, wait—"

I pause, and he looks down at me with agonized hunger.

"Only if you want this," he says. "And not because of him, Averil... I can't..."

"Maybe a little because of him," I whisper. "But mostly because of you. Fair repayment for the other night."

He grimaces as if he wants to say more, as if that isn't quite the answer he wanted. The flap of his pants hangs dangerously low, exposing the flat triangular span of his lower abdomen. I trace a finger across his hot, brown skin.

"Yes or no?" I whisper. "Will you let me have my lesson?"

"Fuck, Averil. Yes."

"Then you must tell me what to do. I like to learn things well, so I can excel at them."

"Shit," he says fervently. "Take me out, then."

My fingers curl into the opening of his pants, and with some difficulty I extract the massive length I've felt on multiple occasions. His cock is thick, straight, and heavy, with a smooth head that glistens slightly at the tip. I lick my lips, wondering how he will taste.

The Sea Witch is facing the wall, and he braces both hands against it as I sink to my knees, like I saw the apothik do.

"You can touch me," chokes the Sea Witch, "however you like. And then—take as much of me as you can into your mouth."

"You're enormous," I murmur. "Much bigger than the prince."

His cock jumps at that, and I smile.

For a moment I explore, running my fingertips along the velvety heated skin, dabbing the bead of moisture at the tip. He smells faintly of sweat, but also salt and sea air, a savory freshness I can't resist. I open up and slide my lips from the wet head along the shaft, until he bumps at the back of my throat. I can't get much of him in my mouth, he's so big.

I close my eyes, listening to the patter of rain on the cobbles, the faint hum of voices from inside the eatery, and the hoarse panting of the Sea Witch as he braces himself desperately against the wall.

"Move your mouth back and forth," he says raggedly. "If you open your throat, you can take more. Try moving your tongue—ahhh…" He groans as I start swirling my tongue, bobbing my head. "Fuck, I knew this wouldn't last long—I can't—you should stop—"

I slide off him and look up, my lips damp. "Why should I stop?"

But he's mesmerized by my face and seems to have forgotten what he said.

"You fucking adorable creature," he whispers hoarsely, staring at me wide-eyed. "You perfect goddess."

I wrap my hand reassuringly around his length. "Why should I stop?"

"Because I'm going to come if you keep going. And I'm not sure you want to swallow on your first time."

"I want it all," I tell him. "Everything you would do if I were another woman."

An emotion I can't name flickers over his face. His features are half-shadowed, half-uplit by the nearby glow from the window. "Then keep sucking me."

I obey, savoring the hot, salty tang of his length, the sweetness of his arousal. He reaches down, guiding my hands around the base of his dick, covering the part that won't fit in my mouth. His body convulses, the strip of stomach muscle I can see hardening, contracting, his big frame bowing over me.

"Open up a little." He pulls back until only the tip of him is nestled in the heated hollow of my tongue, cradled in my open mouth. He wraps his thick fingers over mine, around his cock, and he thrusts twice through the tunnel of our hands. Then he's shuddering, groaning, and his cock spasms, little bursts of hot liquid pooling over my ready tongue.

The Sea Witch lets go of himself, allowing me to stroke him through the ebbing pleasure. He slams one forearm against the wall behind me, his whole body heaving. His hoarse groans sound like sobs.

He came in my mouth. He's broken with pleasure, and it's my doing.

A sweet, warm delight slithers through my heart, easing my bitterness, softening my anger at Kerrin and tipping my entire being into some new sea of emotion, limpid and glimmering.

I'm still holding the Witch's cum on my tongue.

"You can spit it out," he pants, but I don't. I sit back on my heels and swallow carefully.

"Some men would push themselves down your throat until you gagged," he says. "I don't like women sounding as if they're going to vomit when they pleasure me."

"I can understand that." I wipe my lips and rise. "Did I do well?"

He refastens his pants, throwing me a hard look. "There is no possible way you could have done it that I would not have enjoyed, Princess. And now, it is your turn."

"My turn?" My stomach thrills.

"Yes." His eyes darken, a wicked grin sliding across his mouth. "No lesson is complete until you've had the experience from both sides."

The Sea Witch rearranges some of the firewood and places me on a sort of seat he has made. I'm trembling a little, both from the chilly, rainy sea breeze and from the knowledge that if someone came to the window of the eatery and pressed their face against the glass, they might be able to see what we're doing out here.

"It's important to me that you know something," he rumbles, pressing warm between my legs, his broad hands skimming my thighs, pushing up my skirts. "I did not hide from you in the cave because I despise you. I hid because you needed the distance from me. You needed to feel safe enough, alone enough, to enjoy the pleasure. You needed to believe that it did not count, that you were not cheating on your prince, that you were merely enjoying a fair share of the delight he has allowed himself with so many women before you."

"But I'm just as bad as Kerrin," I whisper, mortification heating my face. "I took pleasure with you like he did with Cassilenne. I'm a cheat as well."

"There was a difference of intent between you," says the Sea Witch. "And I happen to think you're far worthier than him." His voice deepens, like black coals, like bones in the blue deep, like pitch-dark sin. "But if you want to think of yourself as very, very wicked, don't let me stop you."

His fingers glide higher, smooth palms against my inner thighs, thick fingers curling around my undergarments, drawing them back down my legs and pulling them off my feet, over my slippers. He lifts the scrap of warm, damp fabric to his nose and inhales deeply. My sex throbs as he does it.

Then he rubs his thumb and forefinger along the material. "These delicate drawers of yours are very wet. Soaked, in fact."

"Perhaps I sat in a rain puddle," I whisper. "Or in some spilled soup."

"Perhaps you did." He surveys me as I sit on my firewood throne, with part of my skirts under my rear and the rest wadded up nearly to my hips. "It occurs to me that you may end up with splinters if I do this here."

"It occurs to me that I don't care." My fingers curl around the edges of two split logs. "You can take them out afterward. With magic."

"Not everything is fixable with magic." He sinks to his knees, pushing my skirts a little higher. Baring my sex to his view. "Although magic can create some beautiful things. Like this exquisite pussy of yours, for example. It's shining, princess. Dripping. Decadent. Delicious—"

"I despise too much alliteration," I gasp. My pussy is quivering, utterly sensitized, and I feel as if a single breath against it might make me squeal. I press the back of my wrist to my mouth as the Sea Witch leans in between my legs.

He looks up at me, and I'm overcome by the raw beauty of him—his mane of darkly purple hair, his thick brows, his rugged, handsome features, and that sly, full mouth approaching my most tender area.

"Your scent is intoxicating," he murmurs, and then he's licking me. His tongue, slick and wide, covers every part of me, over and over, laving between the lips, bathing the tender creases, lapping at the dainty bud near the top. I'm whining, gasping, sharp and shrill and breathy and helpless. It's too much, too much—it's too beautiful to bear—it's better than his tentacles, if that were even possible. An entirely different

207

sensation, delicate and fragile and oh gods, I think I'm going to come already—

He nibbles at my clit, and I come with a squeal, my thighs jerking together around his face, my hands reflexively seeking his head of beautiful hair. He hums between my legs, his face still buried deep.

Embarrassment surges through me. It's humiliating that I came so fast. Now he knows how close I was to the edge, just from sucking his cock.

"You can stop," I gasp, writhing a little as he licks deeper, gripping my thighs, pushing them farther apart. "I came already."

"Why the fuck would I stop at one?" he growls into my sex, and I release a shuddering moan, my neck tilting back and my eyes rolling up.

"You taste so fucking delicious, Averil," he groans, and every rumble of his deep voice is another jolt of scintillating pleasure. Long slow licks shift to a gentle mouthing, then a tiny, quick, lapping sensation right over my clit—

And then the most thigh-melting, belly-softening, mind-glazing, little sucking series of kisses to that tender bud of flesh—

And I break.

Perfectly, exquisitely.

I can't make a sound for a second, or breathe, because the intensity of the bliss is too high, too pure.

And then I'm crashing, panting, holding onto him, rocking my hips against his face, almost sobbing as I ride down the ebbing pleasure. Every nerve in my belly tingles, every muscle in my legs has melted.

"I never want to stop doing this with you," rumbles the Sea Witch against my pussy. "I'll stay here forever if you'll let me."

His words jerk me back to reality, and I stiffen a little.

Never and *forever*. Those words were not supposed to be a part of this bargain.

It's an exaggeration, of course. Careless phrases on his part, brought on by his current enjoyment. He doesn't mean anything serious by it. He cannot really like me that much. Most likely he says that to all the women he pleasures.

"I consider the other half of the lesson complete," I breathe, gently pushing his face back. His lips, his cheeks, and his strong jaw are damp, and he wipes them quickly before rising to his full height.

He gazes down at me where I recline against the firewood, once again dismantled by pleasure of his making.

His eyes darken, a mingling of hot lust, admiration, and something else—something warmer and deeper and—

I tear my gaze from his and pull my skirts down to cover myself.

"Eating a woman out is satisfying, but I'll admit I'm still hungry for other sustenance," he says, low. "Interested in another bowl of soup before you go back to your prince?"

"One more," I say. "And then I should return. It will be harder getting back into the palace than it was getting out."

"I'd assist you with a glamour, but the palace is warded against my magic," says the Sea Witch. "You'll have to hope they continue to think of you as an addle-pated, shipwrecked maiden, apt to wander dizzily about."

I give him a wry glare, hopping up from the firewood stack. My legs wobble, and the Sea Witch catches me against his chest with a low, pleased laugh. "Easy, love. You've had quite the evening."

"Are you ever going to tell me what you did to make King Perindal so furious with you?" I ask, trying to push myself away from him.

For a second I think he might not let me go.

209

For a breathless, warm, pulse-pounding second I think I might stay wrapped up in these sinewy arms forever.

And then he releases me, letting his palm hover at the small of my back as we walk around the building.

"I might be persuaded to tell you the tale," he says. "But not until the prince has proposed and your part in our bargain is complete."

I hesitate, gathering my hair in both hands and twisting it nervously. "The prince did propose," I say. "Tonight. After the banquet. And I accepted his proposal."

The Sea Witch steps in front of me, looming over me in the rain-scented dark. The glow of the window haloes his enormous shoulders.

"You're telling me I licked the pussy of the queen-to-be? I pleasured the fiancée of the Crown Prince?" He splays a hand over his chest. "Gods forgive me."

"You're not angry that I didn't tell you right away?"

His eyes narrow a fraction, a hard sparkle in them. "A little, perhaps. But you did tell me, eventually. And now, before you return to the palace, I must explain the favor I need from you— the one thing you must do for me. This is one task you cannot fail, Averil, or I will have no choice but to cause you harm. Magic, as I've told you, is cruel, and breaking a bargain with me—" He winces. "Let's simply say you'd be better off as a mindless mollusk creeping along the ocean floor."

Dread settles cold in my heart at his words. "That sounds worse than your threat of swallowing my voice."

"Perhaps I did not warn you of all that could transpire in the event of a betrayal. Can you blame me?" He grins, but there is no humor or kindness in it—only the satisfied, icy triumph of a shark. "Come inside for your soup, Averil, and I will tell you the one thing I require."

27

The next day, things proceed exactly as the Sea Witch told me they would.

There's an official announcement of my engagement to the Crown Prince, proclaimed by a herald just outside the palace, while I stand atop the wall above the gate with Kerrin at my side. My name is a concocted fantasy from the froth of Kerrin's imagination— "Lady Aurell DeLongbourne, the lovely and gracious noble daughter of a southern island kingdom." Pure fiction, of course, but at least he didn't announce my name as "Beautiful."

Kerrin hasn't left me unguarded since last night, when I was caught returning from my tryst with the Sea Witch. When the guards intercepted me, I smiled vaguely at them and tried to look very innocent and dazed, as if I'd been sleepwalking. They brought me back into the palace, questioned me, and woke the prince to ask him what should be done with me. When Kerrin arrived, I clung to him, trembling and tearful, pretending the soldiers had terrified me with their inquiries. He soothed me, but he also assigned guards "to keep my bride-to-be from wandering into danger."

I'm not sure how I'll get away to see the Witch again. I'm not sure he wants to see me in person anymore, except as necessary for the last phase of our bargain. He turned so cold and silent last night after I told him of the engagement. We ate our soup, he gave me instructions, and then he stole my voice again.

Once the announcement is complete, Lord Brixeus approaches Kerrin and me. "And now, Your Highness, it is time for the next part of the fidelity rituals—the selection of the engagement jewels. Here is the Priest of Keys." He gestures to a stooped, white-haired man carrying an ornate chest. "If you'll come with us, we'll proceed to the Vault of Queens. For decades, the fiancée of the Crown Prince has visited the Vault of Queens as soon as possible after her engagement, to select her first set of royal jewels. Thus the bond and the promise is cemented between the king and his intended bride. So it is, and so shall it be."

My stomach drops and thrills. This is exactly what the Sea Witch said would happen. He needs something from the Vault of Queens, and I must steal it. Once I'm inside the Vault, I'm supposed to call on him, and he'll tell me what to take.

"You want to go pick out some pretty jewels, Beautiful?" Kerrin asks, smiling warmly down at me. I nod with wide-eyed enthusiasm.

But inside I'm seething. I can still see him thrusting into Cassilenne's mouth. And there's a sharp, saucy triumph in my heart because I sucked the Sea Witch's cock that same night, and Kerrin has no idea.

My heart flinches a little as I think of the Witch, how he said in that desperate tone, *Not because of him, Averil...*

He said those words as if he wanted the act between us to mean something else—not retaliation against Kerrin, but something sweeter.

The way he savored me afterward—the way he asked to stay nestled against me forever—

But he changed when I told him of the proposal. He chilled, like ice creeping over rocks. Like the bite of the cold subterranean air as I descend into the lower parts of the Summer Palace, clinging to Kerrin's arm.

Lord Brixeus and the Priest of Keys lead the way, and a handful of soldiers follow us. We pass a few sets of guards—one pair at the foot of the steps, a trio blocking a gate of wrought iron and gold, and another pair standing before a massive door, which they pull open to allow us entrance.

"This entire palace is guarded by layers of magic," Prince Kerrin tells me conversationally. "A useless precaution, since there aren't many sorcerers left and the ones who exist are weak. But my father is a superstitious, paranoid bastard. Getting worse with age."

I blink up at him, and he lowers his voice, slowing our pace so we're several steps behind Lord Brixeus. "You know, Beautiful, I've traveled through many kingdoms, and I keep seeing the same thing. Hale, hearty, worthy heirs, forced to stand by while their aging parents squander the power of the throne. Ancient kings may hang onto life by a mere thread for *decades* sometimes, holding the crown with shriveled hands while their heirs age and languish, waiting to take over. It's perverse. It's wrong. Why shouldn't an heir take the crown while he is still young and healthy and handsome? Why should an heir be forced to wait for decades, well past middle age, before finally enjoying the power and bounty that a king commands?"

It's all I can do to keep my face smooth and sympathetic and pleasant, when I want to frown at him. It sounds almost as if he *wants* his father to hurry up and die so he can assume the throne.

"There's nothing like the greedy grasp of an old man on power that the young deserve to wield," Kerrin says darkly, staring ahead at Brixeus's back as we descend more steps. "Don't you agree, Beautiful? You believe I'd make a great king, yes?"

I smile and nod, fluttering my eyelashes at him.

He grins, pleased. "Of course I'll be a great king. I will be the most brilliant young ruler this kingdom has ever seen. A golden god. A force to be reckoned with and remembered. And this is where it all begins—with you and me bound by our engagement. The fidelity law fulfilled before my twenty-sixth birthday, and the way cleared for me to be fully instated as the Crown Heir."

Lord Brixeus has paused at the foot of some steps, before yet another immensely tall door. We're so far below the palace I swear I feel the icy breath of the deep ocean, pressing inward from somewhere beyond these rock walls.

This door is an enameled, jeweled wonder, inset with five separate locks, each designed to represent an animal or bird—a swan, an eagle, a bear, a horse, and an octopus. My gaze lingers on the smooth, inlaid, amethyst tentacles of the octopus. Its beaked mouth is a keyhole.

The Priest of Keys hands his chest to a guard, who holds it open while the old man selects one key at a time with quivering fingers. The Priest takes a long time about inserting each key in its lock and turning it slowly, slowly, until there's a decided *click.* Meanwhile Kerrin sighs gustily and shifts his feet and plays with my hair. My long red locks are bound up in intricate braids, but a few tendrils drape along my neck, and the prince seems to be fascinated with them, twisting one around and around his thumb.

"Come on then, old man," he says testily. "Let Brixeus do it—his fingers are steadier. Or I'll do it. It's the Vault of Queens, after all, and queens are owned by the king. So it's my vault, and if I can get it unlocked in half the time, why shouldn't I?"

Releasing the tendril of my hair, he snatches the key from the priest and marches forward, shoving it in the lock. There's a grinding clank, as if the door itself is protesting this breach of decorum. The old priest stands with shaking hands and weak, watery eyes, staring at me and Lord Brixeus by turns as if he expects one of us to intervene. But I cannot, and Lord Brixeus does not, although his grim mouth tells his disapproval.

Prince Kerrin takes no notice. He jams in the last key, then snaps his fingers at the guards, who push the heavy door open. "Stay outside, all of you," he orders. "This is a moment for me and my intended. She and I will enter alone."

"But Your Highness," begins Lord Brixeus, with a suspicious sidelong glance at me. "The priest and I should—"

"No." Kerrin's word is curt, final. He draws my arm through his with a charming smile, a brittle smile, a smile that is just a bit too bright. And I return it with one just as artificial—a pretty flash of teeth for the Crown Prince, the man no one dares to cross now that his father is laid low.

It's strange, this sudden engagement between us. I've been working toward this very thing, of course, with the Sea Witch's help. And among my people, short courtships are common, especially if both parties and the priestesses confirm a "true-mate bond." Though I'm wondering if such things truly exist, or if perhaps my sisters and I, and all our people, have been fooled...

No matter what my people's habits, the prince's sudden launch into this engagement feels dangerous. He wants to fulfill the law and be established as heir—that much is clear. And I'm the convenient pawn to meet that requirement—the voiceless girl to whom he can speak without fear that I might repeat his words.

He obviously favors Cassilenne as a lover. So what, then, does he plan to do with me, and when?

Those dark questions curdle my stomach and quicken my pulse as the prince escorts me into the Vault of Queens, and the heavy door clanks shut behind us.

28

I've been pacing my rented room in a frenzy all morning, waiting for Averil to summon my gaze.

Finally, just when I'm sure I will go insane from suspense, her musical voice plucks at my mind. *Sea Witch. I'm in the Vault of Queens.*

A thrill of terrifed anticipation rockets through my body. Instantly I touch the shell around my neck, and the scene she's viewing spins into colorful life around me.

Stone pedestals about waist-height, rows upon rows of them, each one topped with velvet pillows and bell jars of crystalline clarity. Under those jars, on those pillows, lie the finest jewels and relics in the kingdom. Centuries of accumulated wealth reside in that vault—some of it stolen from other lands, but the rulers of this nation ignore that truth, as they do so many others.

Somewhere in the room lies the thing I seek. Averil is closer to it than I've ever gotten during the long years since it was taken from me.

My heart is pounding so hard I'm afraid she'll hear it. "Give no sign of anything but delight. Wander through the displays, touch a few things, giggle as if you've never seen such wonders. Oh—and kiss him. Kiss him like a fiancée. Throw your arms around his neck and show him your happiness."

She obeys, giving a little gasp of joy and leaping for the prince. Her white arms twine around his tanned neck, and her mouth meets his.

Pain constricts my throat, searing ragged through my lungs. I hate the way Kerrin mouths her with such avarice, laps at her like a dog. I hate the way he thrust his hips against her body, rabidly eager for friction against his erection.

"I want to fuck you here," he pants against her ear. "My father would hate it if I did. My mother too. I want to desecrate this place with you, right now."

"No," I snarl through my mental link with Averil.

I won't fuck him, she says. *But I'm going to do something you won't like. Feel free to look away.*

I growl my displeasure as she backs away from the prince and holds up both hands for him to wait. She gives him a smile so full of sin my stomach turns—and then she steps behind him, pushing her breasts against his back and reaching around his waist to undo his pants.

The prince laughs, breathless, then groans as she takes his dick between her slender fingers. She strokes him softly at first, urging him closer to one of the pedestals. Her delicate hand moves faster—she hasn't done this act before, but she's clearly applying last night's oral lesson to this type of stimulation. She presses her chest to the prince's spine while he moans, helpless to the deft stroking.

"I'm coming," he gasps. "Shit, I'm coming all over the Vault of Queens. Fuck the stupid Queens—fuck the ancestors—ahh!"

Averil points his cock toward the pedestal, and his cum jets out, striping the bell jar, glazing it in milky essence.

I hate what she did. But she managed to satisfy his rebellious pride and his lust, with minimal offering of herself. Clever, clever woman.

Prince Kerrin turns around, his face alight. "You have more potential than I thought," he says with a surprised, breathless laugh. He tucks himself away, then laughs again at the sight of his cum on the bell jar. "When the Priest of Keys sees that, his heart will probably fail. Just as well, so I can appoint someone younger."

He twines his fingers with hers, and they continue walking through the maze of jewels and treasures on display.

Are you alive, Witch? Averil asks me dryly.

"Alive, and plotting your fiancé's death," I retort. "This idiot cannot be allowed to rule."

I might agree with you there. He has no respect for anyone or anything. How did I ever think he was a good or worthy mate? I was so stupid.

"You didn't know him yet." Why do I feel compelled to defend her against her own censure? "You were charmed by a pretty face, easy manners, and a sunny smile."

I was naïve, she says.

"You were open-hearted, sweet, and hopeful. I wish he'd proved himself worthy of your innocent affection. Instead I had to watch you become slowly disillusioned, and that wasn't as amusing as I thought it would be."

I clamp my jaw shut, mentally rebuking myself. I'm giving voice to too many of my inner thoughts. I need to be more careful. "Now, shrimp, look around the chamber. Look for oddments and trinkets. Anything that isn't a necklace, a tiara, bangles, or earrings. What else do you see?"

I watch as she lets her hand casually drift from the prince's, as she wanders away, feigning a dazed enchantment with the luxury around her. Kerrin doesn't seem to mind. He moves a bell jar and picks up the diadem beneath it, making grotesque faces into the smooth, reflective surface of its largest ruby.

Meanwhile Averil wanders farther, toward a long table with several glass cases atop its surface. Through the spell that links us, I follow her gaze, seeing what she sees. A broad golden platter, etched with a historical scene. A goblet from which some past king drank to peace. Another goblet, in which a different ruler used to swirl the blood of his enemies with wine, consuming both at dinner. And then—

"That garnish fork." My voice grates into the empty space of my rented room, echoing into Averil's mind. "The little gold one in the center of the table. Take it. Hide it somewhere on your person. Do it now, while Kerrin is distracted."

Averil doesn't question me. She lifts the tiny glass bowl, plucks the miniature three-tined garnish fork from its pillow, and runs it deep into the mess of coiled braids atop her head.

She has it.

It's concealed. Secure.

Is that all you wanted? Her mental tone is incredulous. *A little garnish fork?*

"Select your jewels," I order in a strained voice. "And then you must come to me as soon as possible."

I'm heavily guarded all the time now, she says. *But there's to be a festival in town tonight, down by the shore. A celebration of the prince's engagement. Food, fire jugglers, music, dancing. Perhaps I can slip away then.*

"Can't you get away any sooner?"

So eager to conclude our business and be rid of me?
There's a sting in her voice, and a corresponding twinge of pain through my heart.

"Yes," I reply.

Because there is nothing else to be done. No sense dragging out the inevitable. No use pretending that the tug I feel when I'm with her is anything but a foolish lust for what's forbidden to me.

Never mind the strange way my soul longs to nestle against hers—never mind that I want to slaughter any man who might touch her or crave her—nothing can come of it.

Last time I wanted a woman I could not have, I lost everything. And that wanting was a watery shadow compared to the full-bodied ache I feel for Averil. If a shadow of affection could cause me so much grief, what would a stronger love do to me? It would kill me. And I do not wish to die.

I can understand your desire to be done with this, Averil says coolly, evenly. *I look forward to the successful completion of our bargain as well. Once I deliver the object to you, how long will I have to decide whether I wish to keep my human form or return to the sea?*

Ah, she still believes she has a choice in the matter. A noncommittal answer will be best. "I can give you one extra day."

Generous of you, she retorts. *Then I'll see you tonight.*

She leaves our connection open while she moves over to a pedestal, inspecting a set of pearl-and-topaz hair combs and bracelets. I can almost sense her delight, her awe at their intricate craftsmanship.

For a moment, I envision her in mermaid form—her dark iridescent scales flashing in the setting sun, her pale arms decorated with the topaz bracelets, her hair a mane of scarlet flame, graced with the combs. In my mind's eye she's naked, her soft breasts and slender torso bared to the sea air. A queen worthy of all worship. A goddess before whom any ruler should bow.

"What's this, Beautiful?" asks the prince, coming up behind her and cupping her shoulders. "Ah, you don't want those old things. I've found something that will suit you much better."

With a snarl of rage, I dispel the link.

When the vision vanishes, I'm alone in the plain bedroom, my palms bloodied by my own claws. I didn't realize I'd extruded them.

My trident is with Averil, on its way to me. I'll have it tonight, and then Tarion will suffer my vengeance. He'll feel a small measure of the pain I've endured for decades.

And Averil will be part of my revenge. Because I've decided not to restore her mermaid form, even if she asks me to. She'll get her voice back once she delivers the trident, but she won't get her tail and gills. Tarion will have lost his daughter to the land-folk he despises. I'll sneer in his face as I show him what I've done to his spawn—the very thing I refused to do for him all those years ago.

The spell that secures Averil's current form is twined with the sacrifice of her voice. I can't shift the magical tether or make the change permanent until I reactivate my trident and regain my full powers. Once that happens, I will have all the magic I need to lock her in human form.

I was careful when I worded the deal with her.

At some point during your acquaintance with the Prince, I will ask you for a favor. And when I ask, you will agree, and you'll perform the task as soon as possible. If you complete it successfully, I will have the power to restore your voice and make your human shape permanent. If you fail, I will swallow your voice, and it will be mine forever.

I did not promise to return her to mermaid form. Nor did I tell her that a deal with me always ends in the bargainer wasting away, once they've realized that the thing they desired has teeth and it's eating them alive.

Once tethered to a deal of mine, no soul is ever truly free. They always return to me upon the breaking of the bargain, or upon their eventual death, whichever comes first, and they haunt my gardens with their wails of regret.

Averil will live out a human lifespan on land, never to dwell under the sea again. She will never inhale through her own gills, or leap from the waves in a glittering arc, or explore the darkest depths of the ocean. She will be a princess of nothing at all. A human girl, land-bound, until the sour truth of her new existence consumes her, fades her, transforms her into a keening, bodiless voice and a bit of sea foam.

The idea pains me deeply. But it is her father's fault, and Perindal's. They caused me grief, and that debt must be repaid. Balance and justice. Sacrifice and solace.

It is the way of magic.

29

I want to go home.

Living on land in this human form has changed me far more than I expected. And I'm not happy about it.

Today I lied. I continued the ruse that I'm happily engaged to the prince, though in reality I despise him.

I stole from this kingdom—a small object, to be sure, but I'm no idiot. I know the little garnish fork must be worth far more than the Sea Witch is willing to say.

Yes, I lied by my actions, and I stole a treasure—and I also used my hand on the prince's cock in the Vault of Queens. I did it so he would continue to trust me, to like me—so he wouldn't insist on rutting with me on the floor of the vault. Knowing Kerrin as I do now, I understood that spraying his cum on the jewels of his ancestors would give him a sick satisfaction. He is a foul, selfish man, utterly blinded by his own perceived greatness.

It's all I can do to stroll calmly through the festival at his side, dressed in my sumptuous gown of heavy emerald fabric, wearing the ponderous, garish jewelry he chose for me. He wouldn't even let me select my own engagement jewels.

The festival is an assembly of hastily constructed, bright-colored tents, lined up in a double row along the boardwalk that follows the curve of the coast. There's a sea wall bordering the area, and a blessed breeze rushing off the ocean, slithering between the booths and tents. The night wind cools and dries the sweat on my forehead.

Prince Kerrin and I are watching a troupe of six fire jugglers. Their talent fascinates and frightens me, though if I felt less sticky and uncomfortable I might enjoy the show more. As it is, the whirling heat of the torches they're using only heightens the sense that I'm slowly boiling inside my gown. The prince chose my dress, of course—and instead of the usual low neckline or plunging back, this garment covers me entirely from ankles to wrists to chin. "Now no one else can enjoy what is mine," he said contentedly, when he first saw me wearing it.

I managed to persuade my maids to leave my hair untouched, in the same coiffure as this morning. The tiny garnish fork is still deep inside the braids; one of its tines is poking my scalp.

Somehow I have to get away from Kerrin and find the Sea Witch. But there are so many guards all around us—so many villagers and vendors.

Reluctantly I shift my thoughts, formulating a wish for the Witch's attention, calling his gaze. But nothing happens. And that means he must be very close by—too close for our remote connection to work. My insides ripple with excitement as I scan the crowd more carefully. Where is he? Can he see me right now?

A scream splits the night, and several horrified shouts erupt as one of the fire jugglers loses control of his torches. There's a bright flash, an explosion of sparks carried high by a sudden gust of wind. Flames burst from the fabric of a nearby tent, and then more sparks land in a wheelbarrow full of oddly pointed sticks—

"Fireworks!" shouts Lord Brixeus. "Get the prince out of here!"

With a panicked jumble of cries, the crowd begins to move, jostling away from the jugglers and the burning tent and the wheelbarrow full of sticks. Guards' shoulders slam into mine, booted feet trample the edge of my gown, and bodies shove past me.

A crackling whistle, and a bang—more thunderous bangs, so loud I can't bear it. I crouch in place and cover my ears, wishing I could scream my terror.

A firm grip on my arm. Someone hauling me to my feet, hustling me toward the sea wall. There's a gap in it—stone steps leading down into cool blue darkness. The hissing murmur of the sea below.

I jerk against the hand gripping my arm. If it's the Witch, he should make himself known. I'm not about to be towed into the shadows by some stranger. He's the right size for the Witch, clad in robes and voluminous cape-like garments, complete with a deep hood. Still, I can't be sure.

Roughly the man picks me up and descends the narrow steps with me, plunging us both into inky dark scented with fish and mildew. Above and behind us, the explosions are still happening, and the acrid stench of smoke tinges the air. Sparkles of color shatter and blaze across the night sky. Between each blast I hear screams and pounding feet, fire crackling and men shouting.

The cacophony fades as my captor carries me down the steps to the bottom of the sea wall and sets me on a ledge slick with spray and seaweed. The water laps at the edge of the cobbled walkway; I'd guess this area goes underwater at high tide.

Tiny glowing motes of golden dust spring to life above my head— formless flecks of light, barely enough to see by. But the intermittent blooming of the colored fire overhead provides a heart-stopping illumination.

My kidnapper's massive body pins me to the wall—saltwater, and fervent heat, and the spice of magic. I inhale deeply of his scent, a smile spreading over my face in spite of my efforts to keep it hidden.

A glow emanates from beneath his robes, and my disembodied voice snakes through the air between us, diving between my parted lips.

Once it settles in my throat, I speak. "Did you cause all of that?"

"A little wind magic to carry the fire and spark chaos." His deep voice sends a shiver through my flesh. "I needed to separate you from His Pestilent Highness."

A few words from him, and I've almost forgotten what he said earlier: how he couldn't wait for our business to be concluded. How he wants to be rid of me for good. No, my body doesn't remember any of that. It only remembers the glide of his tongue, and the slithering penetration of his tentacles. I'm burning hotter than I was before—my entire skin is aflame, and I'm desperate to claw off these clothes.

"It's too hot," I gasp. "I can't breathe. This dress—"

He steps back, his nails lengthening into claws. With several breathtaking, dangerous slashes, he whips those razor-claws through the heavy green dress, cutting it into sections. When he's done, it clings to its form for a few seconds before slowly falling apart around me.

"How am I going to explain this?" I ask, staring at the ruined gown.

The Sea Witch eyes me, clad as I am in an embellished corset, lacy drawers, garters, stockings, and a pair of heeled shoes. "Perhaps you were robbed during all the mayhem."

"And this robber took my clothes, but not my jewels?"

"Fair point." He seizes the garish necklace I'm wearing, snaps the chain, and hurls it into the sea. He does the same with the tiara, before I can stop him.

"Those are royal treasures!" I gasp.

"So they are," he purrs, reaching in to unclasp first one ponderous earring, then the other. I have to admit, my earlobes feel far better without them.

When he turns back to me after flinging the earrings into the sea, I smack his cheek. "You should *ask* a lady before disrobing her and discarding her jewelry."

He snatches my wrist. Rams it against the wall above my head. Leans down to me, his eyes smoky with wicked intent. He doesn't speak. But the intensity of his stare kicks my heart into a frantic rhythm. Mutely I tip my face up, my mouth almost touching his but not quite—a wordless plea, a tentative seduction. My breath ghosting across his lips. I want that hot, smooth, male mouth on mine. I want his tongue tracing my teeth, I want his hands framing my body, dragging roughly along my curves. I want every brutal inch of him surrounding me, filling me up.

I almost *whimper* for him.

"Give it to me," he growls.

Yes. Yes, I will give you anything, all of me—

Oh.

He still has one of my wrists pinned, so I use my other hand to delve into my hair, extracting the garnish fork.

Of course that is all he wants. Our transaction completed. Our business done. No more salacious lessons, no more sensual play between us.

He is the Sea Witch, cruel monster of the deep, master of toxins and torment. He cares nothing for me.

And I can be equally callous to him.

"Here's your precious trinket," I sneer.

He snatches it, and his hand closes around it tightly for a moment before he tucks it away, into some hidden pocket of the tunic beneath his robes. "You did well."

"A compliment on my thieving skills from the Thief of Souls himself. I'm flattered, I think."

He frowns. "I don't steal souls. If they fade and perish because of a rotten deal and linger in my territory, it's their own fault. The same fate would befall me, should I fail to fulfill a bargain."

I want to question him more about that, but instead I ask a more vital question. "What does the little fork do?"

"I'm surprised your father did not tell you that story about me," the Sea Witch rumbles. "I thought he'd have concocted some twisted version of it. No matter. Knowledge of this 'trinket' is not part of my deal with you, shrimp. And our arrangement is now concluded."

"Except you said I could have one day to decide if I want to keep my legs or reclaim my tail."

"Did I say that?" He gives me his shark-smile again. "Very well. Take a day to think over your future."

"So I'll see you again," I say, with more satisfaction in my tone than I intended.

The Sea Witch pushes back his hood and peers at me, his expression shifting, softening a little.

"Not that I *want* to see you again," I add. "Why would I?" I laugh, breathlessly.

His eyes darken. "Why indeed? Why suffer the sight of a loathsome monster any more often than you have to?"

"Loathsome monster?" I snort. "You're anything but loathsome, and you know it."

"In this form, maybe—"

"In either form." The words burst out of me, tugged free by the fervent sway of my body, my blood, my whole heart *toward* him. It's a pull like the strongest current of the ocean, perilous and irresistible.

For a moment of scintillating suspension we breathe, and breathe, and stare into each other.

Then he crashes against me, a tsunami of passion, his lips mauling mine, his palms sweeping over my flesh. I whimper deliriously into his mouth as lightning flashes through my whole being, like fireworks searing my nerves with red-hot desire.

I push down his pants and pull his thick cock into the open. With a violent yank, I rip my underwear and kick the shreds into the sea, because I need his heat, I need him right against me. When he lifts me, pressing my spine to the wall, I wrap my legs around his waist. His cock is pinned between us, against my belly. The shaft nestles between my pussy lips, gliding through them. When I look down, I can see the smooth, arrow-shaped head pointing up, glistening with a few drops of arousal.

One shift of our position, a new angle, and he'll glide inside me. His tentacles have been there before, but this is different. This feels raw and intimate and much too real, and as he begins to adjust, aiming to enter me, I tense in spite of myself.

The Sea Witch stops.

That tiny flinch on my part. The barest tightening of a muscle or two. Not a word, not a sound from me, yet he noticed, and he stopped.

Not inside me. Not yet.

He understands without my having to speak it.

Grateful, reassured, I slide my hands along the ridges of his stomach, pushing up the tunic and cape he wears until my palms skim over his pectorals. With my fingernails I tantalize the taut nipples. He groans deeply, helplessly, and glances down between us, where his erection rests between the lips of my sex.

Lowering his hips, then lifting them, he moves against me, rhythmically, up and down. The hard roll of his shaft over my clit sends sharp, blissful tingles of arousal through my belly. I moan softly and trace his nipples again, tweaking the buds until his whole body shudders.

He comes hard, throbbing against my sex—thick, white, warm liquid spurting and dripping from his cock, slicking my belly, coating my flushed skin. My clit is bathed with his cum. A warm, dazzling rush of sensation swells in my pussy and then crests into glittering pleasure—I'm coming too—I'm coming, while he rubs his cock slowly, tenderly along my center, soothing both of us through an orgasm that's both powerful and gentle at once. I lean in, my forehead pressed to his, gasping against his open mouth, while the tingling bliss chases along my limbs, spinning through my brain.

Something thunks and scrapes nearby—a quiet shuffle of feet against the stone steps that curve up into the darkness. I startle against the Witch, and he swears, pulling away from me, his cum dripping down my sex.

"Fuck," he hisses, dragging up his pants and shucking off his cape. "Someone's there. Put this on and run back to the prince—there's another set of steps down that way. Call on me tomorrow."

Then he's gone, racing after whatever made the sound.

I pull on the rough cape. It smells like him.

I don't know who was watching, how much they saw, or what the Witch will do to them.

Those are the least of my worries at the moment. Because I have to go back to the prince, without the royal jewels, wearing a stranger's cape, with another man's cum coating my inner thighs.

I have no idea what Kerrin will do to me.

I feel my way along the sea wall in the gloom for what seems like hours. At one point, there's a wrenching, searing pain in my throat, and I fall to my hands and knees, retching. I gag out my voice and watch it sail off into the night, a golden thread seeking its way back into the shell on the Sea Witch's chest.

He warned me that would happen. If I went too far away from him, my voice would snap back to him on its own, and it would hurt.

Holding my agonized throat in one hand, pressing my other fist to my chest, I huddle against the wall. Tears trail in burning streams from my eyes as I sob, voiceless.

The Sea Witch kissed me, touched me, came all over me. Gave me pleasure again. How are there so many different ways of finding pleasure with him? I want all the ways, over and over. I think I could be with him a thousand times and not grow tired of it.

But I can't. Because this night marked the end of our bargain—or nearly the end. I might see him once more, and then he won't care to see me again.

What if I never see him, for the rest of my life? Never dance with him, play cards with him, eat soup with him, ride a horse with him, kiss him, just *talk* with him, listen to his gruff answers to my questions, hear him laugh aloud... what if I never experience any of that again?

Because if I choose to remain on land I won't be able to visit him. And if I return to my father, I'll be placed under heavy guard and probably married off within the month. Or perhaps the priestesses will exile me, and I can go live with the Sea Witch and his friends, if they'll allow it.

Why does that kind of exile seem anything but dreadful? In fact, it sounds downright appealing, solely because it means I'd be near *him*.

Something inside me aches for the Witch, sings for him, is brokenly, beautifully wretched because of him. There's a haunted echo in my soul, a cry for him alone.

No. Gods, no. This is not how it's supposed to be—this cannot happen. I cannot feel the Soul Echo—if there is such a thing—for the *Sea Witch*. I'm meant to find some pure-hearted, noble, clear-eyed young male who will be my steady partner in life. Not a two-hundred-year-old witch with granite muscles and cruel magic. Not a monstrous, beautiful man with eyes like midnight sin and a voice like the Deep itself.

Not my father's enemy, an outcast of merkind, a sorcerer and trickster with dark motives he won't disclose.

Not this unexpectedly sweet man who brought me to a place where I could eat all the soup I wanted, who laughs with me, who seems to think I'm genuinely funny and truly clever.

Not this virile, savage creature who knows how to wring every last drop of bliss from my body.

Not this bruised, savage, vengeful heart that can spare no room for me.

Not him.

Not him.

30

I charge up the curving flight of stone steps. There's a figure moving in the darkness ahead of me—not moving fast enough, though. My long legs carry me up three steps at a time, and with a snarl I seize the robes of the figure, hauling them around and shoving them against the stone wall. I spark a tiny glowing illusion, just enough to see by. No use holding back my magic—this person has already seen too much, and must die.

My illusion glows on the ebony skin and close-cropped gray hair of Lord Brixeus. And by the same light, he sees my face. Recognition dawns across his features.

"You," he gasps.

"Brixeus," I growl. "It's been a long time."

"Not long enough."

"The sentiment is mutual," I say dryly.

"And what is *she*? The girl you've sent to play seductress— is she your whore? Your spy, sent to ensure my prince's downfall?" Brixeus rasps the words as my fingers close around his throat.

"She's not my whore."

"Yet you fucked her. I saw it."

"It isn't—she's my—" I grimace, releasing a rumble of frustration. "You don't know what you're talking about."

"She's your accomplice, though. Is she of sea or land?"

Both, and neither. I hold the words back and snarl instead, "You should not be asking questions, Brixeus. You should be begging for my mercy. You know I can't let you go now, after what you've seen."

He lifts his chin, his features calm and resigned. Why does he have to look so fucking noble?

"I know better than to beg for your mercy, Zoltan," he says, low. "You will do as you see fit, like all kings do."

"Yes," I breathe. "I will."

With one hand wrapped around his throat and the other gripping his shoulder, I yank him toward me, and then I leap. Both of us, arching from the steps of the sea-wall, aiming for the surf.

We crash into the ocean, and I thrust my tentacles outward, ripping through the pants I wear, shredding them as I reveal my monstrous self. Brixeus's eyes widen, but he does not shout or gasp. He saw me like this often, long ago.

I'm still wearing the tunic I had on under my cape when I met with Averil. There's a buttoned-up inner pocket over my breast, where I can feel the faint thrum of the garnish fork she gave me. Not a fork—my trident. The one Tarion stole from me. The one he gave into Perindal's keeping when he couldn't fully access its power.

I want so badly to activate it now. But undoing the spell I laid on it will take time, and first I must deal with Brixeus.

With a powerful pulse of my tentacles I shoot away from shore, dragging Brixeus through the churning foam, far out to sea. One tentacle around his neck keeps his head above water, but otherwise I don't concern myself with his comfort.

I should kill him immediately. He saw me with Averil. He might have even seen what she delivered to me. I can't risk him telling the prince and ruining everything. I should end him now—hold him beneath the waves until his lungs fill and his heart stops.

But instead I tow him far, far away from land, until we are alone in the center of a trackless sea, not a ship or shore in sight—only a few jutting black rocks, gleaming wet from the spray, shining in the moonlight.

I crawl up the side of one rock, tentacles suctioning to its surface, and I throw Brixeus on the flat top. "Here you will stay, until my goals are accomplished," I tell him.

He rises on hands and knees, breathing heavily, his robes sodden and dripping. "I'll die of exposure here."

"Maybe not." I slink back down the pillar of rock. "Perhaps I'll come back for you, when it's done."

As I slip into the waves again, Brixeus leans over the lip of the rock and calls down to me. "Kerrin is not Perindal," he shouts, his voice cracked with age and salt. "You would be wise to remember that."

"Should I pity the mewling prince, then?" I shout back with a harsh laugh.

"No." Brixeus vents a hoarse chuckle of his own. "Do not pity him. Fear him. He has no honor, no mercy, no sympathy— none of the emotions that made Perindal your friend before he was your enemy. Kerrin is void of all feeling except love for himself. And he has no good intent toward the girl. I don't know what his plan is, but he's not marrying her out of love. Of course, someone as clever and clear-sighted as you must already know that."

Kerrin has a plan for Averil? What plan? There can be no plan but mine. The prince is a fool. Fools don't make plans.

Brixeus is merely trying to unsettle me, tempting me to return to Crystal Point. He wants me to investigate his accusation, to go closer to the prince so I'll be caught.

I won't fall for it. Averil is perfectly safe. If she suspected otherwise, she would have told me. And if she should encounter some peril, she will call on me. Not that I'll answer. I'm going to be very busy activating my trident and taking over Tarion's kingdom. My kingdom.

"The girl can take care of herself." I can't stop my next words, though I try—they leak out through my gritted teeth. "But if anyone harms her, they will answer to me. As for you, Brixeus, don't try to escape. My mercy and my powers only extend so far."

He doesn't reply, and I plunge back into the sea, heading for the bottom. I enjoyed spending some time on land, but returning to the sea is always a delight. It's refreshing. I like being untethered, not so dependent on land and feet and gravity. Under the sea the world is broader, multi-dimensional, with a dark beauty that thrills me to my core. In the deep, I can fly.

But I cannot reactivate my trident here. I need supplies and privacy for the breaking of the spell, and for those I must go home to my lair by the quickest possible route—a dangerous, fast-flowing current few merfolk dare to use. Taking that channel will hopefully keep me away from any search parties Tarion may have sent out to seek his daughter. Not that I fear them—I'd simply rather not waste time destroying them.

With one hand clutching the fork through the soaked fabric of my tunic, I pause.

I do have supplies in my rented room, items that could help me re-awaken the trident. I could go back there and do the spell on land. It would not be as satisfying as reactivating my powers in the sea—but I would be nearer to Averil.

I left the princess in her corset and garters, with nothing but a rough cape to cover herself. I cut off her clothes, tore away her jewels, and abandoned her in the dark, marked with my release. Her voice came back to me as I was swimming with Brixeus; so she is speechless again, subject to the whims of a merciless prince.

Catching the spy was an urgent matter, but I can't help feeling I've done Averil wrong, somehow.

But of course I have. She's the spawn of Tarion. She was always going to be a casualty of my vengeance. Why should that disturb me?

Yet a sense of unrest gnaws into my bones. I hate it. It feels like guilt.

My tentacles thrash angrily as I hesitate, torn between heading for the rapid current and making for Crystal Point.

31

AVERIL

I can hear Prince Kerrin raging in the hallway outside my bedroom. Cassilenne and the servants have stripped me to my bare skin, and she's inspecting my body, touching the scrapes left on my back from the stone wall, the bruises on my knees when I fell to the cobbles during the fireworks explosion. I wiped most of the cum off on the cape, but the maid recognized it for what it was when they undressed me. And Cassilenne notices a few traces I missed, dried on my thigh.

"The guards found her weeping by the wall, you say?" Cassilenne says to a servant.

The woman nods. "That's what I was told. She was robbed and—and it seems she was assaulted, Apothik." Her voice drops low, tinged with sympathy. "Poor little thing."

"So it seems," says Cassilenne, frowning slightly, meeting my eyes. "Yet there's a lack of defensive bruises or wounds. No skin or blood beneath her nails."

"Perhaps her attacker threatened her with greater harm if she resisted," says the maid. There's a hollow edge to her tone, an intensity to her defense of me. But before she can say anything else, a fist pounds on the door.

"Cassilenne, I'm coming in," bellows the prince.

Quickly the maid wraps me in a sheet from the bed as Cassilenne says, "Come in, Your Highness."

Kerrin storms into the room, his clothes in disarray, stained with smoke and smudged with dirt. There's high color in his tanned cheeks.

"What happened?" he bites out. "Did she—was she—did someone soil her?"

Cassilenne doesn't hesitate. "Yes."

"And the jewels?"

"Gone. Though strangely the thief did not steal this." She touches the golden cord and the shell around my neck.

Fuck. I didn't think of that.

"Perhaps the trinket is only cheaply gilded, and the thief knew it," the prince says. "It's an ugly thing. I don't know why she insists on wearing it. Shit. This is—this is monstrous. Brixeus will rake me over the coals for the loss of those jewels. Where is that old fucker, anyway? He's never around when I need him." He whirls on the maid. "Get out. Go!"

She scurries out of the room, and Kerrin slams the door before approaching Cassilenne, lowering his voice. "She's ruined now. I don't want her."

"Your Highness," she hisses warningly, casting a glance at me.

It's easy to let the tears fill my eyes again, to feign heartbroken shock as I back away from Kerrin. I can fake the wretched disillusionment, the craven sorrow that the Averil of a few days ago might have felt at such rejection.

But I'm not the girl who saved Kerrin from the sea. I've learned the truth of his character since then, and I've learned more of mine as well.

The sweet, handsome prince I rescued was never anything but a fantasy. He represented the hope of true love, yes—and he was also the excuse I needed, a powerful enough reason to take the biggest risk of my life.

But I didn't leave the sea behind for *him*. It was always for me.

And what I feel for him now isn't heartbreak or sorrow. It's unquenchable rage.

Cassilenne is talking to Kerrin in a rapid, intense undertone.

"No," he says hoarsely. "The plan will have to change. The incident at the festival—it was an attack, Cass. An attack on *me*. The fidelity law has been fulfilled—an engagement has been confirmed, which means—"

"We should talk about this elsewhere," Cassilenne says firmly. "First, my lord, you should comfort your betrothed. She has suffered tonight."

Steel runs through her voice, and Kerrin gives her a look of petulant resistance. But then he sighs and approaches me, assuming a gentle smile. His mask. I can see it now—a gleaming film of beauty and charm over his rotten countenance.

"Forgive me, my love," he says soothingly. "I wasn't myself. I've endured so much tonight, you see. In fact, I've endured so many terrible things in the last week—in the last two years—it's a wonder I'm still sane." He chuckles, pulling me against his chest. "Hush now, there's a good girl. The servants will get you a bath, and then Cassilenne will give you something to help you sleep. Things will look better in the morning. And in the meantime no one shall know of your shame. We'll keep everything quiet."

I want to throw him across the room. I want to catch him by the throat and carry him down into the depths with me and watch the life leave his eyes as he chokes on the sea.

I want to tell him that I gave my body to someone else willingly, not by force. I want the prince to know that the one who took me tonight is ten times the man he'll ever be.

I want Kerrin to know that I never loved him. Because I didn't know what love was until—

Until I crouched by the wall and imagined life without the Sea Witch.

The prince frowns, shaking me by the shoulders a little. "Did you hear me?"

I manage to nod, and Cassilenne steps in. "I'll have the servants see to her comfort. You should rest, Your Highness. I'll come and tend to you as soon as I've mixed her sleeping draft."

"I'm counting on it," he says, with a significant look at her.

When he strides out of the room, I can breathe a little easier.

A while later, I'm finally alone, sitting in a milky bath strewn with petals and herbs. Through the open door I can see my bed, and a silver goblet on the nightstand—the sleeping potion I'm supposed to take.

But I'm not ready to sleep yet.

My fingers close around the golden seashell against my chest. "Sea Witch," I murmur. "I need you."

32

THE SEA WITCH

I'm in the current when she calls me. I'm heading back to my lair, because I can't break this spell on land. I can't. I need to be in the sea, in my native element.

I cannot let myself care about Averil more than I care about my power, my revenge.

The current barrels along, a stream so powerful I have to fight to stay in control, to avoid being thrown helplessly about or tossed from its channel and smashed against a reef.

The shell grows hotter, vibrating with the force of her summons.

I'm so close to my destination. I could ignore her and keep going.

But instead I roar "Fuck" into the current, and I throw myself out of its impetuous rush.

I careen through the water, nearly splitting my skull against some rocks, but I manage to grip the stony surface with my tentacles and pull myself to a halt.

246

It's less safe to watch Averil here, in the open ocean. When I'm seeing what she sees, I can't keep an eye on my own surroundings. I'll be vulnerable to predators, or to Tarion's patrols.

But she must need me. She wouldn't call on me if she didn't.

I set my back to the rocky formation I nearly crashed into. It's not much by way of shelter or security, but it will have to do.

I touch the shell floating near my chest. Sand and particles coalesce in the water around me, taking on the image of Averil and her surroundings.

The walls are covered in deep blue tiles. She's sitting in a beaten copper tub that glows in the light of several candles. The water is cloudy white, sprinkled with flowers, cupping the underside of her lovely breasts. Wet strands of her scarlet hair drape her creamy shoulders, and the necklace I gave her shines below the hollow of her throat.

And her face—

I have never seen such delicate strength embodied in one person. Every crisp line of her features cuts my heart, and every soft curve heals it again. Those blue eyes hold the sea in them, and the sky as well. Cleverness and courage, persistence and passion.

She is altogether beautiful.

She can't see me unless I allow it. Until now, a vision of me would have been a distraction. But in this case, perhaps I can permit her a glimpse.

I rub the shell between my fingers and murmur the words of a spell to communicate my image through the connection between us.

She cocks her head, speaking to me in her mind. *That language again. What is it?*

247

"Godspeak," I answer. "The Eldritch tongue, from days long gone. I learned it at great cost, when I was very young."

Did you catch the person who saw us by the sea-wall?

"No," I lie. "They got away. But I doubt they saw much. A little magic, a couple fucking."

The prince believes I was raped, she says reluctantly. *I suppose if anyone did recognize me and told Kerrin what they saw, it would fit into his assumptions. You are rather forceful in your attentions.*

I frown. "I would never hurt you like that."

Of course, she says quickly. *I—I enjoy the forcefulness. And you wouldn't take me against my will. I know you. That's not who you are.*

"You don't really know me," I reply.

So tell me about yourself, she urges, pulling her knees up and hugging them. *Tell me the story you promised. What happened between you and Perindal?*

"That's a long tale. You should finish your bath and sleep."

I don't want to sleep. Her eyes snap with defiance. *I want to know... please.*

The *please* finishes me.

"You won't like the story," I warn her. "You may hate me when it's done."

Then we'll be even, she says. *Because you already hate me.*

"Do I?"

Don't you?

"Do you want the story or not?"

She dips her chin, lifts her eyebrows, and gives me such a pointed, disapproving look that I laugh. It's a gurgling rumble under the water and she smiles, amused.

"It happened about forty years ago," I begin. "Perindal was twenty, I believe, newly crowned after his father died of plague.

He wasn't married then—didn't marry until twenty-six, as the law requires, and Kerrin wasn't born until ten years after that."

I don't know how she'll react to my next words. My fists curl at my sides, and my tentacles writhe along the surface of the rock behind me. "At that time, I was not only a powerful witch— I was also King under the sea. Your father was my best friend and closest advisor."

Averil is shaking her head. *No,* she says in my mind. *No, my father has been king under the sea for many, many years.*

"A few decades," I tell her. "He and the historians and the priestesses have conspired to erase me from history. They've reduced me to a crawling monster of nightmares, the subject of children's stories. Once I was king, as my mother was queen before me. When I took the throne, I focused first on strengthening my domain under the sea, accomplishing certain goals for the betterment of merkind. And then I turned my eyes to the shore, determined to attempt what previous monarchs had failed to achieve—a treaty of friendship between land and sea. Peace and shared prosperity."

Averil is staring at me, eyes wide and bright, clasping her knees.

"Your father, Tarion, advised me against it," I tell her. "He was suspicious of humans. But against his wishes and those of my council, I devised a spell to give myself human form, and I began to make contact with humans. First I did so in disguise, learning their ways quietly. I wanted to understand them before I went to their king in my official capacity.

"Finally, when I had learned much about human customs, I traveled to Crystal Point, where the young king Perindal was staying at the Summer Palace. I entered his court, made myself known as the King of the Sea, and explained my desire to form a friendship, royal to royal. Perindal didn't believe me until I showed him my magic and my true form. He wasn't revolted or frightened—he laughed with delight, and eagerly pledged to an alliance between us.

"For a while we had golden days of true friendship. Merfolk helped to ensure the safe passage of Perindal's ships, and in return, humans shared their technologies, food, and knowledge. Perindal was fascinated with the culture of the mer, so he visited the Summer Palace often. He transformed it into an important royal residence. And then, one summer, Perindal's sister came to Crystal Point for the first time."

Averil lifts her chin from her knees, and her gaze sharpens.

"Tarion and I visited a beach near Crystal Point to meet with Perindal," I continue. "Sometimes he would come out on the royal barge, and other times we'd swim into the shallows. I took human form occasionally, but I never gave human aspect to anyone else. And until that day, Tarion had never asked. But when he saw Perindal's sister, he was enchanted. Obsessed."

Not my father, Averil says. *He hates humans.*

"Yes, he was always wary of them, just as Perindal's best friend Brixeus was suspicious of merfolk. Yet the four of us managed to enjoy each other's company—gambling, drinking, dining, indulging in music, mayhem, and merriment of all kinds.

"But when Tarion became obsessed with Perindal's sister Prella, he changed. He spoke of her constantly, haunted the shoreline watching for her, composed long poems praising her beauty. He started to hint that he wanted human form. Then he begged me outright to give him legs. But I knew if I changed one mer in that way, others would ask. Each transformation would require sacrifice, and a significant amount of my power. I didn't want to lose my subjects to the land, and I wanted to retain that sort of magic for myself. So I told Tarion I could only alter my own form, and that changing him into a human was beyond my skill."

250

Averil's mouth is tight, and her brows slant inward. But she doesn't speak her thoughts in my mind, so I go on with the tale.

"Tarion's fascination with Prella prompted me to notice her more. I realized she was indeed beautiful, graceful, and intelligent. I liked her, and I began spending more and more time on land. When Perindal noticed my attention turning toward his sister, he made it clear I was not allowed to pursue anything sexual or romantic with her."

I give Averil a wry grin. "Of course, since I was forbidden to pursue Prella, I became more eager to have her. I visited her secretly, without Perindal's knowledge, or Tarion's. She and I fucked often and eagerly. We were friends who liked each other's bodies, and perhaps I loved her in a way—but not with the all-consuming passion Tarion felt for her. He was convinced she was his one great love of a lifetime. That was the first seed of the concept merfolk now worship—the law of the 'one true mate.'

"We were discovered eventually, of course. Someone saw us, without our knowledge, and secretly reported to Tarion that I was fucking his great love. He was enraged, firstly because I'd refused to give him the magical transformation he wanted, and secondly because I'd stolen the woman he craved. And then, in his pain and fury, your father did two terrible things, Averil. Are you prepared to hear them?"

When Averil nods, pale and wide-eyed, I continue my tale.

"When Tarion found out about me and Prella, he didn't confront me at once. He planned his revenge first. I still had no idea my secret had been discovered, so I took no precautions.

"As my trusted best friend and advisor, Tarion had access to my chambers. He entered them one night, paralyzed me with a virulent toxin, and stole my trident.

"I'd inherited the trident a century before from my mother, who was Queen of the Sea and a witch as well. It carried some of

251

her power, and over the decades I'd infused it with power of my own—some natural and some acquired. A witch can encapsulate some of the natural power they're born with and place it into an object, where it becomes more focused and easier to wield. In my own foolishness and desire for convenience, I'd placed far too much of my natural ability into that single object.

"Paralyzed as I was, I couldn't prevent Tarion from taking the trident. With the assistance of another witch, of far lesser power than myself, Tarion began to transfer some of the trident's power into his own body. But I was able to speak a handful of words, just enough to activate a protective spell I'd laid on the trident long ago, as a preventative against such theft—an unbreakable locking spell that would stagnate the trident's magic and prevent anyone but me from accessing it. As a side effect, the trident also shrank to the size of a garnish fork."

Averil gasps, pressing both hands over her mouth. Her gaze sharpens with realization. *The garnish fork I stole for you.*

I smile a little, nodding. "Tarion only got a little of my water magic before I locked the trident. Once he realized he couldn't get any more, he went to Perindal and told him about my relationship with Prella. Perindal was furious, of course. He agreed to take the trident and lock it away where I could never reach it again. He hired human witches who laid spells to prevent me from entering the Summer Palace, glamoured or not.

"Meanwhile, Tarion kept me imprisoned, dosing me with paralytic toxin whenever I began to recover. I floated in my own filth for days, barely allowed enough food to sustain life, repeatedly poisoned so I would stay docile. Slowly I began to develop a resistance to the poison Tarion was using, though I pretended to suffer its effects just as strongly.

"Tarion concocted a story that painted me as a traitor, and Perindal corroborated the tale. And then Tarion began to sow an idea in the people's minds, that my magic was wicked and my form was corrupted. That I was a wretched monster, the spawn of a witch who had grossly mated with a mindless sea-beast.

"When my mother ruled, no one questioned it when the occasional mer who was born with an unusual form. No one blamed the parents of the child, or ordered immediate exile, as they do under Tarion's reign. Back then, those with different forms were neither maligned nor celebrated, but simply accepted. But Tarion and his priestesses incited a new hatred, an intolerance of those with differences of body or belief.

"After convincing my people of my unworthiness and treachery, Tarion assumed the throne under the sea."

Averil speaks softly in my mind. *Why would they believe evil things of you?*

"I was not always the kindest or wisest ruler," I admit. "I had a vision for our civilization, and my methods of carrying it out were sometimes strict, even harsh. I can be cruel to those who oppose me, or to the foolish who refuse to listen. I abolished the noble class among merkind and forced the redistribution of wealth and property, which made me many enemies among the former nobility. They were all too willing to back Tarion, especially when he promised a return to the class system."

I've never known any other system, she says. *You must tell me more of your economic theories sometime. But please, continue the tale.*

"Tarion upheld a cautious peace with Perindal for a while, but he couldn't overcome his craving for Prella. Eventually he broached the topic to Perindal, and when he was sharply rebuffed, he hired human mercenaries to capture Prella and bring her to him.

"The witch working for Tarion had promised she could help Prella breathe underwater. And it worked, for a while. But Tarion didn't consider the other effects of prolonged submersion on the human body. The pressure, the gases, the toll on the skin and membranes—Prella could breathe, but she couldn't survive down below."

My throat tightens as I'm speaking, and I have to pause. Strange. I thought I'd moved past all twinges of grief over Prella's death. But recounting it bathes me in sadness, and regret.

"Tarion finally came to me, when Prella's condition was dire and the other witch's spells were failing. He begged me to fix Prella with magic so she could stay under the sea with him. He said he'd mated with her a few times—with or without her consent, I do not know. But when they brought her to me, she was already gone. Her skin was so covered in sores I barely recognized her, and though her eyes were open, they were sightless.

"The priestess of a small religious sect had begun to whisper in Tarion's ear, and she convinced him that I refused to help because I was cruel and wicked. Tarion scheduled me for execution the next day. But that night, I was able to regain enough mobility to escape.

"I fled to a cave system I knew, one Tarion and I had explored when we were much younger. There I surrounded myself with toxic plants and protective spells, and Tarion feared me enough to leave me alone. He had Perindal to deal with.

"Once Perindal discovered what had happened to his sister, he and his soldiers set about capturing as many mer as they could, scaling and filleting them, leaving them for Tarion to find. So merkind withdrew, learned to stay far from humans, and became the isolated, fearful community they are now, bound by a religion devised by your father and that first priestess—who later claimed to be Tarion's 'true mate' and gave birth to all his children before she died spawning the last one—you."

33

AVERIL

I'm shivering in the tub. My pulse is rapid, my breath comes short and quick, and I can't stop the panting, or slow the frenzied beat of my heart.

"Averil," says the Sea Witch, frowning. "Averil, are you all right?"

I shake my head violently, repeatedly. It's too much, all of it. He must be lying. I never knew my mother, and though I have conflicted feelings about my father, I do respect him—I think. I've always mostly believed him.

But no… that isn't true.

I've known for years that my father wasn't being honest with us, that he was twisting true stories just enough to scare us into obedience. Perhaps the stories were more falsehood and less truth than I thought.

"Take a deep breath, Averil," says the Sea Witch. I can't see much of his surroundings—just a cloudy dark blue and some blurry black rocks—but I can make out his tentacles shifting and coiling restlessly.

I speak to him through our mental connection. "You had me steal the trident for you, so you can unlock your power. You're planning to take your kingdom back, aren't you? You're going to hurt my father, my family, the priestesses—"

I can't focus my thoughts anymore. My breath is too fast, too frantic, and my head is spinning.

"Averil," snarls the Sea Witch. "Breathe. Or at least get out of the tub before you faint and drown. Get *out*, shrimp. Now."

I manage to stand on shaky legs and climb out of the tub. I collapse on the rug beside it, slick and wet and naked, bowed over and gasping, trying to suck in a deep breath while my hair plasters my back and shoulders.

"Don't kill my father," I plead in my thoughts. "Don't kill him, or my sisters, please don't kill my sisters. Please. Oh gods, what have I done?"

"What has your father done, is the question," growls the Witch. "Established a false religion to shore up his cowardly reign. Exiled countless merfolk for spurious reasons based on fabricated theology. Do you know what happens to exiled merfolk, shrimp? Far from the safety of the mer settlements, they die. Some found their way to me, but most made foolish bargains, left my domain, and perished one way or another. Graeme, Liris, and Ekkon are the only ones who ever stayed. Your father has been responsible for so much misery and death, starting with Prella's murder. Yes, it was murder. I may have done Tarion wrong, betrayed him as a friend—but he killed Perindal's sister. Her death was his fault!"

He's practically roaring now, his voice reverberating through the water that surrounds him, transferred to me through his shell and mine, thundering in my head. I curl into myself, holding my skull in both hands. I can't stand the force of his anger, or the flood of clashing emotions in my chest. I feel as if I'm being suctioned by two opposing currents, a few seconds from being violently ripped apart. Tears glaze my cheeks. I would give anything to be able to scream.

"Unless your sisters resist my conquest of the kingdom, I will not harm them," says the Witch. "But you need not worry about what's going to happen under the sea, Princess. You won't be there to see it."

His meaning registers slowly, a point of blazing realization in my head, centering my thoughts.

"You're not going to change me back." My thought-voice sounds stunned, distant, detached.

"Changing you, taking you from your father, using you to retrieve my trident—it's all part of my vengeance on Tarion." The Sea Witch bites out each phrase, and I can't tell if the emotion behind the curt words is regret or rage.

"I hate you," I hiss into his mind. "You used me. You—I let you do things to me. I—"

"Consider it a learning experience," he says. "And now you have the skills you need for life on land. I wish you a full and happy existence as a human. And I mean that."

"You're despicable."

"I never pretended to be anything else, love." He's about to say more, but a sleek black shadow whips across his body, and he snarls in pain. Dark blood spirals from a wound in his stomach. "I have some unfortunate company to entertain. I shall return your voice tomorrow and secure you in your human form, once my trident is active again. Goodbye, little mermaid. Good luck with the puny prince, or whoever takes his place in your heart."

The connection between us ends.

Whatever is attacking him, I hope it kills him.

No. No, I don't hope for that, I can't. But I hope they cause him as much pain as I'm in right now.

I crumple onto the rug, curled into a ball, shaking, my mouth open in a soundless wail of agony.

This hurts so much more than when I found Kerrin with his dick in Cassilenne's mouth. This betrayal cleaves my soul, wrenches me open, floods the room with my heart's-blood and my salty tears.

Finally I stagger to my feet, clean my face, and empty the tub. Dully, mechanically I move, drying myself, putting on a nightdress, drinking the potion Cassilenne left for me. I crawl into bed.

I will have to sleep in horribly stagnant, motionless beds for the rest of my life. I will forever be rooted to the ground. Yes, I'll be able to swim sometimes, but it won't be the same. I won't be able to dive deep, to breathe beneath the waves, to flick my beautiful tail, to feel the quiver of my gills.

The Sea Witch betrayed me. Of course he did.

I wasn't careful enough. I should have realized that he never actually promised to restore my mermaid form. He only promised to restore my voice.

I was nothing but a tool in his hand, for his vengeance and his pleasure.

I meant nothing to him.

That knowledge hurts the most—worse than losing my mermaid form forever. Worse than being trapped in this palace with the deplorable prince. Gods help me, it even hurts worse than the thought of losing my father.

I actually thought the Sea Witch might care. That under his sworn hatred, he actually liked me. Of course I was wrong. He can leave me behind easily and move ahead with his purpose, his goals.

The potion is taking effect, blurring my thoughts, softening them into a muddled swirl so I can rest.

Tomorrow I will have to leave Prince Kerrin. He doesn't want me anyway. I'll avoid the guards somehow, get out of the palace, and flee this region. Perhaps I'll travel along the coast and find work at the "Fiddling Albatross."

Maybe then I'll see the Witch again someday. If he comes in for a drink, I can surprise him, poison him, kill him.

No—not kill him—but definitely bind him. Chain him in some dank cellar, stark naked, and pummel him with my fists until he's bloody and beautiful—and then kiss his terrible, wicked face over and over…

No, I can't think that way.

I turn onto my side, my heavy eyelids drooping, closing.

No kissing of the Sea Witch. Never again.

In my dreams someone is speaking, low and soft. Telling me that the king needs me. An aroma of herbs and roses slithers through the haze in my mind. Are my eyes open or closed? I'm not sure.

The voice keeps speaking, half-whispering. I can't tell if it's a man's voice or a woman's, and though its echo lies somewhere in my memories, I can't tease it out, can't link it to the countenance of its owner. My brain is a blurry, agreeable, mushy space within the globe of my skull.

Kerrin's father is dying of thirst, the voice says, and I must bring him a cup of water. I'm the only one who can save his life. I must make him drink, or he will die.

Over and over the voice repeats the instructions, low and firm, until I nod. I like the voice. It sounds kind, and I like kind things. I want to make the voice happy.

Blinking, I force myself to rise from the bed. A cup is pushed into my hands, and I grit my teeth, doing my best to walk smoothly and not spill its contents.

The walls and floor of the palace are tilting, swaying, flexing. I can barely keep hold of the cup in my hands—some of the liquid sloshes out over my fingers. It stings.

At last I reach the room where the king lies sweating and muttering among his sheets. There are two guards, but they don't stop me.

The king refuses the water, but he's weak.

The gentle voice said he must drink, or he will die. I won't let Kerrin's father die. There has been too much death, too much pain.

I can help him live.

I cup the back of his skull, lift his head, force him to gulp the contents of the cup. Once he's drained it, I shuffle back to my room and collapse across my bed, which spins and tilts until I slide sideways off its edge, crashing into a writhing pool of black water and gray tentacles. A tentacle jams itself down my throat, thickening until I'm sure it will split me apart.

Then suddenly it withdraws, and I gag.

I'm awake, sitting on my bed, vomiting onto the blanket. A goblet lies on the mattress not far away, purple drops staining the sheets.

When I'm done spilling my stomach's contents, I crawl from the bed and peel off my sweat-drenched nightdress. Naked I stumble into the bathing room. Too nauseated and shaky to turn up the lamp, I shove aside the drapes on the window to admit the pale, watery light of dawn.

My fingers hurt, and when I look down at them, they're dotted with blisters.

Is this still a nightmare?

Frantically I scrub my hands, but the blisters remain.

Dimly I remember liquid sloshing from a cup onto my fingers.

Was that real? Did I go to the king's chamber to give him a drink?

A drink of *what*?

My skin breaks into a panicked chill, hot and cold at once. I stagger back into the bedroom, staring at the goblet and the purple stain.

What happened last night? What did Cassilenne put in that potion she gave me?

Why did I drink it?

Muffled shouting, the rumble of footsteps in the hallway outside my suite. Then the door to my room bangs open.

Guards pour in, along with a few lords or nobles I recognize vaguely from the court. I cringe away from them, trying to claw a sheet off the bed and wrap it around my bare body, but they won't let me cover myself. Hands seize my arms, and one soldier grips the back of my neck.

"Look, there, on the bed! The goblet with the poison!" exclaims one of the noblemen. "She's the one the guards saw entering His Majesty's chamber. They did not stop her because she is the prince's betrothed."

"Those guards will die for their foolishness." Another man shakes his head, his eyes glittering as he scans my body. "Our king is dead, poisoned by this girl. Such wicked treachery. Take her to the dungeon, and wake His Highness!"

I motion with my hands, forming a protest with my lips— but no one pays attention. They're dragging me out of the room, into the hallway.

"A terrible tragedy," says one of the lords. "Did you see the king's body? Bloody foam filling his mouth, blisters all over his chest where he vomited out poisoned bile. A wretched end for our liege, to be sure."

"The prince will demand an equally wretched end for this traitorous bitch," replies another noble.

"She deceived him most wickedly. But His Highness wouldn't be the first man to have his head turned by a fuckable mouth and a set of juicy tits."

Their laughter fades as the soldiers haul me farther along the corridor.

"I've heard what our Crown Prince does to those who run afoul of his good nature," mutters one of the guards to another. "There's a rumor among those who sailed with him—that he mutilated a woman while he was traveling in Lourne. Cut off the wench's lips after she told some embarrassing things about him. A prostitute, she was."

"Cut off her lips?" says another guard.

"Aye. Both sets, if you know what I mean. She'll not be getting that sort of work again." He laughs coarsely. "I've no doubt His Gloriousness will do something worse to this one." He gives my arm a shake.

A mindless fear seizes me. Struggling against the choking nausea, I call up my years of battle training under the sea. Fighting is different beneath the waves—it's all about grappling, strategic holds, and pressure points. But in the thin air, without the resistance of water, achieving the force I need is actually easier.

Twisting my body and ramming my hip against one of the guards, I wrench my right arm free and use the side of my hand to strike the man's throat. Another twist and some brutal leverage, and the wrist of the second guard snaps. He yells in agony, while I whirl and crush the larynx of the guard behind me with quick grip-and-twist.

Someone else reaches for me—I seize the oncoming hand, step aside and turn—another wrist pops, jagged bone splitting the skin.

Then I'm overcome by a pile of male bodies, slamming on top of me, shouting and sweating, nearly crushing me against the cold tiled floor.

"She's an assassin!" cries one of the guards. "Only a trained assassin would have such skills!"

Shit. No use trying to claim that I'm guiltless now.

Sea Witch, I call through the shell.

But there's no answer, no warming thrum of magic. The shell grinds against my breastbone.

Sea Witch, please. I'm in trouble—they're hurting me. Please. I'll give you anything if you answer me, if you help me.

Still nothing. A new fear flickers inside me—the fear that perhaps something did kill the Sea Witch. Does that mean my voice is lost forever? Does that mean he's gone, really gone, and I'll never see him or speak to him again?

He can't help me. I must save myself, somehow.

With a desperate squirm, I manage to slither out from the pile of guards. The chain around my neck catches on something as I wriggle free, and it snaps. My fingers scrabble for it, but it's stuck—no time to stop and pull it loose.

I lurch to my feet, preparing to run.

Something cracks against my skull. My vision sparks, then blackens.

34

THE SEA WITCH

I'm almost ready to perform the ritual and reclaim my powers.

Getting to this moment took me longer than I hoped. I was wounded by a shark during my conversation with the princess, and I had to fight it off before I could continue my journey to the lair. And then I had to dress my own wounds, since Liris and the others have taken refuge elsewhere.

But I'm healed now, and everything I need is assembled.

After decades of waiting, a handful of extra hours could barely be considered a setback.

I pluck the garnish fork from my inner pocket, which is still miraculously intact despite my battle with the shark. The human who wove this material and stitched this garment knew their craft well.

I uncork a bottle—my own ink and tears, blended, and I guide the cloud of murky liquid around the garnish fork until it's nearly invisible.

I only produce ink in my aquatic form, and only in the rarest moments of distress. I captured this ink and these tears after the death of my mother. Strange that I had the presence of mind to collect them at all, mired as I was in grief. But I did preserve them, and they are among the most powerful spell ingredients I possess. The pain I paid back then was stored in these elements, and that old agony will serve as the necessary sacrifice to unlock the spell on the trident.

To the inky cloud wreathing the fork, I add beads of silver-blue memory from a former servant of mine, one who was exiled by Tarion after my downfall. The beads hold recollections of my former power, before I was betrayed, before I sealed the trident. They, too, are a necessary ingredient to help my old weapon remember me and unlock for me.

The merman gave me the memories in exchange for a new face so he could return to the mer kingdom. Unfortunately he was killed by a razenfish swarm a year later. So often these bargains of mine seem to doom rather than aid the people who come to me for help. Not that I care. I've worked hard to eradicate the last shreds of compassion from my heart.

A fruitless effort, perhaps, because I keep picturing the little mermaid princess crumpled beside the tub, broken by the weight of what I told her. I hear her plaintive voice in my mind, pleading for the lives of her family. Each thought she pressed into my brain is like a taut thread, winding around my heart, tightening until my entire body twitches with pain.

I keep remembering that other moment, when I was coming against her smooth stomach, painting her with my release, and she throbbed against me, panting in the throes of her own ecstasy. We stood there, foreheads touching, synchronized in pleasure. I wanted so badly to be inside her. But she held back part of herself, and I respect her the more for not giving me everything. She did not trust me entirely, after all. Wise woman.

We played our sensual games, and now it's done. All I want is to reawaken the trident, reclaim my power, and take back my kingdom, my birthright.

Once I've conquered Tarion and claimed the throne, I will bring down the nobility again, spreading their riches among the less fortunate. And I'll go one step farther. I'll make the choice I wasn't strong enough to make last time.

During my previous reign, I tried to force equality on everyone else while still retaining my own ascendancy and wealth. This time, once the kingdom has stabilized, I will establish a new form of government, where all the people have a voice and a vote. Once that is in place, I will leave. I have no interest in listening to the petty daily concerns of the people who rejected me.

The magic is mine. It will be the prize I take with me when I leave the kingdom under the sea. Beyond that, I have no desire to rule.

I add a few more ingredients, using my control over water to hold everything in place around the trident until I'm ready to speak the spell. It's a long one, twined with words of incredible power in the tongue of the gods, and I must have complete focus when I perform it.

To prevent any distractions, I remove the golden shell from around my neck and close it into a drawer.

Then I lift my hands and begin the chant.

At my first words, the garnish fork begins to shake, throwing off beams of purple light that arc against the sides and roof of the cave. One beam splinters a cabinet, another cracks the rocky wall, and more snake along the ceiling. Their heat filters to me through the water.

My heart thunders, pounding blood through my veins. Over the crackling roar of the magic my voice rises, a fell sound, dark with indomitable purpose.

Keep control of the spell. Every word is vital. Enforce your will on the magic.

Drawers begin sliding out, cabinet doors bang open, and their contents spill into the cave, whirling in the heightened current that's circling the trident. I send out my tentacles, pressing cabinets shut and holding drawers closed while I keep bellowing Godspeak, the fiery words that can sear through the magical chains around the trident's power.

The spell I laid on the trident is incredibly powerful, intended to defy the skills of any other sorcerer. No one but I can undo the magic, and even I am struggling. Every muscle in my body strains, and my head and throat begin to ache as power flows from me, crashing against the locking spell.

Why did I have to make it so damn effective?

Louder I chant, forcing the words through my seared throat, through the rippling water. The trident is larger now—not full-size yet, but growing. More purple light flashes from its tines; the water around it bubbles and steams.

I'm coming to the end of the spell, and still I haven't fully conquered the magical lock on the trident.

The last words erupt from my throat with all the power I can muster. The trident vibrates, stretching, growing—the walls of the lair quake. A threatening rumble overhead, and the roof of the cave splits wide.

I made the spell too strong. Magic is cruel, vengeful. It turns upon those who wield it.

But I refuse to back down. I will have what belongs to me, and I will have it now.

"Mine!" I roar, and the shockwave of my voice collides with hissing water around the trident.

A searing explosion. Coils of ink threaded with flashes of violet light. I crash against some cabinets, pain blazing through

269

my body. A secondary pulse impacts my chest, keeping me pinned, while the trident spins wildly in a purple sphere of light.

Snarling, I use my tentacles for leverage and push myself away from the smashed cabinets, reaching for the trident. My hand passes through the sphere around it, and a slow scream of agony claws out of my throat as the sizzling magic peels back the skin from my fingers and wrist, flaying off thin slices of red muscle.

"I am your master!" I bellow. "You are not mine!"

My ravaged, bleeding fist closes around the shaft of the trident. Another blast of magic, and I shut my eyes against the hissing whirl of objects raining sharp against my body.

But I don't let go. Because I must see this through, and achieve my revenge. I cannot have betrayed her for nothing.

A booming shockwave blasts outward, and my eyes pop open in time to see my lair explode into chunks of rock and countless pieces of detritus. Everything I've gathered and created so carefully over the past few decades, broken and destroyed. The last sacrifice required by my terrible magic.

The trident goes quiet, except for an obedient thrum against the raw muscle of my palm.

Chunks of rock are settling, crunching onto the remains of my cabinets and drawers.

I have to find what supplies remain so I can heal myself. I need to—

Shit. *Shit.*

The shell necklace with Averil's voice.

It must be somewhere in this wreckage—hopefully not crushed.

Shit. It could take hours to find it.

35

I'm lying on a chilly, bumpy, hard surface. A rough stone floor, grainy with sand.

I'm still naked.

My joints hurt, and my flesh is sore in places—bruised, I think. My head aches. When I touch the place where I was struck and knocked out, pain radiates through my skull, generating a fresh wave of nausea.

It's so dark. The faintest orange light seeps down the hallway outside my cell, but I can't see its source. Probably a torch on the wall, just around the corner.

I crawl to the bars and wrap my fingers around the cold metal. But when I try to call out, not a sound comes from my lips.

I forgot my voice is still with the Sea Witch. Stupid of me.

How long before he returns it, I wonder? My part of the bargain is fulfilled, and I truly believe he will honor his. He might be a trickster and a bastard, but he keeps his word when it comes to bargains. And while he avoided actually promising to return my mermaid form, he did vow to give my voice back.

Without my necklace, I can't call him or speak to him. Not that he'll notice or care. Beyond the return of my voice, he's done with me. He has made that abundantly clear.

I've been accused of something horrible—the murder of the human king. I was framed for it, that much I know. I'm not sure if it was Cassilenne, acting alone, or perhaps Kerrin himself. Or maybe someone else. Lord Brixeus seems to be ever-present at Kerrin's side, yet I did not see him last night, after our return to the palace. Could he have had something to do with the king's death? Surely not. By all appearances he's a loyal servant to the crown, even if the heir to the crown is often rude and dismissive to him.

There's nothing in my cell, except a hole in the ground where I can relieve myself. Reluctantly I avail myself of the opportunity, then crawl back to the barred door of the cell, clinging there in silence, waiting.

After a long, long time, there's a murmur of faraway voices, and then footsteps coming nearer. Just one person, I think.

A shadow looms on the wall, cast by the torch or lantern around the corner. Immense and menacing at first, the shadow shrinks slightly, sliding to the floor, merging with the rest of the darkness as its owner approaches my cell.

Kerrin looms over me, beautifully dressed in a black-and-gold doublet over a silky white shirt with ruffled sleeves. His pants are a soft, pale leather, and his black boots have gold embroidery up the sides. He's wearing a rapier at his hip.

The distant light bathes one half of his pretty face, but the other half is shadowed. His glossy black curls gleam as he crouches beside my cell.

"Hello, Beautiful," he croons. "Give us a smile, would you? And maybe a squeeze? If you're nice to me I'll get you a blanket." He slips an arm between the bars, his palm approaching my breast, but I scuttle backward, out of his reach. I pull myself to a standing position, but when I'm this dizzy it's hard to balance my torso atop my human legs. My head spins, and the floor of the cell undulates, so I have to brace my back against the wall to stay upright.

But at least I'm standing.

"So that's how you're going to play it." The prince rises too, his eyes glittering. "Fine. Let's talk about why you're here."

I nod, then press a hand to my temple as the pain in my head spikes.

"You killed my father last night," Kerrin says. "Poisoned him. A dreadful thing, for a man to be poisoned by his future daughter-in-law."

I take an unsteady step forward, shaking my head, miming a drink.

"Yes, you gave him poison to drink," says the prince carelessly.

I shake my head again, trying to explain with gestures.

A slow, satisfied grin crawls across Kerrin's mouth. "You can flail around all you like. No one will understand you. That's why you're so perfect for this, Beautiful. Because you're *silent* in my presence, as a woman should be. You guard my secrets, whether you want to or not. And I can tell you things—all the wonderful, clever things I can't tell anyone except Cassilenne.

"See, Beautiful, you were going to be my queen, and Cassilenne was to be my mistress—*our* mistress. I planned to have you framed for the king's murder much later than this, after Cass and I had a chance to enjoy you awhile. After a suitable number of months I would have disposed of my father and blamed you for it—you, the mute spy, sent by enemies to destabilize our kingdom. But then you had to go and get yourself roughed up and robbed. I can't have a wife who might be carrying some thieving wretch's spawn in her womb. It's a pity, really. I wanted you quiet and clean and perfect and *mine*."

I bare my teeth at him, clenching my fists. Despite my dizziness, I take a threatening step forward—and Kerrin actually retreats. Perhaps the guards told him how I fought so fiercely in the hallway, before I was knocked unconscious.

"I do not approve of your attitude," Kerrin says. "If this is your true nature, perhaps it's a mercy we hurried the plan along. I'll have to find another wife now, but at least you've been a useful tool, removing one obstacle from my path. With my father gone, I, the bereft son and betrayed fiancé, will have the people's hearts in my hand. I'll be able to assume the throne quickly, easily, since my engagement has already fulfilled the fidelity law. And you—well, you can't talk. You can't refute the charges against you. I swear, you're such a perfect scapegoat—it's like the gods sent you to me, as a blessing on my plans. Cass and I could scarcely believe our luck when we found you on that beach.

"Cassilenne has been part of my plans from the beginning," Prince Kerrin continues with a chuckle. "Secret lovers, she and I, ever since we were far too young to be fucking. She traveled abroad with me, helped me take care of more than one delicate situation. She loves me, and she'll do anything for me. She is the one loyal woman in a world of treacherous whores. Just before we voyaged home, she hired a man to conduct the first poisoning attempt on my father. It had to be done before I arrived, so no one would suspect my involvement. Cassilenne made sure the assassin wouldn't betray us; she put a slow-acting poison on the gold we paid him with. The toxin killed him shortly after he poisoned the king. Brilliant, really.

"Unfortunately the king didn't fully ingest the first dose of poison, or else he is tougher than I thought. During our voyage home, a passing merchant ship hailed us and told us of the assassination attempt, and its failure. Cass and I had to alter our plans quickly. We had a few ideas, but nothing was settled—and then came the storm. Cass managed to get to a skiff, and somehow I made it to shore as well. I'm beloved of the gods, I swear."

No, I think fiercely. *I saved your life, you asshole. Most idiotic thing I've ever done.*

"Then you washed up into our laps, so lovely and helpless," the prince continues. "I sent Cass to my father's side so she could pretend to help him, while continuing to quietly weaken him. She had to do it gradually, so she wouldn't be suspected. I stayed with you, to determine whether you were as mute and mindless as you seemed. And the rest of the story you know. My darling Cass concocted the potion that made you so pliant and suggestible last night. She's brilliant, truly. Wicked as they come."

And I thought Cassilenne was kind at first. Just as I thought the prince was sweet and charming when I met him.

I press the half-circles of my nails into my palms until my nerves shrill in painful protest. How am I such a terrible judge of character? If I survive this, I must strive to do better. I must be wary of everyone until I get to know them. My trust and affection will be closely-guarded treasures, difficult to earn. Suspicion and apathy will be my default—

But that perspective seems all too familiar.

That's how the Sea Witch views everyone, with caution and suspicion, with hatred and keen calculation. He cares only for what he can take from others. He's too afraid to let anyone into his heart again.

And he has that mindset because he went through a pain like *this*—betrayed by those who claimed to be his friends.

Like me, he was falsely accused. Like me, he was drugged, imprisoned, torn away from all sources of help. He had to save himself, through agony and endurance.

Sympathy wells in my heart, tightening my throat. The back of my nose prickles and tears fill my eyes.

The grief and anger in my heart—those same emotions made the Sea Witch into the person he is. That's why he can't care for me, why he chose revenge over the connection we have. He's broken, the same way I'm breaking.

I finally understand him.

"Why are you smiling?" says Kerrin warily.

Vaguely I touch my mouth and realize he's right. I am smiling, even as a few tears trace my cheeks.

The emotion I feel for the Sea Witch surges up, wave upon wave, until it's a tsunami crashing through my heart, filling the trenches carved by his betrayal.

He might never speak to me again. He might never beg my forgiveness, or change his mind. He might tear apart my father's kingdom, end my father's life, and leave me stranded on land, stuck in this form. All of that will hurt me, deeply. But I will love him anyway. Not because he deserves my love any more than Kerrin does—gods know he doesn't.

I love him because I can't help it. Because in the Sea Witch, I hear the deepest echo of my own soul.

Like me he is a wanderer, a risk-taker, a wayfinder, a breaker of rules. He is curious about all things far away and forbidden. He is forever learning, forever exploring. Determined, like me. Proud, like me. Full of heart and humor that he keeps hidden away.

I love him, and I don't even know his name.

Prince Kerrin stares at me as I smile, my cheeks wet and my whole body brimming with a wild, incandescent certainty.

I love the Sea Witch. He's mine.

I will survive this, and then I will find him. I'll learn magic, I'll cast a spell so I can breathe underwater, and then I will hunt him through the depths of the sea.

I'm still smiling, savagely now, and Kerrin backs away, eyeing me. "I need to speak to my people and mourn my dearly departed progenitor," he says. "Then I'll have to settle the matter of your punishment. We might have a trial—a formality, of course—and then I'll decide on your sentence. A good hard whipping and then life imprisonment, I think—execution would be a waste of those lovely, silent lips. Remember, Beautiful, I'm always happy to make your surroundings a little more comfortable in return for good behavior." He smirks and wraps a hand over his crotch. "Care to begin behaving now?"

In answer I smile wider and snap my teeth together. His eyebrows shoot up, and he cups his dick protectively.

"Very well," he sneers. "Enjoy your solitude."

He strides away.

For someone like me, who appreciates action and mental stimulation, time spent in a dark, empty prison cell is torture. I lie on the floor, careful of the sore spot on my head, and I ponder ways to communicate with anyone who might attend my trial— ways that I might be able to express my innocence and cast suspicion onto the prince.

When I become frustrated with that, I amuse myself by recalling every time the Sea Witch has spoken to me, and all possible meanings of each phrase from his mouth, particularly ones like "I never want to stop doing this with you" and "I'll stay here forever if you'll let me" and "Someday I will make you scream until the sea itself trembles."

Voices startle me in the middle of my reverie. One voice protesting, another murmuring quietly, firmly. Neither is the voice I most crave, but one of them sounds familiar. Brixeus?

Slow footsteps are approaching my cell. I don't bother trying to conceal my nakedness.

Lord Brixeus pauses at the door and pushes a thin cloak between the bars. "Cover yourself, princess."

Princess?

Startled, I accept the cloak and wrap it around myself, my eyes locked with his.

He nods. "Yes, Averil. I know who you are."

Lord Brixeus knows who I am.

How?

Did the Sea Witch tell him? Have the humans captured or killed him? Maybe that's why he hasn't restored my voice.

Weakness floods my limbs, and my legs fold under me.

"I've suspected you of malice since the beginning. You know that." Brixeus wraps one of the bars with a gloved hand, his spine curving a little. He's trying to maintain his courtly posture, but he's exhausted, nearly to the point of collapse. What happened to him?

"I was watching you and the sorcerer yesterday evening, by the sea wall," he says. "Until I was caught."

So the Sea Witch lied. He *did* find the person who was spying on us—Lord Brixeus. Why didn't he tell me about it?

"After Zoltan caught me, he took me out to sea and left me on a rock."

I stare at him, uncomprehending. I mouth the word *Zoltan?* with my most quizzical expression.

"Zoltan. The Witch of the Deep. Former King under the sea."

Delighted shock zings along my nerves because finally, *finally* I know the Sea Witch's name. Zoltan.

I like it. It feels powerful and solid, like him.

"I might have died there," Lord Brixeus continues. "Or Zoltan might have returned for me—I'm not sure. He is not a merciful man, but he is a fair one, true to his own code. He does not kill without reason."

I spread my hands, palms up, shaking my head, wordlessly asking how he came to be here.

"One of your father's patrols found me," says Lord Brixeus. "King Tarion's people have been combing the depths for you, from the Fathomless Trench to the Ice Reefs. They discovered me atop the rock, and jeered at me. They would have left me there, but I shouted Tarion's name and everything I know of him, and they came closer. I explained that I've dealt with their kind before, long ago. I mentioned the Sea Witch, they told me they were seeking a lost princess. With the bits of information we each possessed, we put a few things together."

Lord Brixeus leans closer to the bars. "They brought me to shore with one purpose only—to find you and the Witch, and deliver you both to Tarion, King under the sea. I swore I would do so, yet I felt some compunction about returning you to the ocean when you so clearly desire to be ashore. I was going to give you the chance to run away, to go inland. But imagine my surprise when I returned at dawn to find my king poisoned by your hand."

Getting to my feet again, I shake my head rapidly.

"You killed him for Zoltan, didn't you? You gave him your voice and vowed to commit murder, in exchange for your human form?" Brixeus's dark eyes sparkle with angry tears. "Perindal had his flaws, but he was my friend. He did not deserve this. His one fault was getting himself and our kingdom involved with merfolk. I warned him about your kind."

I shake my head again, but I can't explain. This is too complex a matter for rudimentary hand signals. I can't tell Lord Brixeus that if I'd wanted to kill the king, I wouldn't have staggered into his room in full view of guards, dumped poison down his throat, and clumsily spilled the same poison all over my bed and my hands—which are still blistered and stinging. Several of the blisters opened when I was fighting the guards, and the liquid that oozed from them has dried on the backs of my fingers.

If I were an assassin, I wouldn't be that clumsy and stupid about it.

But I have no way to express that to Lord Brixeus.

"I have told Kerrin nothing of your true origins yet," Lord Brixeus says. "But I will. He may demand proof of what you are, which means we will have to break the spell Zoltan has placed on you. I have a variety of charms and potions which may be helpful with that. I've collected them over the years. I always knew he would come back." His voice fades, and he stares into the dark corner of my cell as if it's a window to the past, when he and Tarion and Zoltan used to gamble and drink together in the bright sun, by the glimmering sea.

In this moment, I'm so terribly desperate for my voice. I think I might burst with the ache of everything I need to say.

And then, I have an idea.

I step toward the bars, urgently miming the act of writing while trying to hold the cloak around myself.

Lord Brixeus frowns. "The prince told me you only write in a foreign tongue…" Then his eyes widen. "The language of the merfolk. That's the written language you know."

I nod and point to him, hopeful and questioning.

He nods slowly. "Zoltan taught Perindal and me how to read your written language. The words are the same; it's the symbols and their assigned sounds that differ. I only paid attention because I didn't like the idea of him communicating with Perindal in symbols I could not understand. I thought he might betray the alliance between our kingdoms."

Again I pretend to write, begging him with my eyes.

"I'm not sure what you could have to write that I would want to read," he says slowly.

Please. I mouth the word, clasping my hands. *Please.*

Lord Brixeus frowns slightly. He's considering my request. I wait, barely breathing.

"I will bring you something to write with, before I tell Kerrin what you are," he says. "One more thing—Kerrin says you were found half-clad last night, with signs of a man's release on your body. He seems to believe you were assaulted. Is that true?"

Blushing, I shake my head.

"I thought not. I suspected the signs were from your tryst with Zoltan, but I wanted to be sure." He runs a hand over his short gray hair and sighs. "If you *had* been harmed in that way, keeping you naked in a cell would be beyond cruel, assassin or not." He tugs sharply at the cuff of one glove, then the other. "I will see that you have food, water, paper, ink, and a quill. And you will tell me your truth, all of it."

Thank you. My lips form the soundless words. It's a relief to have someone who will actually look at me and watch my mouth, and try to understand. The prince never did, even when he was pretending to be good and charming.

Lord Brixeus is nearly to the corner when he halts. "One more thing. The mer patrol who took me from the rock and brought me to shore—they will have returned to your palace and told your father about all this by now. Tarion will likely set a bounty on Zoltan's head for kidnapping the princess. Which means if any of Tarion's patrols encounter the Witch of the Deep, he'll be killed on sight."

I suck in a sharp breath and press my hand to my chest, as if my fingers could still the frantic beat of my heart.

Lord Brixeus's mouth tightens. He nods as if I've confirmed something he suspected. "You care for him. Foolish child. He cares nothing for you." His frown deepens then, and his eyes grow distant, as if he's recalling something. "Or perhaps… but no. It's not possible. He's a selfish, cruel creature, with no capacity for love."

And with those words, he disappears around the corner.

36

The magic of my trident vibrates through my body whenever I touch it, a pulsing force so powerful I can barely maintain my grip. Given time, its magic will synchronize with me fully again, and the bone-jarring effects will settle. Until then, I need to keep it in contact with my skin.

My lair has been destroyed, but some of my healing supplies are intact, lying in a half-broken chest near me, so I can mend my ravaged hand. I don't have everything I need, and it's not a perfect spell. I will have scars thatched over the skin of that hand from now on.

I need something to keep the trident secure against my bare back while I search for Averil's voice, so I fashion a makeshift harness from some seaweed rope I find in the wreckage.

Then I continue my search for the shell necklace.

The shell wasn't crushed, or her voice would have been lost to the sea, and I would have felt the snap of pain inside me, the gnawing ache of a bargain broken.

No, the necklace is intact, trapped somewhere in this mess, maybe protected by the remnants of the drawer in which I stowed it.

I suppose I could shove the debris aside with the power of my trident, but if I do that, the shell might be permanently damaged. I can't risk it.

Or I could speak the spell now, and if I'm near enough to the necklace, Averil's voice should slip out. I could capture it in something else. But as I glance around for a proper vessel, I don't see anything I could use. I don't have to be right next to her to return her voice, but I certainly can't return it from this distance. It would dissipate on the way and be lost.

So I'm left with the task of sorting carefully through the rubble by hand, searching for the shell, when I should be heading for Tarion's palace.

"Fuck," I snarl aloud.

Once again, I'm faced with a choice between what I want, and *her*.

With my tentacles I shift a few slabs of rock and check some of the broken drawers. But this search could take hours. Hours I don't have, because I must destroy Tarion, and then I must take Brixeus back to shore before he's too parched from sun and thirst. I can confine him somewhere on land until my business with Averil is done and she has gone her own way. Perhaps I can bribe Brixeus not to tell Prince Kerrin about Averil's connection to me—though I doubt it. He's possibly the only man I know who is too noble to accept a bribe.

I must get her voice back to her soon, or I'll have broken my end of the bargain, and I will suffer the consequences. I'm not immune to the price of my own magic. The pain will eat away at me for months, even years, until I fade and become a restless spirit like those which haunt my garden.

Grinding my teeth, I force myself to stop the frantic search for the necklace.

These other concerns and tasks can wait. Nothing is more important than my vengeance. Nothing.

Brixeus is tough. He will survive on the rock a little longer. And I'll return later to find Averil's voice.

With the burning magic of the trident searing my bare back, I spring away from the wreckage and glide through my garden. I've gained a resistance to some of the poisons; others I must still be wary of.

When I pass the fringes of the garden into open water, I pause. Dark shapes fleck the murky blue distance. Torsos and tails. Merfolk.

They've seen me. They're advancing, and their hands bristle with weapons—spears, swords, and crossbows, all designed to function with lethal accuracy underwater.

During my spying forays into Tarion's domain, I've glimpsed the merman who leads them. Tattoos on his chest, a tail covered in sickly white scales. He's the captain of Tarion's forces. Dyrei, he's called.

Behind him, several of the mer soldiers are carrying a huge spiked net made of thin chains.

"Is that for me?" I point to it, grinning. "You shouldn't have."

I half-expect Dyrei to retort, but he doesn't. He lifts his hand, and two dozen darts whiz through the water toward me.

Automatically I lift both hands, the impulse for self-defense flooding my body, forcing my magic outward in a great shockwave. The oncoming darts are knocked aside, thrust backward, tumbled around in the churning deep, while Tarion's soldiers thrash their tails and fight to stay upright.

I can control more of the ocean now, not just thin streams. Long ago I had godlike power over the sea—my birthright combined with what I earned myself—and it feels glorious to have that control back.

Laughing, I create a maelstrom that catches all of Tarion's soldiers and spins them in a violent circle until they're nothing but a ball of fins and bodies, tumbling over and over each other. My tentacles pick up the net they would have used for me, and I wrap the flailing ball of mermen in it. No point in bringing them with me, so I leave them behind and proceed toward Tarion's court.

There are numerous settlements under the sea, but most cluster near the central city where Tarion holds sway. Proximity and numbers offer more protection against the dangers of the deep. The farthest settlements like those in the Southern Sea have their own minor leadership, but all are under Tarion's rule, and none may shelter anyone he has exiled.

For decades his word has been law. That changes today.

37

I've been writing my confession for what feels like forever. I have no way of telling the time, but I've written several pages, front and back, in the mer script.

Under the sea, we etch letters in stone. Writing with ink is easier, although it took me a while to adjust to using quill and ink. Despite the relative ease of writing with a pen, my right hand is cramping, and my wrist sends flickers of pain up my arm. Yet I keep going, until I have poured out every bit of my story.

When I finish, I lay the stack of papers, the ink bottle, and the quill near the barred door. Then I move to the opposite side of the cell and lean back against the stone wall, wrapped in the thin cloak Lord Brixeus brought me.

I have not slept nearly enough in the past week. I can't tell if it's my head injury or pure exhaustion making me dizzy, even while I'm sitting down. My vision is blurry, and my eyelids feel swollen, thick, and heavy.

Pulling the cloak more tightly around me, I curl up on the floor, using my arm as a pillow.

Sometime later, a sound wakes me—the crisp swish of paper on paper.

Lord Brixeus is standing outside my cell, reading my confession. How long has he been there?

He's frowning intently at the paper, perhaps concentrating hard to recall his knowledge of the mer script. Or perhaps he's frowning at the implications of what I've written.

I have little hope he'll believe me. He's Perindal's loyal friend, equerry to the Crown Prince.

Even if he does believe me, he may choose to ignore my accusation against Kerrin. I have no proof that I was drugged and manipulated. No proof that Kerrin and Cassilenne were behind the first poisoning attempt. Nothing but the word of the prince himself, which no one else heard, and I can't repeat aloud.

Lord Brixeus takes the page he was reading off the top and places it underneath the stack. I'm not sure how close he is to the end of the story, but I can hardly bear the waiting.

At last he sighs, moves another page to the back, and straightens the pages. He tucks the sheaf of papers under one arm while he puts his gloves back on.

I sit up, my long red hair tumbling around me, hands clutching the blanket in place. I don't look at him with the vulnerable, "protect me" look the Sea Witch taught me. I meet his gaze straight-on, unflinching.

Whether he believes me or not, I have told him the truth.

He pulls the papers from beneath his arm and curls them into a roll between his hands. "I believe you," he says simply.

A lump rises in my throat, and I choke on an exhale.

He nods. "There was a scandal while the prince was abroad—some words repeated by a woman he slept with. Since then I have wondered if he was capable of plotting his father's demise and his own early ascent to the throne. I suppose I came to you the first time because my heart knew the truth I refused to accept—that the little boy I taught to ride a horse has become a patricidal monster."

I bite my lip, nodding. My fingers find my hair, gathering the locks, twisting them round and round. The texture of my hair is different in human form, but acting out the habit is still satisfying, comforting in a way I can't explain.

"I did not know about the trident," Lord Brixeus continues, "but it makes sense. It explains why Zoltan was so eager to enter into this bargain with you, and risk your father's wrath as well as Perindal's. He must have activated its magic again by now. Do you think he will limit his conquest to the sea, or send some calamity to plague us here as well?"

I lift my shoulders, shaking my head. I have no idea what the Sea Witch will do once he has conquered my father—if he succeeds in doing so. My father has large armies and well-trained bodyguards.

But Zoltan was powerful even without the trident. I cannot imagine the magnitude of his magic once the trident is fully his again.

Lord Brixeus keeps talking, reviewing certain points of the document I gave him, and I answer his questions as best I can with nods, head-shakes, mouthed words, or short sentences written on the extra paper.

"The prince is occupied with funeral arrangements and coronation plans today," says Lord Brixeus. "He will likely arrange your trial for next week."

I nod, grateful for the information. I've been dreading another visit from Kerrin, and it's a relief to know that I probably won't see him again today.

But I have a question of my own, one that won't let me rest until I ask it. I turn over the last sheet of paper and write, "What will you do with the information I've given you?" Then I hold up the paper to Lord Brixeus.

"I could keep silent and tell no one about your true identity as the mermaid princess," says Lord Brixeus. "I could preserve my own station as the Crown Prince's equerry, and let you take the blame for the king's murder. But if the Witch gives your voice back and Kerrin finds out you can speak, he will kill you on the spot. He won't let you expose what he has done."

He's right. Kerrin will kill me rather than let me accuse him. And even if he didn't, it's unlikely that any of his court would believe the word of a strange shipwrecked girl.

"If I reveal Kerrin's role in his father's death, I must also reveal your true identity," says Lord Brixeus. "No one will believe the prince's guilt without the full story. However, if I reveal that you are a mermaid, I don't believe the nobles will let you go, even after they depose Kerrin. They'll keep you imprisoned."

I lay the paper down and write again. "You could help me escape. I can pay you in treasure from my father's realm."

Lord Brixeus meets my gaze, pity in his eyes. "Your father's realm and its treasure may not belong to him anymore. And I will not accept a reward for doing what is right. I will find some way to free you, but it may take a little time."

Tears well in my eyes. I can't speak or write how I feel, but I try to pour my gratitude and admiration through my gaze.

Stern and stiff though he may be, this is a good man. A noble, wise, just man. He would make a far better ruler than Kerrin.

Lord Brixeus's dark eyes soften when he sees my tears. He clears his throat. "Trust me, Princess, I will find a way to ensure that you are liberated and the prince brought to justice for what he has done."

"What *he* has done?" A clear voice rings out, startling me and Lord Brixeus. A woman's silhouette rounds the corner of the hallway, black against the torchlight. "What about what *you've* done, Brixeus? Betraying your lord and king, making deals with his enemies?"

"Apothik Cassilenne," says Lord Brixeus evenly. "Have you been listening 'round corners? I know your mother taught you better."

"Save your insolence for His Majesty's interrogators," says Cassilenne. "It's a pity, Brixeus—I liked you, I truly did. You would have had a place of honor in the kingdom. But now you'll have to face the same fate as this assassin—pain, silence, and death. Guards, seize him."

Three uniformed figures advance, moving past her, surrounding Brixeus. He doesn't resist as they shackle him.

Cassilenne snatches the papers Lord Brixeus is holding. "You'll read this document aloud to His Majesty," she says. "Or you'll suffer. Gag him and take him to the torture room."

As I watch the guards obey her, immediately and without question, I realize how much power this woman has amassed for herself. Not just power through Kerrin—power of her own, influence that she has obviously woven throughout the ranks of the kingdom's military and probably through the court as well.

For a moment I'm not sure if she is Kerrin's partner—or his puppet-master.

Once the guards have hustled Lord Brixeus away, Cassilene approaches the bars of my cell.

"You, fish-girl," she says, lowering her voice. "Kerrin and I will deal with you later, once we have the whole story. I only overheard bits of your conversation, but I look forward to making Brixeus tell us more. It's very interesting, this tale of a powerful trident. Imagine the things one could do with so much magic!"

With a soft chuckle, she walks away. I remain standing until I'm sure she's gone, and then I crumple to the floor.

I wrote it all down. Every secret. My infatuation with Kerrin and how it transformed to hate; my deal with Zoltan and how it transformed into a heated, intimate connection.

Lord Brixeus will have to read it aloud to the Crown Prince. They'll torture him if he doesn't.

And once Kerrin knows how deeply I've deceived him, what I've stolen from him—

He's going to kill me himself. And he'll make it hurt.

38

THE SEA WITCH

I have never belonged to the sea, but it is mine.

Mine to push outward before me in a great, all-consuming wave as I sail through limpid blue waters, riding a current of my own making.

Schools of shimmering fish swerve out of my path. Predators give me a wide berth now, sensing my dominance.

The Royal Seat, chief city of the kingdom under the sea, is ringed with watchtowers that extend from the ocean floor nearly to the surface, with enough space to avoid scraping the hulls of passing ships.

Those towers are usually poorly manned by lazy soldiers who prefer to chew dreamweed and play bilge-bones instead of minding their duty. I've slipped past the outer rings a few times, clad in a false mer form, with one of their sleek tails instead of my own tentacles. Farther in, around the central part of the city, Tarion has some magical barriers in place, just as Perindal did—

charms to dispel glamours and disguises. Magic intended to prevent me, specifically, from entering without being detected.

Weakened as I was, I did not dare challenge Tarion openly. But now the trident glows hot in my palm, intermittently sending a bolt of purple lightning from its tines. I can't dispel the grin that bares my teeth, can't calm the triumphant thunder of my heartbeat.

Enough with glamours. No more hiding. I am here to reclaim what was stolen from me, and I want everyone in this place to know it.

As I approach the royal city, crossbow bolts streak through the water, trailed by bubbles. They're being fired from the watchtowers—from guards who are alert and ready, not sluggishly taking up their posts after noticing my approach.

Tarion was warned. I have no idea how, or by whom. No matter. Every missile that streaks toward me is repelled, knocked aside by a bolt of lightning or a surge of current. I barely have to think about it. My power encircles me, flows around me, protects me.

Just for good measure, and as a message to the others, I send a rolling pulse of water against one of the towers. The impact shatters its side, knocking it from its foundation, and it crumbles slowly, its stones settling to the bottom of the sea.

I move on, buoyed by the ocean itself, carried into the city in all my dark glory.

I've not been in the presence of so many merfolk for a long time. There's a cloying flavor to the water, trails of savory warmth from bodies—the alluring fragrance of pheromones, the freshness of vegetation from the gardens, and the biting scent of fish and other seafood being prepared for meals.

Under the sea our settlements are far quieter than those of humans. Murmuring voices, the burbling eddies and gurgling currents of movement, the reverberation of a gate closing, the grind of a wheel rotating, and the occasion mellow strains of undersea music. But when I sweep into the channel between the tall rows of podlike homes, the sounds around me begin to change. I smile as the voices shift into cries of alarm, as the doors to the houses slam shut, as people abandon their usual tasks to flee or hide from me.

Some attempt to fight. Pathetic. I seize several in my tentacles, choking them until they're limp and unconscious. Others I slam against houses with a pulse of water like a punching fist. Their heads strike rock, and thin streams of blood issue from noses or skulls.

My aim is temporary dysfunction, not death. Although if a few of them never wake, I will not feel guilt over it.

Resistance is stronger around the palace itself, so I dispense a shockwave of water, laced with purple lightning. The lightning catches some of the soldiers, crackling around their bodies while they scream, while their skull-bones and teeth show in startling flashes of purple and white. Their tails spasm with agony.

Another shockwave, and the gates meant to keep me out collapse into rubble. I soar through the entrance to the palace, careless of the debris swirling in the water around me, of the bodies drifting behind me.

I'm crawling along the halls now, tentacles clasping walls and pillars to pull myself along faster, faster.

The great hall with the royal bower is empty, so I continue on. Tarion has changed many things in my palace, but not the layout. I know where my chambers were. I know he took my rooms for himself.

A few servants cringe away from me and clutch each other as I pass, their tails quivering. I can only imagine how I must look to them—a massive, brutal form, hair streaming, a flickering trident gripped in my fist, my lower half a mass of writhing tentacles. I am a monster to them. Perhaps I always was. Thanks to Tarion, the seeds of hatred, the fear of the Different and the Other, have taken deep root in my people. I'm not sure I can ever repair the evil he has wrought. Nor will I try. They do not deserve my efforts.

I surge on, past the whimpering servants, and I dispatch a dozen more guards. Tarion has a gate barring the way to his chambers; I grip it with my tentacles and snap the metal like twigs.

Like a storm of retribution I erupt into his rooms. My head is roaring with the thunder of my heart, with the force of my rage, so long subdued. It swells hotter inside me when I see him.

Tarion has changed. He is about two centuries old, like me, but two hundred and fifty is the longest recorded lifespan for one of merkind, and Tarion possesses no magic to keep him young.

Like the spells that allow me to change my form, I have kept the secret of my youth to myself. I earned it shortly after my mother's death, through great effort and agony, but never was I more glad of that sacrifice than I am now, looking at Tarion's loose, wrinkled skin, his gray hair, and his dull gray scales. His features still have a noble cast, but neither his jeweled chestplate, nor the bracers on his arms, nor the rings on his fingers can restore him to the beauty he once had when we were young, when we were the most handsome, powerful, and desired males under the sea.

My mother's crown—my crown—is fastened into his hair. Thin gray braids are wrapped around it and through it, as if he's desperate to hold it tight to his head despite the pull of the sea.

I have not seen my crown in years, but it is as beautiful and imposing as it was the day I wore it to Perindal's court for the first time, when I walked on human legs into the Summer Palace, presented myself as the King of the Sea, and proposed an alliance. The crown is black obsidian, crafted with an ancient magic long lost to merkind, studded with ice-white diamonds.

Tarion is staring at me, clasping a bag, his tail flicking with agitation.

"Too soon," he mutters. "They were supposed to hold you back until—" He breaks off the sentence, dropping his gaze to the half-filled bag he holds. There's a gold medallion glinting in the mouth of the bag, threatening to slip out, and he shoves it back inside.

Tarion is packing up his treasures. Preparing to flee.

My stomach hollows, and it takes me a moment to recognize the feeling.

I'm disappointed in him.

"Running away, Tarion?" I say, in my deepest, most threatening tones. "I thought you would fight to retain the rulership and the luxuries you've enjoyed all these years."

"I'm not a fool, Zoltan," he hisses at me. "My patrols found Brixeus stranded on that rock where you put him. They brought me word that you gave Averil legs and made her seduce Perindal's son. The moment they told me, I knew you must be sending her after the trident, that you might already have it in your possession. So I made preparations accordingly."

"Preparations to run from me." I swirl around him, my tentacles unfurling through the water, ready to grab him if he tries to bolt.

"I've seen your power. The soldiers I sent were supposed to slow you down until I could escape."

"You fed them to me like chum for a shark, rather than leading them into battle." My lip curls. "Do your own people mean so little to you? And what of your daughters and their mates? Your grandchildren? Your priestesses? You would leave them all at my mercy? What if I showed them the same kindness you showed to Prella?"

Tarion recoils, his features contorting. "Do not speak her name to me."

"Because it reminds you of your foulest deeds? Your worst moments?" I slink nearer, forcing a menacing sneer onto my face although I'm screaming inside, caught in the grip of emotions I can barely manage. Smoky ink is beginning to leak from my body, curling in the water like an unspoken curse. "You caused Prella unspeakable pain. She disintegrated under your care, swelled and rotted while you played king. You're abhorrent. You disgust me. But if you want the last dregs of mercy left in this dark heart of mine, you'll confess the truth in front of your people."

One of my tentacles snakes out and coils under Tarion's jaw, just above his gills, while another wraps his arms against his body. I leave his tail free to move. He can't escape the suction of my grip. Perhaps he knows that, for he doesn't fight me. Another disappointment. We used to enjoy some spirited wrestling matches, he and I.

Ever since we were young together, when my mother was still queen and I was a prince, I've known that Tarion and I were similar. He would latch onto an idea or a thing he wanted and pursue it without care for anyone else until he possessed it. I shared that passionate persistence, but I've been able to temper my desires, most of the time. If there was something we both craved, I let him have it.

Until Prella.

Perhaps even back then, a part of me knew that if Tarion ever lost something he desperately wanted, it would be a disaster. He was a noble's son, spoiled by his parents—and perhaps I spoiled him too. He was my dearest friend, after all.

That weakness in him—that incapacity to handle disappointment—it has shifted and grown into something else. His worst loss transformed into the terror of future loss, and that fear spurred him to create this foul religion, this altered society darkened by the absence of honest pleasure, the desperate

299

devotion to purity, and the idea of the "one true mate." Along the way Tarion became a coward—a grasping, cringing, greedy creature who cares nothing for his children or his priestesses.

I shouldn't be surprised that he'd abandon them. After all, he turned on me, when we'd spent much of our lifetimes together.

I tow him through the halls of the palace, seething inside, angry words boiling in my head. But when I finally speak, the words aren't what I intended to say. "Do you remember the night near the lava pools, when we were celebrating my sixtieth? The sisters with the green hair? You took one and I took the other—"

"Mother Goddess forgive me for the failings of my past life," Tarion drones. "I have rejected all foul speech and impure thoughts. My old sins have been purged."

"Have they indeed? That's a pity. You made that mermaid come six times, I do believe. Remember how she followed you back to the city, begging for more? What was her name—Lea? Brea? Six months you spent with her. I thought you were going to marry the girl."

"Why are you saying this?" Tarion grits out.

"I'm not sure. Perhaps seeing you again has made me sentimental. Don't worry, I will not allow sentiment to spoil my revenge."

I haul him out the front gates, and I call out to the wounded guards, who are slowly returning to consciousness and mobility. "Summon everyone in the city! Bring them here, so their former king may tell them a truth long denied."

It takes time for the injured soldiers to carry the message. Impatience sends my tentacles into a twisting, crawling frenzy— impatience for Tarion's final confession and the culmination of all this.

Urgency grates at my soul, whispering *Averil, Averil* in my mind. Her voice. I must return her voice.

Perhaps I won't simply swim near Crystal Point and release it, letting it find her. Perhaps I'll take human form again and give it back to her myself. I'll see her once more, and ensure that she's safe before I leave her to her new life.

Unless—

My chest feels suddenly tight, and my tentacles cinch correspondingly tight around Tarion, until he groans.

"You said your men found Brixeus," I say. "What did they do with him?"

Tarion's gills are half-covered by a tentacle now, and he can barely move them. His eyes bulge with stark desperation.

"They took him back to shore," he chokes.

The blood drains from my face. My tentacle loosens, and Tarion's gills quiver wildly, sucking in water.

"What have you done?" I growl. "If the prince finds out she's a mermaid, that she's been fooling him—he is not a good man. He might hurt her."

"Whatever happens to her is the goddess's just punishment," Tarion says. "She disobeyed her father, rejected our faith, and betrayed her people. She committed foul treason by bargaining with you, and a worse sin by taking on the form of the two-legged plague. She consorted with the son of my enemy—she has probably been fouled and invaded by that human prince. She is no longer my pure, sweet daughter."

Despite my anxiety for Averil, I can't resist this moment of delicious revenge.

"Your pure, sweet daughter *has* been invaded," I say, curling the tip of a tentacle under his chin. "But not by the human prince." And I smile, with all the wicked sensuality I can manage.

Shock and horror blaze in Tarion's eyes. It's everything I've wanted to see, almost as satisfying as reclaiming my magic.

"No." The word is almost a sob from his throat. "No. You—you raped my daughter?"

The tentacle around his waist constricts, and he barks with pain.

"I would never take her by force," I snarl. "No, Averil was willing. She asked for the pleasure, craved my tentacles. She was wet for me, trembling and pulsating as I invaded her body…"

"Stop!" Tarion screams, his gaze averting from mine, fixed on something over my shoulder.

I'm facing him, with my right shoulder toward the gate and my left toward the gathering crowd. But when I glance behind me, there's a small group of merfolk—two females with reddish hair, wearing fine corsets and jeweled crowns. One of them is holding a child against her breast. And behind them are a handful of mermaids clad in armor crafted of limestone and black shells. They wear tall headdresses of the same materials. How do they swim properly with those?

"Let our father go," says the young mermaid with the child. Her lips are trembling. "And speak no more lies."

I turn fully to face them, wrapping another tentacle around Tarion for good measure. The trident hums in my hand, but I mentally restrain its power. I do not want an errant bolt of lightning to harm the little one.

"You're Averil's sister," I say quietly. "Even without the crown and corset, I can see it. The same sweetness is in your face."

She lifts her chin. "I am Ylaine."

"Well met, Ylaine. And where is your mate?"

"He was injured trying to keep you out of the city. Monster."

She throws the last word like a dart. It pierces me, destroying the twinge of compassion I felt for her.

302

"Yes," I murmur. "Yes, your father has taught you that I am a monster. Perhaps he is right. But if I am wicked, so is he." I give her a broad smile. "And either way, I am the monster who fucked your sister."

"Averil is a little bitch," the other princess bursts out. "I can believe that she asked for it, wanton wretch that she is. She has always been a devious, rebellious brat."

"Serra!" exclaims Ylaine. "Don't speak of Averil that way. She likes adventure and excitement, that's all. Sometimes it leads her into dark places—"

"Dark places?" I raise my voice, cutting her off and turning toward the assembled crowd of merfolk. "I'll use those words, Princess, if I may. Let us speak, friends, of dark places. I would have you hear the truth of your king's ascension to power—a truth he has tried to erase. A story stained with innocent blood."

I pause with a sigh and send a blast of power toward a group of soldiers trying to sneak up behind me, and a few more attempting to descend on me from above. The shockwaves send them careening into the deep or crashing into the palace walls.

"Make no more attempts on my life," I say. "They will come to nothing, and will only cause you pain. I am not here for a slaughter, only to make the truth known and take back the crown. Let me rephrase that—I am here to kill *one* person. Tarion, son of Annessin and Rochtar, my one-time friend and advisor. If he refuses to confess before you today, I will kill him. And the rest of you will bow to your true king."

39

AVERIL

A voiceless scream builds in my throat as Prince Kerrin
douses my body with another potion from Lord Brixeus's
collection. My belly caves in with every agonized breath, and my
skin sizzles from the harsh magic.

I'm hanging naked by the wrists in the palace's torture
room, my body filmed with sweat and my toes barely touching
the floor. Lord Brixeus lies unconscious and bloodied on a table
several paces away. It looks as if he resisted a while, but
eventually they wore him down. He read aloud all the pages I
wrote, and he must have told Kerrin and Cass about the potions
and charms that could break Zoltan's spell. They seem
determined to return me to mermaid form.

"Why isn't it working?" Kerrin says petulantly. "Three
potions and she's still human. Maybe this is all an elaborate ruse.
If someone is trying to make a fool out of me—"

"Patience, darling," says Cass. "The potions were meant to
break powerful spells. Let's try one of these charms—they're

designed to undo magical transfigurations." She picks up a strange-looking amulet and loops its chain over my head.

The instant the pendant contacts my skin, spokes of white-hot pain stab through my chest. It feels as if they're incinerating my heart. Tears pour from my eyes, and my mouth opens in a silent shriek.

"It's a very powerful spell. Let's add another." Cass drops a second pendant around my neck.

The agony redoubles. This is worse than the anemones, worse than my change into a human. I will die from this. I'm glossy with sweat, writhing, my shoulders screaming from holding my weight. My body jerks involuntarily, a ripple of magic rolling through me from head to toes.

"It's a pity she can't scream." Cass tilts her head. "I do love a screamer."

"I'm getting so hard," says Prince Kerrin, staring at me.

Cass reaches over, rubbing the front of his pants lightly. "We've sent the guards away. Indulge yourself, my love."

"I'm going to come all over her," he murmurs, pulling Cass in for a hard kiss. "Watch me, won't you?"

"Gods," she moans, squeezing her thighs together. "You are so wicked. It makes me so wet."

But before Kerrin can take things any further, a searing surge of magic convulses my body. My thighs and legs pull together, seamed to each other. My leg bones begin to thin, to snap, to melt away. I can feel my flesh thickening. Gashes split open along my neck—my gills returning.

The pain is excruciating. My teeth grind together so hard I'm afraid they will crack, and my eyeballs roll up until they ache.

Just when I think my skull will crack open and my eyes burst, the pain begins to ease. I'm shaking, dripping with sweat, yet I'm not sweating anymore. I can sense my gills, sealed shut for now, but ready to take over my breathing once I'm back in the water. Iridescent scales sheathe my lower half. Where my feet were, a fin spreads out, wide and translucent.

"Shit," says Prince Kerrin, wide-eyed. "It's all true. She's a mermaid."

My natural body feels both strange and familiar at once. I'm glad of it, and terrified as well, because now I'm more helpless than ever—I can't run away from Kerrin and his horrible lover. Such a pair they are, smiling and charming everyone, while they secretly revel in the pain of others. I have never hated anyone like I hate the two of them.

"That's done, then." Cass taps her chin thoughtfully.

"Now I want the trident," Kerrin says. "How can we get it?"

"The Sea Witch she speaks of in there." Cass jerks her head toward the papers I wrote, scattered on a nearby table. "She obviously loves him. Perhaps he returns the feeling. She makes it sound as if he betrayed her, used her, but if you read between the lines, and put that together with what Brixeus said—"

"You think he would come for her?"

"He has to return her voice, doesn't he? It sounds as if he takes his deals seriously. Honors them, whether he wants to or not." She purses her lips. "I'd like to see this powerful brute of a sorcerer."

Kerrin's face darkens, but Cass appears not to notice. "Here's what we'll do. You know the Deathlock, that arch of rock that comes off the cliff north of here? The one in Mariner's Cove?"

"With the deep pool below?" The prince raises an eyebrow. "Of course I know it. I've been shark-hunting there."

"That's where we'll do it. We'll hang her from the arch, chum the water, and lower her down. The Witch will come to save her, and then we'll bargain with him. The girl for the trident."

"Why in fuck's name would he give up the trident for *her*?" Kerrin shoots me a disdainful glance.

"For love," Cass says sharply. "Wouldn't you give it up for me, if you had it?"

"Why, of course, darling," the prince croons. "And you'd do the same for me."

"Of course, my king."

Neither one looks the other in the eye while they say it, and I almost smile. Selfish, power-hungry people, both of them. They deserve each other.

"Let's make preparations then," says the prince, moving toward the door. "We can skip the trial—I am the acting king after all, so I can dispense with that tedious business and move right to the execution. I want a big spectacle, mind you. A crowd gathered to witness the demise of my father's assassin. Lots of fanfare and food. Plenty of wine."

"We need a plan if the Sea Witch refuses the deal," Cass adds, but I can't hear anything else because they've left the room.

I prop my long tail against the floor, using its strength to take some of the strain off my shoulders. The sweat is drying rapidly on my skin, which is just as soft but more resilient than a human's—more resilient in water, that is. In the air, I will dry out quickly and begin to desiccate.

Those two fools were so focused on their scheme that they forgot to consider the nature of their bargaining chip. Unless I get saltwater soon, I'll be dead.

40

THE SEA WITCH

Tarion's confession is long and difficult to extract. I have to tighten my tentacles warningly several times when he tries to portray events in a light other than the absolute truth. Although truth, I suppose, is subjective, and memory can fail.

Still, he manages to tell it all, more or less as I would have wished. His words bring back memories, shards of glass long embedded in my heart, shifting while he recounts the tale, blood seeping from wounds I'd thought healed. And there's a fresh wound, for he admits the thing I suspected—that Prella did not welcome his desire, and that he acted on it anyway.

He speaks in a cold, detached tone, as if he's telling someone else's story. Perhaps he feels that he is.

At the end, he says, "For all that I have done, I have begged and received the forgiveness of the gods, and especially the clemency of our treasured Mother Goddess, Lady of the Ocean. I am guiltless, purged of the past and worthy to lead you. And I have led you well, my children, have I not?"

The crowd of merfolk begin to mumble to each other, but I can't discern their words. In this case, I'd prefer air. Much easier for sound to pass through.

But one gray-haired mermaid's voice resounds above the others. "What of the reckoning you performed? The priestesses sacrificed my daughter and two others to find your precious little princess!"

"And the sacrifice worked," says a priestess, her voice tremulous. "The gods revealed the location of the princess. They arranged the meeting of the King's soldiers with this human Brixeus. Rest assured that your daughter walks with the gods on the paths of the wind—"

The gray-haired mermaid shrieks, baring her teeth, and charges toward the priestess. A few merfolk catch her and hold her back.

But her anger has incited more unrest among the crowd. Like all leaders, Tarion has enemies, and they begin to make themselves heard with shouts and protests. I recognize some faces—older merfolk who lived under my rule. When they backed him decades ago, they had no idea what he would become, or the changes he would make to the mer way of life.

Not that I care about their regrets or their unhappiness. I was not a perfect leader myself, and I don't intend to take up the responsibility again. Since I was deposed, I've had a clearer perspective on politics, and it sickens me.

I should be savoring this, drinking in every angry shout of the onlookers with vengeful delight. I should be smiling as they turn on Tarion, like they once turned on me. I should be savoring every savage hiss and sorrowful whimper from his daughters. More of the princesses have gathered now, along with their mates. The oldest princess, Serra, looks as if she wants to slice off each one of my tentacles and make me watch while she eats them. Ylaine is swishing her tail, rocking herself and the baby, her eyes sealed and her face a mask of sadness.

The crowd grows louder, restless and uncertain. It's time for me to act.

"Tarion, I take back my crown, and my rightful inheritance." My voice rolls through the water, loud enough for every ear to hear. With one of the three sharp points of my trident, I cut the braided locks that bind the crown to my enemy's head. My tentacles seize the crown and place it on my own head, while my hair winds around it, securing it at my direction.

"And I take back my magic." With the trident in one hand, I press my other palm to Tarion's chest. I can feel it inside him— the bit of water magic he was able to siphon from the trident before I activated the locking spell. It's *my* magic, and it rushes to me, flowing out of him into my body. Tarion's back arches, and I vent a low rumble of satisfaction as the magic returns home. This time I will hold it within myself, and not entrust it to anyone or anything else.

"You are no longer King under the sea," I tell Tarion. "For the kidnapping, rape, and murder of Prella, sister to King Perindal, as well as the sacrifice of three innocent merfolk and the exile of countless more, I commit you to death."

"What?" Tarion gasps. "You said if I confessed—"

I give him a mirthless grin. "I lied."

Serra darts forward, knives flashing in her hands, but I'm ready for her. Two of my tentacles catch her wrists and then rise, carrying her high above everyone else.

She hangs there, shrieking, while the priestesses cover their ears in horror at the curses that spill from her mouth. Like most religious rulers, the priestesses are useless in a crisis. They cannot defend Tarion's right to rule, not after the confession of his sins from his own lips. Not when the gray-haired mermaid is still wailing for her dead daughter.

"It looks as if your priestesses are not so certain the Goddess has forgiven you," I murmur to Tarion. "I certainly have not."

My tentacles cinch around Serra's wrists until she cries out and releases her knives, which twirl slowly downward through the water.

Carefully I deliver her into the cluster of princesses. "Hold your sister back," I warn them. "Next time she attacks I will not be merciful. I promised Averil I would spare everyone except your father, and I wish to keep that promise."

Why does my voice falter over her name? My stomach twists and sickens at the thought of her in peril, in the hands of the merciless prince, with her secrets laid bare to him.

I need to go to her. But I must finish this first, then find her voice.

I will kill Tarion, and then I will go to her. I can see to the creation of the new government later.

Looping more tentacles around Tarion, I lift him high.

"Witness the justice of Zoltan, Witch-King under the sea," I roar. My gaze sweeps the crowd—their eyes are wide, tails flicking. They lean forward, eager to see the death of the one who has ruled them for years.

The princesses wail louder, long ghostly howls of impending grief. No tears under the sea, only voices.

Rising on my tentacles, I grip my trident in both hands and prepare to run it through Tarion's stomach.

But first, I look into his eyes.

A mistake.

Because though I've never seen him in Averil, I can see *her* in his features. The slant of the cheekbones. The angle of the brows. The blue of his eyes, almost the same as hers—just a shade darker.

I imagine her seeing him dead, clutching his body, weeping. I remember how broken she looked beside the tub, after I told her what he did. What *I* have done.

Cruel wretch that I am, I left her to bear that pain alone.

I could kill my one-time friend, the man who betrayed me, my worst enemy.

But Averil's father? I can't do it.

I'm frozen, my teeth clenched so hard that pain shoots through my jaw. I shake my head and refresh my grip on the trident.

I *must* do this. Justice, and revenge.

I hate that I can't do it.

A gentle hand on my arm, and my head whips aside with a snarl.

It's Ylaine, Averil's sister, still holding her child—a baby mermaid with enormous green eyes, a tiny mouth, and a froth of orange hair that waves gently in the water. She is the most adorable infant I have ever seen.

"Ylaine, you fool," screeches Serra. Her sisters are gripping her arms as she tries to lunge forward. "Get away from the monster."

Ylaine ignores her. She looks only at me, her eyes soft. "You don't have to kill him. You've already won."

My voice grates out through my tight throat. "She wouldn't want me to do this."

"She?" Ylaine frowns slightly, and then her eyes widen. "You mean Averil."

"Yes."

"You can imprison him instead of killing him," Ylaine suggests. "You have your trident, and the kingdom. You can do anything you want."

"My trident, and the kingdom," I repeat. "But what I want is—"

What I want is the sweet, fiery mermaid who bargained with me for legs. I want *her*, determined and passionate, clever and curious. I want her body, her heart, her mind. I want to fuck her and worship her. I want to laugh with her, and dance with her. I want to leave my lair behind and go with her anywhere she wants to travel, until we have exhausted all the beauties and knowledge of the entire world.

Understanding brightens in Ylaine's eyes. "You want Averil."

"I must go to her. Now. The human prince—he may harm her."

"Go then," she says.

A flood of purpose galvanizes my body, heats my blood. I drop Tarion and order, "Guards, restrain him. Put him in the darkest cell of the palace prisons. I have something to do. But I am still your King, and when I return, I expect to be welcomed and honored, or my next invasion of your city will be far more catastrophic." Impulsively I add, "Princess Ylaine is in charge in my absence."

I wait until the former king is in chains, and then I explode upward in a tempest of purple lightning, tentacles, and whirling water. The noise of the crowd is part fear, part awe—it fades rapidly as I streak through the waves, making for my ruined lair at top speed, buoyed by all the magical power I can summon. Everything I encounter, I blast aside with a pulse from the trident.

I will not berate myself for my weakness in sparing Tarion. His reign is done. I have given the people the chance they needed to free themselves.

And if he becomes a problem, I can always kill him later.

313

I need to find Averil's voice and get to her as fast as possible. Nothing else matters. Nothing. The very throb of my heart seems to echo her name. My nerves vibrate with anxiety; every fiber of my body urges me to find her, go to her.

Find her.

Go to her.

41

AVERIL

Once again I'm hanging by my wrists, and I hate it. At least this time there is a rope around my middle, too, and it takes a little of the weight. Still, my shoulders hurt, and so does my ribcage. I can't cry in mermaid form. Nor can I scream, so there's no relief, no way to vent a little of the agony. All I can do is squirm and twitch my long tail.

Brixeus is hanging beside me. He regained consciousness shortly after Kerrin and Cass left the torture room, and when he saw me panting, fading, drying out, he yelled until the guards came. He insisted they immerse me in saltwater.

Thanks to him, I survived. But as punishment for his outburst, Cass cut out his tongue.

If she was afraid he would talk to the guards and spill secrets, she could have gagged him. But no—she had to be immeasurably cruel.

The former equerry's mouth is stained with dried blood, and two of his fingers look broken. I can hardly bear the sight of him in so much pain.

Neither of us have been allowed the dignity of clothing, but my long hair hangs over my breasts, covering most of them. Not that I care about nudity at this point. I care more about the bloodied surf below me, and the triangular fins slicing through the pink foam. Sharks circling, waiting to devour Brixeus and me.

But in spite of my terror and my pain, when the fresh wind rushes through the rocky arch, I lift my face to it and close my eyes. It carries the scent of home, the fragrance of both saltgrass and seaweed, of dark depths and rocky shores. Land and sea, blended.

Gulls dip and cry overhead. A few crows sail among them, too. They can sense our impending demise, and they hope to snatch a few bits of our flesh.

This is how it ends, then. My body shredded by sharks, my blood filtering through the waves, my bones settling to the bottom of the blue pool.

Because I can't imagine the Sea Witch coming to save me. He's busy with his new kingdom.

Yes, he promised to return my voice, but he can likely do that from a distance. His bargain fulfilled, he will go back to the future he has worked so hard to achieve. He'll be King under the sea, shaping our people to his will, like my father did.

I wonder if he'll think of me sometimes. There was a glorious intensity to his kisses, so much tender passion in the way he touched me, held me, danced with me. What if maybe... maybe...

It's too much to hope for, and yet I hope, as I hang by my arms, high above the swirling sharks.

Maybe he will come.

But he wouldn't give up the trident for me. It's the one thing he's been wanting for decades.

Prince Kerrin has emptied the town for this occasion. Everyone from Crystal Point is here, clustered along the strip of beach down below, or standing along the windblown ledges of the bluffs. Mariner's Cove is like the arena in the royal city under the sea, where we have public gatherings or celebrations. Citizens cluster in rows along the perimeter of the half-circle, waiting to be astonished or entertained.

The arch of rock where I'm hanging joins with the cliffside to my left. There's a wide ledge nearby—perhaps as far from me as the height of a very tall man, like the Sea Witch. On that wide ledge stands the prince, with a few nobles, guards, and a servant or two.

Heavy clusters of cloud hang in the blue sky, and the bright sun lances between them, bathing Prince Kerrin with its light as if the gods themselves are blessing him. His raven hair gleams, his crown sparkles, and the white suit he's wearing shines until I can barely look at it. Perhaps that was his intention—to look like an untouchable, radiant young god.

The ropes around my wrists and body are secured to a horizontal pole, which hangs from a thicker rope that runs through a pulley bolted to the rocky arch above me. The pulley looks weathered, which tells me that someone—Kerrin or his father—has done this to prisoners before. Brixeus is hanging from an identical rig.

Behind Kerrin, a pair of burly guards hold two taut ropes— one connected to me and the other to Brixeus. They can lower us slowly, or let go altogether so we fall straight into the pool three stories below.

I'm not sure where Cassilenne is. Perhaps she's in charge of the backup plan they've made, in case the Sea Witch arrives but refuses to yield the trident.

There is no universe in which he would give up the trident for me.

Kerrin lifts both arms, and the crowd quiets as he begins to speak.

"Gentlefolk, loyal citizens, you have come here today to witness a terrible wonder. You have heard tales of the creatures beneath the sea—those which are half human, half fish. They have not been seen in decades, so perhaps some of you doubted their existence." He sweeps a hand toward me, his fingers flashing with rings. "Behold, the daughter of Tarion, King under the sea."

Gasps hiss from the crowd, mingled with astonished swears and murmurs.

"Beautiful, isn't she? Some of you may know her as the silent yet lovely noblewoman I had chosen as my bride. I found her on the beach, helpless and injured, and I assumed she had lost everything in the storm that nearly took my own life. I thought her sweet, kind, and altogether wonderful. I—gods help me—I fell for her." He splays a hand over his chest. "What can I say? I have a generous and loving heart. And truth be told, my passion for her muddled my senses, stole my logic. Rest assured, I will never again allow a woman to mar my good judgment. Forgive me, my people."

The prince bows his head, while the gathered citizens murmur their understanding and sympathy.

"She was sent from below to kill my father!" screams the prince, so suddenly that I startle in my bonds. He's pointing at me, every muscle in his body rigid with rage. His eyes are bright with furious tears. A vein pulses along his temple. "She crept into his room one night and forced him to drink the poison that killed him. She and her people were the orchestrators of my beloved father's death. And Lord Brixeus was the girl's accomplice—a traitor to humanity."

The voices in the audience swell as one, growls of anger merging with wails of pity and horror.

"Will we let this stand?" cries the prince. "Will we allow the slithering monsters of the deep to reach up from their foul murk and claw at the foundation of our kingdom? Will we let them get away with murdering my father, your good and venerable king?"

"No!" bellow the people.

"No," says Kerrin, panting, eyes flaming. "No, we will call this what it is—an act of war. And we will treat this princess, this foul assassin, as a prisoner of war. We will judge her according to her crime. She broke my heart—" his voice cracks, and he pauses, bowing his head, pinching the bridge of his nose.

He's a consummate actor, I'll give him that.

"She betrayed me, her devoted lover," resumes Kerrin after a moment, his voice thick with feigned emotion. "She probably would have killed me in our marriage bed. And my own equerry—that he would join with her, turn against his own people, after all my family has done for him—it is unforgivable."

Another roar from the crowd—more menacing this time, strident with a growing lust for vengeance against me and Lord Brixeus.

"Justice," Kerrin says, slowly and heavily. "Justice for my father. That is why we are here today. To enact justice, and to send a message to the dark denizens of the sea. Treachery will be met with nobility. Violence will be answered with decisive punishment. And murder—" he looks back at me, meets my gaze. There's glee in his eyes, triumph on his beautiful face. "Murder will be repaid with justice."

I narrow my eyes at him, wishing I could speak what's on my mind. I doubt he came up with that speech himself. I'd bet my crown Cass wrote it for him.

"Chum the water again," says the prince to the guards holding the ropes. "And begin lowering her, slowly." His voice drops, his eyes still locked on me. "We'll see whether or not her

Witch will come to save her. Frankly, I doubt he considers her worth the trouble."

The pulley groans, and my body drops suddenly. My stomach thrills, horror skating along my nerves. But it was a short drop, and the guard holding my rope lowers me slowly after that—painfully slowly, hair by hair, it seems. I rather wish he'd hurry and get it over with.

I've been hanging here a while already, and my skin is becoming parched. I can almost feel it crinkling like paper, ready to burst into flame at any moment. The pain in my shoulders and ribs is almost too much to bear.

The Sea Witch won't come. How would he even know where I am and what's happening to me?

In this form my eyes are more sensitive to light. I can't handle any more pain, so I have to close them. The hot sun presses on my eyelids like burning, insistent fingers.

I wish I could faint. Then I wouldn't have to be conscious for this.

I wish I could speak to Lord Brixeus, and thank him, and tell him how sorry I am that he's here because of me.

I wish I could see the Witch again. I picture him, swirling dark hair and eyes of indigo and violet, heavy brows, huge tattooed forearms, that fiercely handsome face, the sensual mouth that pulls into a smile so often when he's with me. I love how he tries not to smile, and then it breaks out anyway. I love the impetuous way he kisses me, like he can't help himself. As if I possess some powerful magic, some mystical force he cannot resist.

A startled, excited murmur from the crowd, voices rising with panic and anticipation.

I open my eyes a sliver.

A wave is approaching the wide mouth of the cove—a strangely even wave, a long roll of water precisely the same height from one side to the other. Another swell of water rises behind it, and a third billow, higher still. None of the waves crest or break; they approach steadily, purposefully.

It's unnatural.

It's magic.

My heart was already pounding with fear, but it kicks into a new, more joyously violent rhythm.

It's him. My terrible, beautiful Witch.

All three waves roll into the cove, surging higher as they approach the bluffs and the cliffside. They're mounting one atop another, piling into an enormous, destructive wall of water that could wash every citizen off the ledges and into the shark-infested sea.

"Your Highness," says a nobleman, in a high, nervous tone.

"Give me the girl's rope," snaps Prince Kerrin.

The guard hands it over. Kerrin lets me drop a little more.

"Halt!" he roars toward the mounting wave. "No more magic, or she falls to the sharks!"

For a moment, I don't think the Sea Witch hears him. How could he? He's somewhere below, buried beneath all that water.

But then the waves recede, slowly smoothing themselves out, rolling back toward the sea, away from the coast and the cliffside.

One moderate swell remains, a hill of glimmering water in the center of Mariner's Cove. The Sea Witch rises from it, his broad torso glowing bronze in the sunlight, glittering with drops. His tentacles writhe, frothing the surf around him. On his chest, nestled between those powerful pectorals, is the golden shell necklace containing my voice.

The people on the bluffs and the beach retreat, clutching at each other. A few of them scream.

In his gloved right hand, Zoltan holds the golden trident. The tips of its tines look sharp enough to slit the air and make it bleed. A purple glow flickers along it intermittently.

Odd that the Witch is wearing a glove. Perhaps he needs to grow used to the trident again before he can manage it barehanded.

"Prince Kerrin," he says, in that night-deep voice of his. "Quite the spectacle you have here."

"This mermaid is a murderess. An assassin of the deep. By killing my father, she has incited war between our people."

"Yes, I heard of your father's death, just a short while ago. Very suspicious, that. You return from your travels, and suddenly he dies? How convenient for you."

"I will not permit such painful and untrue insinuations," says the prince. "This girl poisoned him. There are witnesses, and proof of the act."

"Perhaps she was forced or manipulated into doing so," says the Witch.

"Enough!" Kerrin bellows, and he lets me drop a little more. "The girl also stole *that* from the royal treasury." He points to the trident. "My father took it from the people under the sea, so that your kind would not have the power to destroy us. If you want the girl, you must give me the trident. The security of my kingdom is my first priority."

"Power is your first priority," says the Sea Witch coolly. "You ask too much. If you've learned the trident's history, you must know that I went to great lengths to obtain it. I sent Averil to fetch it, true. But she did not know what she was taking, or the power that lay within it. She's been nothing but a pawn for both of us, I suspect. A little fool swayed by the commands of powerful men."

Anger pierces my heart and I seethe silently as I hang there. I stare hard at Zoltan, willing him to look at me, but he doesn't.

"If the price is too great, go back to the deep. Or stay, and watch her die." Kerrin begins lowering me. "Lower Brixeus too," he says over his shoulder to the guard. "Faster. Let him feed the sharks first, and show this Witch of the Deep what is going to happen to the little mermaid."

As Brixeus is lowered past me, I try with all my might to scream. I want to shriek the truth, to beg for mercy, to plead with Zoltan to do something. But all I can do is open my mouth, the cords of my neck straining with desperate silence.

He could return my voice right now. Why doesn't he?

The pulley screeches, and I drop lower. Brixeus is far past me now, approaching the water at a terrifying rate. Below his bare, dangling feet circle the sharp fins of hungry sharks, churning the bloody surf, angry that when they came expecting a meal, they only found bits of chum.

"Precious moments are passing, Witch," taunts the prince. "Brixeus will die in a few moments. I know you care nothing for him, but his death will be a vivid picture of what awaits the girl."

Lord Brixeus makes not a single sound. His bloodstained mouth is shut tight, his face as stern and noble as ever, even as his feet come within an arm's length of the churning water.

"Stop!" The word explodes from the Sea Witch. "Spare them both, and I'll give you the trident."

"Both of them? You want me to spare both the traitors?" Prince Kerrin sweeps his gaze over the stunned crowed. "Should I let the traitors go? In exchange for the power to control the sea itself?"

A smattering of conflicted answers rises from the crowd.

"Pull Brixeus back up," growls the Sea Witch, lifting his trident. "Or you die where you stand."

"Do not forget that I hold the mermaid's rope," snaps Kerrin. "Harm me, and I'll drop her immediately. No magic of yours can save her once she plunges into that water. In fact, it seems you're a little too close to the hungry sharks yourself."

One of the dark shapes has broken off from the others and is heading for the Sea Witch, its fin slicing the surface. My breath quickens with terror. But he's powerful now. Surely he can defend himself.

The Sea Witch sends a burst of water at the shark, pushing it away. "I do not fear these creatures anymore, nor do I fear you. Now pull Brixeus up, and bring him and Averil safely back to land. Then I will give you the trident."

Joy races through my body, from head to tail.

He would give up all that power, his rightful possession, the thing he's been wanting for decades—he'd yield it, just to save my life.

It's beautiful, tragic, unbelievable. Fresh tears pool in my eyes.

But Zoltan can't give the prince the trident. That much power in his hands would be disastrous. I can't even imagine the kind of terror and trauma someone like Kerrin could wreak with a weapon of such potent magic.

I can't speak. I can't tell Zoltan that he needs to leave with the trident and let me die.

Why doesn't the idiot give me back my *voice*?

Prince Kerrin lets me fall a bit more. The guard behind him stirs, shifting forward a step.

"I'm not a fool," Kerrin says. "The moment I let them go, you'll attack me with magic. No, you'll come here and toss the trident to me, and then I'll let them go."

"Not 'let them go,'" clarifies the Sea Witch. "You'll bring them back safely to land, and then they are free to leave unmolested. Be warned, a deal with me is not easily broken."

Kerrin scoffs, but he says, "Very well. They will be brought back and allowed to leave safely. Satisfied?"

"We have a deal," says the Sea Witch.

He rises on a column of water and moves toward the cliffside. He seems a little unsteady in his control of the water that's carrying him along. Perhaps his emotions affect his magic? Or maybe he's still acclimating to having all his powers back.

"Hold this," clips the prince, handing my rope back to the guard who had it earlier. "And you there—pull the equerry up."

Brixeus is hauled out of harm's way, and the other guard pulls me up as well, his muscled arms bulging as he works the rope.

"He's wearing a glove to hold that trident thing," Kerrin mutters. "Lord Thespin, hand me your gloves."

The noble passes them over, and Kerrin pulls them on.

I wish they would hurry up with the exchange. My skin is so dry and tight it feels as if it might split apart. I think I feel a few small cracks opening along my stretched torso, near the rope that encircles my waist. Looking at the delicious liquid beauty of the water is torture. I need to be in it. I have to submerge myself entirely, breathe it in, soak myself in saltwater. *Please please hurry*, I beg in my mind.

Why doesn't Zoltan give me my voice back?

The Sea Witch rises higher, borne aloft on his shining column of water. He's lifting the trident. He's throwing it to the prince.

Prince Kerrin reaches out. Catches the trident in both gloved hands. Lighting snakes along its shaft, and he nearly drops it, but then he laughs aloud, gripping it more firmly.

"Mine," he says. "All your power is now mine."

No. No, this cannot happen. This is all wrong.

The Sea Witch backs away, the water beneath him sinking rapidly until he's at sea level again. Not entirely powerless, though—he still has a bit of control over water. What else can he do? I tally the abilities I know of in my mind—the spell for faster travel, illumination magic, a little control over water and wind, glamours—

"Honor our bargain," urges the Sea Witch. "Release my friends."

Friends. My heart sinks a little at the word.

Of course Brixeus is an old friend, and I'm a new one. I'm just the Sea Witch's ally in a scheme, his partner in some meaningless pleasure. Nothing more.

But he gave up the trident. He wouldn't do that for Brixeus. Would he? I'm almost sure he did it for me.

"Of course! I must release your friends." Prince Kerrin flashes one of his warm, charming, brilliant smiles. And I know what he's going to do the instant before he does it.

He whirls, and with the sharp tines of the trident, he slashes both ropes.

My severed rope whips free, charred and sizzling.

The pulley whines, circling rapidly as I drop, helpless and voiceless, toward the deadly pool below.

42

AVERIL

I'm falling—

A bluish-gray tentacle snakes down from above and whips around my waist, jerking me to a stop.

Another tentacle catches Lord Brixeus.

I'm being pulled up, up, toward the ledge where the prince stands gaping, trident in hand.

The burly guard who held my rope has transformed. He still looks like the guard, but his lower half has transformed into coiling tentacles.

I can't breathe.

I look down toward the far end of the pool, the area away from the sharks, where the Sea Witch swirls in the water, looking up, watching us—and the glamour slips away from him and it's not Zoltan at all. It's Graeme, gray-skinned and yellow-eyed, grinning triumphantly with all his pointed teeth.

The real Witch—my Witch—is poised on the ledge, holding me and Brixeus aloft while the other guards and nobles draw their swords and attack him. Carelessly he seizes each one with his tentacles and flings them off the ledge into the pool. He throws them far out, away from the sharks.

A smile breaks over my face. And he told me he wasn't merciful. My darling liar.

His glamour falls away, and my smile vanishes. The Sea Witch's handsome features are contorted with a rage so violent my whole body shudders. His blazing eyes are locked on Prince Kerrin, even as he pulls me and Brixeus onto the safety of the ledge.

"I'll be taking the trident back now," the Witch growls, his tentacles creeping along the ground toward Kerrin's boots. "Give it here."

"How—" gasps Kerrin, holding the trident defensively, tines toward the Witch. "How did you—you were there." He glances down at the water below. "But you're here—and—"

"Your father or Brixeus could have warned you about my glamours and told you how to dispel them," says the Sea Witch. "But you despise the wisdom of the previous generation. How unfortunate for you."

I'm lying on the grass now, pinned down by the weight of my sleek scaly tail. Brixeus is next to me, teeth clenched, eyes bright with pain—but alive.

My wrists are still bound together, but I can use my hands. A short sword lies in the grass, left behind by one of the men Zoltan threw from the cliff. It's nearly within reach, so I squirm over and grasp it. At my nod, Lord Brixeus holds up his hands, and I begin carefully cutting the rope that binds his wrists.

I have to be careful not to cut Lord Brixeus, so I can't watch what's happening between the prince and the Sea Witch. But I can hear the crackle of lightning, a hiss of pain from the Witch, curses from Kerrin.

"How does this fucking thing work?" the prince screeches. "Shit!"

"Such a broad and varied vocabulary you have," Zoltan says dryly. "Did your father teach you nothing of merfolk and magic?"

"Not much," snarls the prince.

"Perhaps he realized that the more you knew about sources of power, the more dangerous you would become," says Zoltan. "You are neither intelligent nor persistent. You grasp at each new shiny thing, destructively, foolishly, selfishly."

My sword severs the rope, and Brixeus shakes off the pieces. He takes the short blade from me, but two of his fingers are badly damaged. His progress cutting through my ropes is slow.

I risk a glance behind me. Zoltan's back is to me, his muscled torso clad in the guard's coat, his thick tentacles holding him up like legs. Beyond him is Prince Kerrin, standing at the narrowest part of the ledge, where there's a path sloping down to another shelf on the cliffside. Soldiers have clustered there, but the path is only wide enough for one at a time, so they can only stand behind their prince—they can't move around him to attack Zoltan.

Movement above me catches my eye. Along the bluffs and on the clifftop, figures appear, dark against the bright sky. Some have longbows drawn, and others hold crossbows.

This, then, is the prince's secondary plan. If Zoltan hadn't yielded the trident, they would have killed him and taken it anyway.

I can't shout at the Witch and warn him. I can't run to him and alert him to the archers' presence. He seems entirely fixated on the prince and the trident.

"I don't want to kill you, princeling," says Zoltan. "Wait— yes, I do. I desperately want to kill you. But I'd rather not sully my tentacles with your blood. So hand me my property, and I'll be gone with my friends."

"What are you waiting for?" yells Kerrin toward the clifftop. "Shoot him!"

Bowstrings twang, and a hail of arrows arcs toward the Sea Witch. He lifts his hands, and wind stirs around him, catching some of the arrows and sending them off into midair. But he can't divert them all. One bolt lodges in the back of his shoulder, while another pierces his side.

My scream is soundless, but he voices a roar of pain. All his tentacles rush toward the prince, who slashes with the trident while more arrows fly.

My hands are free. I throw aside the ropes and lunge toward the Sea Witch. He's got the trident wrapped in two tentacles— he's pulling it away from the prince. Kerrin wrenches at the trident, but Zoltan is stronger. The trident itself is jerking, jumping, throwing off bolts of purple lightning that strike both of them, and judging from their bellows of pain and the smell of burnt flesh, it hurts.

I'm crawling toward them, propped up on both arms, pulling my stupid tail along, determined to help Zoltan somehow.

And then Prince Kerrin's frenzied eyes lock with mine.

"The girl!" he screams up at the archers. "Shoot the girl!"

Zoltan whirls, alarm flashing across his face.

The twang and whine of bowstrings.

The whistle of dozens of arrows.

The Sea Witch throws himself on top of me, his body braced over mine, his tentacles curling around to protect my head. I don't know if he even tries any wind magic.

I'm on my back, and we're face to face, panicked breath mingling.

He flinches, his muscles and tentacles jerking as the arrows strike him. His eyes close, teeth gritted and bared.

He let go of the trident to protect me.

He's slumping against me, a massive weight, heavy and sinking.

This isn't happening. No, no, no.

"Got him!" cries Prince Kerrin triumphantly.

Over the gigantic slumped shoulder of the Witch I can see the prince. His wretched, pretty face glows with triumph. He jabs Zoltan in the side with the trident, and Zoltan's body quivers, but he doesn't try to rise. A heavy groan rumbles through his chest, but there's a sickening gurgle in it.

Someone leans over the cliff's edge above us—someone with a crossbow and a long braid. "Best to be sure he is dead, my lord." Cassilenne's voice. "Perhaps you should push the monster over into the pool and let the sharks finish him."

"A good idea." Kerrin kicks at Zoltan's form. "By the gods, the beast is heavy."

I'm pinned beneath the Sea Witch, and as much as I want to claw Kerrin's eyes out, I can't get my arms free. I writhe, desperate, but Kerrin lays down the trident and gives the Witch a firm shove with both arms. Zoltan flips over the brink of the ledge and plummets out of sight, his tentacles sliding after him.

"There. That's done." Kerrin straightens and touches his crown, which has gone crooked. He reaches up to adjust it.

And I sink the trident deep into his belly.

Then, with a violent heave, I pitch him and myself over the edge.

A moment of bright, sun-soaked air. Stomach-dropping sensation, wind rushing past my face.

The trident pulls free of Kerrin's belly on the way down.

He's spraying blood, tumbling—

We crash into the sea together.

Blissful liquid, embracing, gurgling, comforting me.

Thank the gods, I'm saved… I'm home…

No, not yet.

I have to save Zoltan.

He's floating unconscious in the depths, his hair an inky cloud and his tentacles listless, inanimate. His guard's coat is shredded, peeling away, and his body leaks blood from so many wounds. I want to cry an ocean of tears for him.

The sharks had started to lose interest, but with the scent of fresh blood in the water, they're coming back, dead eyes surveying my Witch. One of them takes a bite out of a tentacle and I shoot forward, teeth bared, slashing at it with the trident. The weapon is burning my hands, but it also stabs the shark with a jagged blast of lightning.

More sharks sail past, some calmly surveying the situation, others whipping by in a frenzy. I spin and strike, jabbing at them, trying to keep them away from Zoltan, but I can't protect all sides of him, all the tentacles—

Suddenly Graeme is there on my left, his eel's tail ribboning behind him, his body flashing with electric light, his pointed teeth snapping. Several sharks change the angle of their approach and swim away, apparently deeming him more trouble than they want to deal with.

Then Ekkon glides in from the right. The orb dangling from his forehead fascinates two of the sharks and they hover near him, blank eyes staring a few moments before they turn and wander off.

Liris comes up from below, his poisonous spines fanned out, grazing a few of the sharks. The rest of them swerve away, disappearing into the blue.

Liris turns to me. "We have to get him out of here and get him conscious so he can heal himself."

"He needs supplies for that." Ekkon's voice is fragile, distant.

The trident isn't scorching my hands anymore, or shooting lightning. It's humming against my palms, a vibration that feels intimate, almost musical. It sounds like wind over waves, like the murmur of distant thunder, like the fall of rain, or the whisper of fins through the stillness of the deep.

It sounds like the sea, and I am a princess of the sea. It's almost as if the trident has recognized me in a way it refused to recognize Kerrin. It quiets in my presence, thrumming with suppressed power.

I swim closer to Zoltan, wrapping one arm around his body, and I press the trident flat against his chest. I have a strange instinct that perhaps its nearness will help him. He has put some of himself into it. Maybe part of that energy can flow back into him. Anything to help him survive this.

I can't speak, but I press my whole self against him, with the trident pinned between us. And I touch my mouth to his motionless lips.

"The human prince is dying," says Ekkon's faint voice. "Would you like him taken ashore, princess?"

I shake my head. Let the sea have him, as it was supposed to on the night when his ship sank. He would have died without my help, and now he dies at my hand.

I turn my head aside for one last look at Kerrin—crisp beautiful features, panicked eyes turning glassy as the last few bubbles leak from his mouth, as the blood threads from his body, dissipating into the water.

I'm glad the last thing he'll see is me, clasping Zoltan close to my heart.

Perhaps I should feel pity, or guilt, or a mild sorrow. But Prince Kerrin has killed all the soft things I felt for him at the beginning. I feel nothing for him at all, except the satisfaction that he will never be able to hurt anyone else.

His body spasms one last time, and he's gone.

I turn back to the Sea Witch, my pulse thin and frantic. I'm not sure my Witch can survive so many injuries. I need to tell him what he means to me.

Desperately I glance at Graeme. He's wearing the shell necklace with my voice, and I point to it.

"I'm sorry," he says, shaking his head. "I don't know how to free your voice. I don't really have magic—Zoltan only gave me a temporary fragment of water magic so I could fool the prince. Only Zoltan can return your voice."

Damn it.

Wake up, fool. I press my mouth to the Sea Witch's lips again, thinking all the words I want to say. *Don't die. You haven't come this far just to perish at the hands of some puny humans. Come on, wake up! You have to heal yourself, you have to—*

Hysteria rises in my throat, and I crush myself and the trident harder against him—one hand locked around the trident and the other clasping the back of his neck. I can't feel a heartbeat, and his chest doesn't move. He's not breathing.

You bastard. Wake up, wake up! Don't do this, please, please.

The trident jerks, sizzling and sparking in the water. Ekkon's transparent fingers seize my arm, yanking me back, away from the intermittent forked lightning shooting from the weapon. Some of it catches Zoltan in the chest and I startle, cringing against Ekkon. I can feel the heated static of the lightning through the liquid around us.

But the lightning isn't harming the Witch. It's shifting, melting, enveloping him in a purple glow. That glow seems to soak into his torso and tentacles, right through his skin, until it's gone.

And Zoltan opens his eyes.

43

My eyes fly open.

I'm in the blue deep, weak rays of yellow sunlight shining through water like arrows.

I'm not entirely healed. But I am sustained somehow. There's a new energy inside my body, keeping me alert, maintaining my damaged organs. I'm not sure how long it will last.

The trident floats in front of me, though it should be sinking. It is a strange weapon indeed—it seems to have assumed a latent sentience of its own—a protective instinct where I'm concerned. I'm not unhappy about it.

Reaching out, I seize it.

And then I see her. Blood-red hair unfurled through the water. Her slender body, bare to the waist. The dark, shimmering scales of her long, sinuous tail. Her blue eyes, wide with shock and relief and—anger? She looks very, very angry.

Ekkon is behind her, flanked by Graeme and Liris. And to my right, drifting slowly to the bottom of the deep pool, is the inanimate body of Prince Kerrin.

Averil seizes the shell pendant floating in front of Graeme's chest, and she jabs a finger at me.

"All right, love." My voice is thicker than usual, and my lungs suck oddly around the arrows still lodged in my back. "A deal is a deal."

The spell I placed on the necklace keeps the chain from floating over the head of the wearer, a preventative measure so it does not drift away underwater. But the chain yields to Graeme's touch when he removes it, and I take it from his hand.

The moment my fingers close around it, I give the order for Averil's voice to return, permanently this time. Our bargain fulfilled. Our connection closed.

The threads of her voice slip out of the pendant, traveling back to her. The gold fades from the shell, and the chain becomes simple twine once again. I let both fall from my hand, and they drift away in the water.

"You were supposed to call if you were in trouble," I say. "Where is your necklace?"

Her voice settles into her throat, and she snaps, "Is that really your first question after coming back from the dead?"

"I'm not back yet," I say heavily, pressing a palm to my chest. "I need to heal myself, and soon."

"Shit." Alarm flares in her gaze. "What do you need?"

"I have some supplies in my rented room near town. Again, what happened to your necklace? And who broke my transformation spell?" I frown, surveying her form. "How did the trident and the prince end up down here?"

"So many questions."

"A taste of your own medicine."

She fixes me with a steely look. "I lost the necklace while I was fighting some guards. After Kerrin pushed you off the cliff, I grabbed the trident and ran him through, and then I jumped in after you. I thought you might need the trident, and it was still stuck in Kerrin, so he had to come along."

My blood heats, and joy spirals through the haze of pain in my body.

She killed the prince and then leaped into shark-infested waters after me, bringing my trident along for good measure. My sweet, violent, clever darling.

She cares. In spite of everything I have done, she cares.

"As for my form," Averil continues, "Kerrin and Cass broke your spell using some charms Lord Brixeus had—oh gods— Brixeus!"

She shoots upward immediately, heading for the surface.

"Don't," Graeme calls. "The archers are still up there."

"He saved my life," Averil throws back. "I won't leave him to be executed."

Refreshing my grasp on the trident, I use its power to propel myself toward the surface as well. Pain tugs through my body, a festering ache in my muscles and organs. "Let me get him, Averil."

"You're wounded."

"I have magic. A good thing, or I'd be dead."

"Don't remind me." Her voice quakes, but she keeps swimming, refusing to look at me.

"Averil, stop!" With a pulse of power, I shoot up beside her and wrap my arm around her waist, pulling her down before she breaches the surface.

"You think I protected you so you could go up there and die?" I snarl. "I'm sustained by the trident right now, and I have its magic. I can go up and get Brixeus, as long as I know you're safe down here."

"What if they shoot you again and the energy from the trident isn't enough?" Her body is rigid, her voice keen with anxiety.

"Brixeus is all the way up on that ledge, love. How do you propose to get to him? You don't have legs."

She bares her teeth, growling her frustration. It's adorable, and also threatening enough that I release her and back away a little.

"Go and get him," she says at last. "But come back *alive*, do you understand?"

"Why do you care?" I hold her gaze. "I'm the monster who overthrew your father. And you haven't yet asked me what I did to him."

"It doesn't matter. If you had to—to kill him, because of what he did to Prella—I—I understand."

"You understand?" I choke on the words. "You *understand?* How can you say that? How can it not matter, Averil? You begged me to spare him!"

"Yes, yes, I did—and I don't want him dead, and I hope you spared him, but—and maybe this makes me a monster of the worst kind but—whether you killed him or not, it doesn't matter—"

"Why not?" I shout.

"Because I fucking love you!" she screams.

She holds my gaze, her whole face blazing defiant and beautiful amid the cloud of her scarlet hair.

From somewhere below us, Graeme says "shit" softly.

I gape at her, stunned. "You—you fucking love me."

"Get Brixeus," she hisses, her eyes shining. "Then you need to heal. And then we can talk."

339

44

I blast out of the sea like a conqueror, like a destroyer, riding the tallest wave I've ever conjured. More waves crash against the shoreline, drenching the humans who still cluster along the bluffs. They've been rabidly watching the pool for signs of death and mayhem. Vultures. They deserve a good drenching.

Arrows hail at me again, but this time I have no one else to protect. When Averil was in danger, my mind went blank—I couldn't think of a spell in time to save her, so I used my body, my tentacles. This time my mind doesn't stutter with terror. Instead I send long whips of water high, high above me, and I use them to sweep every archer off the clifftop. Some fall onto ledges, others into the sea.

Rising high on my column of water, I locate Brixeus. He's still on the ledge, and they've bound his arms behind his back, but no one is really watching him. The nobles are shouting over each other in a confused panic, while the guards stand uncertain, without their king to give orders.

With a couple of tentacles I pluck Brixeus off the ledge.

A terrified silence grips the crowd. Peasants, guards, merchants and nobles, they all stare at me, like a flock of dull-eyed birds robbed of their leader. It's laughable how they turn instinctively to the most powerful creature around, desiring to be commanded, to be led.

"The king is dead," I announce to the crowd. "Do with that what you will."

Then I sink back into the surf, carrying Brixeus with me.

Averil, Graeme, Liris, and Ekkon join me as I swim out of the cove, carrying Brixeus along. I'm careful to keep his head above water. "All right, old friend?" I call to him, but he doesn't answer.

"The apothik Cassilenne cut out his tongue," says Averil.

"Fuck." I will heal him as soon as I can. But first, I must heal myself.

We swim along the coastline until we're nearer to the boarding house where I rented a room. My lungs are laboring, and there's a deep warning ache inside my body. The energy the trident gave me won't last much longer.

As we halt in the shallows, Liris says, "Hold still for a moment, Zoltan. Let me pull those arrows out of your back."

"I barely feel them." My tentacles set Brixeus safely on the beach. Immediately he lies down in the sand with his eyes closed, breathing deeply.

Liris gives me a weary half-smile and shakes his head. "The arrows, Zoltan. It needs to be done."

"And I need to go back to the sea," murmurs Ekkon. He cringes from the sun, shrinking into the waves.

"Go on, then, my heart," Graeme says. "We'll join you soon."

Liris leans down and plucks a broken crossbow bolt from one of my tentacles. The flesh quivers with pain, and I snarl a little.

"Let's take your mind off it," says Averil. She's lying in the shallow surf, bare-breasted, her tail flicking little sprays of water. "How did you find us? How did you know Brixeus and I were being executed in the cove?"

I'm glad she didn't ask the deeper question—why did I abandon my conquest of her father's kingdom and come looking for her. I want to tell her, but not here. Later. When we're alone.

"When I left Tarion's palace, I took human form and went into town to ask about you," I say, grunting as Liris tugs an arrow out of my shoulder. "There were plenty of rumors floating around—servants and guards talk, whether above or below the waves—and I managed to extract most of the truth. I couldn't go into the palace because of the magical barriers, so I went back out to sea, determined to raise a tsunami that would smash half the town. Then I planned to threaten more destruction unless the prince set you free."

"That would have destroyed so many homes and killed hundreds of people!" Averil frowns. "What a terrible plan."

"It would have worked. But before I could carry it out, Liris, Graeme, and Ekkon found me. They have apparently been hovering nearby, keeping an eye on me, even though I ordered them to go hide in the Sounding Waste." I twist around, glaring at Liris.

He only smiles placidly and jerks another arrow out of my back. "I suspected this wouldn't end well if Zoltan was left to his own devices. We were waiting near Crystal Point, ready to come alongside when he needed us."

I hiss as another bolt tears out of my flesh. "The three of them persuaded me that it would be wrong to cause so much death. Which I already knew. I was—beside myself. Not thinking clearly."

I can't endure Averil's gaze, so I look away, conscious of hot blood creeping up my neck into my face—and more hot blood trickling down my back from my wounds. "Liris helped me devise an alternate plan, one that would let us extract you and Brixeus with minimal loss of human life. I gave Graeme a brief taste of my water magic, just enough so he could create the right effect. I also glamoured him to look and sound like me. After such a long time under the locking spell, the trident is still too volatile for anyone but me to hold, so Graeme had to wear a glove. But he is more resistant to lightning than Ekkon or Liris, so he was perfect for the role. After that it was simply a matter of finding one of the vile prince's guards and putting myself in his place."

"You fooled me." Averil casts an admiring look at Graeme. "I really thought you were him."

"He has a grand and prideful way of speaking, this one," Graeme says, with a jerk of his head toward me. "I believe I mimicked it well."

"Off with you both to the deep," I growl. "I have just enough energy to transform Averil and make it to my room."

"You'll be all right?" Liris tugs one more arrow out. That one must have been lodged in something important; I can't help a bellow of pain.

"I'll be fine once you stop torturing me," I snap.

"Very well." Liris retreats into the waves, with Graeme at his side.

"Thank you both," Averil says. "And please thank Ekkon as well."

"Gratitude?" Graeme splays a hand over his heart. "How refreshing. We're not used to that, are we, Liris?"

"Begone," I snarl.

Graeme throws me a "fuck you" gesture and a saucy grin. Then they both leap into the sea and disappear.

Trying to stifle my groans, I transform my body slowly, changing my lower half into legs, then altering my skin, eyes, ears—every part of me. There's an element of innate transfiguration magic that lives in my bones and blood, making me capable of altering myself and others. I used to need a spell in addition to my intrinsic ability, but I've done this so many times over the years that I can *think* the spell, and the change occurs.

I wish the shift could heal me, but the wounds remain.

Next I speak aloud, weaving the spell to give Averil back her legs. Her transformation into human form is just as painful this time as it was the first time, but she bears it with her usual determination.

"A sacrifice of pain for the magic," I tell her. "But this time I don't need to take your voice, because you won't be far from me."

She's naked, and so are Brixeus and I. I have no clothing for any of us. My energy is low, and I need to save some for healing.

"I will glamour us into some simple clothing once we're within sight of the boarding house," I promise them.

Neither Averil nor Brixeus protest.

As I stumble up the beach, I sway on my legs, sudden dizziness slanting my vision. I'm falling—I crash onto loose, dry sand mixed with broken shells and driftwood.

I'm weak—pathetically so. The energy the trident gave me is fading.

Shaking, I plant the trident in the sand and use it to pull myself up.

Slim fingers grip my wrist, pulling my arm across a pair of smooth shoulders. Averil presses against my side, shoring me up, supporting me.

"Don't be afraid to put some weight on me," she says. "I'm strong."

"Don't I know it," I say hoarsely.

With labored steps we move away from the coast, working on way inland along a sun-baked path. Each breath drags through my lungs reluctantly; each step is a dreadful triumph.

"I have questions," says Averil.

I choke on a laugh. "Of course you do."

"They might keep your mind off things until we get where we're going," she suggests.

"Fine."

"How do you breathe underwater without gills?"

"An oddity of my birth, like the tentacles," I tell her between ragged breaths. "All those mechanisms are internal for me."

"Fascinating. I wonder why you're different. Why Ekkon, Liris, and Graeme are different."

"Remember how I told you that powerful magic changes you? Each of their family lines contains a witch or two. My mother believed that her use of magic had something to do with the uniqueness of my natural form."

"So your magical ancestry gave all of you special shapes and rare gifts." She looks up at me, delight in her eyes.

I expected her to say something unconsciously hurtful—that my own tentacles and my friends' bodily differences are the unfortunate result of some dark magic. But she has opened her mind wider, as I told her to do on the first day we met. She views my natural shape, my friends' forms, as assets. In her eyes we are gifted. Not monsters or outcasts.

"Yes," I reply, low. "You could say that."

"I have another question—well, more of a statement. You said the trident was still volatile, that no one except you can wield its magic."

"Yes."

"But I did."

I almost stop walking. But I force myself to keep moving, because we must reach the boarding house before my body gives out altogether. "You did *what?*"

"I held your trident. It hurt me a little—my palms are a bit raw—but then it calmed down. I put it against your chest and held it there." She hesitates. "When I was holding it I could feel something—a response. It was waiting for me to use its power. And I think it wanted me to help you. It could tell that I—"

She stops short of repeating what she told me earlier. That she loves me.

Loves me. That can't be possible.

My whole haunted, wretched soul yearns for it to be possible.

I haul in another breath. "When this is over, I will teach you more of magic. You don't have your own, but such power can be collected, if you have the courage and persistence to pursue it."

"I do," she says fervently.

"I know."

A few moments' silence, and then I force out the words I must say, the words that rattled in my head while I stood behind Prince Kerrin on that ledge, dressed in a guard's uniform, while Averil hung helpless above the pool of sharks.

"I left you." My voice is hoarse, thick with emotions I have not felt in a long time, and never with this intensity. "I left you by the sea-wall, alone. The things I said to you later that night—I am sorry for all of it. I made you part of my revenge, but I need you to know that even if Kerrin had not threatened your life, I would have come back. I was coming back—"

"To return my voice," she says calmly. "I understand."

346

Why is my throat tightening, my eyes stinging? I am weak from these gods-damned wounds, that's what it is. Weak and foolish.

"No, you do not understand. I wasn't returning just to give you your voice. I wanted... shit." A bright slash of pain spears through me, and I have to breathe through it before I can speak again. "I apologize. For letting you believe that I would leave you in human form forever. For thinking that I could actually do it. But I could never make you so miserable. That's why I could not kill your father."

"You didn't kill him?" Her voice is faint with relief.

"No. I deposed him and put your sister Ylaine in his place until I return. Your sister Serra may try to assume control, but I think Ylaine can withstand the challenge."

"Thank you." The words burst from her, cracked with emotion.

"I could not betray you." I say it harshly, because I cannot bear to be soft with her, or I will break before we reach safety.

"You're forgiven," she says.

My throat tightens still more, my eyes burning, tears gathering—

Before I lose all my dignity, Brixeus stumbles on the path ahead of us. Averil pulls me forward until we're alongside him, and she pulls his arm around her waist. He nods gratefully, and we continue like that awhile, both of us leaning on her.

As we walk, Averil fills in the parts of her story I did not know—how she was drugged, framed, tortured, and forcibly transformed. I don't have the strength to show my rage, but it burns inside me, galvanizes my clenched jaw.

Finally Averil falls silent, too. Strong as she is, she's breathing hard by the time we glimpse the boarding house up ahead.

I glance down at her body, grimed with dust and shiny with sweat. Her full breasts sway and her strong thighs flex with every step. If I were not straying near the gates of death, I would have her right now, grime and sand and all. My wild, cunning, lovely, indomitable princess.

Claiming her will have to wait. First, I need to heal.

I manage an illusion of simple garments, just to get us through the door of the boarding house. For Brixeus and Averil, I cast facial illusions so no one will recognize them—nothing complex, just a tweak of the features here and there. Then I turn my trident temporarily invisible.

The magic takes a toll, and my vision begins to darken at the edges.

When we enter the house, I request an extra room for Brixeus. I paid for my chamber with plenty of gold in advance, so the landlady agrees, even though I have no coin in my possession at the moment. I also order food, fresh clothes, and hot water for washing, promising full payment in the morning.

The three of us struggle up the staircase and see Brixeus to his room. He is weak, but the glint of purpose in his eyes and the lordliness of his bearing still remain.

"I will repair your tongue as soon as I'm healed," I promise him. "For now, wash and rest."

He points to the ring on his heartline finger, a gold band etched with words of love.

"You have a husband?" I ask. "Or maybe a wife?"

He nods to the second question.

"She'll be worried about him," says Averil quietly. "Write a note, my lord, and I'll give it to the landlady so she can send a messenger to your wife. Zoltan, you need to gather your supplies and heal yourself."

I nod. I can't spare breath for any more words.

With my last dregs of energy I stagger down the hall, using the trident as a walking stick and pressing one hand to the wall for support.

Once I'm in my room, I collapse. My limbs are wracked with excruciating spasms, and my lungs quiver. My heart is beating huge and desperate, trying to keep my body going.

I crawl to the bags containing my healing supplies. Tonics, tinctures, raw ingredients. Everything I need.

But my vision is blurring. I blink against the oncoming darkness, gripping the trident, trying to draw strength from it.

I refuse to die. Not when I'm so close to everything I didn't know I wanted.

Words resound in my mind, a whipcord of savage passion lashing me back to consciousness.

I fucking love you.

I repeat those four words in my head, over and over, gripping them like a lifeline.

I fucking love you.

I fucking love you.

45

AVERIL

When I've finished delivering Brixeus's note to the
landlady, I climb the stairs to the second floor again. There's a
maid standing uncertainly outside the door I saw Zoltan enter.
She's holding clothes and towels, and on a cart beside her is a
large basin of steaming water and a covered tray.

"The things the gentleman ordered, milady," she says. "But
he won't open the door, and he sounds dreadful ill."

"It's all right—I'll go in," I tell her. "Come back for the cart
later, please."

She nods and hurries away, with a final apprehensive glance
at the door.

I look down at myself, at the blue dress the Sea Witch
glamoured onto me. It looks real enough, but I can't feel the
fabric against my body. When I place a hand on my belly, there's
no cloth, only my bare skin. So strange.

At least Zoltan is still conscious. I suspect if he'd passed
out, I would be suddenly naked to all eyes. Very awkward
indeed.

Tucking the basket of clothes against my hip as I saw the maid do, I shove the door of the room open and push the little cart inside.

The Sea Witch has let his own glamour fall away. His great sinewy body lies naked on the floor, dripping with the tinctures he has poured over himself, hissing steam as his wounds slowly close. He's groaning, grunting, not bothering to hold back the sounds of his agony anymore. His inky violet hair straggles over his face.

As I move inside with the cart and close the door, he anoints himself with another potion, muttering a spell. A fresh burst of steam rises from his torn flesh, and he hisses with pain, pounding the floor with a fist. "Fuck, fuck."

I move toward him, drawn by the echo of his pain in my own soul. "Can I help?"

"Pour this over the wounds on my back, if you would."

After handing me a small bottle, he turns onto his stomach, exposing the brown expanse of his back—mountains of muscle with the valley of his spine between them. I bite back a gasp at the sight of the injuries, some half healed already. I knew he had taken several arrows for me, but I didn't realize how many.

"Your injured tentacles—you switched forms, so when you revert, will they be healed?"

"No. I take on the form exactly as I left it. I'll need to heal them when I change back—shit, Averil!" He groans as I pour the contents of the bottle onto an especially angry-looking wound.

"Hush now." I smooth my palm over the round cheek of his ass, stroking its curve. He stills instantly, breathing heavily.

"You said your hands are injured," he mutters. "Let me fix them."

"In a moment. You first."

"No." He pushes himself up to a sitting position, and though I try not to look, I can't help noticing that his cock has stiffened and lifted, in spite of the pain he's in. "*You* first." His tone is deep and fervent.

"But—"

"Let me do this for you, Averil."

Sighing, I hand over the bottle and hold out my seared palms.

The Witch cups one of his huge hands under both of mine and lowers his mouth to my inflamed skin. He kisses my palms tenderly, one after the other, then murmurs words over them as he pours the tincture. My skin tingles painfully, but the discomfort eases quickly, and the redness disappears.

"There," he says, lifting his eyes to mine.

My pulse throbs faster, and there's a quivering throb between my legs too, because I love him with all my heart and my body.

"I have a question," I whisper, and he nods.

The way he's looking at me—he's already saying it. Communication without a voice. Emotion without words.

But I want to hear it, too.

"You let go of the trident to shield me," I say. "Why?"

His voice, deeper than ever, dark and beautiful. "You are worth more to me than the trident."

"No," I whisper through a sob, through a smile.

"Yes." He leans in, his hand cupping my cheek. "I fucking love you, too."

Teeth clenched, tears beading on my lashes, I crawl forward into his lap. He sets the bottle aside on the floor and wraps his massive arms around me while I bury my face against his neck.

"I have a question for you, princess," he murmurs into my hair. "Why do you love me? I'm a wicked wretch, and you know it."

Words swirl through my head—so many reasons, piling one atop another. But I give him just one, for now.

"You listened, even when I couldn't speak," I whisper.

"Not as well as I should have."

"Hush." I press my lips to the heated skin of his throat, right over his pulse, and I feel it quicken. A telltale hardness twitches against my thigh.

A flare of delicious awareness floods my sex and I shift my body, scooting in close as we sit face to face on the floor. The tip of his cock prods my bare pussy, sending little eddies of pleasure through my stomach.

When I glance down, the glamour of the blue dress is gone.

"Naughty witch," I murmur, grazing his mouth with mine.

"Can't help myself."

There's sand on our bodies, sweat filming our skin, salt in our hair. I don't care about any of it. But I do care about him.

"You need to finish healing," I breathe against his lips.

"Fuck that," he whispers. His broad hands sweep down my back, gathering my bottom, lifting me slightly. Then he grimaces, his muscles going rigid.

"You're hurting, aren't you?"

"Maybe," he grumbles.

"Let's get you healed, and then we'll wash up," I tell him. "And then…"

He reaches down, sliding his thumb from my clit along my center. "Then I'm going to slide my cock into this soaked little pussy of yours and fill you up."

"Gods," I breathe. "How fast can we get you healed?"

46

Once all his wounds are closed, Zoltan sponges the sweat and sand from his body. I sit in the corner with my hands clasped while he does it, fighting the urge to run to him, hook my legs around his waist, and tuck him inside me. I don't think I've seen anything more beautiful than his taut, muscled body shining wet, flexing as he washes himself.

But then he towels off and puts on clothes. "I'm going to heal Brixeus's tongue and fingers," he says. "Be ready when I return."

"I'm always ready."

He grins, hooks his satchel onto his shoulder, and leaves the room, closing the door behind him.

My entire body is a cage full of fluttering birds. I wash myself with trembling hands, and then I nibble a little of the food on the tray—cold sliced meat, hard cheese, dry bread. I know the names of all the human foods now. So much more variety than we have under the sea, because they can blend ingredients and cook with fire.

I could never go back to a life entirely underwater. And it seems as if I may not have to. Zoltan said he loves me. He said he will teach me magic, which sounds as if he wants me around for a long time.

Maybe he'll teach me the secrets of transformation and of his perpetual youth. Maybe we can live together, ageless, exploring both sea and land at will.

My eyes latch onto the trident, which leans against the wall in the corner of the room. Its glow is nearly bright enough to rival the lamp on the rickety dresser. Almost as if it wants me to touch it.

It's a mark of Zoltan's implicit trust that he left it here with me. If I were a different sort of woman, I could take it and leave. I already know I can use it; I could run off on my own and do anything I wanted, with such power at my disposal.

It's a despicable impulse, one I reject instantly. I can't bear to imagine the anguish my Witch would feel over such a betrayal.

"Not now," I murmur to the trident. "Perhaps later we can become better acquainted."

I drape myself on the bed, which has a much thinner mattress than any I've slept on before. The timbers of the frame squeak loudly every time I shift my position, so once I find what I hope is an alluring pose, I lie very still.

Zoltan is taking a long time, and I'm so dreadfully tired.

Sometime later I wake, bleary and blinking. The lamp has been turned down, and the room is dark except for the golden glow of the trident in the corner. A heavy male arm is draped across my body, and the heat of a broad chest warms my back.

The tattooed forearm and veiny hand cupping my waist belong to Zoltan. His thick fingers bear a few rings, and I touch them lightly, my brain still muzzy with sleep.

I wish I hadn't fallen asleep before he returned. I wanted him inside me.

Slowly I turn over under the weight of his arm, until I'm facing him.

I've never seen him asleep before. His rugged face looks smoother than usual, peaceful and beautiful. His lashes sweep black against his cheeks, and his hair swirls over the pillow like spilled violet ink, the ends of the locks moving and curling slightly, as if they have a mind of their own.

He's naked—he must have stripped again before climbing into bed with me. I smooth my hand over the hulking rise of his shoulder, over the bulge of his bicep. His pectorals are squished together as he lies on his side, the groove between them deepened. Lightly I touch one of his nipples, delighting in the way it tightens.

"Princess," his voice rumbles, sending my pulse sky-high. "Are you trying to take advantage of me?"

"I'm sorry," I whisper. "You just looked so beautiful."

"Never apologize for caressing me like that." His lashes lift slightly, showing his glittering eyes. "It's been an age since I was touched by someone who cares."

The statement is unusually vulnerable for him. I shift closer, pleased by the prod of his growing erection against my belly. "I'm sorry I fell asleep before we could—you know."

"Say it, shrimp."

"Before we could fuck," I murmur.

"Good girl. That's my little sinner." His warm, broad palm glides up my back, then down to my rear, where he cups my ass cheek, squeezing the flesh with a rumble of satisfaction. "And don't apologize for your body's needs, love. You say you're sorry far too often."

"I'm used to apologizing to my father and sisters for everything I do, I suppose." My breath hitches as his hand travels down the crease of my rear, all the way to the back of my pussy. He dips a finger deep, then traces the wetness against the skin of my bottom. He's writing something on me in my own juices—I think it's the mer word for strength.

He dips again, writes another word—beauty.

"You're so wet for me, Princess," he whispers, and his cock throbs against my stomach.

Scooting closer to him, I slide my free arm up his chest, thumbing his nipple before circling his neck and sinking my fingers into his hair. I tilt my face up, meeting his mouth. Hot, smooth lips. A flick of wet tongue. A deepening press of his mouth, and my tongue sliding into his space, traveling the edge of his teeth.

He squeezes my bottom again, then delves into my pussy from behind, sinking his thick central finger deep into my insides. I release a mew of helpless pleasure over his tongue, and he chuckles, a gravelly sound of satisfaction.

When he removes his finger, I squirm in protest.

"Take me," I gasp. "Take me now, please."

"Not yet," he murmurs. "I want to savor this."

With a whimper, I tuck one knee up higher, looping my leg over his hip, giving his hand better access. Humming low in his chest, he traces my sopping slit with his fingers, stroking along my pussy over and over, swirling through my wetness, coating me with slick need.

Ripples of pleasure flood my belly, widening and intensifying, and they're delicious but I crave more. Slowly I become aware that I'm whispering, "Please, please, please" over and over.

"Please what?" he growls.

"Please make me come. Please."

"Why don't you make yourself come, sweetheart?" He shoves his thumb inside me, a quick plunge and then he withdraws, while my inner walls quiver at the absence. "Spread those gorgeous thighs and play with yourself until you come. While I watch."

A fresh rush of heat rises to my cheeks. What he's suggesting is so wildly wicked.

But he's seen me play like that before. And now I know my body even better than I did then.

I think I can do this.

He props himself on one elbow. Licks my wetness off his fingers. "Fucking delicious," he mutters.

"Gods, you're filthy." I shift onto my back, trying to ignore the creaking of the bed, and I spread my thighs. When I touch my pussy, it's dripping, sloppy, soaked. "You do this to me," I whisper, lifting my glistening fingers so he can see them.

His eyes widen, his chest heaving. "Touch your clit, love."

I place one fingertip on it and begin circling. It feels so good that my head tips back and my eyes close, a soft moan skating through my throat. Round and round I circle, and then I massage it rapidly, a steady rhythm while the pleasure builds and builds inside me, tightening, brightening—I press all my fingers against my pussy and swirl them around—and I come hard, my thighs tensing, belly tight. Floods of bliss wash through my body.

The Sea Witch is on his knees, grasping my legs, pushing them apart again. "Move your hand. I want to see."

I obey, and he watches me quiver and spasm through the ebbing pleasure. "Fuck, he says hoarsely.

"I need you," I whisper. "I need you inside me."

"I've wanted nothing more since I first saw you," he answers.

"Really?" My eyebrows lift.

"Yes. You don't know how I've craved you, Averil, how I've hungered for you—" He's pushing my legs wider, moving in, aligning himself with my entrance. "Are you—"

"You ask me if I'm ready, and I'll stab you with your own trident," I hiss.

He laughs, breathless, and plants both hands on either side of me on the bed. His enormous body hovers over mine, and his mouth grazes my cheek. "I'm big, little princess. I used my most slender tentacles on you before, but this—" He props himself on one hand and uses the other to pat his hot, heavy cock against my wet folds. "This is harder, and thicker."

"Shut up and fuck me."

"As Your Highness wishes."

The head of his cock pokes into my soaked slit, pushing my softness apart, making its way inside like his tentacles did, except his cock is so much harder and hotter and *gods* I've never been stretched so much or filled so full.

I tense up without meaning to and he pauses, teeth clenched as he struggles for control. "Relax for me, precious."

I inhale deeply. My thighs fall completely open, entirely relaxed, and I let him all the way in.

The sound he makes is guttural, heart-wrenching relief. Fully seated inside me, he halts, his chest heaving, arms braced rigid on the mattress. His eyes are closed, his dark hair tumbling around his face.

I press both hands to his cheeks. "Open your eyes, Witch. Look at me."

When he opens them, they are swirling indigo-violet from corner to corner, white pupils shining like stars.

"Does it frighten you?" he says, and I think he means his eyes but maybe this act, too, or maybe the monumental, cataclysmic emotion rolling through both of us in this moment.

"No." I pull him down to me and I kiss him, feeling his exquisitely hard length flex inside me. Joining with him like this—it's everything. Everything I wanted.

His tongue curls around mine, a liquid heat to match the glow between my legs. I pull back from the kiss, my lips wet. "Come inside me," I whisper.

"Yes." He extends the word in a low growl.

He pulls out of me all the way, and I frown, but then he's straightening upright, throwing my legs over his shoulders, lifting my rear with both palms. He sinks in again, and it's so slippery, so easy, no resistance this time, just my body sucking him in, craving every surge.

He impales me to the hilt, then pulls all the way out—rams in, draws himself out. I'm making sounds now—weak, wanton sounds, and he reaches forward, covering my mouth.

"Everyone's asleep, love," he says, half-smiling. "Your screams will have to wait. I don't fancy getting kicked out of our refuge."

I want to point out that the creaking of the bed is a lot louder than my cries, but I just nod frantically, and he removes his hand, using a fingertip to jiggle my clit. I almost squeal.

"I need to come again," I gasp as he removes his hand and pulls all the way out again. "I need to come, I need to, please, please—"

The Witch laughs quietly, and it's not a mockery, it's pure joy. "This is exactly what I've wanted to do with you. To make you melt and beg like this, you strong, beautiful woman—"

"Bastard," I hiss, and with a twist of my body I swing my legs down, sit upright, and plant my hands on his shoulders instead. I push against him—he's mountainous, but he lets me

360

shove him back onto the bed, which groans louder than either of us.

His cock stands up, thick and flushed with arousal, gleaming with his precum and my wetness. Carefully I kneel astride him and insert his length into myself, sinking down on it, reveling in the fullness. My hair spills down my back, a lock or two falling over my shoulders and draping his stomach.

The Sea Witch grips my hip with one hand and thumbs my clit with the other until my eyes roll back in my head.

But when I'm right on the edge, he stops the motion, with a breathless chuckle and a saucy grin.

"You wicked—" I gasp. My thighs work desperately, pumping me up and down on his length—and now it's his turn to writhe, and throw back his head, and moan with delicious agony. I have never seen anything more gorgeous than him, right now.

He helps me move, lifting my hips as I drive us both closer to the peak. It's harder for me to climax in this position—I'm straining, sweating, desperate.

And then he touches me again. Two fingers, wiggling over that little sensitive place, and I let loose with a half-scream, half-gasp as I come around him, ecstasy chasing along every nerve, my insides pulsing and my brain a glazed, glowing muddle of delight.

47

The pinnacle of my two centuries is Averil coming on my cock.

Nothing I've seen or experienced compares to it.

I've slept with many women, mermaid and human. None of them were *her*.

The little flutters of her body around my shaft are the most exquisite torture ever invented. I can't last any longer—I spill myself inside her, my balls tightening, my hips jerking upward into her heat, my cock thrilling, my whole body contracted with ecstasy. It's explosive perfection. It's beyond anything I've felt before.

I fucking love you.

Why didn't anyone tell me that love makes pleasure more powerful?

I'm staring at her, caught in the storm of her beauty, the brilliance of her eyes, trying to think of words that will contain everything I feel…

And then, with a creak, a crack, and a groan, the bed collapses. The mattress sags to the floor in the middle of the broken frame.

"Oh shit!" whispers Averil, clapping a trembling hand over her mouth. "Shit, Zoltan."

My name in her mouth is inexpressibly precious.

I sit up, still deep inside her, and I wrap her in my arms, pulling her to my chest while we both shake with helpless, stifled laughter.

"I'll pay the landlady for it," I whisper.

Averil kisses my mouth, lightly—and then she's kissing me again and again, sowing tender kisses all over my lips and cheeks. A drop of liquid smears on my jaw. She's crying.

I'm instantly enraged at myself. "Did I hurt you?"

"No, no. I'm just—I wish I'd seen you sooner, and I hadn't seen him at all."

Him. The dead prince. "Without him, we might never have found each other. It's the one good outcome of his pathetic life."

"I suppose so. But still." Sighing, swiping at the tears, she lifts herself off me. My cock pops out, sated and soft.

She curls her lithe body against mine, one long leg hooked possessively over my thigh, her dainty foot tapping against my shin. Her head rests on my chest. I gather a handful of her blood-red hair and run it through my fingers, over and over, until I'm too drowsy to move.

I'm vaguely aware of her sitting up sometime later, pulling the sheet over us both before lying down again. My consciousness tips over into sleep, but I wake to her silky skin gliding against mine, her fingers creeping down the planes of my stomach toward my cock. I hum deep in my chest to let her know I'm awake.

Emboldened, she starts to play with me, and I try not to think of how she made the prince come in the Vault of Queens.

It's dark in the room, but by the dim glow of my trident I watch her slender fingers stroking my length. My body heats, blood pumping the lust straight to my groin until I'm fully erect, achingly hard.

My hands tighten into fists and I make myself lie still while she experimentally tries to curl her thumb and forefinger around the base of my shaft. They don't quite meet.

Then she slides her hand lower, cupping my balls, fondling them. Playing with the sensitive skin behind them.

Eventually she sits up and licks the beaded moisture off the head of my cock with her dainty tongue.

I can't hold back any longer, broken bed or not.

With a snarl I pounce, tumbling her over, flipping her onto her belly and hitching her bottom into the air. I swipe a hand along her pussy to make sure she's ready—and of course she's slick, eager to take me. She whimpers a soft "yes" against the sheets, so I plunge in.

Every nerve, all the sensitive skin of my cock roars with delight as I glide through her. We fit together so perfectly I can hardly breathe.

I grip the curve of her hip with one hand, and I spread my other hand across her lower belly, right above her mound.

I pound into her at a hectic pace, and the sound of my flesh slapping against hers fills the room. She's grunting softly with every slam of my cock into her body, and when she starts to whisper staccato curses I know she's close.

My hand slides from her belly to the small of her back. In the golden light I admire the creamy smoothness of her skin, the ledges of her shoulder blades, the gentle valley of her spine, the way her waist tapers and then widens into those luscious hips and round ass cheeks. Her scarlet hair pours over her shoulder onto the mattress, swinging with each thrust of mine.

I love the way she rocks to meet me. How she has abandoned her inhibitions altogether and leaped into carnal lust with all the passionate abandon of her wild heart.

"I love you, Averil," I rasp.

And she comes, shoving her ass compulsively against me. I brace her with my hips and hands while she's bending, breaking, muffling her soft shrieks in the mattress. She writhes, her trembling insides clenching around my cock.

"Gods, Averil, I'm going to come," I pant, bowing over her. "Shit... yes..."

I pour myself into her, a release so violent I can't hold back a loud visceral groan. My body quakes with the force of the bliss cascading along my limbs.

When I pull out and collapse beside her, she nuzzles her face against my neck and kisses me right below my ear.

No one has ever kissed me exactly there.

"I love you, too, Witch," she murmurs, stroking the center of my chest, where the shell necklace used to hang.

"I could do this for days," I reply. "For years. Endlessly."

She laughs a little, but then she props herself on one elbow. "But are we safe here? What about the humans? I killed their king, and you stole from them. Won't they look for us? Maybe we should leave, and return to the sea. Or at least travel farther from Crystal Point."

"After I repaired Brixeus's tongue, I cast an illusion around this place so it looks like a thicket of trees. The illusion won't stay in place for much longer, but it should last until morning. And then we can leave."

"After we find Brixeus a safe place. Him and his wife."

With a gusty sigh, I look away. "I've done enough for him."

"He's your friend. You called him your friend in front of Kerrin."

"That was Graeme, not me."

365

"Zoltan." She sits up, flushed, her tone dripping with rebuke. "He's marked as a traitor now. We can't just leave him to fend for himself."

"He's a wise man, a lord, with connections at court."

"Connections that have been severed since his link to the prince was broken. You know better than anyone how quickly courtiers and nobility can turn when someone falls out of favor."

"I am not merciful, Averil—" I begin, but she only smirks at me. "What?" I growl.

"Of course you're not. You're a big, bad, terrifying witch." She places her warm palm in the hollow of my hip, right above the slanted ridge there, and though I've been sated, the sensation is still irresistibly pleasant. She begins stroking me, from my abs to my thighs, caressing every ridge and groove.

"You can't pet me into agreeing with you," I tell her.

"I'm enjoying you," she says. "Because I can." And she lays her cheek on my stomach, her hair swirled across my chest.

Something deep inside me, something cruel and calcified, breaks apart, softens, and melts away. The tension I always carry, the caution, the fear of betrayal—it unspools, loosening into utter relief. More at ease than I've been in years, I drift into a deep sleep, soothed by her quiet breathing.

And I'm awakened by her screams.

48

The slow rise and fall of Zoltan's torso as he breathes is just enough subtle motion to lull me to sleep.

Until my body is jerked off him.

I'm dragged upright, my arms pinned back and snapped into metal cuffs at my back. The world is a muddle of darkness and armored figures, the smell of metal and salt air and sweat. Blood pounds in my head as I try dizzily to make sense of what's happening.

"Douse him with the magic repressor and the paralytic, and then cut his throat," says a voice, low.

A voice I recognize, a voice I hate. Cassilenne.

"No!" I scream.

A guard steps forward and throws the contents of two bottles onto Zoltan's chest. The liquid activates immediately, a sickly green glow. His eyes blink open, bleary and confused.

I'm still screaming, my body lurching against the coarse hands that hold me. "No, no, wait, please wait—let me—please, you need him—you need him!" My voice rises to a keening shriek as the guard begins to slice across Zoltan's neck.

"Stop," says Cassilenne. "If he talks, kill him."

The soldier pauses. The edge of his knife is slick with blood, but the cut he made looks shallow and small. Thank the gods.

Cassilenne comes around to face me. Deep hollows circle her eyes, and messy tendrils straggle from the braid over her shoulder. "Why do I need him? The last thing I want is him casting another spell to lock the trident's power. Speaking of which—gag him as a precaution," she throws over her shoulder.

While the guards obey, I scramble for words. "I don't think he can lock the trident again, not without preparation and supplies. He's the only one who can teach you how to wield it. You saw Kerrin try to use it—he couldn't manage to control its power. You need the Sea Witch."

"But not *you*." She takes my chin in her hand, smiling. "I don't need you."

"I'm leverage, to get him to do what you want," I gasp.

A smile breaks over her face. "Clever girl. I knew I liked you. Or perhaps you're not so clever, since you had the gall to spend the night *here*, halfway between Mariner's Cove and Crystal Point. Of all the foolish choices. Did you really think I would let you murder my lover and escape with your stolen treasure?"

"How did you—"

"How did I find you? Simple. I knew you couldn't keep Brixeus in the sea with you, not in his condition. You'd have to bring him to shore. Maybe you'd leave him alone, or maybe you'd accompany him on land to care for him—I guessed the latter. And I was right."

"But the building is concealed by an illusion," I protest.

"I picked up a few things when we raided Brixeus's home to fetch those charms, the ones that turned you back into a mermaid." She holds up an ornate hand mirror. "In his private vault I found this beauty, which detects objects that have been tampered with through magic, from quite a distance away. It can also reveal the truth of illusions. Brixeus had everything so neatly labeled—really quite thoughtful of him. His wife tried to stop us when we came for his treasures. Silly old thing is deep in the dungeons now, rethinking her choices."

My gaze travels to the half-dozen guards crowding the room. "And you're in charge now? Why would the nobles allow you to take power?"

"I'm an apothik, darling. One of the best physicians in the kingdom. And as such I've had access to the private chambers and innermost secrets of many a noble house. Yes, I've been away a while, but two-year-old secrets can be just as powerful and persuasive as fresh ones. Scandalous secrets and confidential favors are the most reliable currency in this kingdom or any other. I grew up at court, sweetness. Do you think I was idle the whole time? No."

"You want to be queen," I murmur. "It's what you've always wanted. But Kerrin wouldn't marry you because his father demanded he have a bride of noble birth."

Cass leans in, her lips brushing my ear. "After he married you and framed you for his father's death, he was planning to marry me next. The condition of a noble bride would have been fulfilled, and then he could take whomever he wanted without his father around to prevent it. But you and your Witch fucked everything up."

"Did you love him?" I ask, low. "Did you love Kerrin, truly?"

She pulls back and stares at me, her eyes burning, her teeth clenched.

"My lady?" It's the guard holding the knife to Zoltan's throat. The Sea Witch's mouth has been stuffed with cloth, and he's glaring at everyone in the room.

"My lady, shall I kill him?" the guard asks, a touch of morbid eagerness in his tone. Perhaps he wants the dubious honor of being the man who killed the Witch of the Sea.

"No," says Cassilenne, still staring at me, and I'm not sure whether she's answering my question or the guard's. Maybe both.

"Are you sure?" says the guard. "He's a nasty brute, this one, full of foul magic—"

"I know what he is." Cassilenne turns and stalks toward the guard. Her voice is perfectly even, her movements tight and controlled, but there's a subdued threat in her diction, a forbidding tension in each step she takes. "Give me the knife."

The guard hands it over, and Cass whips the blade across his throat savagely. Eyes bulging, mouth open, neck gushing blood, the guard topples over.

"Would anyone else like to question me?" Cass says calmly, wiping the knife on the edge of the fallen man's tunic.

"No, Regent," mutter the rest of the guards.

Cassilenne leans over the Sea Witch, who lies naked, gagged, motionless, and furious on the broken bed. "Look at you," she murmurs, trailing a hand down his body. "So powerful, and yet powerless. You and I are going to do great things together. And perhaps one day you'll see that joining me is much more fun than resisting." She strokes his inner thigh.

I twist in the grip of my captors. "Get your hands off him or I'll kill you," I choke out.

"With what, little mermaid?" She smiles at me. And moves her hand higher.

With a screech of rage I thrust my manacled hands upward, landing a hard blow to the groin of the guard behind me.

He's wearing a piece of leather armor over his crotch. Shit. Pain radiates through my fingers, but I shift my weight onto one foot, hooking my other leg backward, around the guard's leg. A quick sideways tilt, and both he and I are off-balance, teetering, then crashing onto the floor.

Now I can use my legs as weapons. I haven't had training in human form, but I know my leg muscles are strong, so I kick as hard as I can, aiming for stomachs, wrists, ankles, knees— anything not protected by armor. But my feet are as bare as the rest of me, and the guards are well-protected. I manage a flailing kick to someone's nose, cartilage and bone crunching under my heel—but then I'm hauled upright again, smashed against the wall by a huge guard with hot, stinking breath. He leers into my face, seeming far too pleased that I'm naked.

Cassilenne has been watching my attempts at fighting with an amused smirk on her face. "I really do like you, Averil, in spite of the fact that you murdered my prince. You're loyal, a fighter. And you kill when you need to. I could use someone like you at my side. Too bad I need you for leverage. Which will likely entail fairly frequent torture—"

Something rises behind her, a huge bulk with eyes of swirling violet. Zoltan's tattooed forearm slams across her throat, securing her in a choke-hold. His other massive hand clamps to her skull.

"Don't move," he warns the guards. "Or I snap your regent's neck."

When I was fighting, all the guards in the room gravitated toward me, to help subdue me. And Cass turned her back to the Witch. Who is apparently not paralyzed at all.

"You may have temporarily suppressed my magic," he growls. "A weak potion, which will wear off in minutes. But the paralytic has no effect on me. I have built up an immunity to quite a few poisons. A little hobby of mine over the past couple of decades."

Cass's eyes widen, but she doesn't speak.

"Take the shackles off the princess," orders the Witch.

When the guards hesitate, Cass wheezes, "Do it!"

I'm not sure how secure her control over the soldiers may be, now that she's in someone else's power. But they honor her enough to obey, removing the manacles around my wrists. There's a simple dress on the pile of clothes the maid brought us last night, so I seize it and pull it over my head.

"Now, Averil my love," says the Witch. "If you would take my trident and persuade these brigands to leave the building."

"With pleasure." I pick up the trident bare-handed, and it hums a pleased response against my fingers, its light flaring brighter. When I point it at the guards, a surge of intent passes from me into the weapon, and forks of purple lightning snake out with a searing hiss.

The guards flee, armored shoulders jostling against each other as they all try to squeeze out the door at once. Several of them are stung in the ass, and two of them are stricken by the magical spears of light, collapsing onto the floor and twitching violently. The air crackles with the smell of singed flesh and acrid magic.

There's a thunder of distant footsteps as the rest of the guards pound down the stairs to the first floor and rush out of the boarding house. The two who collapsed struggle to their feet and flee as well, howling with pain. More shouts outside tell me there must be additional soldiers encircling the building.

"I'll check on Brixeus," I tell Zoltan. I don't have to ask him if he's got Cass under control. She's purpling, gasping for air, probably a moment away from passing out.

I rush into the hallway with the trident. Towards the end of the hall are three nervous-looking soldiers, keeping Lord

Brixeus, the landlady, and a couple of maids under guard. As soon as I brandish the trident toward the stairs, they abandon their post and hurry after their comrades.

"What is happening?" quavers the landlady. "First the squealing and the creaking, and then the grunting and the pounding—I don't mind that so much, had plenty of lovers come through here for a bit of nookie in private, you know—I rather like the sounds—but then the crash came—sounded like furniture breaking, and I have a business to run, can't be buying new bedframes every fortnight—and then the soldiers tromping in, pulling law-abiding folk out of their beds—"

Lord Brixeus takes her hand. "My good woman, you will be well compensated for the anxieties of this night, and for any broken beds. I am sure the Sea Witch and the princess will be all too happy to settle our account to your greatest satisfaction. Please, let us go down to the kitchen and I will make some tea."

He looks so much better, healed and rested and clothed. He's once again the genteel, solemn man I first met on the beach, but with a bit less grim suspicion around his mouth.

"Your wife," I tell him. "Cassilenne says she's in the dungeons. We'll help you get her out, and we'll find you two somewhere safe to go."

"I can do better than that," says a deep voice behind me—a voice brimming with dark fury.

Zoltan strides out of the bedroom. He's wearing pants now, and dragging a limp, unconscious Cass. "I've decided to take control of this kingdom's future, as well as the one below the sea. And why shouldn't I? I have power. And what is power if it cannot do some good, am I right, love?" His eyes meet mine, a hint of warmth swirling through his gaze despite the rage.

"What did you have in mind, Witch?" Lord Brixeus's tone is cold and cautious.

"You'll be the new king." Zoltan points a thick finger at Brixues. "Best one the place has had in an age. Don't protest. You've got plenty of good years left. And you'll have my power behind you, so if anyone says shit about it, I'll end them."

"Perhaps killing anyone who disagrees with you isn't the right move," I suggest.

"Fine," growls the Witch. "I'll toss them around on my trident until they see reason."

"Better, I suppose. We'll work on it." I glance at Lord Brixeus, who looks utterly stunned.

"A king," murmurs the landlady, her fingertips fluttering over her mouth. "A future king, and a witch, and a princess—in my boarding house... oh merciful gods..." Her eyes roll up, and she tips over.

Lord Brixeus catches her just in time. Her weakness seems to have restored his senses. "I'll take her to the kitchen. She needs rest, and some tea."

"I like tea," I say. "I've had it a few times... very soothing."

"I will make you a cup as well, Princess." And he gives me a smile. It's a tight, polite smile, but a smile nonetheless. From him, it's as good as an embrace.

Lord Brixeus hesitates for a moment, then picks up the landlady. As he straightens, he shoots Zoltan a look of blended suspicion and awe. "You healed more than my tongue and my fingers, Witch. I feel better than I have in years."

The corner of Zoltan's mouth tilts up. He doesn't thank Brixeus for saving my life, nor does Brixeus thank him for the healing. The two men simply give each other curt nods, and then Lord Brixeus descends the steps, carrying the landlady.

"Tie this one up, the two of you," the Sea Witch orders the maids, letting Cassilenne drop to the floor.

Half-clothed and muscle-bound, Zoltan is as stunningly virile as he is menacing, and the two maids toddle toward him on shaky legs, their cheeks flushed as they move to obey him.

But Zoltan moves past them to me, and plants a hot kiss on my mouth. "Warrior Princess."

"Trickster Witch," I whisper back.

When I hand over the trident to him, it glows brighter for a moment, a pulse of recognition. "It has finally settled," he says, a touch of relief in his tone. "I'll go inform the soldiers outside of the change in leadership. I believe the trident and I can make them listen. Though it may take time to ensure that everyone accepts Brixeus as the new ruler." He shakes his head, half-smiling. "A king who makes tea for a boarding-house landlady. I like it."

"I like it too. It's a wise choice, setting him on the throne."

"High praise from the woman who called me a fool and a bastard."

"Oh, you are both of those things," I confirm as I descend the steps behind him. "But you are sometimes wise, too."

"I do know many things."

"Wisdom and knowledge are not the same."

"As vengeance and happiness aren't the same." He sighs, tossing back his dark hair. "I know, I know."

"But your knowledge—I do crave more of that. Knowledge of magic, and youth, and long life."

He turns to face me. He's two steps below me, which puts us at eye level.

"I will give you everything I possess," he says quietly.

My heartbeat quickens, warmth racing through my body.

"The trident," he continues. "Magic can be siphoned from it, if one has the right spells and supplies. That's what your father began to do with the help of his witch, so many years ago. What I denied him, I will give to you freely. Half the power of the trident, infused into your body and blood. My mother's magic, and mine. You'll take half, and I'll take the rest."

"But the trident will be empty then," I gasp.

"We can leave a little defensive magic within it. I would never think of discarding such a precious family heirloom. But in its current state, it is too powerful. It was a convenient way to store my magic and wield it without sacrifice, but it makes me vulnerable. I suppose that was the price I paid for the ease of using it. But now that I'm risking not only my safety, but yours as well—" He shakes his head. "No, I will let it diminish, and it shall be no more than a mildly magical tool. You and I shall hold equal shares of its former power. And I will teach you Godspeak, so you can use the magic you will possess."

The enormity of what he's offering settles in my soul, a gentle weight, a wondrous, comforting assurance.

"You'd trust me with so much?" I whisper. "After all you've been through? Zoltan, you haven't known me very long at all."

"Long enough." His gaze bores into mine. "I left you alone with the trident last night, and you didn't run."

My eyebrows lift. "That was a test?"

"One I already knew you'd pass."

"Perhaps I should test you." I narrow my eyes at him. "You deserve it, for twisting our bargain, and for making me believe you didn't care."

"You said you forgave me," he counters.

"A woman may forgive, but she remembers."

"Then is it truly forgiveness?"

"Gods." Aggravated, I push at his chest, and he laughs. "Go deal with the soldiers outside, Witch. And then you and I are going to have a long discussion."

"I do love a good discussion," he purrs, leaning in to kiss my forehead.

"No, not sex. A *discussion*. With words."

"You're welcome to discuss anything you like, as long as I don't have to reply. My tongue will be occupied elsewhere." The smile he gives me drips with wicked promises.

"Bastard," I whisper, because I simply can't think of more words when my body is thrumming and melting for him. "I'm going to keep an eye on Cassilenne."

Turning my back to him, I start to mount the stairs.

"As I mentioned, putting Brixeus in power will take time," he says from behind me. "And securing your sister as Queen under the sea will take time as well."

"We have time now, for everything we may want to do."

Something in my tone must give me away, because he says, in a voice as dark and smooth as waterworn stone, "Is there something in particular you have in mind?"

I press my lips together, blushing, unable to face him.

I have cracked open the barriers that were molded around me, the guides and guards for my life. I dipped my toe into pleasure, and then I dove in, heedless and joyful. But I'm still a little shy about speaking of such things openly.

"There is something I want to do," I tell the Witch. "When we've stabilized Brixeus as king and we return to the sea, I'll tell you."

"You want to fuck me in our mer forms."

I freeze, my hands clenching. Slowly I turn around, my face blooming with scarlet heat. "How did you know?"

He's grinning, his sharp eyeteeth looking more like fangs than ever. "You're easy to read, love. Most of the time."

He saunters down the rest of the stairs, calling back over his shoulder, "And my answer is yes."

Then he swings out the front door, trident in hand, to face the soldiers.

378

49

Three weeks later, Brixeus is firmly established as regent, with an official coronation set to take place in a month. Zoltan has made several trips back to the mer kingdom to check on my sister Ylaine. According to his reports, she is taking to her new position surprisingly well.

I've been in human form the whole time, wearing gorgeous gowns that suit my status as a princess of sea. When Zoltan is gone, I'm his representative to the humans, supporting Lord Brixeus, participating in meetings, lending my voice to conversations.

Now that they know who I am, the nobles and generals will actually listen to me. In some ways I believe they prefer me to Zoltan—he tends to insist on being obeyed at once, whereas I'm more likely to work through the issues and hear everyone's point of view.

The humans are deeply unhappy with a mer dictating whom they should place on the throne. But Lord Brixeus does have a strong number of supporters, especially once our tale was told and Cassilenne's full confession was extracted.

Brixeus supervised Cass's interrogation. She didn't look much worse afterward, so I'm not sure how he managed to get her to tell the truth—perhaps some magical talisman or other. Several nobles and notaries witnessed her verbal confession, after which the resistance to Lord Brixeus's ascension diminished significantly. King Perindal's funeral was celebrated in grand style, while the patricidal Prince Kerrin was buried quietly.

Lord Brixeus's wife has recovered from her ordeal in prison, and she's strong enough to stand beside him as he works to secure his rule—which means I can confidently step away from the court and go to the sea with Zoltan to visit my family.

We don't take to the sea from Crystal Point, though. Zoltan insists that we ride up the coast together on the horse he stole from the seaside village. He brings the stallion to the courtyard of the Summer Palace, where I'm waiting, dressed in flowing pants and a loose shirt.

Zoltan wears black leather pants that make his rear look squeezeably delicious, and a baggy cream-colored tunic, half-tucked, that billows in the breeze. His purple-black hair is tied back, a few tendrils brushing his temples. The trident is slung on his back, secured by a leather harness.

"I suppose I should return him," Zoltan says, patting the horse's long nose. The stallion shakes and tosses his head, then nuzzles against Zoltan's palm.

"You could buy him," I suggest. "Board him at the inn, and use him whenever we're on land."

"I think I'll do just that." Zoltan's gaze shifts, his eyes fixing on someone behind me. "Lady Felton," he says coolly.

Lady Felton has become one of Lord Brixeus's most vocal supporters. I doubt it's because she believes in him—rather because she senses the turning of the tide, and she's prepared to flow with it as long as it brings her prosperity and security.

"Princess Averil." She nods respectfully to me. "Your Excellency—I mean to say, Lord Witch, Your Eminence—"

"Enough, Lady Felton," interrupts the Witch. "You've shown your respect. What brings you here?"

"The Regent wanted you to have this." She unfolds a velvety cloth. In its center sits a golden ring with a garnet in the center and two tiny black diamonds on either side. The band is marked with unfamiliar symbols.

"This ring dispels glamours." Zoltan picks it up with a short laugh. "And Brixeus is giving it to me?"

"A sign of trust, he said."

I can't hide my smile of delight. Gently I squeeze Zoltan's arm as he stares grim-faced at the ring.

"That's quite a gesture," I murmur. "It means a lot to you, doesn't it? Him giving you this?"

Zoltan clears his throat and drops the ring back into the cloth. "Give it back to him, Lady Felton, with my gratitude. Tell him he should keep it and wear it. I am not the only being in the world with the power of glamour and illusion. Others have it too, and are far more dangerous. He should protect himself."

"As you wish, Eminence—I mean, Excellence. Your Lordship." Lady Felton curtsies and hurries off.

"Stop looking at me like that, Averil," growls the Sea Witch.

I give his arm another squeeze. "You're adorable when you're soft like this."

"I'm never soft."

"Of course not. Help me mount, would you?"

He boosts me into the saddle, then swings up behind me. We ride out of the gates, down the winding streets of the village, and onto the dusty, sun-soaked road beyond.

The sky is piled with creamy clouds, washed blue between them. Beyond the sway of the sea-grass on the bluffs, the ocean glitters a glorious azure. I lift my head and close my eyes, drinking in the salty fresh air, the spicy warm aroma of the grass, and the tantalizing male scent of the man behind me.

"I needed this," I say. "I've been shut inside rooms for too long. I need to be outside, with you. I need the sea."

"Of course you do." He kisses my temple. "We'll ride to the village and purchase the horse, and then we'll walk down to the beach."

He doesn't have to specify which beach. For us, "The Beach" is the strip of sand where I dragged Kerrin after I saved his life, where the Sea Witch taught me to walk, and where he made me climax for the first time.

With the sea breeze rushing over me and the sun warming my skin, I feel more alive than I have in days. Zoltan and I have made love a few times since that night at the boarding house, but we've been busy, exhausted, and frequently apart when he needed to check on things under the sea. Our rooms at the palace were good, but there was a busy corridor outside where servants passed often, and although Zoltan didn't care, I felt self-conscious about people hearing us please each other.

Out here, with Crystal Point growing smaller behind us and the road lying empty before us, I feel no such embarrassment. In fact, I'm determined to make the Sea Witch come in his pants against my ass, like he once threatened to do.

He's already half-hard—I can feel his firmness rolling against my rear as the horse jogs along the road.

And we have hours of riding together like this. Gods, it will be such fun.

50

THE SEA WITCH

Finally Averil and I are alone. Not alone in an overstuffed palace chamber with countless servants and guards passing outside at all hours of the day and night, or alone in some back hallway where all I can snatch is a taste of her mouth.

Now we are truly alone, like we were at the beginning. She and I, wandering the world, savoring its wonders, free to go anywhere we like and do anything we crave.

Of course, we do have a destination—her sister's palace under the sea. I've yielded the throne and the royal title for good now, but I kept my mother's crown. Ylaine understands my vision for the eventual dissolution of the monarchy so the people can rule themselves, and she is a better choice than me to shepherd that transition.

To Ylaine I will continue to be an advisor, and to both kingdoms Averil and I will be a warning. Our magic, once it is drained from the trident and divided, will serve as a deterrent to those who might desire war instead of peace.

But I don't have to ponder that now, not with the air casting silken lines of Averil's red hair across my cheek. For the next several hours, she and I do not belong to any kingdom or ruler. Nor do we belong to the grassy windswept land on my left, or to the glittering ocean on my right.

We belong only to each other.

The sea and the land are ours, and will be ours for as long as we both live—if she agrees to it. Until now, our ongoing relationship has been an unspoken, expected thing, mentioned only in connection to her education in magic or our exploration of lands beyond. But I crave clarity on the matter. I want her to be mine, and I want to be hers—not for some indeterminate span of years, but forever.

My life was a shadowed chamber, and when Averil came she swept back the curtains. My existence was murky, poisoned water, and her presence cleared away the filth until the waves sparkled clear again.

"I think you saved me," she murmurs.

I inhale sharply. "Did you read my mind? I was just thinking that you saved *me*."

She chuckles. "I wish I could read your mind. But it's more exciting to watch you, and figure you out. And yes, you saved me, Zoltan. If I hadn't met you I'd have wandered too far alone and perished in some dangerous trench full of toothy sea monsters, or I'd have resigned myself to a staid existence, mated to a mildly pleasant merman. I would be spawning his children—"

"Hush, shrimp," I rumble. "I don't like to think of anyone else taking you."

"If you keep calling me shrimp I'm going to call you 'octopus,'" she says, with a petulant shift of her body in the saddle. The friction sends a thrill skating along my cock.

"I'm not an octopus. I have more than eight tentacles."

385

"Tentacles of varying sizes, too." She settles back against me, shifting her rear again. Is she doing this on purpose? I grit my teeth as more blood flows to my dick.

"I remember those tentacles fondly," she breathes, with another squirm.

Oh, yes, she is doing this on purpose.

"Averil," I say in a strangled voice. "Do you want me to stop the horse?"

"No need," she replies airily. "We have too much ground to cover. And anyway we're just talking."

"We could stop awhile, and then I could use magic to help us travel faster for the rest of the journey."

"But it's such a nice morning. And it's so lovely riding like this, don't you think?" Another wiggle, and I groan as more ripples of sensation flow through my hardening dick.

"Little sinner," I growl, my mouth at her ear.

Averil looks all around carefully, as if checking for any farmhouses or other travelers. Then she scrapes her blousy, wide-necked shirt off both shoulders and pulls her arms out of the short sleeves. She pushes the shirt and the lightweight corset down around her waist so her breasts are bared to me, satiny and warm in the sunlight.

I'm too shocked for words. Silently I shift the reins to one hand and press my other hand to her chest, just above the arches of her breasts. My fingers glide along her soft skin and she sighs, tilting back against me, working her hips again. Her bottom rubs against my cock, and my eyes close.

"Fuck, Averil—" I moan as my hand slides over one breast, gently squishing and squeezing it, feeling her peaked nipple roll between my fingers.

"Don't touch yourself," she orders. "Come in your pants, Witch. I want you to come because you crave me and you can't help it."

I vent a short, breathless laugh. She has gotten bolder since a few weeks ago, when she couldn't voice her wish to me. Sometimes she is wild and free and naughty like this, and other times she retreats again, uncertain and shy. Either phase of hers is a delight—I meet her where she is, and it always ends with her writhing and spasming on my dick, my tongue, or my fingers.

She's rubbing against me more shamelessly, moving with the rhythm of the horse, and my mind blurs into sunshine and sensation. I can't think of anything else now. Nothing but her lovely rounded ass cheeks rolling against my inner thighs, teasing my sensitive length over and over.

"Take the reins," I gasp.

"No touching yourself."

"Take them!"

She gathers them, and I clasp her luscious breasts in both my hands, grinding myself into her rear as hard as I can.

"Come for me, Witch," she whispers, and with a harsh moan I erupt, pulsing against her backside, bliss flooding through me. My release soaks a large wet spot on the front of my pants.

"Gods," I hunch down to press my forehead against her bare shoulder, gasping through the waning thrills of my climax. "There now. My clothes are soiled. Is that what you wanted?"

She leans forward a little, pushing the reins back into my nerveless hand. When I straighten upright, she pulls up her corset, tucks her breasts into it, and rearranges her shirt. Then she twists around to give me a sidelong smirk.

That smirk seals her fate. "One hour, Princess." My lips brush her ear. "And then you are going to regret teasing me."

51

AVERIL

For an hour we ride, while Zoltan explains the rules of Hangman's Yoke as coolly as if he didn't promise to make me regret the teasing.

I begin to think perhaps he forgot about his revenge. Which would be a pity.

And then he pulls the horse aside, toward a meadow surrounded by a low stone wall. A creek sparkles nearby, curving between grassy banks.

He dismounts, gazing around. "This looks like a good spot for your punishment."

"Punishment?" I squeeze the saddle with both thighs, unwilling to dismount.

He tethers the horse to a low-hanging branch, gives the stallion water, and then comes back to me. "Get down, shrimp."

I shake my head. "No."

"Averil. Come here."

Every part of me is excited and terrified, thrilled at this new game. I'm fairly sure my arousal has soaked through my pants and left a damp spot on the saddle.

"Come and get me, Witch." And I shoot him a rebellious grin.

At my challenge, Zoltan's eyes flash, and his mouth twitches. But he manages to hold back the smile. He removes the trident and its harness from his back. Setting it against a tree, he casts an illusion to make it temporarily invisible. Since the night at the boarding house, he never takes the trident off without concealing it, even when we are in our own chambers. Usually he adds some protective charms as well, but not this time.

He strides back to the horse and seizes me by my upper arm and my leg, lifting and dragging me off the horse. I struggle, though not as hard as I could if I really wanted to get away.

Zoltan carries me, twisting and bucking and flailing, to the low stone wall. Then he throws me down in the grass and begins removing my clothes—first the shirt, dragging it over my head while I squirm, then unhooking my corset. He seizes one of my feet and tugs the boot off while I kick him with the other.

"If I wanted to hurt you I could," I gasp, while he captures the other boot and jerks it off my foot.

"By all means try it, love," he answers. His fingers catch the waistband of my pants and draw them down, exposing my bare sex.

"No underwear today?" He looks at me, his eyes a storm of wicked lust. "Naughty girl. Is this for me?" With a broad thumb, he strokes the tender skin right above my clit.

"Maybe," I whisper.

Grasping the pants again, he yanks them all the way off my legs. I'm entirely naked now, half-lying in the lush grass at his feet.

We're still within full view of the road. When I bared myself to him, we were riding between some dunes and a strip of forest, but here we're much too close to a small hamlet and a few farms. Anyone could ride or walk past and see us.

"I thought we were going somewhere more private," I protest.

"You thought wrong." He pulls off his own shirt and spreads it over the wall, while I take the opportunity to flee.

I have never run naked on land before. The whisper of grass blades against my toes and calves, the faint chirping and humming of insects, the heat of the sun on my skin, the soft swirl of the breeze—it's almost more sensory delight than I can take.

And then Zoltan's sinewy arm wraps around my waist and I'm lifted clear off my feet, curled against the firm muscle of his side.

He totes me to the wall and bends me over the place where he spread his shirt. My nipples are tight and sensitive, and when they're pressed to the fabric, with the cool stone beneath it, they tingle unbearably. My entire ass and pussy are exposed to anyone who might pass by.

"Are you comfortable?" Zoltan asks.

He's not just inquiring about my physical comfort. If I asked him, he would take me somewhere more private.

But I want to do this with him. So many ways of enjoying pleasure, and we're going to try them all.

"I'm fine," I reply.

Being bent over and exposed like this—it's making me helplessly wet. I'm quivering, my breasts pressed to the top of the wall, my fingers gripping the stones.

I want so badly for the Witch to touch me.

I expect him to tuck himself inside me right away and give me a pounding I won't soon forget.

Instead his warm lips land just below the nape of my neck. Right between my shoulder blades.

Sensation explodes from that spot, radiating along my nerves. I hold my breath.

He kisses me again—the left side of my ribcage, near my breast.

Then again, right over the base of my spine, above my bottom.

"I love you," he whispers against my flesh, and I whimper, overwhelmed with desire and joy.

"Zoltan," I breathe. "Zoltan, come into me. Please."

His broad hands sweep over both my ass cheeks, spreading them. A rustle of grass as he kneels behind me, and then his tongue—oh gods, his tongue. He curls its tip over my clit and then draws it all the way through my folds. I squeal and shiver while he does it again and again.

Then he begins to mouth me, his lips sucking and working, and my consciousness is a taut, brittle, shining thing suspended in crystalline ether, trembling on the verge of a cataclysm.

When he stops I whine, nearly sobbing.

"What do you want, Princess?" His deep voice is both a comfort and a command.

"Your cock, please. I want your cock."

"And do you care if anyone walks by, if anyone sees you coming undone for me?"

"I don't care," I gasp. "I don't care."

"Good girl."

The thick, blunt head of his cock nudges into me, pushing, sliding, stretching, filling. I'm stammering *yes*, half-sobbing his name. But he moves slowly, so slowly—just forcefully enough to keep me on the edge but not firmly or quickly enough to let me come.

After a few minutes, my arousal shifts to a desperate, clawing anger. "You fiendish monster," I gasp as he thrusts. "This is torture."

He squeezes my rear with both hands and vents a long shaking moan. "It is. For both of us, trust me."

"So end it, gods, please."

"Pleasure deferred can be more intense." He shoves himself in deeper, and I choke on a gasp. "You feel so good, Averil—I could nestle in these silky folds forever."

"Forever is too long," I whisper savagely, and I move one hand, reaching between my legs.

Zoltan seizes my hand. Pulls me off the wall—bends me over with my face nearly brushing the grass. He pins both my wrists to the small of my back and he fucks me harder than he ever has. I thought I was on the brink, but he's taking me farther, higher—I'm jerking, shaking—when I come I shriek, full-voice, careless of anything but the ecstasy soaring through my body, shearing all thought into fragments, ripping my own will to shreds.

It's intense relief beyond anything I've felt with him before—a tsunami of mind-shattering ecstasy, washing into exquisite bliss.

The Sea Witch is roaring too, jetting heat inside me, clutching me tight, pulling me against him—deeper, deeper, we both need to be deeper—I want tentacles of my own so I can wrap myself around him and never let go, never, never.

When his throbs of pleasure have eased he pulls out, and we both crash into the feathery green grass. He hauls me to his chest, collecting my last whimpers with his mouth. "I love you." He kisses me frantically, each press of his lips more fervent. "I love you beyond reason, Averil. I want you. I need you to say you'll be with me forever, my darling, my—" And then he breathes one shining word against my mouth. "Mate."

52

THE SEA WITCH

Averil pulls back and sits up in the grass beside me. She's flushed with orgasmic bliss, a little sweaty, her pupils still dilated from arousal. Her lips are swollen, cherry-red. Delicious.

I move to kiss her again but she presses a hand to my chest.

"You said 'mate.'" She stares at me. "But you don't believe in mates."

"Not the 'one true mate' your priestesses speak of—someone you must wait for at the expense of experiencing life and pleasure," I counter. "I still despise that sort of mate. But a partner, a fellow wanderer, a friend beyond all others—one lover for a lifetime—that kind of mate, I could believe in."

"One lover for a lifetime? Are you sure?" She traces my lip with her finger. Tears shimmer in her eyes.

"I will never want anyone else." The truth of the words reverberates through every bone and muscle I have.

It's her, forever.

I will say it, if it kills me. I will commit to this—to her.

"I belong to you," I tell her, in a tone rich with all the certainty I feel. "I've been yours from the moment Graeme brought you to me, when you were swollen and helpless, yet fighting so hard against the poison. That day and beyond, I watched you endure, and persist, and grow. You changed me. You pulled me out of the darkness I had lurked in for decades, and you brought me back to life. I adore you, Averil, every part of you. I would do anything to be your mate. If you will have me."

"You want *me*?" Tears are sliding down her rosy cheeks. "I'm young, and I have nothing to offer you, no secret magic or wisdom, little knowledge of pleasure or the world."

"Nothing to offer?" I glare at her. "You think so little of yourself? You are wiser than I am, in many ways. Intelligent, clear-sighted, kind, diplomatic, a quick learner—you charm people, my love, and not in the false way the prince did, but in a genuine way, because they can feel that you care. Kerrin taught you a lesson, but he did not erase your sweet capacity for hope, your inner belief in a person's potential for goodness. And beyond all that you are—fun."

I grin at her, and she gives me a small smile in return.

I reach out, brushing the tears from her cheek with my finger. "I enjoy your company, whether you're sad or angry or saucy or blooming with happiness. Dark moods come to everyone, and I know that you and I can draw each other out of them—or sit together in the darkness awhile, if we need to. Nothing to offer? Bullshit, Averil. You give me everything. Everything I could want in a partner, a friend. Not to mention your delectable body." I lunge toward her, pushing her down into the grass and burying my face between her breasts, nuzzling her skin. She's laughing, shaking with each peal.

But I can't help noticing she hasn't answered me yet. And I wonder if, now that I've reassured her, she's realizing how unworthy I am.

Why would she want to bind herself to someone like me? Someone with two centuries of dissolution and desperation hanging like an anchor around his neck, someone violent and vengeful, someone with base appetites and melancholic moods.

I kiss her belly one more time, softly, and then I rise, heading for my clothes.

Why would I ask a woman as bright, clever, and charming as the princess to chain herself to me for life? I cannot believe I had the gall to pose the question. I am a fucking idiot.

I jerk my stained pants into place and button them. When I turn to grab the shirt, Averil is there, holding it, looking at me with a keen, steady understanding in her eyes. The knowing in her gaze unsettles me.

"Thank you," I mumble, taking the shirt and turning my back.

"Zoltan."

"What?"

"Look at me."

I haul in a deep breath and face her.

"You're doubting yourself," she says. "Hating yourself. Don't do that."

"Why not?" I scoff. "You did."

She sighs. "Perhaps when you love someone so much and cherish the best of them so deeply, it's natural to wonder why they love you back. But I do. And I always will, you wild, sweet, weary, wonderful Witch."

"That's far too much alliteration." My voice is a hoarse, choked whisper.

"Sometimes a little poetry is required." She cups the back of my neck with her fingers and pulls my mouth down to hers. "You're mine forever. My darling mate."

53

AVERIL

Our stop in the village takes longer than we expected, since messengers from Crystal Point have been sent throughout the small kingdom with word of the change in rulership, and everyone in the town is eager to see us and speak to us. Far from being unhappy, the townspeople seem thrilled to have played a part in the greatest drama of the past decade. Prince Kerrin wasn't especially kind to any of them—downright rude and cruel to some—and they don't seem sorry he's gone.

But the Sea Witch and I—we are treated like a king and queen. It turns out that Zoltan stole the mayor's horse—but when he offers gold, enough to pay for its absence and its purchase, the mayor insists, "The horse shall be yours! We will keep him for you, and you must use him anytime you like."

They try to persuade us to stay for dinner, and we're only able to escape by promising to return soon.

"The Witch and I enjoy being on land," I tell them. "I'm sure we'll visit often. After all, he has promised to teach me more card games."

"Is that so?" chuckles Mayor Throanfeld. "He's going to make a gambler of you, eh? You know, my lord, I believe I may have played you once, in a hovel of a tavern up the coast. The 'Fiddling Albatross,' I think it was."

The Sea Witch nods. "A good game. You lost, I believe."

"As did everyone who played you that night. You have skill."

There's an unspoken suspicion behind his words, and Zoltan says, "All skill, and no magic, I assure you."

"Oh, of course, of course," says the mayor. "Wasn't a question at all." But he looks pleased, just the same.

Finally, with the help of an illusion or two, we manage to slip away, taking the narrow path out of town down to the strip of beach. Zoltan uncovers a chest where we can store our clothes until we come ashore next time. While I undress, I eye the shadowed cave-like recess where Zoltan tossed my naked body around and pleasured me with his tentacles.

"If we weren't in a hurry," I murmur.

"What's that, love?"

I glance at him and immediately forget what I was going to say. I'm not sure I will ever get used to the sight of him naked. He is absolutely glorious—power and muscle and rugged beauty.

"I, um—I want you to teach me 'Hangman's Yoke' soon."

"Even if I trounce you every time?" He flashes me a grin.

"Cocky bastard. Surely you've lost to someone before."

"Well…" He stalks toward me, his dark eyes hooded and mesmerizing. "I gambled my heart once. And I lost it to you."

I suck in a quick breath. "Don't try to seduce me, Witch. We're late to our meeting with my sister."

"Lateness is fashionable among royalty."

"Zoltan…mmm…" But I'm already tipping my face up to his, accepting the firm warmth of his lips on mine. His tongue slides in, and I yield entirely, my body caving toward his, hungry for the heat of his skin, the strength of his frame.

I'm not sure how long we stand there, twined together, our mouths melting into each other. I'm still wearing my corset, which Zoltan has pushed down so he can feel my breasts.

"We should stop. Someone from the village could come down to the shore," he rumbles at last.

"Says the man who rutted me in full view of the road and a few farmhouses."

"Distant farmhouses. And those people were strangers. The villagers know us now."

"So you won't take me in front of people who know us. Good to know you have some boundaries." I fondle one of his nipples, and he hisses sharply, his cock bumping my stomach.

Somehow his reluctance makes me feel all the more wicked. Backing away a few steps, I unhook the corset and toss it aside, freeing my breasts entirely. Then I seize his wrist and pull him with me into the shadow of the rocky ledge.

"Remember the waking dream?" I whisper. "You did such wonderful things to me here. I was ruined for anyone else." I'm sinking to my knees, my palms sliding over the hard, bumpy muscles that line his stomach. Then I'm sucking his shaft into my mouth, savoring him. He's salty, warm, delicious. A little hum of pleasure escapes me as I take him deeper, pushing him down my throat. I almost gag, but I stop myself, remembering that he dislikes the sound.

"Gods, Averil," he gasps. "Shit, shit." He gathers my hair and holds it back while I pump my mouth on him, stroking and circling the base of his shaft with my hands.

I pull off for a moment to look up at him—this powerful sorcerer, his chest heaving, muscles rigid, slave to the magic of my tongue.

"Come in my mouth, sweetheart," I whisper to him. "Come for me." And I slide my lips over him again.

He cries out, hips thrusting forward convulsively, and his cock bobs against my tongue. I swallow everything, and I lick him clean.

When I stand up, my knees are coated with sand, sore from kneeling.

Zoltan seizes my arm, drags me back against his chest. I can feel the thunder of his heartbeat against my spine.

His hand wraps between my legs, two thick fingers sinking into my slickness. His thumb grazes my clit, working it with clever, exquisite little touches. Then his fingers adopt a merciless, rapid rhythm, pounding into my sex until I'm squealing breathlessly, clutching at his other arm with both hands, squeezing his bicep for dear life.

He pauses, sliding his fingers out so he can massage my clit and pussy lips, round and round, round and round until I'm going to go mad, I'm going to scream—

"Scream if you need to," he growls, and then his fingers are back inside me, thrusting wetly—and with a faint shriek I come around them.

"Yes, love, yes. I can feel you squeezing my fingers," he says in my ear. "That's it, Princess."

After a few more pulses, he withdraws his hand and cups my sex, providing pressure just where I need it while I come down.

I'm too shaky to stand, so when he lets me go I slide to the sandy floor of the hollow and sit there while he buries the chest with our clothes. He leaves my corset on the sand—a wise move, since some clothing is expected in the kingdom under the sea. I can't go into the city or my sister's court with bare breasts.

When he's done the Witch stands beside me, arms crossed, an insolent smirk on his face. "Well, shrimp? Can you walk?"

"Of course." I get to my feet and wobble a bit.

He catches me, laughing, and helps me take a few steps. "This feels familiar."

"I can manage on human legs very well now, thank you." I pull away and walk farther, swaying a little.

When I bend over to pick up my corset, Zoltan hums with appreciation. "The first time I saw that ass of yours—gods. Divinely beautiful. I was so hard for you I went behind a rock to relieve the pressure."

"Oh." I hook the corset and jog it a bit, settling my breasts into the cups. "I remember that. I asked what you were doing back there."

Zoltan tosses me a small woven bag, and I sling it across my body without questioning why we need it.

"I had to leave my hiding place unsatisfied," he says, "or you would have gotten suspicious—even more suspicious than you already were."

"It feels like so long ago... and yet it really wasn't."

"We've been through a lifetime's worth of danger and intrigue since then," says Zoltan. "And pain, of course. Unfortunately I have to cause you more pain with the transition back to your natural form. Are you..."

"Ready," I say, and he smiles.

But his smile vanishes as he speaks the spell over me and my body contorts and shudders, returning to its original shape. The pain is less than the agony I endured when Cass forced my transformation, but it's still sickening, bone-cracking, and horrible.

When it's over I'm a mermaid again, flopping in the clear water of the shallows.

Zoltan has reverted to his mer form as well, and his tentacles glide over me, touching and testing my altered flesh and my scales. Once he's satisfied, he moves deeper into the waves, and I follow him.

The bliss of returning to the sea is practically orgasmic. A slow descent isn't enough—I plunge in, skimming through the shallows and then diving once the sea floor drops. I surge back up to the surface and leap, spray flying as I laugh aloud.

Zoltan catches me when I splash down, and he swirls me in a circle, a maelstrom with the two of us at its center.

"We need to make up for lost time, and I seem to remember a certain little mermaid once claiming she could swim faster than me," he says. "Care to test that boast?"

Every fiber of my being roars *yes*. "Race you to the Royal City."

The Witch laughs. "So confident, shrimp."

"You have to promise not to use magic."

"Agreed."

"And don't let me win."

"I wouldn't dare, love."

"Whoever reaches the first watchtower wins." I give him a saucy flick of my tail and shoot away into the blue gloom.

"Little cheat!" he bellows, far too close behind for my liking, and with a squeal I whip my tail, propelling myself even faster.

He's bulkier, less streamlined, but he has all those powerful tentacles. He pulls ahead. A few minutes later I manage to gain the lead.

Streaking through the ocean at top speed has its dangers—rocks, shipwrecks, reefs, and predators with teeth or toxins. I haven't swum like this in a while, but I know how to outrun predators under the sea, and there is no predator more threatening than the imposing male chasing me.

He barrels ahead again, snapping a tentacle against my backside. It feels different against my scales than it would in human form, but a wicked tingle still races through my body.

Straining every muscle I have, I surge forward, coming abreast of the Witch. He flashes me a wild, savage grin, and I'm grinning back, but only for an instant. Another pulse of my muscles, my tail whipping like mad, and I'm ahead again, creating and then widening the gap between us.

So it goes, until finally, in the distance, I can see the murky shadow of a watchtower. My gills are working frantically, the muscles in my torso and tail are screaming—I'm speeding toward the column with all my might. Getting closer—closer—I stretch out my hand to touch the stones—

But a tattooed brown arm is also reaching for the tower wall. Thick fingers, flashing with rings.

We slam our palms against it at the same moment.

"A tie," Zoltan says, his tentacles coiling and crawling along the stone.

"You were carrying the trident," I admit. "And I had a head start."

"So you did. But you might have won anyway." He curls a tentacle under my chin. "Excellent technique, love. You're very good, and I do like a challenge. We must race again soon. Maybe next time I'll catch you."

There's a dark, sensual intent in those final words, but before he can say anything else, three mer guards drift down from the tower entrance. They're holding weapons, but they aren't pointing the weapons at us. They touch their foreheads respectfully to me and Zoltan.

"Witch-lord," says one of them. "And Princess Averil, welcome home. You're expected. We can escort you to the palace if you like."

"Thank you, but that's not necessary," I reply. "Don't let us keep you from your duties."

They return to the tower, while Zoltan and I swim on into the city.

I've grown comfortable with human towns and their streets, and it's quite different to swim along channels instead of walking on roads, to see the podlike structures instead of houses, with randomly placed entries instead of neatly cut first-floor doors. The warmth of familiarity suffuses my heart. Even though I never quite belonged here, it's good to be home again.

The merfolk we pass cheer for me, shouting a welcome, crying out their joy at my return. It's odd because, as the youngest princess, I've never been cheered personally like this. Of course the people knew me and paid me respect, but there's a palpable freedom and gladness in the water that I've never felt from them before. Could it be that my father's rule had weighed everyone down more heavily than I realized? Maybe I wasn't the only one feeling repressed, forced into a life I didn't want.

The merfolk who approach to clasp or kiss my hand do so warily, cautious of the Sea Witch. Yet they seem to welcome him too. They watch him pass with awed expressions, fear and admiration blended.

We're admitted to the palace without question, with bowed heads and reverent salutes from the guards. I greet several servants on the way to the royal reception room.

The colonnades and colorful lights are just as I remember— except the lights seem brighter, more golden. No priestesses hover in the alcoves, tasting delicacies and watching the supplicants with faint disdain. No dignitaries cluster around them, or around the royal bower. Instead of merfolk drifting dully in a long lines, hoping for the unlikely chance to speak to my father, there are stations in two rows across the chamber, each one manned by a pair of merfolk. The supplicants gather in much shorter lines before each station.

"These representatives were my idea," says the Witch, low. "Two at each station, as you see. They are leaders among the people—not nobles by birth, mind you, but mer nominated by their peers, whose wisdom, skill, or personality make them fit to answer questions and resolve disputes. They've been hastily chosen, and the system isn't yet perfect—but having them here takes some of the pressure off Ylaine. If the representatives cannot solve an issue, it is passed on to the Queen."

He points ahead, to where Ylaine floats in the royal bower. She is speaking with someone I recognize—a merchant from a southern settlement. Her mate, Ardoc, is playing with their daughter nearby. As I watch, he swirls my niece around and touches his nose to hers while she bursts into giggles that ripple throughout the room.

"He's the perfect royal consort." The Sea Witch's mouth quirks as he watches them. "Kind and simple, with no ambitions to be anything but a reliable support to your sister, a defender of his people, and a good father."

"Simple?" I raise an eyebrow. "Seems he has more true wisdom than many other men."

"Fair point." The Witch nods to me. "Go, Averil. I can see your tail twitching with eagerness."

Laughing, I rush past the representatives, heedless of the current I cause, and I shoot straight up to my sister just as the merchant is leaving.

"Averil!" she screeches, flinging both arms around my neck, pinning my gills shut like she always does. I tap her arm, and she lets go. "Sorry."

"You've always hugged like a human."

"Says the girl who *became* a human. Can others try this transformative magic? I would ask the Witch, but—I'm a little scared of him. We all are. I pretend not to be because—Queen." She touches her crown.

I glance back at Zoltan, who is speaking with one of the representatives.

I understand why the Witch denied human form to anyone else. Perhaps someday we can devise a way to make shifting into human form easier, but until then, I refuse to put that burden on him.

"No," I say slowly. "It's not a magic that can be shared. Not yet, anyway."

"Ah, well." Ylaine shrugs. "You must at least bring some human food down to the shore so I can taste it. Tell me everything you've eaten, in detail."

"Gods, the soup," I exclaim, my eyes closing at the memory. "You must try soup."

We talk for a long while, and then I inquire about my other sisters. According to Ylaine, most of them have returned to their lives and homes, resigned to the new regime. Serra, the strongest objector, has been temporarily confined until she adjusts her perspective.

"She insists that she should rule," Ylaine says. "I don't know—maybe she's right."

"Nonsense. You and I both know how she is—cruel at heart. She'd be no better than Father—worse, I suspect. You are ideal for this role. And Zoltan says you're doing a wonderful job."

"He said that?" She lifts her eyebrows.

"Yes." It's a paraphrase, but I know he admires the way Ylaine has taken to the rulership. "I hope one day you'll come to think of him as a brother."

"You truly love him, then?" Ylaine's blue eyes pierce mine, her features suddenly serious. "I hoped and believed that the love between you was true, but I wanted to see you in person to be sure."

"Yes, I love him. More fervently than I thought possible. Not because I have a false view of him—I see everything that he is, good and bad. And he's mine."

She clasps both my hands. "It's wonderful, isn't it?" Her gaze slants toward Ardoc, fondness glowing in her eyes. "So the Sea Witch is your one true mate. How strange! We'd never have imagined such a thing when we were young."

"I'm not sure I believe in the 'one true mate,'" I murmur. "But if such a thing exists, then he is mine."

The Witch is approaching us, and every head in the room turns to follow his progress. I don't blame them—he's an imposing figure.

"Your Majesty." He bends his head and salutes Ylaine. "Averil, I thought you might want to visit your father."

"'Want' is probably not the right word," I mutter. "'Should' is probably nearer the mark."

"Go on," says Ylaine. "I'll order refreshments and you can have some when you return."

54

THE SEA WITCH

Tarion is floating in a dark cell beneath the palace, a bolted metal grate preventing his escape from the cell. He is not shackled—a mercy of his daughter Ylaine. He doesn't possess his former strength or any of my magic, so I haven't insisted that he be put in chains.

"Come to finish the job at last, creature?" he sneers.

"No."

"Come to taunt me then, about your carnal assault of my foolish daughter? She was always the most headstrong of them all. I should have confined her and married her off when I had the chance, before you could spoil her with your foul seed." He practically spits the words at me.

"Tarion—" I start to warn him, but he continues the tirade.

"Maybe you've done me a favor. The little fool is gone now. I don't ever have to see her face again."

Gritting my teeth, I move aside, allowing him to see Averil behind me.

His eyes widen. "You… You traitor, you idiot child. Do you see what you've done to me? You've wrecked the kingdom. Ruined everything. The priestesses and your sister Serra are imprisoned because of you! Everything I've worked for, all that I've striven to accomplish, undone in a handful of days, because you were stupid enough to make an alliance with my sworn enemy. What were you thinking, child? I loved you, in spite of all you did to make my life harder. Do you realize how much worry you caused me? These gray hairs are not from my concern for your sisters—no, they are all from you. Who would have believed one of my offspring could be so stupid? After I warned you about him for years. And now one small, foolish spawn of mine has yielded her purity to a fiend, and thus destroyed our family's legacy."

He pauses, a choked sound issuing from his throat. "You betrayed me, daughter. Betrayed your father who did nothing but love you, preserve you, protect you. You have broken my heart. My will to live is gone. I will likely die soon, not as a respected and beloved king, but as a disgraced wretch. That's what you wanted, isn't it? Because I would not let you indulge your wayward passions, because I discouraged you from your interest in humans, you decided to have revenge upon me. Look at me now, Averil. Did I deserve this? Is this a just end for the father who loved you?"

Averil moves forward, ready to speak, but Tarion keeps spewing words. "How could you soil yourself with a monster like him? I could tell you stories of his past deeds that would make your ears curl and turn your heart sour. He is a brigand, a thief, a dissolute rake, a monstrous divergence, a freak. He is a pestilence, a toxin polluting the world with his foul magic. He will use you up and cast you aside, and then you will have lost everything and everyone who ever cared for you. And *you* made the choice. You listened to his lies. You let this creeping beast invade you, when I fought so hard to keep you pure. I can't bear to look at your face—sin is scrawled upon it. You should be ashamed of yourself, child. Pray—pray to the gods that you may be forgiven. Make a sacrifice, flay your flesh in penitence, wail for the sins you've committed in your youth and idiocy. No honest merman will want you now. But perhaps you may be forgiven if you live a life of quiet seclusion, bowed to the will of the Mother Goddess."

It's all I can do not to reach between the bars and throttle him. I want to defend my darling, to close Tarion's lying, manipulative lips forever.

"Say the word," I growl to Averil, "and I will tear out his tongue."

When I glance at her, I half-expect her to be cowed or distressed. I wait for her expression to change when she looks at me, for her eyes to fill with hatred, loathing, and self-doubt.

But her features are calm, her eyes clear and keen.

"No need for violence, Zoltan," she says. "I've been around enough poison lately to recognize it, and to develop a certain resistance."

At the words, my heart beats faster, warm and glowing with my adoration for her. She surprises me over and over with new reasons to love her.

"I am glad you still live, Father," says Averil. "Though I don't believe you deserved Zoltan's mercy. Perhaps your time here will allow you to rethink your actions and find some true remorse. As for your abhorrence of my face—don't worry, you won't have to see it again. Zoltan and I will be traveling, and when we do return here for visits, I won't disturb your solitude. May you find your own kind of peace with who you are and what you have done."

She turns her back on him and sails back along the corridor.

412

"Your one great deed in life was spawning her," I tell Tarion. "And Queen Ylaine, of course. I'll see to it that they're well taken care of." And I give him my most wicked smile.

That smile is purely vindictive on my part, because I have every intention of truly seeing to Averil and Ylaine's well-being. I intend no harm to either of them, now or in the future. But I want Tarion to have something to stew over while he languishes in his cell.

I am done with him forever. And it seems Averil is, too. I don't fault her for it. She does not owe him her forgiveness. If she chooses to give it someday, I will support her, but I will not encourage it. A child does not owe a parent the gift of peace after years of lies and pain.

When we join Ylaine and Ardoc in a royal parlor for refreshment, Averil is quiet and subdued at first. Ylaine eyes her appraisingly, then shoves her infant spawn into Averil's arms. I would defy anyone to be solemn or sad with a creature of such impossible cuteness babbling and smiling at them. Soon enough, Averil succumbs to the little one's coos and questing fingers, and she begins kissing her niece's tiny round cheeks.

When we've eaten and conversed, Ylaine asks, "Will you be staying here tonight? We have rooms for you—or a single room if you prefer to share." She wiggles her eyebrows.

Averil opens her mouth to answer, but I interject, "I'm taking Averil home with me. But we'll return soon."

Averil frowns at me, confused. "Home? What home? You told me your lair exploded when you reactivated the trident."

"Oh, *home*, of course!" Ylaine giggles, practically squirming with excitement. It's very unqueenly, but I don't protest. She knows the secret I've been keeping from Averil, and she's eager for her sister's joy to be complete. "Off you go, then," she crows. "Safe travels!"

55

We leave the palace and swim through the city channels, pausing to greet more citizens along the way.

"That went as well as could be hoped, and rather better than I expected," I tell Zoltan as we swim clear of the ring of watchtowers. "What did you mean, you're taking me home? Your lair is broken."

"Indeed." He keeps swimming, but casts me a sidelong half-smile. His eyes glitter with suppressed delight.

"Fine, keep your secrets." I skim alongside him, conscious of the dramatic difference in our size and shape. He's immense, and he has all those blue-gray tentacles surging and writhing as he swims, while I'm much smaller and slimmer, with a long lithe tail covered in dark, iridescent scales.

We don't hurry this time. We meander through the ocean together, pausing to admire a beautiful school of fish or a particularly large and gorgeous anemone. The Sea Witch halts a couple of times to collect bits of this or that from the ocean floor or the nooks of a reef, and I stow the items in the bag slung across my back.

"For magic?" I ask.

He nods. "I always bring along a bag for specimens and supplies."

As we swim farther, one of his tentacles curls around my forearm like a bracelet, its tip caressing the underside of my wrist.

I begin to notice more toxic plants and creatures dotting the ocean floor. The warning signs of the Sea Witch's domain—the area I used to avoid. Strange to think that if it hadn't been for the shipwreck, I could have lived my whole life without ever meeting him, or knowing him. I shudder at the thought, and he turns to me instantly, his features tightening, an alarmed question in his eyes. The tentacle around my wrist relaxes and slithers away.

It pains me that I ever recoiled from him, that I ever hurt him like that. I hate that he thinks I would recoil from him now.

"I was thinking about how I used to steer away from this area," I explain. "How I might have gone a lifetime without meeting you. A terrible thought."

"Oh." His features relax, and a tentacle slithers out, wrapping my waist, drawing me closer to him. "Terrible indeed."

Ahead of us rears the wall of his poisonous garden, a rainbow of deadly hues in the azure deep. Plants and living things overgrown and stretched out, wider and higher than is natural.

"You enhanced their growth with magic," I say.

"I did."

"You're incredible." I stare at the gently waving fronds and luminous anemone tentacles. "You did all of this without the trident."

"A tedious process, I admit. But it was good for me to relearn the slow way of magic, without the convenience on which I'd come to rely."

"And you'll teach me everything."

"I will. If you promise not to leave me afterward." He's smiling, but there's a twinge of real uncertainty in it. "You don't have to promise," he adds. "I will take whatever time you give me and consider myself the most fortunate soul in the world."

I face him, linking my hands behind his thick, strong neck and pulling myself close to his chest. My hair swirls with his, ink and fire mingled.

"I love you," I tell him, with all the passionate certainty I can inject into the words. "Someday I will make you believe it. I will erase every last bit of your doubts."

His muscled arms close around me. "I look forward to it. Hold tight now, love. We must pass through danger to reach our haven."

Just as he did on that first night, he clasps me against his massive body. This time I'm not afraid at all—only awed and delighted. Well... perhaps a little bit afraid, because there are things in this garden I didn't see the first time—toothy plants snapping from shadowed hollows, slack-jawed fish with malevolent eyes, strange gelatinous blobs that slide between anemones as tall as trees.

But I am safe with him. He won't let anything hurt me.

I close my eyes and inhale the rich masculine scent of the Witch, laced with pheromones that seem much more potent here, beneath the waves, in this place of toxic magic. Desire courses through my body, and my tail twitches, my caudal fin fluttering against his tentacles.

The Witch hums deep in his chest, clutching me tighter.

My arousal intensifies, centered beneath the scale-flap, in the widest part of my tail. The mating slit there is warming, tingling, widening. I can smell the liquid seeping from it—my own scent, my own pheromones spiraling through the water. It's beyond my control. Blood rises to my cheeks, heating them.

"Your fragrance, little sinner," he rumbles. "It's intoxicating."

My heartbeat ratchets up, and I press harder against him. The space inside me feels hollow, a sweet ache growing there, a craving for fullness.

We break out into the safe waters, the zone in front of the entrance to his lair. I glimpsed it just once, and the memory is blurred. Still, I can tell that the area has changed. It's wider, and it looks as if broken bits of rock have been laid together and cemented to form walls and columns. Instead of a craggy cave, I'm looking at the entrance to a rugged sort of palace.

"I thought you said it blew up," I say blankly.

The Witch uncoils his tentacles from my body and lets me float forward to survey the dwelling. "I fixed it. Those visits I made to the sea—they weren't all political meetings with your sister. She's quite capable, in fact. No, most of them were trips I made here, to repair this place. And I had help."

"A lot of help." Liris drifts into my view—I'm not sure whether he came from the garden or a side entrance of the new lair. Behind him floats the ethereal Ekkon, and Graeme swirls up beside them both, his eel's body undulating, his sharp teeth bared in a grin.

"We had to help him," Graeme says. "Zoltan blew up our home too."

Liris wears a smile on his scarred face, and his beautiful cream-and-brown-striped fins are fanned out wide. "We're all rather proud of the place. Less dark and gloomy. Better suited to everyone's needs."

"Our quarters are far from yours," says Ekkon in his distant voice. I can't look straight at him—the light bobbing in front of his forehead is too distracting—dangerously enticing. "That way we won't hear each other while we're fucking."

"Gods, can't you say 'enjoying each other' or 'pleasuring each other?'" Liris protests. "Something less crassly human?"

"Off with you," grunts the Witch, but he's half-smiling. "I want to show Averil around."

"We know what *that* means, don't we, darlings?" says Graeme. "Come on, let's leave them to it. Enjoy 'showing her around' your cock, Zoltan."

Zoltan lunges at him, but Graeme zips out of reach with an electric flash and a merry laugh. The three males hurry off, disappearing through a nearby arch.

"That's the way to their quarters," Zoltan says. "You and I will enter here. There is still much work to be done."

He leads the way inside, while I marvel at the height of the columns and the ceiling, the delicate multicolored glow of luminescent plants and creeping things.

"How did you manage all this in so short a time? You must have had more help than theirs."

"I used a lot of magic," he admits. "The entrance is complete, and a few of the chambers, but I have plans for more."

We pass out of the entrance hall into a wide room decorated with—

I stop immediately, shock vibrating along my spine. My gills spasm, and my tongue feels numb.

This great room is full of familiar things, precious things. Items I've spent years accumulating. Heavy, ornate frames feathery with green growth. Shining cups and bowls. A chandelier with crystal pendants—I remember how long it took me to drag that back from the wreck where I found it. I was nearly lunch for a giant squid.

My fiddle is there, bracketed to the rocky wall. It will never play again, of course, but I used to like looking at it and imagining the sounds it might make. Now I know what a fiddle sounds like. I never have to wonder again.

"How did you know about all this?" I say quietly. "How did you find it?"

"Ylaine is deeply invested in your happiness," Zoltan says. "She told me."

"She used to go with me sometimes, to explore shipwrecks." I drift forward to a piece of human furniture he has placed against the wall—a sideboard, I think it's called. When I pull a drawer open, my collection of mismatched silverware winks back at me. Another drawer holds jewelry and baubles and trinkets I've gathered.

"Zoltan," I murmur. "This is—it's beautiful. It's more thoughtful than the soup thing."

"The soup thing?"

"When you took me to the all-you-can-eat soup place. Flay's Kitchen."

"Ah, yes. I should hope this is more meaningful. It certainly took longer."

"I can't even imagine how hard you must have worked to do this."

"And look here." He points to a crystal case at one side of the room. Inside it are two crowns. One of them is the tiara he promised to keep for me, on the night he first turned me human. The other I've seen on my father's head every day since I was spawned—but now I understand it wasn't his by right.

"That's my mother's crown, the one she passed on to me," Zoltan explains.

"It's beautiful. And mine—you kept it safe."

"Of course, love." He grimaces sheepishly. "I may have touched it and fondled it a little too often while I was thinking of a certain persistent, delightful mermaid princess and wishing she would call on me."

Those words, uttered in a gruff, embarrassed tone—they finish me. If I were human right now I'd be crying buckets full of tears. As it is, I'm trembling, wracked with emotion. I need an outlet. I need *him*.

I've grown used to the clarity of sound on land, to the ease of motion through air. In mermaid form, my ears are more sensitive, tuned to catch and interpret sound underwater; and my voice is sharper, designed to carry through liquid. I'm still not sure which element I prefer, despite the fact that I was born to one and a guest in the other.

Just like I'm not sure which form I prefer for the Sea Witch—his strong, capable, long-legged human body or his majestic, extraordinary tentacled form.

It's a relief that I don't have to choose.

"What's your penis like in this form?" The question tumbles out before I can think better of it.

The Witch's eyebrows rise, and his mouth curves up at one side. "Long and flexible, like every merman. Just right for slipping inside a little mermaid's tail and breeding her."

Breeding—oh gods.

"I didn't ask before, when we had sex on land," I murmur. "But—about the idea of spawning—I don't want—I'm not ready—"

"I'm teasing you, love," he replies, sweeping closer and taking my chin in his hand. "You don't need to worry about that. I have magical precautions in place, for myself. I can't impregnate anyone unless I remove those spells."

"Oh." My body relaxes a little. "Good."

"I really scared you, didn't I?" He grins. "Good to know that the mere mention of offspring is enough to make you stiff with terror."

"I like them," I say defensively. "Just not from me. Not now. Maybe—maybe someday. It would be interesting to see

420

what they would look like." My mind begins to conjure tiny tentacled creatures with iridescent skin and scarlet hair.

"Shrimp, you're drifting," he warns. "I can see that clever mind of yours questioning and theorizing. Remember, we were talking of sex."

"Hmm," I feign a vague disinterest. "You may have to remind me."

His lashes droop lower, his eyes hooded and burning with wicked glee. "My pleasure."

The next second his tentacles snake out—half a dozen at least—binding my arms to my body, coiling around my tail so I can't manage the barest flick of my fin.

"Zoltan!" I squeal as he bundles me up and carries me out of the big room, down a short hallway and into a chamber glimmering with bright stones. Their orange glow pulses softly, suffusing the chamber with gentle light.

"Lava crystals and a touch of magic," Zoltan explains.

He grabs the small satchel I've been carrying and removes the trident harness from his own back. While he's setting them aside, I remove my corset, and I take a scant few moments to notice the sleeping alcove, filled with feathery plants; the dressing table, decorated with more items from my collection; and the big wardrobe.

Then Zoltan's tentacles flip me upside down, and with one hand clasping the back of my head, he brings my mouth to his.

Bubbles rise around us, tiny sparkling orbs I barely notice before my eyes close. Kissing him underwater is strange, beautiful, ethereal. The sea flows through both of us, fills us, slips in and out of throats and gills, whispers in our ears. We are one with it, but it does not define us, because we are more than the sea, more than the air. He and I—we are something altogether beyond.

Zoltan eases back from the kiss and turns me upright again, my body aligned with his. The tentacles crawl around me, tightening against my rear, drawing me in. One of them nudges beneath my scale-flap, teasing it open. Inside I'm warm and wet, pulsing, hungering, yearning for him.

The Sea Witch angles his body, and I see it then—at the center of his tentacles, protruding from an aperture similar to mine. His cock is similar to a tentacle, though much shorter and slightly more rigid, and it's adorned with tiny bumps. My insides practically vibrate with eagerness to know how those little bumps will feel rubbing inside me.

Clasping, tugging, softly pressing my skin, the tentacles writhe along my spine and spiral around my arms. They creep across my breasts, plucking at my nipples with the same gentle yet urgent suction I remember from the cave by the beach. My whole body sings in response, my torso and tail lurching toward Zoltan, mutely begging him to come in.

The Sea Witch's gaze is dark with lust, heavy with the same yearning I feel. There's something different about this joining, here in the amber glow of the room he made for us—both of us secure in the forms we were born with. No glamours, no disguises, no transformation.

He hooks his great hand around the back of my neck and hauls me in, my scarlet hair bleeding into his, our lips colliding, crushing against each other with insistent need. Our tongues entwine, and as they do Zoltan's tentacles constrict around my body, angling my spine, adjusting my tail for entry. He's sliding in. Writhing deeper and deeper inside me, farther than any human cock could go. My inner channel is as long as his shaft; and past the entrance, it is lined with exquisitely sensitive tissues. The nubby surface of his cock skates along those nerves, lighting up every one of them.

422

I've never had anything in this part of me. I've never climaxed in this form. I never knew it could feel like this, and I'm whining into Zoltan's mouth, bucking against him, eager for more, and yet the rippling glide of his length is almost too much stimulation to bear. It's as if my entire inner channel is as delicately sensitive as my human clit, capable of a hundred times the pleasure.

I break our kiss, whimpering, "Zoltan, Zoltan," over and over.

"Averil," he says through his teeth, his eyes reflecting the amber light of the crystals. He's groaning, shaking. "Averil... gods..."

"It's new for me," I gasp. "You—you've done this with others."

"It never felt this good," he moans, throwing his head back. "Gods, love, I don't know how long I can last."

His length shifts and rolls inside me, and I scream. No thoughts—only the white, dazzling heat of pleasure vibrating through my channel. Only burst after burst of stimulation until I'm sure my mind will break—it will explode—I can't bear any more.

The delicate sucking pull of the tentacles on my back and shoulders.

My breasts, flush with Zoltan's chest, my hardened nipples grazing his.

The scent of him—heavy, masculine, a spicy musk fringed with savage power, saturating my gills and my nostrils, soaking my skin.

His textured length tantalizing every inner nerve I possess. The hum of his throaty groans through both our bodies as he plunges, and plunges, surging, thrusting. Yes, yes, yes—

A sharp, pure, piercing shriek leaves my throat as I come.

It feels like my entire tail is coming, every nerve firing at once. It's like fireworks—one massive burst of orgasmic pleasure and then a thousand tiny, sparkling climaxes following that one.

Zoltan's entire body lurches, and all his tentacles clamp my tail tighter. He's coming—roaring—a bellow that shudders through the water in visible waves. His heat pours into me, filling all of me. It's blissful—a blessing.

I have never felt so sated, so loved, so perfectly happy.

The ecstasy fades, but we stay wrapped together for a long time. Finally the Witch eases himself out of me. His cock is much shorter now, easily withdrawn into its hiding place. My scale-flap seals his release into my body. And it's over.

"It's less messy in this form," I murmur against the heated skin of Zoltan's neck. "And far more intense."

"It has never been so intense for me, not in all my years," he admits. "Though I've heard of a few mated pairs reaching that level of bliss. Even for those rare couples, the intense matings only happen once a month or so, when their fertility cycles align. The rest of the time the pleasure is milder than it is in human form."

"So we get to do *that* once a month, and the rest of the time we'll fuck in human form," I say firmly. "I wonder *why* only certain couples enjoy that intensity? What if there's some truth to the 'one true mate' idea after all? Why is the pleasure less strong at other times of the fertility cycle, and how will we know the perfect time to mate, to enjoy maximum pleasure? Because I certainly want that again, as many times as possible. When do the pheromones—"

But I stop, because he's laughing, grinning more broadly than ever. That smile, on his rugged face, when he's usually so serious and growly—it's a sheer delight. I could stare at it forever.

"What?" I say, my own smile reflecting his.

"You," he purrs, cupping my face. "With your neverending questions."

"You must help me find answers to all of them."

"It will be an honor." He leans in for a kiss.

We explore our room then, including the wardrobe, which contains two new corsets for me and a breastplate for him—durable for underwater use, and removable as well, unlike the one my father made me wear.

Next Zoltan shows me the adjoining chamber he has begun to furnish as his new place for spells and supplies. He explains the spell he's working on, the one that will split the trident's power and infuse an equal share into each of us. And he answers all of my questions with consummate patience.

When we return to our bedroom, he dims the glow of the crystals with a single word. We float together in our sleeping bower, him drifting face-up and horizontal while I drape myself over his body.

"There is one thing I miss about our deal," he says.

"And what is that?" I prop myself on my elbows, against his chest.

His lips twitch the way they do when he's trying not to smile, and his strong hand slides up the back of my neck, a possessive grasp.

"Sing," he says, and his deep tone vibrates my heartstrings.

Cradled on his chest, enticed by the velvet darkness of his eyes, I sing for him. The song is wordless, because we don't always need words, he and I. The music carries every throb of desire, every quiver of fear—every delicate, indomitable thread of hope for the future we plan to share. And it carries the pulse of my love for him, a melody of two wanderers drifting blissfully together under the sea.

MORE FROM
REBECCA F. KENNEY

The IMMORTAL WARRIORS adult fantasy romance series

Jack Frost
The Gargoyle Prince

Wendy, Darling (Neverland Fae Book 1)
Captain Pan (Neverland Fae Book 2)

Hades: God of the Dead
Apollo: God of the Sun

Related Content: *The Horseman of Sleepy Hollow*

The PANDEMIC MONSTERS trilogy
The Vampires Will Save You
The Chimera Will Claim You
The Monster Will Rescue You

FOR THE LOVE OF THE VILLAIN series
The Sea Witch
The Maleficent Faerie

The SAVAGE SEAS books
The Teeth in the Tide
The Demons in the Deep

These Wretched Wings (A Savage Seas Universe novel)

The DARK RULERS adult fantasy romance series
Bride to the Fiend Prince
Captive of the Pirate King
Prize of the Warlord
The Warlord's Treasure
Healer to the Ash King
Pawn of the Cruel Princess
Jailer to the Death God
Slayer of the Pirate Lord

The INFERNAL CONTESTS adult fantasy romance series
Interior Design for Demons
Infernal Trials for Humans

MORE BOOKS
Lair of Thieves and Foxes (medieval French romantic
fantasy/folklore retelling)

Her Dreadful Will (contemporary witchy villain romance)

Made in the USA
Coppell, TX
02 December 2023

25167044R00236